Portrait of Paloma

Harry W. Crosby

PORTRAIT OF PALOMA

SUNBELT PUBLICATIONS
San Diego, California

This is a work of fiction. Names, characters, and incidents are either products of the author's imagination or are used fictitiously, and any resemblance to actual persons, living or dead, is entirely coincidental.

Copyright © 2001 by Sunbelt Publications, Inc.
All rights reserved. First edition 2001
Edited by Jennifer Redmond
Book design by Kathleen Wise
Project management by Jennifer Redmond
Printed in the United States of America

No part of this book may be reproduced in any form without permission of the publisher. Please direct comments and inquiries to:

Sunbelt Publications, Inc.
P.O. Box 191126
San Diego, CA 92159-1126
(619) 258-4911, fax: (619) 258-4916
www.sunbeltpub.com

05 04 03 02 01   5 4 3 2 1

Library of Congress Cataloging-in-Publication Data

Crosby, Harry, 1926–
    Portrait of Paloma: a novel / by Harry W. Crosby.
       p. cm.
ISBN 0-916251-56-X (pbk)
    1. San Diego (Calif.)—Fiction.   2. Middle aged men—Fiction.
    3. Young women—Fiction.
  I. Title.

        PS3603.R67 P67 2001
        813'.54--dc21

        2001032772

A Visitation

After devoting half of my many years to pursuing Baja California's past, tracking its ghosts onto high mesas and into deep arroyos, it seems entirely right that Paloma found me in a peninsular backwater.

In June, 1998, I was mapping the three-hundred-mile route of the 1769 expedition that founded San Diego in the company of significant Baja California aficionados: explorer-writer Graham Mackintosh, publisher Lowell Lindsay, and photographer Bill Evarts. It was our second night in Arroyo de Valladares, ninety miles southeast of Ensenada and twenty miles from the Pacific, our camp near the spot where the expedition's padre, Juan Crespí, buried Manuel Valladares, his valued helper and a convert from far-off Misión de San Ignacio.

The day had been something of a triumph. In a morning's hike, we'd located the pass that must have been used by the 1769ers to make the difficult transition from Arroyo de San Antonio to that of Valladares. We celebrated by resting in a grove of giant yucca, then trekked three hours back to camp and the first water we'd seen all day. I had carried only a quart with me—shame on me, a greenhorn mistake—and I got to camp so dehydrated that my legs and lower back went rock-hard with cramps. I drank water nonstop, but remained in excruciating pain only partially relieved by lying flat on my bedroll and willing myself to relax. That ordeal began at five in the afternoon, didn't subside until long after midnight, and all the while I lay there *con ojos cuadrados*, "square-eyed," as the locals say.

My comrades turned in for the night and I was soon desperate for anything to take my mind off pain and boredom. I indulged in male fantasies, necessarily older male fantasies, thinking of the young women who have, over the years, frequented the coffee house where an Old Boys Club — a group of old friends — have held informal daily meetings for many a year. One of our ring leaders, Russell Forester, no saint himself, gives me a hard time about my shameless ogling of young women. Ogling, and even having the nerve to chat them up.

I lay there on my bed of pain and thought, "All right, daydreams are one thing, but how does one visualize a real-life 'Older Man, Younger Woman' affair?" I turned the question over and over and every answer seemed ugly, impersonal, materialistic, every relationship a shared embarrassment leading to a dead end. Turning to other things, I tried to commune with the past, tried to summon the spirit of Manuel Valladares, abroad in the moonlit canyon — but it was a handsome young woman who stepped from the shadows. "Older Man," she said, "I am Paloma. I heard your question — and your answer. Don't be so sure. Let a Younger Woman tell you how it was with her."

Well, I wasn't fooled. Plainly, I'd called her up; she was a product of pain and fantasy. I imagined myself mouthing her words, she the puppet, I the ventriloquist. I blinked my eyes, but, open or shut, I had no power over her — quite the contrary, she captivated me. I hung on her every word and expression as she sat like Sheherazade and spun a tale so hypnotic that I moved into her world and became a participant in its provocative affairs.

And as we interacted, my original question found unexpected depths. I experienced a poignant sense of an older man's relationship with a younger woman — no, of man's community with woman, blossoms, thorns, and all. Intoxicated by that, I finally drifted off to sleep.

In the morning, my visitor was gone but her essence lingers to this day and her story is engraved in my head. I took it home with me, like it or not, and wrote it down because I had to. Wrote it down as an Old Boy whose idle inquiry had launched a spellbinding journey. "Fiction," I'd always thought, "is the calling of others." Until this. Until Paloma.

Out of Baja California.

For every evil under the sun
There is a remedy or there is none
If there be one, seek till you find it.
If there be none, never you mind it.

— MOTHER GOOSE —

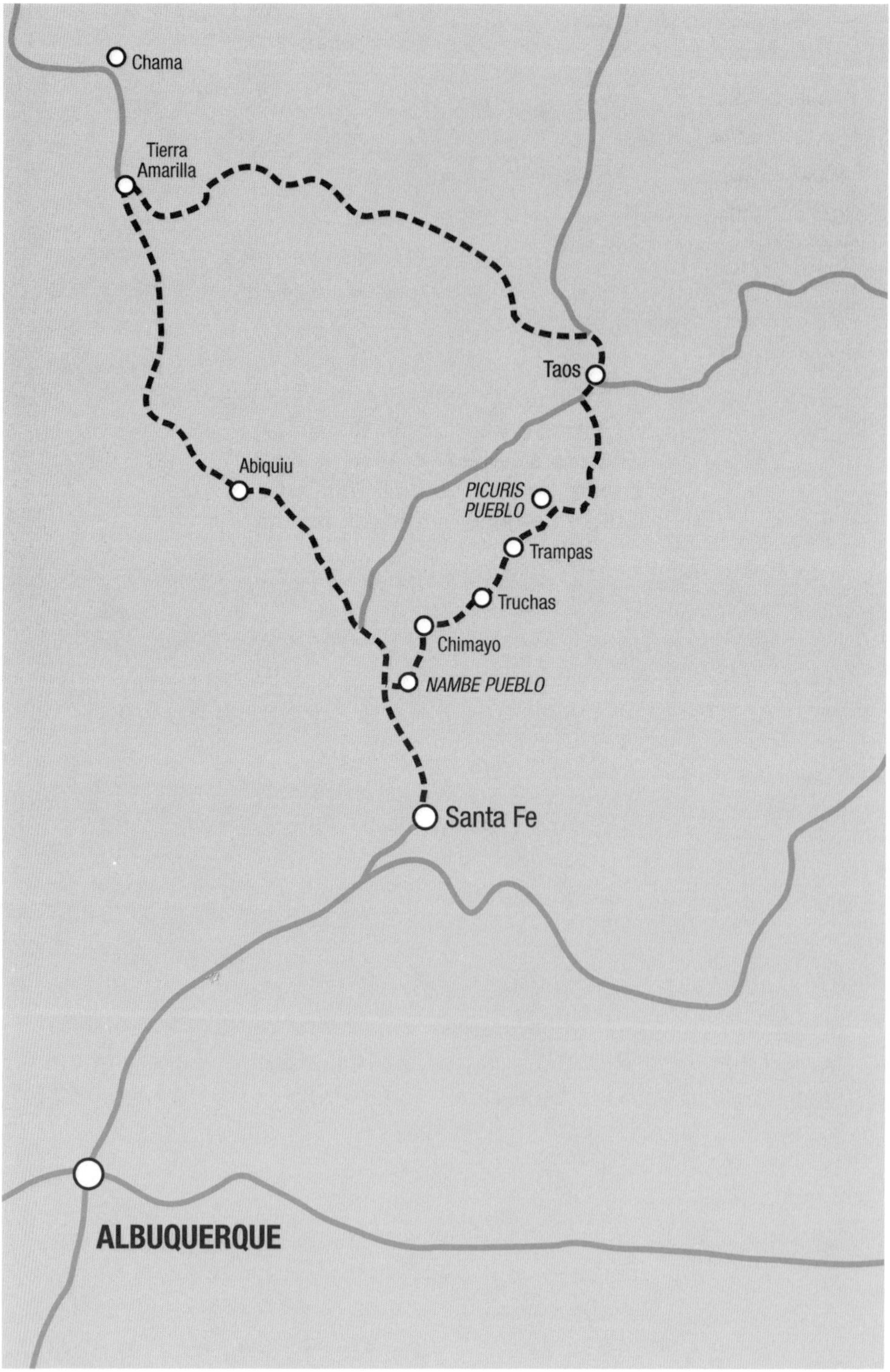

Chama
Tierra Amarilla
Taos
Abiquiu
PICURIS PUEBLO
Trampas
Truchas
Chimayo
NAMBE PUEBLO
Santa Fe
ALBUQUERQUE

I Paloma

Santa Fe, New Mexico — Friday, September 20, 1996

I awoke with the optimism of first consciousness, that instant in which we know no age or infirmity, that moment limited to "I'm me. I'm here. It's a new day." But memory, in full detail, was only a step behind — with my next breath I was all too aware that I was sixty-eight, no longer had the powers of youth, and was waking alone as I had for twenty long months. Miserable reality. Well, no use lying there wallowing in all that.

I rolled out with no clue that I was taking the first step on an unimaginable path.

Parting the curtains in my hotel room showed me nothing but a blur. "Big dummy," I muttered, and clapped on my glasses to scan Santa Fe in the first flush of dawn. I dressed, thinking dutifully of the conference I'd come to attend and how I'd almost stayed home but finally caved in to my daughters' urgings. "Try getting out," they'd said, "do something, anything."

I went down for a turn around the block in the crisp New Mexican air and got back to the hotel's coffee shop minutes before opening time. I waited at the locked door with no special enthusiasm — until I caught sight of a tall young woman in a bone-white pants suit striding up from the lobby. I managed a hurried smile as she joined me, then

1

was captivated by large dark eyes and a heart-shaped face framed in glossy, chestnut-brown hair.

She nodded politely despite my bold gaze and I was encouraged to lean her way and confide in low tones, "Rumor is, coffee in five minutes or less."

"I've heard," she returned in her own stage whisper, "the night clerk knows all."

No clever rejoinder came to mind, so I tried peppy. "You're up early. On your way this morning?"

"No. I'm always out at the crack of — scouting for tea."

We kidded around about our shared penchant for early rising and I took note of a light accent, a winning smile, and nearly perfect teeth. I say we kidded around, but honestly, I wasn't all that nonchalant. Just standing there at ease, the woman radiated a vital femininity — and had me feeling like a tongue-tied teenager. I got a break when the door behind us opened and a bright-eyed Native American hostess gave us a friendly "Good morning" and waved us in.

"Sit anywhere you want. I'll bring you some coffee."

My companion reacted quickly. "Oh thank you, but could you bring me instead a pot of really hot water?"

"Of course, no problem."

As the hostess moved off to fetch and carry, I ventured, "Would you join me?" and got back a gracious, "By all means. Thank you."

The place was typical Santa Fe, with tile floors, a grand corner fireplace, high ceilings, and Southwestern decor. We chose a table away from the door and sat facing each other. I raised my eyebrows and she did the same — neither of us spoke. I grinned, trying to look receptive. She returned a sweet smile, a bit overdone. It flashed on me that this was not an awkward pause, it was a game, and one of us had to make the opening move. Well, etiquette was on her side and I finally remembered my manners.

"Haley Talbot, San Diego." I offered my hand.

"Paloma Grey, Laguna Beach — almost your neighbor." She shook my hand more firmly than most women do. For several electric seconds, I gazed into big, brown, wideset eyes enhanced by shapely eyebrows and strong cheekbones. "Swear to God," I thought, "those eyes have the hypnotic effect you get from Byzantine portraits." When it hit me that I was staring again, I glanced around the room. Weird. I'd come in with the impression that the long, plastered space was cold and impersonal. Now it seemed colorful, intimate, warm. And more than that, I was warm — and so distracted that I fumbled the conversational ball.

Paloma Grey filled the gap. "You're the first Haley I've met. Is that H-A-L-E-Y? And is it a family name?"

"Right on both counts. And yes, if you're tempted to ask, I do get hit with a lot of comet gags."

"Not," she said firmly, "from anyone able to spell it or pronounce it."

Her accent by now was a tease and I took the bait. "Surely your manner of speech predates Laguna. Am I hearing England English and maybe something else?"

She smiled. "Good for you! It was all English till I was taken to Spain at age eight. And there I was for six years, the sole native English speaker in a Spanish school."

"Aha! But wait — how does that relate to your Spanish name?"

She sounded amused. "It doesn't, really. I was born, believe it or not, in Roanoke, Virginia. 'Paloma' was my mother's whim, but her family did have Spanish connections. And then I spent my first eight years in London with an English nanny. But truly, I've had to unlearn some of what I picked up from her."

I wasn't buying that. "Unlearn what? Your English is a jewel in your crown. You must have an excellent education and a fine ear."

Now she wasn't buying. "Thank you for kind intentions, but I have less education than you seem to suppose. As to my ear, I can't say, but you are generous." That came with a warm smile.

Paloma opened her purse, found a packet of tea bags, and put an Irish Breakfast in her cup just as the waitress arrived with hot water for her and coffee for me. We traded reasons for being in Santa Fe and found that we'd both come for conferences — I to present a paper at a Western Historical Society event, "Spain in the American Southwest," and she to attend a conclave called "Folk Art Looks at Its Roots." We'd seen each other's conference posters displayed in the lobby.

She stirred her steeping tea and asked, "Are you then a university lecturer?" Her low-pitched voice contrasted with the tinkle of spoon on cup.

I admired her long fingers and noticed manicured but uncolored nails — and no wedding ring. Then I snapped to and tried to answer her question. "No, actually I have no university affiliation."

Her raised eyebrows looked politely skeptical, so I pressed on. "I got into academe by a side door — and quite by accident. I had an idea to write something popular on California's pioneer Hispanic families, and I headed off, casually enough, to hunt up data in The Bancroft Library at U.C. Berkeley. Well, there's nothing casual about The Bancroft. I got into their documents and I was like one of Ulysses's lotus eaters — hooked, and lost to the world. Willy-nilly, I had a new career, 'Studies of Spanish California.'" I mentioned my publications.

Paloma looked beyond me and seemed to think aloud. "So you write. Interesting. I'm fascinated by the process, always have been. I practice a bit by keeping a journal — but that's not really writing, is it?" Clearly she didn't expect an answer for she went on more briskly. "I must say, I'm puzzled by the idea of an unaffiliated historian. Highly unconventional, I should think. Do I detect a story behind this apparent contradiction?"

She puzzled me. Her manner was friendly, yet she spoke formally and sounded old-fashioned. I wondered, "Is she mocking me, or is that just her way?" I suppose I'm extra-sensitive, having been accused of sounding pedantic myself. Anyhow, to play her game, if it was one, I replied in similarly formal terms.

"Fact is, I've had more than one career. I came into this one in mid-life with some resources — which let me indulge my passion for research without devoting myself to the politics and paperwork most of my colleagues have to accept."

"I see, fortunate you. May I ask what you'd done before — that had such a happy outcome and yet permitted you to walk away?"

"'Fortunate' is a good guess. I was grandson to a man whose hobby was finding opportunities, and who made it his business to roll up his sleeves and turn a profit, enough that some came down to me. And I've been in the right place at the right time for investments that grew improbably, also no credit to me."

She looked dubious. "I get the sense that you haven't lived the life of the idle rich, nor of the gentleman investor. Am I that wide of the mark?"

That was perceptive — and flattering. Not your garden-variety youth, I thought, then admitted, "No, you've got me pegged, and thank God there is more to my story. I married an artist when I was twenty-four, and she and I raised two daughters. And I taught high school for eighteen years before I got into history and writing. Along the way, I designed and built three houses, our girls married, both live near me, and thanks to both, I have four grandchildren." I decided that was enough about me. "What about you? What do you do?"

She seemed not to hear as she pursued her own inquiry. "Does your wife not travel with you?"

That jolted me. The exhilaration of the moment had lifted me out of an enveloping sadness, but now I slipped back. I managed, "My wife died nearly two years ago," then I was too shaky to add a word. My throat felt like old dry wood and I reached for my water.

Her face, and her voice too, softened. "I'm sorry. I know how it is to lose the people who count." There was a moment of quiet before she picked up the thread. "Excuse me. You asked about my interests. Well, folk art, obviously, and I'm involved in several ways." She sipped her tea without losing her look of sympathy.

To my surprise, my emotions had subsided. I hurried to follow her lead. "So you're a craftsperson? A collector? Scholar?"

"Mmm, not easy to explain. I'd say I'm here primarily to act as eyes and ears for a friend, but I have an interest in folk art publications as well. And I'm studying the influence of folk art on mainstream design — regional architectures, for example."

She went on with what I'm sure was an intelligent overview of her conference's agenda, and I was as attentive as I could be, but I got lost in the person and missed the message. When she paused and looked expectant, she caught me thinking ruefully about the age gulf between us, and I could only retreat to the last point I actually took in. "You mentioned a friend that you're scouting for?" I'm not sure I fooled her at all.

"Right," she said, "an old and dear friend who supports herself by creating pictures with fabrics and stitchery. She can't travel, so you might say I'm her field agent. I'm here basically for the textile session tomorrow. And yes, I have asked myself why I signed up for all three days."

"Friday, Saturday, Sunday?" Somehow I needed to know.

"Exactly. Amazing, isn't it, how three days has become the universal format?" She leaned in and lowered her voice, "Don't tell me your 'Spain in the Southwest' breaks my rule."

"Not a chance, fits right in. My God, do you realize that you're toying with the ingredients of a new law? You could find a place with Murphy, Parkinson, et al. Let's see, Grey's Law could be 'A conference is created as a three-day vacuum with a stated purpose that will expand to fill the void.' Something like that."

She gave me a crooked smile. "And the magical number of three days arises from considered input by—wouldn't you say—airlines, hotel chains, and chambers of commerce?" I offered her a high five, which she met with no hesitation.

We'd emptied our cups and refills and I was acutely aware that our time together was about to end. I asked, as casually as I could, "Have you made plans for breakfast?"

"Not really, but I have nothing on till ten. I'm told there's an exemplary Old Santa Fe neighborhood just east of here. I thought I'd walk over to look around, and while I'm at it, keep an eye out for a likely spot to get a plate of what I call 'eggscetera.' Would you care to come along?"

Would I! It was tough to contain my surprise and delight. "I'd love to tag along. And would you join me for a bite at Pasqual's—the best eggscetera in town?"

"Perfect," she said. "Been there. Loved it. Shall we meet in the lobby in, say, fifteen minutes?"

I allowed as how that was perfect with me.

I needed that fifteen minutes. I touched up my shave, went after nose and ear hair, polished my coffee-stained teeth, and practically drank mouthwash. As I cleaned up, I mused, "Eggscetera, huh? Not bad." I ran a comb through my old gray hair, thanking God most of it was still there, and I was out the door. I passed on waiting for an elevator and hurried down the deserted stairs.

I wasn't late, but neither was Paloma Grey. As she crossed the lobby I saw that her square shoulders and erect posture gave her an athletic look that I'd missed in our closer encounter. She arrived beaming, her outfit now topped off with a broad-brimmed straw hat, a flying rusty red ribbon tied about its crown. Fetching and quite chic, I thought, but my objectivity by then was highly suspect. We headed off for the plaza to take our proposed route, east along Palace Avenue.

I'd done my share of talking, so I inquired about her previous visit to Santa Fe. Turned out, she'd come two years before with a board member of a Los Angeles folk art museum, a man who wanted to introduce her to the related local facilities. She mentioned other trips with him to observe regional craft practices in Africa, Indonesia, Eastern Europe, and Central and South America, maybe more. I lost track as I marveled at the amount of travel all that must have involved.

We stepped along briskly. I exercise regularly and I'm six-foot-two, but I'd guessed Paloma at five-foot-ten, and I soon suspected that she was taking it easy on me. "And I thought I was a serious walker," I said at last.

She sounded dismissive. "Well, it's my principal exercise. I try to get in three miles a day."

I pressed for more. "No gym near your place?"

"Yes — but gyms, to me, are noisy hothouses. I'd rather be outside, feel free, see things, have time to think. As we are here. Compare this with the gym at our hotel." Her gesture included the neighborhood, the sky above, and the ground below.

I winced to think of my well-used weights and rowing machine, and felt like a hypocrite when I pointed to a topiary tree and said, "None of those back at the gym."

"Exactly."

Our exercise took us out of the business district and into a neighborhood of traditional Santa Fe homes. We marched abreast and I welcomed the opportunity for sidelong glances. A profile depends a lot on the nose, and, while hers was nicely formed, it wasn't large enough to create a strong silhouette. But then, there were those full lips, admirable cheekbones, and splendid eyelashes. I relished the chance to admire discreetly.

We made our way along quaint streets and viewed adobe homes behind guardian walls. We peeked into gardens and courtyards and commented on whatever took our fancy. Before long, our discussion of Santa Fe's mixed Spanish and Indian roots led us to compare our ideas about the blending of cultures, and finally about the ways in which cultures express themselves. I began to realize that Paloma saw "folk art" and "culture" as almost synonymous. I asked about that, and she admitted that, for her, folk art was the substance of humankind's regional differences.

"Folk art," she insisted, "is not just traditional objects. It's language, religion, cuisine, the way societies are organized — really most human activities. It bothers me that so many people think of folk art as trinkets and trivia. For me, it's a big part of who we are."

She seemed dead serious, but she wasn't on a soap box, there was a twinkle in her eye. "Wow," I ventured, "your definition is pretty inclusive. Why don't you just throw in racial differences as elements of folk art?"

She stopped and faced me, looking very solemn. "Oh, I do! Don't you? I'm sorry for anyone who doesn't admire the richness in humanity in the same spirit in which he admires diversity in art objects." Her smile was such that I decided she was serious and spoofing me at the same time.

"Touché," I admitted cheerfully, "and 'gotcha' and all the rest. I never made the conscious connection, but that's exactly how I've always felt."

"Well then," she said with a note of finality. She linked her arm with mine and I couldn't tell whether she was gloating or consoling me — nor did it matter.

Before long, she made a sweeping gesture toward several handsome homes. "See how pleasing these adobes are. This mix of pueblo and Mexican architecture looks as if it just mushroomed out of the ground. For me, these variations on one theme are attractive and restful, especially when I compare them with most places in the U.S."

"Not just a little too self-conscious?" I was needling her again.

"Oh, I suppose. But it's still a charming relief from the typical American hodgepodge — you know, unrelated themes, no themes at all."

"Careful now, your overseas antecedents are showing. Every red-blooded American property owner has a right, almost an obligation, to choose what he wants for architecture, to express his individuality."

"OK," she retorted, "pull my leg. But suppose I play your game. How do you reconcile your precious American individuality with all that look-alike housing tract yardage draped over our southern

California hills? Come on! What do Americans travel overseas to admire? Things like English villages and Italian or Iberian hill towns, harmonious expressions that date back centuries, places I call folk art. Doesn't it bother you that a lot of American children grow up with no sense of that beauty, no tie with the past?"

"Peace! I'm a rotten leg puller. I'm in your camp all the way, just wanted to hear what you'd say. So thank you."

We had fun for a full hour, pacing the streets and kicking around ideas and opinions. She responded enthusiastically to my turn of mind and I took solace from that. It helped me to cling to my cherished belief that my poor old brain was in better shape than my body. And every step revealed how much more there was to Paloma than an admirable physical presence. Throughout our walk, she one-upped me with her grasp of the successive cultures around the Mediterranean, not only the facts, but her ability to peel them off the pages of history and use them among her examples and arguments. Dear Lord, I thought, there's an awful lot going on behind those big brown eyes.

At one point, I was really tested. Our opinions coincided so closely that she drew back, squinted, and asked, "Are we sure we just met?" I had to battle a rousing impulse to take her in my arms. How intoxicating it was to be so drawn to a young woman, and in a way I hadn't felt in — what was it? — nearly fifty years. Even the mental image of the oldish face I'd shaved that morning didn't stop me from feeling younger and more optimistic. I had to watch my tongue for fear of bubbling over.

At last we were at Pasqual's corner doorway. We came in through a draft of warm air scented by coffee and cinnamon rolls and I was pleased to find the small place not yet packed. Trying to keep up with Paloma physically and mentally had me hungrier than I'd felt in ages; everything looked and smelled delicious. We gave our order to a finely chiseled Hispanic waiter — and raised our eyebrows at each other as he left. Paloma lowered her voice, "What do you think? The poster boy for my conference, or yours?" Then she questioned me about Spanish activities in New Mexico and I'm afraid I delivered a mini-lecture — as well as I could manage in the face of such a distracting audience, this beauty who sat so erect and appeared to listen with her eyes. Or was she reading mine?

In good time, our waiter made his way down the narrow aisle, moving like a dancer balancing a tray on high. He served our colorful plates of papaya, eggs, and *sopaipillas* with a flourish, and we ate amid increasing noise and the packing in of bodies. Throughout our walk, Paloma had diverted me with her good humor and her delight in ideas. Now, across from her in a booth, I could better enjoy her gestures, expressions, and accent—and rejoice in the cheer she'd imparted to me in less than three hours. I sat there feeling blessed and praying for some device to keep this encounter alive, but it was over all too soon.

I tried desperately to think of a way to stop everything, or slow it down, or change the direction in which it was headed—but all that came to me was the bill. I paid, got gracious thanks, and we shouldered our way through the waiting throng out into the brightness of the street.

Paloma turned to me, momentarily more formal. "I must be going. Perhaps we could take tea or meet again somehow while we're here?"

Hallelujah! I went for broke. "Is dinner a possibility?"

"Oh. Afraid not. This is banquet night for our affair. I've promised to join a couple of women with whom I share interests." She put her hand on my arm and added, "But what do you say to four or so this afternoon? The late session should be out, and I'd actively enjoy skipping the cocktail hour."

"Enchanted. Meet again in the lobby?"

"Perfect! I'll look forward to it." She hurried off.

I had a rotten morning. I found the history sessions poorly presented, of little consequence to me, or both. The lunch break struck me as equally hollow, strangers making labored attempts to connect in a vast space full of forced laughter and soulless food. It did finally dawn on me that I was the problem—"Spain in the American Southwest," had taken a distant backseat to "Tea with Paloma." Time couldn't pass quickly enough to suit me.

My panel was set for two o'clock and I'd be the final speaker. Three colleagues presented their pieces and I got up to give mine. I looked out on an audience of thirty or more, and there in the back row sat Paloma. Suddenly obligation felt like opportunity. I dredged up a couple of anecdotes I'd cut out in pursuit of brevity, and delivered my largely improvised essay with unusual animation. Applause was politely brisk and questions from the floor were elementary — as usual, not many listeners were familiar with my neglected period.

Afterward, I shook a few hands and worked my way over to Paloma. "Ready for a drink?"

"More than. But let me observe, Mr. Non-professor, you do the professor bit rather well — and your audience is entirely taken in. My, such humble pie I was fed." My, how stern she looked as she twitted me.

"Oh come off it. I never said I wasn't the world's foremost authority, I merely stated that I wasn't a card-carrying academic. And I'm not."

She stood squarely in front of me and very straight. "Dear sir, I shall spare you my thoughts on the letter of the law versus the spirit." She dropped the pretentious air and lowered her voice. "I enjoyed your show. I like to hear you think. Now it's teatime. You may take my arm." We stepped into the hall and set off for the café patio.

"You surprised me," I admitted. "What happened to your last session?"

"Simple. I found myself more curious about Spanish California than about Afghani sweatshops. I'm glad I switched. It was all new to me, especially your points on the relatively greater importance of common folk in frontier settings. I'd never appreciated the degree to which the elites who created colonial projects had to depend on humble, faraway people to put their programs into effect. And I liked the way you explained why it took a many-layered bureaucracy to bridge that gap."

"Well, thanks. And that's a very tidy synopsis. Too bad there was no test, you'd have got an A." I grinned and she grinned, and then we were in the patio and I set about to be host. "Where shall we sit, and what's your pleasure?"

"Lemonade, if you please. I never got over my little-girl passion for Spanish *limonadas*." She looked around, sizing up the space. "Let's sit where we can see the sun on the square."

The outdoor area was filling and cheerful chatter resounded off hard glass and concrete. We found a table for two, sat, and got the attention of a waitress as discreetly as the bustle permitted. We ordered, and my guest leaned forward, looking and sounding rather serious.

"Haley, how did you get into your work? And what do you want out of it?"

My heart jumped. "Haley," I thought, "she called me 'Haley.'" I leaned forward myself, caught the sweetness of her breath, and my reaction was so far afield that I had to struggle to focus on her question. "How and what? The essence? Good question." What man my age, I wondered, could resist an invitation to lay out his cards for such an apparently sincere young woman? Why resist?

"Well, it was back in the sixties when San Diego and California were getting cranked up for the two hundredth anniversary of their Spanish settlements. I contracted to do a study of the Hispanic people who'd been involved, and when I looked up some of their descendants, I was so taken by their history that I decided to get into the act. I told you about going to The Bancroft Library. OK, after that I wrote a book, and first thing you know, twenty years had passed, I'd done four books and got some recognition. But I can't simply quit. I need the stimulation."

That last part was less than frank. I couldn't let it go at that. Not with her.

"To be honest, my problem's not as simple as I just made it sound. The truth is, right now I need to be involved, but I'm not, really. Marian's, my wife's, suffering was a nightmare and I've been floundering ever since. I know this'll be hard for someone your age to even imagine. Marriage, family, middle age—they all lie before you, one big step at a time. But Marian and I'd been through all that and more. And I got so much from her along the way. Now I see that she always did more than her share. She had her work—she was an illustrator, things like children's books, greeting cards, and product labels—but first and most important, always, she took care of our home, raised the kids, shopped, cooked—God, I was spoiled. When I had fieldwork or archival research to do, I'd go off hundreds of miles for weeks or months and she'd stay home and do it all, keep the home fires burning. And then, when our girls grew up and moved out, we had a sort of second honeymoon, built a new house, decorated, traveled, ate out more—great times. And we went right on living and working under the same roof and being best friends. I don't think either of us knew or even guessed how dependent we were on each other. After we found out what her condition was, we never really talked about dependence. Maybe she felt guilty about going. I know I felt guilty about staying."

I'd never really worked through those feelings, and it felt odd pouring them out for a stranger. But it also seemed right and Paloma seemed receptive. I went on.

"I was lost. When two become one, what's one left alone? Most of my adult memories stayed alive and mattered because we'd gone on sharing them. When she left, it was as if she'd taken them with her. Now my world's that much smaller and I'm a different person. And not being a good sport about it, or very mature about getting out of the dumps. But, you know, today things look better, and I *am* trying to be better. And you, young lady, are a brick to sit through this long lament. Thank you for letting me get it off my chest."

She reached across our tiny table, put a hand on top of mine and said, "Listen, you're going to be fine. I heard you coming through in your lecture back there. I admire anyone with a real *afición*. From what I've heard, you're the ones who do cope, come what may. I've admired your outlook from the moment we met."

"Paloma, I'm flattered as hell. I can't tell you what a good time I had this morning. It's not often in my experience that a man my age has the company and the voluntary attention of a young woman with any semblance of your gifts. I want you to know the compliment's not lost on me."

For some reason, my appreciation made her brusque and businesslike. "Really, you protest too much. I enjoy sharing ideas and experiences with older people. I hear more pith and less jargon. So! No more of that. I need to pick your brain."

The waitress brought our drinks and gave me a moment to compose myself. I paid the bill and then took up Paloma's implied question. "My brain's available. Any particular crevice you'd like to dig into?"

"Your database on Santa Fe. The Santa Fe area. I've heard it's delightful, but I know only what I've seen from the shuttle bus, here-to-Albuquerque. On Sunday the conference is offering a couple of cattle-call bus tours and I have to decide which to take, or what else I might do. I don't know when I'll be here again, so I'm casting about for ideas. What do you know? What do you recommend?"

"OK, I don't know the itineraries of your bus tours, but I'd say the closest thing to instant gratification would be the back road from here to Taos, the one through Chimayo and a couple of other pueblos on a high ridge. A few years ago, Marian and I did that as part of a memorable day-and-a-half circle tour. High mesas, pines, picturesque pueblos, churches, lots of neat stuff. Ever been to Taos yourself?"

"Never. Here sits a New Mexico novice."

"Fine, you're in for a treat. As I see it, scenery improves as you head toward Colorado. 'Go north, young woman, go north,' that's my advice. You've mentioned kindred spirits in your group. Maybe you could rent a van and go where you wish. When do you have to be back in Albuquerque?"

"Oh, Monday, noonish. I'm tied in with a couple who left their auto in Los Angeles. They'll drive me home when we get there."

"Good, that gives you all day Sunday. You could cover more ground or be less hurried." Then I went on a bit about the pleasures of Taos and a sprinkling of pueblo attractions to highlight the to and fro.

Paloma was attentive until she glanced at her watch. "Oh, oh! I really do have to get dressed. Any chance you'd care to meet once more at six *por la mañana*?"

"Every chance. I wouldn't miss it. Now run along." She ran.

Luckily, I managed to dine with congenial colleagues. Inwardly, I rejoiced and gave thanks; fellowship helped to pass time while I exulted in my latest invitation. Actually, exulted and agonized. I'd wasted parts of our previous encounters in worrying about when they'd end, but there I was, another bid in hand, and still fretting. Why, I grilled myself, was Paloma hanging around with me? She must have admirers, lots of them! I wondered what had happened to the museum board member who'd taken her around the world. Don't ask, I told myself. Don't rock the boat.

We finished dinner and I stayed on for chitchat until the party broke up, then got to my room weary, but still inspired. There, alone at last, I came to grips with the euphoria I'd experienced all day. Something important had happened, something exciting, welcome, long overdue—and now I put my finger on it. My seemingly endless depression was gone, and the emotional contrast was overwhelming. I sat there with no control over the foolish grin on my face. I wanted to sing. I can't really carry a tune, but I tried anyhow, tears streaming down my cheeks.

When my outburst of witless jubilation subsided, I looked back on my two years of dejection and acknowledged that togetherness with my wife had shielded me from loneliness and kept the specter of aging at bay. The two of us had aged together, we'd shrugged our shoulders over wrinkles, blemishes, and diminished stamina; we'd sighed over the onset of handicaps and setbacks. When dilapidation is shared, it's easier to take. You grieve less over the loss of your young self and you compare yourself less with others. With Marian gone, living was like trying to stand on one leg. As I struggled to keep my balance, my age and vulnerability became oppressively apparent and I came to see myself as ineffectual, unproductive, and just going through the motions — all in a lonelier, emptier world.

In the midst of those ruminations, my thoughts swung back to Paloma and the hopes and fears I was building up from our slight relationship — hopes raised by the relief I'd experienced, and fears that her magical effect would fly out the window when she tired of me. And there was that other nagging element, this delicious attraction to a very young woman — out of character for me and unsuitable from any sensible viewpoint. "Doomed to fail," I mourned. "Damned if I do and damned if I don't!"

So there I was, exhilarated, but acutely ill at ease. I'd lost Marian but I hadn't shed my married state, the habit was too ingrained. In the presence of this young woman, I fancied myself young again, capable of romance and intimacy — only to look nervously over my shoulder and experience what might be the gut feelings of an unfaithful husband. I went to bed, my head full of asteroids in alarming orbits. I saw and felt Paloma from every angle — her gestures, her warmth, her body, seen or imagined. I feared I would never sleep, but I finally did.

Saturday, September 21st

No need for an alarm clock — I awoke in the dark and knew it was for good. As I dressed, I hit on a desperate scheme. I'd offer to take Paloma to Taos myself. I'd ask if there were someone else she'd care to invite. I was sure she'd turn me down, but what the hell? I had nothing to lose and I was perfectly game to look like an old fool.

I went out into the glimmerings of dawn and set off to round the block, enjoying the chill. I'd covered maybe fifty yards when I heard hurrying feet. It was Paloma.

"Saw you leave and decided you might put up with me a few minutes early."

"Put up with you! Ha! I'll take every minute I can get. Good morning."

"Good morning to you. You're sweet. You make me feel right at home." She bounced on the balls of her feet, breathed into her cupped hands, and added, "Could we step over to the plaza and back?"

Could we! I clapped my hands and let out a low, "Away we go!" And away we went, briskly, greeting a surprising number of early risers, some in athletic wear, most at work cleaning up streets and sidewalks.

We made it back to the coffee shop on the stroke of six. It was open, and we ordered from an expectant waiter, then sat and watched him head for the kitchen and backtrack with carafes of coffee and hot water.

I took one sip, savoring "hot" and "coffee," and drew a deep breath. "Paloma, I've got an idea and I'm going to blurt it out so we can either talk about it or forget it, *de pronto.*"

"I told you I enjoy your ideas. Why shouldn't I like this one then?" She sounded reproachful.

"Because it could be presumptuous. You tell me. First, I get a car, and second, I show you my route to Taos and thereabouts, and if there's someone else you'd like to take along, fine, plenty of seats."

She froze for an instant, wide-eyed. "You can't mean it! Sorry, that was rude. What a surprise! What a generous thought! The instant winner, no competition. And no chaperone, thank you. Not a full day of three-cornered conversations. But are you sure you want to do this? I mean, it's a lot to offer a stranger."

"That's the presumptuous part. To me, you're not a stranger at all. You told me that I made you feel at home. OK, ever since we met, you've made me feel alive and charged up. You're a wave I've somehow caught, and I want to go with it while I can."

"Well! We beach people take comparison to a wave as a high compliment. I accept with pleasure, and I'll cover half the costs, of course."

"Miss Grey, when I come into your world, you may do the honors. In mine, I'm the host. Please, let's leave it at that." I couldn't believe I could sound so pompous.

"Take it or leave it? You do strike a hard bargain — I'm speechless. I can only say 'thank you, thank you' — but I can well and truly mean it."

"Umm, more than enough. The pleasure's mine." I couldn't go on just beaming like an idiot, so I raised my cup. "May the adventure live up to your expectations. But I'm not too worried. Remember that line in the old song, 'The bear went over the mountain to see what he could see'? Well, I detect a wide streak of him in you. I'm guessing that you're ready for whatever presents itself."

She threw up her hands. "Heaven forfend! I am found out through some unguarded act."

"I'll never tell — and I'll go make car arrangements and get a map. Any other preparations I, or you, or we need to make?"

She leaned forward. "Oh dear, I know I'll sound greedy to a fault, but I have to ask. How involved are you in your afternoon sessions?"

Oh, I liked the sound of that. Wherever that was going, I wanted in. "Not much for me. No colonial issues. I might skip it all, find some kindred souls, get drinks, sit around the pool, ogle scantily clad maidens — you know, like that."

"Well, I hesitate to interfere with such a high-minded agenda, but as I say, I'm greedy. So — and here I take a deep breath — how would you feel about heading for Taos after lunch? What's proposed for my afternoon sounds pretty tame compared to that. Then we'd have tomorrow for your whole circle tour and still wind up here Sunday night." I nodded encouragingly and she pressed on. "Of course, it's an extra night's hotel bill for each of us, but let me handle that. Now it is I being presumptuous." She sat up straight, pursed her lips, and looked hopeful.

Now I was doubly elated, but I tried to keep the lid on. "Shoot, I don't know. Why not? I'd never have had the guts to propose it, but I'm glad you did. Let's do it. I'll get on the ball and round up the car and make reservations in Taos. I'll bet the Inn's full, but maybe they still have a chauffeur's room for me and a maid's room for you."

She bent forward, more confidential but also more animated. "I'm embarrassed to be so pushy, but I'm thrilled. I was supposed to come here with someone, and that fell through, and I wondered if it'd be a mistake to come alone. Well, it wasn't. I met you, I've had a great time, and now there's this to look forward to. I could jump up and down and squeal 'goody, goody!'"

"Later, please," I urged, "there'll be places where that'll cause less public alarm."

"Spoilsport! No, just now you can do no wrong." She peeked at her watch. "Oops! Haley, you know, I have to go. I'm taking breakfast with some of the stitchery crowd, and the session I'm mostly here for is at nine. I suppose I'll be out around eleven-thirty. Where can we meet?"

"Let's see, I've got a must-go-to panel at ten, friends involved, but I'll be out around that same time. Let's just plan to plop down in the lobby when we're finished. One of us is bound to be first and hard to miss for the other."

"You're so clever. I'll be there. And I can't tell you how much I'm looking forward to this, practically holding my breath." She got up and clenched her fists in front of her, gave me a little-girl grin, mouthed "goody, goody," and was gone.

The car rental was no trick, done in minutes in the lobby. The Inn at Taos was full, but the first motel I tried had two nonsmoking singles. I even had the foresight to reserve a table at Doc Martin's for dinner. Then I was off for a morning of history and clock watching.

At eleven-fifty I was finally in the hall and hurrying to the lobby. No Paloma. My heart sank. I sat, I stood, I roamed in small circles. At twelve-fifteen I headed for the desk to try her room. As I waited at the counter, a low voice behind me said, "Boo." It was Paloma. Order was restored in the universe.

In short, the circle tour went splendidly. All my ideas panned out — it's hard to go wrong in northern New Mexico — and Paloma and I got on famously. In fact, for me, it was more than that. I'd been entranced from the moment we met, but after two days together, I was also relieved. When strangers are cooped up, they can run out of things to share, togetherness can pall. But that didn't happen with us. One thing led to another; we seemed to stimulate each other. A telling moment came when she knocked on my door to start our Sunday pre-breakfast hike; both of us were full of ideas that had come to us in the brief time since we'd said good night.

Even in the early hours of our acquaintance, it was easy for us to exchange interests and opinions. On the road, we went farther and deeper and became sillier and more serious. And with that, I began to understand why our age gap posed so few problems. Paloma had read most of the books I'd loved in my youth, the gamut from children's books to classics to writers popular before either of our times, Americans included. I was amazed that she knew my lightweight favorites, H. H. Munro, George Ade, James Branch Cabell, and Don Marquis, as well as I did, and we had a great time sharing our enthusiasms. All of which made me more curious about her background.

"You've had a hell of a liberal education," I guessed. "Was a lot of your reading college related?" Boy, did I get a surprise.

All the fun went out of her face and she answered slowly and seriously. "I never went to college. My mother died when I was sixteen and I had other responsibilities. I've been alone a lot and I've been a reader all my life. It's great company." Then she turned resolutely to something else — clearly she wanted to drop that topic.

While we were sharing our personal passions, I told her of my love for the music of Johann Sebastian Bach. "Let's see," she responded, and began humming *Sleepers, Awake!*, bobbing her head to emphasize the compelling rhythm. Then she added snatches of *For God So Loved the World* and *Hold in Remembrance*.

"Amazing," I gushed, only half joking, "my all-time-favorite medley."

"Thanks," she said, "Bach does get around."

She told me of her delight in Jane Austen, how she'd identified with each of Austen's heroines and felt that she'd lived the works, not just read them. I couldn't hum those themes, but I did the best I could with a fair grasp of English life in Austen's times. We talked on. At one point, Paloma made an odd but touching declaration. "I can't begin to tell you what a pleasure it is to have someone with whom I can truly commune."

And I couldn't begin to tell her what a pleasure her company was to me. Or how grateful I was for her tact, her uncanny knack for ignoring or downplaying the subject of age. She never deferred to me in a way that reminded me of my seniority. How important that was to one who had glumly and passively begun to accept old age.

So that was the upside of our interaction, and I'd have to say that, on the surface, everything was positive. But a day or two later when I looked back on our little trip, I saw that she'd kept me busy answering her and talking about my past and my current work while she turned aside or gave short answers to questions about herself. Even so, during our far-ranging conversations, I got glimpses of another side of Paloma. She made a few references to her family — actually to her lack of family — but when I questioned her, her answers were rather guarded. Her blood family was gone, she said, and hadn't amounted to much anyhow, no siblings, or cousins, or aunts and uncles. I realized that I'd raised another touchy subject, so I dropped that too.

But I did pursue a question that had puzzled me all along. To what did she devote her evident energy and intelligence? That line of inquiry wasn't greeted with open arms either. She mentioned part-time library work and managing a small residential complex, but she described those as chores done on the side. She sounded more involved in helping her friend to market fabric art, but I knew by then that crafts weren't a primary interest for her, that her ties to the field were through others. Nothing she'd revealed added up to a profession, a passion, or much of a life. She acted embarrassed, and by the time we'd parted for the night I was sorry I'd pressed the point.

In my room that Saturday night, alone in my bed, my thoughts went back to Marian, and to her death, against which she'd fought with such fortitude and to which she was so unresigned. Why did it still seem possible that I'd go home and find her upstairs in her studio?

And what would she think of me, squiring around a woman almost young enough to be our granddaughter? She'd find it unsuitable and unconscionable, surely. And yet Paloma seemed much the sort of woman Marian admired — forthright, honest, unaffected, not petty, not self-centered, displaying taste and restraint. If a friend had brought her into our lives as a bride, Marian would have welcomed her with open arms.

I pictured Marian when we first met. I tried to picture myself. We were so sheltered, so inexperienced. She was eighteen, a freshman at our small college, and we were married when she was twenty-two. I compared Paloma with each of us as we were then. Paloma would've frightened me to death and I'd have bored her to death. But I thought of Marian's inborn determination and sense of direction, evident from the start. She had given me the confidence to imagine our shared life even though I felt ill-prepared. Resolution and goals, Marian's strengths, were elements that seemed missing in Paloma. She'd told me she was twenty-four, two years older than Marian at the time of our wedding, but unlike Marian, she appeared to lack a compass and a purpose. I wondered why.

We returned to Santa Fe on Sunday evening in time for dinner under the high ceilings at La Escalera, a delightful, unhurried meal during which I did not hesitate to stare at my traveling companion, paying her back for her own intense gaze. After a bit, she managed a blush and lowered her eyes. We both smiled. We knew it was coming to an end, the party about to be over. I told her in the frankest terms how much I had enjoyed our time together and how I hoped we might meet again. She thanked me once more — she'd done so piecemeal as we went — and suggested that we postpone our good-byes, take a last dawn walk, and say our farewells at Pasqual's. I was flattered. She could easily have bid me *adios* after dinner and gone out of my life. Somebody raised a nice girl, I thought, wishing I could deliver that message to somebody in person.

We walked back to our hotel and prepared to part in the lobby — I hate saying good night in an elevator. She took my hands, drew back, and said the strangest thing. "Look at me. You'll never see me quite this way again." She pulled herself up to offer one cheek, then the other. I put her strange instruction out of mind and kissed each side lightly, my heart full. She gave me a wistful smile and was gone.

I strode off, puzzling still, but forcibly reminded of the spring in my step and my renewed optimism for the whole path ahead. I prayed that the change in me was there to stay, even as I dreaded the good-bye awaiting me in the morning.

Alone in my room, my bravado faded. I knew, deep down, that my renewal was due to Paloma and that my time with her was running out. Some corner of my mind closed the door on reality and allowed me to dream. "What a godsend," I fantasized, "if I could keep up this acquaintance, woo her, and start a whole new partnership."

"Ridiculous," I countered, coming back to earth. I thought of my age and of a body that showed the ravages of time and functioned at half the capacity it once had—and I thought of public opinion and my family's opinion.

A few moments of that and I came to and laughed aloud. There I was, an old fool juggling absurd pretensions. What did I, or my family, or the public have to do with it? It all depended on Paloma, and why in the world would a woman of her station and attainments give a second thought to pairing up with her figurative grandfather?

I wrestled with those and other gloomy thoughts for an hour, still wide awake. I took a sleeping pill but spent a fitful night anyhow, alternately dreading a return to solitude and trying to imagine some substitute for Paloma.

Monday, September 23rd

I found Paloma in the coffee shop and looked her over carefully in the light of her parting admonition. No surprises—other than a certain seriousness, she appeared as sightly as ever. As we sipped our tea—I'd joined in her habit as a parting gesture—she was in the mood to reminisce rather than anticipate, and I thought she sounded a little blue. Or was I listening to my own anxieties? Certainly, I had to struggle to look and sound upbeat. The coffee shop, so cheery the morning we met, now felt darker and cooler. After one cup, I proposed that we march.

This time we hiked higher and farther, into the wind as we went, facing it on our return. The sun came up and pierced the blowing clouds to sweep us with dazzling light and deep shade, but we hardly noticed. We tried to recapture the spirit of our trip to the north, but that seemed behind us, fading. I saw our images reflected in tall windows across a street and my heart leaped—there we were, the two of us, company. I felt a desperate need to stop time, to cling to this blessed state, but my legs walked on. Inexorably we came to Pasqual's. This was it, the end was at hand.

Inside, we had the worst luck. All tables were taken, but two of Paloma's acquaintances had a booth and invited us to sit—it was awkward, either we accepted, or excused ourselves and left. Paloma appeared immobilized, so I cut in with thanks and waved her into a seat. Despite our disappointment, we had a cordial get-together. Our benefactors were gearing up for a flight home and full of inspiration and new ideas. Breakfast was good.

Then it was over. Paloma insisted on paying, we pushed out into the busy street and I turned to her for direction. She'd brightened up now that we were alone, and her voice was urgent. "We'll have to make it quick, but could we take a few steps along the river?" I took her arm and hustled her across the street to emphasize my approval. A block brought us to the river, and another to an expanse of grass with a picnic table.

Paloma had been quiet. Now she looked up and spoke. "I'd hoped for an opportunity over breakfast, but.... Could you sit down with me for a minute or two? I have something to tell you."

We sat on opposite sides of the table and she took off her broad-brimmed hat and laid it between us. The wind from behind blew her near shoulder-length hair forward around her face and made her collar stand up and flutter. She gave me a somewhat rueful smile. As so often in the past three days, I was enchanted.

"The truth is, I haven't been entirely candid with you." She glanced down, then raised her eyes to me. "I hope you'll see that I was not in a position to be as open as I'd like. My occupation, or whatever you may wish to call it, doesn't lend itself to forthright discussion with strangers. I liked you from the moment we met and I feel that you like me. But I needed some acquaintance, something more than mutual impulses to go on. Now I have a lot to explain and I haven't left much time." She leaned forward, very earnest and, as usual, looked me right in the eye. She took a deep breath, and that little hesitation seemed like an eternity.

"Haley, I support myself by acting as a professional companion, a traveling companion if you wish. I make travel arrangements, if that's desired, and I accompany one client at a time, from a very select group, on whatever travels he chooses. My fee is six hundred dollars a day, plus, let's say, bed, board, and transportation. I do not require a second room."

She signaled that she'd spoken her piece by resolutely setting her jaw and sitting back. She looked relieved, but I was speechless, transfixed by the enormity of what I'd just heard — in all my years, no revelation had caught me so off guard.

Was it some hoax? In her attempt to sound businesslike, she'd come across as insecure and vulnerable. I raced through a wild phantasmagoria of reasons why such an evidently superior person would put herself in this position. Or pretend to. I got nowhere, couldn't make it real. It was as if we were on stage. The woman addressing me was an actress delivering lines, and not delivering them well. I heard myself as critic. "See here, Paloma, surely this demands a bit more drama.... " For another second we remained shimmering figures in that vision, then the full import of her words hit me like a resounding slap across the face.

I flushed, I burned with humiliation. This perfect woman with her intriguing background and tailor-made interests had conned me, taken me in, led me on. I'd walked into her trap and snapped up the bait. I felt betrayed. I'd responded to her blandishments, released a flood of sincere sentiments, and accepted hers at face value. I felt used, and made to look foolish in the process.

Before I could whip myself into a properly self-righteous frenzy, the absurdity of it all jumped out at me. Who was I that anyone would plan such a campaign? I had no state secrets and no covert plans for anything but another volume of history. And six hundred dollars a day sounded like a relatively modest jackpot for a reasonably adept con artist.

And how, exactly, had I been humiliated? How betrayed? I hadn't. Disillusioned and disappointed, yes, but only because I'd idealized Paloma as the perfect woman, the ministering angel of my blessed restoration. Well, there she was, looking right at me across the picnic table, and no actress playing a part. She'd simply brought herself to Santa Fe and revealed herself to me — and she didn't look happy at all. If anyone was humiliated, it was she, and she'd done it to herself. With that, I felt contrite, and — though I couldn't have said why — sorry for her. But all I could do was stare wonderingly across the table, still at a loss for words.

Paloma must have sensed my state and felt compelled to rescue me. She reached across and put her hand on mine, her touch as apologetic as her voice.

"I hate breaking this to you in such a blunt fashion. It makes me sound as if I've been a hypocrite all the time we've been together. Well, I wasn't, truly I wasn't. But I really did have to know you better. And when I began to think that I did, I was having too much fun and I was too selfish to take a chance on spoiling our adventure. Anyhow, I need to be open now. I want to deserve one bit of your praise. Remember? You found my candor refreshing and my logic straightforward?"

Her look was almost pleading, but I just sat there, still stunned. She opened her bag and took out a slip of paper with a telephone number written on it. "Here's how to reach me in case you care to do so. This number isn't easy to get. If you should call, you'll reach my answering machine. Leave a message and I'll call back. I have your card."

Now it was my turn, but I hadn't the heart or the composure to discuss her proposition. In some corner of my mind, I was weighing my shock over her sordid business against my feelings for her and the blessed changes in me — but all that came of that were visions of our rapport and the joys I'd just experienced. Well, here she was, offering more, and — never mind the conditions — I needed to ante up or drop out. No contest there either — at that point, I could not have turned my back on her if my life had depended on it. I reached for her hands and gave them a long squeeze, trying to reassure both of us. I struggled for words.

"Paloma, I can't imagine what you're really up to or why. None of this matches my vision of you at all.... " I hesitated; she was trembling and looking more distressed. "Uh-oh," I thought, "wrong tack."

She tried to speak, but I held up my hand. "Please. My turn." She withdrew, looking absolutely blank, childlike. I couldn't stand to see her that way. I felt an overpowering need to reassure her, to express the positive feelings I so sincerely felt.

"OK, true confessions. I've been a little in love with you from the moment we met. Every time we've got together I've prayed for another chance, and I was surprised and thrilled every time it happened, I didn't care how or why. You pulled me out of a ditch — no, a lot worse than a ditch — and I was happy. You couldn't possibly imagine how much I hated the thought of this morning, saying good-bye with no clue how a man my age could go on seeing you and having the fun I've had. Now you're telling me it's possible. The way I see it, you just handed me a reprieve. OK, you've got me baffled too, scratching my head, but I'm sitting on Cloud Nine while I do it. So come on, perk up! Pretend you're happy because I'm so relieved."

She didn't say a thing, but she looked more relaxed. I came around the table and picked up her hat and placed it gently on her head. I helped her to her feet with "Shall we go?" and led her off. When I caught her eye, she gave me a tiny smile, and we set off for the hotel, arm in arm, no words. I stepped along, my mind blank but for a sense of togetherness — until I realized with a pang that I was allowing myself, as I had not before, to dwell on the outlines of her womanly form. I might have looked as I would escorting a daughter, but I felt unmistakably otherwise.

In the lobby, there was no embrace or farewell kiss. She took my hands, held them for a long beat, gave me a little smile, and fled.

A shroud of isolation and loneliness settled on me as soon as Paloma disappeared. The shuttle ride to Albuquerque felt prolonged and drab, a constricting tunnel back to my life as a widower. I had no interest in looking out the window and nothing to do but rehash the morning's stunning surprise and my ridiculous state of mind. I told myself that the palpitations I was experiencing were those of an old fool, that I should pass off my adventure with a shrug and make it grist for the conversation mill at coffee shop get-togethers with cronies.

But I didn't kid myself for one minute with all that worldly logic. True, I'd never resorted to a prostitute, but I'd been around enough and heard enough and read enough to know that Paloma had none of the telltale traits associated with even the most elite women-for-hire. She should have been to some degree flirtatious, insincere, jaded, cynical, passive, shopworn. She was none of those things. The mystery, the total mystery in all this, revolved around the woman she clearly seemed to be. What possible circumstances might have seduced such a one into this profession? And if it really was her profession, why was she so hesitant in approaching me? Why wasn't that whole scene as smooth as silk? Or was all that uncertainty and uneasiness part of the act? Ridiculous, utterly non-Paloma. And, on top of that, I remembered my earlier daydreams of a relationship with her — and that raised the eerie suspicion that this incredible offer had come as wish fulfillment.

The whole thing was incomprehensible, but even in my confused state every instinct told me I'd met a fascinating person whose story I needed to know and whose presence I wanted so badly I ached. I wrestled with exhilaration and shame as I flew, and that conflict continued as I faced up to the chores accumulated at home.

Tuesday, September 24th

Back home, chores were all I could face. I answered calls, paid bills, filed papers, and tended Marian's potted plants, indoor and out. Beyond that, I fidgeted, couldn't concentrate. And the house felt changed. I'd been away only four days, but it struck me as strangely stale and empty. It was a shock to find that Marian now seemed gone for good. I felt lonelier than ever.

Gwyn, our younger daughter, invited me to dinner on my second evening home. She and her kids, seven-year-old Lynne and four-year-old

Birk, are as dear to me as life itself, and I've always been close to my son-in-law Ted. But it was tough going over to their place, knowing that any account of my trip would have to be stripped to the bone.

"Well, how did it go?" Gwyn asked cheerfully after she opened the door and gave me a hug. I handed her a luxurious Christmas cactus I'd found in bloom when I came home, and told her she'd been right to suggest I go. I had gotten out of myself, I said. (Which was true, sort of. But what had I gotten into?)

I rattled off a humdrum summary of my junket and Gwyn asked if I'd met anyone at all interesting. I couldn't imagine giving a realistic account of Paloma, so I settled for trivialized remarks about enjoying the company of a well-traveled Spanish woman I'd met at the hotel. Gwyn looked pleased. I was afraid she'd press for details, but just then Lynne slipped her pet mouse into my shirt pocket. It stuck its wee head out, whiskers all ashiver, little Birk laughed like a hyena, and I got down on the floor for a romp. That got me off the hook but I felt like an old fraud. After dinner, I was glad to find Ted and Gwyn preoccupied with a new computer, and to be taken on a tour of its wonders until I could plead travel weariness and go home.

Thereafter, particularly at night, I was obsessed by conflicting images—the impressive person with whom I'd spent so many hours, and a woman who would accompany a paying customer around the world and into bed. The entire proposition clashed with my intuition. Try as I might, I could not make Paloma into a sordid person. I'd lived a long time and dealt with many diverse individuals. I had seldom, almost never, been betrayed by my judgment of people. My life had been tranquil, partly on that account.

Unexpectedly, and perhaps for the first time, that conviction sounded self-congratulatory and hollow. Hadn't part of my tranquility come at a price? Wasn't there an element of aloofness in that method for sidestepping problems, particularly those in human relations? I'd been comfortable, sure, but hadn't I missed a lot of life's experiences by confining myself to the proverbial straight and narrow?

No doubt. But what's wrong with that? I'd been a lifelong believer in conventional wisdom. Most of it had seemed advantageous, not just blind devotion to society's rules. I'd preached it in good conscience to my students and my daughters. Had I simply been conforming to a goody-two-shoes formula? Of course not. I believed in it, and it worked—then. But then I'd had Marian, we had each other. We felt that our life together was good. We wanted to pass along what we'd learned and, in a way, proved.

But that was then, I reasoned, and now is different. Marian's gone, the girls are grown and raising kids of their own. I'm getting old. I'm in the "now or never" time of life, and temptation, even casual sex, looks different. Casual sex? Come on! I couldn't think of one thing casual about my feelings for Paloma—the thought of her was more tantalizing than ever. I'd run the full course of sincere marital fidelity, and accepting Paloma's offer would open aspects of life that I'd missed.

Fine—but it was wrong and I knew it. I shouldn't be doing this any more than Paloma should be doing this. Two wrongs don't make a right. What would happen if my daughters and grandchildren found out? How would I live with that? "Turn your back and walk away," I told myself, but I couldn't. I'd been lonely and unproductive for so long that I was frightened—and heartily sick of myself. And now that I'd been rescued from that state, I doubted that I could stay clear of it on my own. Which scared me. I hated the idea of alone; all I wanted to think about was the exciting alchemy I associated with Paloma.

Why, oh why, did it have to be Paloma, so impossibly young, so impossibly employed? Dumb question, I reminded myself. I fell for her days before I found out what she did for a living. The woman herself is the potent drug and I'm the instant addict—I responded, I turned a corner, I began to feel and act like myself again. The more I hashed it over, the clearer it became that mine wasn't some abstract debate about whether or not to deal with a prostitute. It was a decision whether or not to deal with Paloma.

Looking back, I see that I was playing with a stacked deck all along. The game never really revolved around reason or morality— old, foolish, whatever, I was in love with Paloma. And for the moment all I could do, and I did that well, was recall her in every graphic particular. For some reason, the most precious and damnable recollection was the scent of her hair, something I'd caught fleetingly during our brief encounter.

Monday, September 30th

After a week, I stopped fighting myself, emotion took over, and I swiveled my desk chair and stretched for the phone. My heart began to pound and I caught myself holding my breath while I punched in the numbers from Paloma's slip of paper. I listened—and thanked God at the first ring. After the fourth, her recorded voice cut in, low-pitched and precise, "Please leave your name and a number where I can reach you. I'll get back to you sooner than you imagine—perhaps sooner than you deserve."

I hadn't rehearsed, I just poured out my hopes. "Paloma, it's Haley Talbot. I very much need a trip and you're the trip I need. Maybe a couple of weeks, if they're available, and how would you like to do the Spanish-Portuguese border country? Call me. I'm sure I could get away 'most any time. You have my card, but here's the number...." I rattled it off and hung up.

Then I was in a new state. That day and the next, I was the caged lion, didn't dare go out. I carried a cordless phone when I stepped out front for the paper, or to the backyard to water, or, more likely, to stand there staring blankly at my unweeded jungle.

Each time the phone rang, which was mercifully seldom, I made a convulsive leap for the nearest handset and did my best to be brief with whomsoever.

Tuesday, October 1st

The next day, noonish, I heard the phone and ran for it. Paloma was on the other end.

"Haley! Good to hear your voice! You were such a dear in Santa Fe and I handled the whole parting thing badly—so awkward, my first attempt at that revelation and all. I'm so glad you weren't entirely put off."

"God no. I'm delighted to hear from you. But is it, or is it not, sooner than I deserve?"

"Oh, that! That wasn't for you. A friend left me in the lurch, no explanation. It's all cleared up, but, hey, it's a bonus if it gave you the odd giggle."

"Sorceress! You read me even from the far end of a wire — but can you become a presence?" I tried to sound flippant, not easy with the suspense I'd built up inside.

"The earliest I could arrange would be around the eighteenth, this month. Would that fit your schedule?"

"Paloma, I have no schedule. My schedule is your schedule. Let's fly to Lisbon for starters, rent a car, and I'll show you off-the-beaten-track goodies you haven't dreamed of."

"Stop! Not another word. I'd love to be landing in Lisbon this minute." She paused. "Speaking of that, should I make airline arrangements? And what about hotels?"

"Yes, for sure to the airline thing, but let me do lodgings. I've stayed in some, I've looked at some, and I've collected a slew of tips."

"Perfect, but let me arrange the auto. My airline contact has great deals on related auto rentals. You'll get my bill and one for the airfare, and both should be paid immediately. And Haley? One other thing I have to ask. I'm going to send a doctor to your house to take samples of, shall we say, bodily fluids? He'll be a real doctor, and he works for insurance companies when they need quick medical exams. I'm sure you can imagine why I need this routine checkup."

"Of course I understand. You're worried about some old geezer who might just pop off from the impact of your charms."

"You're bad! But thank you for understanding. Oh, and you should know I've had the same checkup, but you'll have to take my word. I'm not in a position to give out my doctor's name. And don't worry about contraception. I'm prepared."

"Listen Paloma, I'd be more than happy to take this trip the same way we did in New Mexico. I mean it's you I want to see, and I don't want you to be thinking of intimacy as an obligation. Do you know what I'm saying?"

"Yes, and you're sweet. You don't want to impose on me and I promise not to impose on you. But is this a bridge we need to cross today? We'll have two weeks. Why don't we just go and get acquainted and follow our feelings?"

What could I say? I was in over my head, the whole affair was mad, I was mad, I might as well be hopelessly mad. "OK. OK to everything. I trust you. Count on it."

"I do, and I won't let you down. Oh! Hold on. While we've been talking, I've worked out something I really like—saves you money and me two days of travel wear and tear—and we start earlier. How 'bout that? This way, I book you San Diego to Lisbon, arriving the thirteenth, and I fly in from Vienna the next morning. You could pick me and the auto up at the airport. Will that work for you?"

"Work? It sings! Do that, and I'll get after my end of things as soon as we hang up. Now, what else? Any other ideas?"

"Yes. What about clothing? What do you have in mind in the way of accommodations and restaurants? And what about recreation or night life?"

"Well, at risk of sounding like a dull thud, I'm not much for night life. Outside of Lisbon, I thought we'd stay mostly in those neat government-sponsored inns, you know, the *pousadas* and *paradores*. I'll take a couple of ties and a blazer, but I'd rather not wear them. Think of outfits to go with an old fellow dressed in a khaki bush suit."

"Right! What you wore in Taos. Good. Comfortable. I'll bring things that won't embarrass you. And Haley—I should've said it sooner—I'm truly looking forward to meeting again. Now don't be cynical. I really am."

"OK, Paloma. All I'll say is my one word of Portuguese, *obrigado*, much obliged."

"See you in two weeks. Be good!" Then she was gone and the line went dead.

I sat there dazed, disbelieving. Did I just do that? Did I just buy Paloma for two weeks? I thought of her voice, her last words. I thought of her high humor, her smile, her body—and I was galvanized. I'd been too fearful of a jinx to get guidebooks before I had her signed up, but now I hot-footed it to a bookstore. Within three hours I had my travel agent busy with a list of two-bedded rooms to reserve—and much admonished as to the need for immediate results.

Saturday, October 5th

Some small magic seemed to hang over my preparations. Was it possible, all but one lodging confirmed in three days? In the same period, a Dr. Lachner called to arrange a next-day appointment at my house. When the hour rolled around, he was at my door, short, somewhat nervous, middle-aged, and sporting a remarkable fund of all-purpose wit with which he entertained me as I gave blood and cooperated in a certain examination. He relished the view out my windows while I went to procure the final sample, and departed whistling something lively from *Carmen*. No words passed between us as to the particulars of this order, not who had requested it, who would evaluate it, or who would pay for it.

The doctor left me encouraged, not embarrassed. Paloma might have sacrificed her morals but she had enough self-respect to be concerned for her safety. Fine, but my euphoria didn't last. Before long I was overcome by the eerie feeling that this entire affair was a dream and I might awake to find all traces gone aglimmering. Still, I had no alternative. I had my marching orders and I marched.

Monday, October 7th

A bill arrived from an accounting firm in Orange County. I checked its two items, "Fee.......$8,400.00, Airline Tickets........$1,873.00," and compared their total to what I imagined might be the costs of protracted counseling to deal with my depression. In that company—hell, in any company—Paloma was a bargain. I wrote a check, walked it to the post office, and sent it by overnight mail. Back home, I faxed her a copy of our accommodations schedule and, later, got back a fax detailing a Lauda Air flight departing Vienna at 6:40 A.M., stopping in Barcelona, and arriving in Lisbon at 10:30 A.M., all on the fourteenth of October.

I outlined my trip to the family and mentioned that I would join the Spanish woman I'd met at the conference. Everyone applauded;

they'd encouraged me all along to seek company. But when they asked for details, I resorted to barefaced sins of omission, an oh-so-casual report that my companion-to-be was a travel expert who knew the territory well. I winced, even as I spoke, to think how they'd react if they could picture the woman and the circumstances.

Then, my preparations complete a week ahead, the countdown became agonizing. I had too much time, and doubts proliferated. How would our contract affect the rapport Paloma and I had enjoyed? Could I keep my hands off her and still enjoy the relationship we'd started? Clearly, she thought not.

But if we proceeded into bed, what might happen to the innocent camaraderie we'd shared in Santa Fe? And how would I manage as a sexual partner? What with Marian's progressive medical problems, it'd been ten years since I'd made love to a woman, and I wasn't the man I'd been ten years ago. After all that time, even imagining unrestrained intimacy set me to trembling with fear as much as fever. Would I be a lover or a laughingstock?

And there were other night horrors, and not only at night. I conjured up alternate visions of Paloma, my sense of the woman I'd met, and the specter of another, a prostitute who created illusions and drew men into them. I was aroused by alluring promises and chilled by the fear of seeing them turn to slime. I was ashamed of myself for accepting companionship on terms that few would find acceptable, and I had no one with whom I could share my turmoil.

On the other hand, I clung to one shred of evidence that all this might be less ugly than imagined. On the phone, Paloma had let slip that I was the first to whom she'd disclosed her "profession." Really? What might that mean? I wracked my brain to no avail. I've never been good at riddles.

Saturday, October 12th

Getting to Lisbon was hell. I was in a sweat over so many things, it's a long flight anyhow, and I got hung up in one of those damnable delays that plague the airlines. We were late leaving San Diego, too late for my connection in New York, and I was lucky to get to Lisbon in time for dinner when I should have been there for breakfast. To make it worse, all through the flights and delays I'd hadn't so much as dozed — too many palpitations over Paloma on the one hand, too much shame on the other. And, in the back of my mind, there always loomed a doubt that this escapade would really happen. In some weird way, I half hoped that she wouldn't show up, that she'd send me the equivalent of an April Fool's greeting and explain that it was all a prank. I half hoped, but I also half feared. I was a mess.

And when I finally got to Hotel Metrópole, I was handed a fax. "I am truly sorry to report that I must stay over one day at an international meeting. Expect me same flight on 15 October. I look forward to our adventure more than ever. Paloma."

Great. More suspense. And that shot down one of our three days in Lisbon — no way I was going to start changing our whole lineup of reservations. I was exhausted. I went to my room, crashed in one of the beds, and slept, jet lag and all.

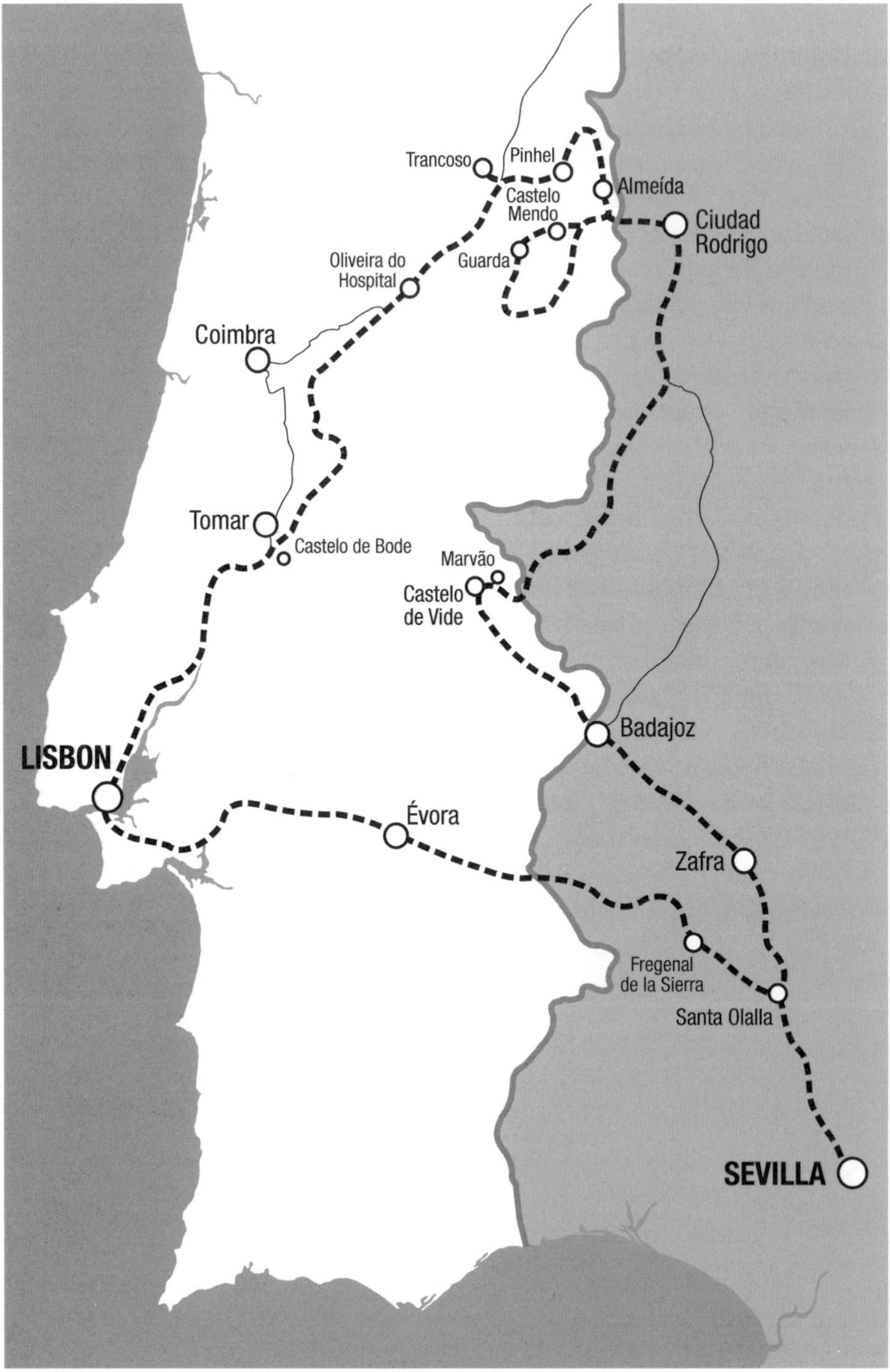
Trancoso
Pinhel
Almeída
Castelo
Mendo
Ciudad
Rodrigo
Guarda
Oliveira do
Hospital
Coimbra
Tomar
Castelo de Bode
Marvão
Castelo
de Vide
Badajoz
LISBON
Évora
Zafra
Fregenal
de la Sierra
Santa Olalla
SEVILLA

II IBERIA

Lisbon, Portugal — Monday, October 14, 1996

I awoke in the dark, then lay there. Remembrances of Paloma floated randomly by, playing and replaying — and somehow leaving me more at peace than I'd been in three weeks. Even her tardiness now seemed a blessing, a day to recover from my travel ordeal and time to prospect for places to take her.

Slowly it dawned on me that overnight my anxiety had taken flight. I happily anticipated the woman — and bother the circumstances. I had accepted that she meant more to me than whatever part of my principles or good name had to be sacrificed. As naive as it might seem, I had the gut feeling that I'd found a friend and started a relationship, not made a business deal. I was doubly drawn — I needed her, and I needed to know more about her.

Eventually I stirred my bones, rose, and drew the curtains. Before me was the Rossio, Lisbon's principal downtown square, all set about with trees, plantings, and shops, and crisscrossed by streams of cars and pedestrians. There, too, was the start of a fine day, autumnal, soft around the edges.

I dressed, went down, walked past the elaborate National Theater, and crossed to the handsome strip park that graces the broad median of Avenida da Liberdade. I strolled in sunlight filtered through fine-leafed elms until I came to an open-air café with invitingly shaded tables. Finding myself more thirsty than in need of stimulants, I had a *limonada* in honor of Paloma—no, in hope of Paloma. And with her in mind, I inquired about black teas and was offered three choices, all Twining's, a brand she favored. I ordered an omelet with leeks and ham, a pleasure that moved me to ponder one of Western culture's profound mysteries: How is it that every European nation serves ham more flavorful than ours? My newfound peace of mind permitted me to sit back and enjoy the passing parade as I sipped a rousing *café americano*.

I was struck by a shameless inspiration—go out and explore routes to propose casually to Paloma for the walks I presumed she would expect and enjoy. I leafed through my guidebook, bent the corners of promising pages, armed myself with a city map, and set out to evaluate nearby attractions.

The botanical garden on the hill to the west proved tidy but colorless, so I headed southeast, hiked up a crowded slope, and stood before the ruins of Castelo de São Jorge. The approach through a colorful hillside neighborhood, the picturesque ruins themselves, and the views of rooftops and river traffic made the place a sure winner. I stepped down to reacquaint myself with an ancient, once-Moorish neighborhood, the Alfama, a maze of crooked streets, tiny squares, and buildings faced top to bottom with blue or yellow tile. Nearby, I found more treasure, The Espirito Santo Foundation, a museum of decorative art whose many handsome displays, even at a glance, promised to engage Paloma.

By then, the easy walk suggested by the map had become an effort, and when I'd finally made my way back to the hotel, I was tired, damp, and thirsty. I sent for iced tea and slumped into an overstuffed chair in a nook off the lobby. Two leggy young women in tennis outfits attracted my eye and led me to wonder about Paloma's legs—after all, I'd seen her only in slacks. I blushed inwardly. Here was the old goat in full pursuit of his Quixotic romance, but still wondering about the conformation of his lady's legs. I had visions of my own sagging form and was properly ashamed of myself. And tired. Lured by thoughts of bed, I retreated to my room, no matter that a nap could end my chances for sleeping that night. Regardless, it was wonderful to lay me down in dim light and close my eyes.

I awoke late in the day and needing supper. I got up, enjoyed my view of lights winking on in the square, and turned to consider the untouched second bed. If I were joined, would it be the friendly spirit I'd conjured up? Or a relative stranger, somehow changed by our scandalous contract? I puzzled on as I hunted out a small restaurant on the Rossio and used crusty peasant bread to soak up a vast bowl of savory onion-and-seafood soup.

When I'd pushed away my plate and paid the bill, I stepped out into the warm evening and headed for the strip park, hoping for a busy scene. I walked into a visual delight, trees and buildings festooned with strings of tiny white lights, but found little action—people must go elsewhere for evening meals. I enjoyed a glass of sweet Madeira and retraced my steps. En route, I spotted a stand with buckets of cut flowers and bought a bunch of pungent pinks for Paloma to find in our dressing area—my concierge supplied a vase. After a protracted shower and yet another effort to scrub, trim, polish, or file whatever needed attention, I went to bed and I did sleep.

Tuesday, October 15th

I slept, that is, until 4 A.M. At that hour I awoke one hundred percent, the motor running. I got up, already in a sorry state of nerves, pulled on some clothes, and found the room so lonely that I couldn't wait to flee. I moved through silent halls, a silent lobby, out into a dark street, and up to the long park for a third time. Nothing was open, most lights were off, but then I made out, far ahead, a brightly lighted stand with Brazilian pop music blaring. I joined a cluster of coffee drinkers, half of whom proved to be semi-English speakers eager to practice, and right through my three cups, they kept me busy fielding questions that ranged from baseball to NATO policies in Bosnia. It was flattering to be treated as an oracle and it took my mind off Paloma. I rejoiced to find another hour come and gone.

I returned to my room, tidied it up, and went down for the breakfast I'd counted on to kill more time—a forlorn hope. My state of nerves was such that I couldn't eat and I had to fight the urge to down more coffee—the last thing I needed was heightened jitters and the odor of coffee exuding from every pore. I backtracked to my room for another round of tooth brushing and mouthwash. I shaved, buffed up the bathroom and the separate vanity area, then changed into my best pants and a cheery salmon-colored shirt.

A final checkup in the mirror did nothing to calm my nerves. Staring back at me was a lined visage with gray hair and slack flesh, emphatic reminders of the implausibility and inappropriateness of my coveted tryst. Who did I think I was? I peeked at my watch—it was still minutes before eight, but I was too agitated to sit down and stay seated.

I gave it up and made for the airport, never mind that I could be two hours beforehand. Surely dealing with the car rental people would take a bit off the clock. An airport limousine pulled up and conveyed me and two others at a sedate pace through Lisbon's teeming morning traffic.

No luck killing time with EuroCar. Their office was so efficient that our business was done in fifteen minutes. I arranged to leave my newly acquired Opel Astra with them, then took my time getting to Lauda's gate where the ten-thirty arrival was confirmed. I still couldn't sit. I visited the men's room. I downed an orange drink. I toured the soulless terminal, absently aware that it mimicked, or was mimicked by, a hundred others around the world. I returned to the men's room. At long last it was ten-thirty, the witching hour, but nothing happened. Ten-forty-five, and nothing. No announcement proclaimed delays. I moped—then, abruptly, it was there, a fuselage with "Lauda" in rust-red letters sweeping by the tall windows. In moments the plane reappeared and taxied up to the gate. I began to shake, a schoolboy again with the dream girl approaching—also an old man amused by his own knocking knees.

I hurried to wait outside the closed-off customs area, a dozen other expectant folk fidgeting with me. Twenty minutes passed and newly arrived passengers began to emerge. I craned my neck, and suddenly, incredibly, there was Paloma. She flashed a wide smile and hurried her cart forward while I stood there gaping, only half-believing at the end of all that suspense. As she presented her cheeks for traditional European pecks, I caught the scent of her hair and a shiver rippled down my spine.

She looked me over and observed, "Must be warmer than I'd expected." My shirt was soaked below each armpit.

"Dear Paloma, I cannot tell a lie. What you see is a trifle compared with the lather I have churned up inside."

"Why ever for?"

"I've never done anything like this. I've been in a fever of speculation. For weeks. Uncertainty. I'm not good at it."

"Silly man. Did you really think I might not be a woman of my word?"

"That's not it at all, but please don't press. If I try to explain, I'll get myself in so deep that two weeks won't begin my rehabilitation."

"My, my, I'm that formidable then?" This with the sweetest of smiles.

"No, Paloma, contrariwise. One glimpse of you, really, truly here, and my private chorus burst into *The Heavens Laugh! The Earth Rejoices!* I'm terribly glad to see you and I can't wait to find a quiet spot where we can have tea and talk."

She crooked her finger to draw me in. "And commune? Do let's commune. I'm glad to see you too." Then, somewhat reprovingly, "I suppose I wanted some reassurance about us, but I must say, I've looked ahead with excitement, not sweats and fears." She pretended to slap my cheeks, but her face appeared serenely free of misgivings.

"She came," I thought nonsensically, "she's really here!" I took a deep breath and felt light as a feather.

Paloma was grateful in a smaller way. "Haley, thank you for not getting into a big hug-and-kiss routine. You couldn't know, but I hate public displays of affection. Affection is personal, at least it is to me."

"Me too — and in your company, I feel extra conspicuous. But if I get careless, if I slip up, you kick me."

"Is that an order?"

"Absolutely. I can forget where I am and what I'm about. I need a keeper."

She grinned, I assumed the cart duty, and we traversed the long corridors. In minutes we'd loaded up our blindingly red car, quitted the rental lot, and wound down onto the boulevard headed for the Rossio. Whenever I glanced over, my new roommate's glowing presence made my rosiest dreams seem pale and wispy. The demons I had conjured up were banished.

We were back at the hotel by noon, and when Paloma stepped from the car, it was plain that I achieved a new status with the doorman — just what status was anybody's guess. We followed our porter up to the room. I handed him a tip and left Paloma to scan the place while I dived into the bath to sponge off and change my shirt. I returned to find her fully approving the size of our room, its high ceiling and prime view of the great square. She excused herself, and minutes passed before she reappeared, coat and shoes off, her blouse sleeveless. For the first time, I saw the long, strong arms that so fitted her eloquent hands. She came to me, holding up one stem of pinks. She put it to my nose, then to hers.

"Dianthus! How could you know? My favorite scent." She put her arms around my neck, and her hopeful smile seemed to say, "Time for you to decide." Not easy. That fresh face cost me an intense stab of conscience. I imagined a detached view of the two of us, the weather-worn grandfather and the young thing, a veritable poster for the delights of prostitution. But I wanted her and I couldn't imagine trying to explain that all of this was some unaccountable mistake. I felt eons out of practice as I encircled a yielding body and kissed the mouth so invitingly offered up — kissed rose petals, warm and plush, my mind numb, unable to cope with a fulfillment I had fantasized daily, hourly, but never quite believed would be.

We parted slowly, then brushed again. I was afraid to open my eyes, to break the spell. I was afraid, period, and I admitted it. "Paloma, this is too wonderful for words, having you here and in my arms and all. But I'm not ready for anything more. Not yet. Can you understand?"

She put her cheek to my chest and spoke softly to my shoulder. "Haley, there's nothing to apologize for. We're just starting. Be patient with yourself — and with me. We need time to learn each other's ways."

I pulled back with a pounding heart and galloping emotions. I spoke to those great brown eyes. "Dear lady, patience is a good thing. Thank you for understanding the state I'm in." She patted my cheek and leaned in again. I wrapped her in a tender embrace and buried my face in fragrant hair. Sheer heaven.

Paloma skipped to the window for another peek at the bonny Lisbon day. She looked back. "What shall we do? Any ideas?"

Suddenly I felt smug. "Sure. How about stepping out for a just-as-good-as-a-Spanish *limonada* in the shade of a tree? Then we could double back here for a little lunch, or stay in the park for a sandwich."

She did another skip to the dressing room, painted her lips, put on shoes, and gave me a roguish grin as she shimmied her hips in adjusting her slacks. She swung her purse in a playful figure eight, slung it over her shoulder, and by the time she reached the door, was once again a dignified adult.

As we walked in dappled light under the elms, she enthused over the strip park, commented on the varied shops, and stopped to examine underground work in a roped-off area. Peering into the rather deep trench, she feigned disappointment. "Oh, damn. Not archaeology at all, just a new takeoff from some electrical feed."

I was impressed by her grasp of all we'd passed. When we'd placed our order at my favorite café, I commented, "Amazing. You took in more in one jaunt up here than I did in four. If there's a live wire around here, you're it."

"Eww! Please, you're trying too hard. But listen, I'll try not to overdo it — no running commentary on the passing parade. It's just that checking out the street scene is an old habit, and this is my first-ever glimpse of Portugal."

"Paloma, until I get tired of reveling in you — a remote possibility — you may describe anything, retell *The Thousand and One Nights*, or read me the telephone book." For that, I got a thoroughly dismissive look.

Our food arrived, and as we munched, Paloma told me how she'd looked forward to seeing Portugal ever since childhood geography classes in Sevilla. Before long, though, she leaned back and let out a sigh. "You know, the morning wasn't as easy as I'd supposed. I confess I could use a rest." We drained our glasses, and headed back.

I needed a rest. My early rise, the suspense, and all my I hoped not-too-obvious hovering had taken their toll. Paloma peeled off her clothes with evident relief, and the little white nightie she donned in the dressing area settled the burning question of legs. When she came out, I tried not to stare but was so unsuccessful that the owner of those legs lifted her hem to mid-thigh and did a three-step turn with the air of a runway model. *Voilà!* Miss Grey disclosed no flaw.

"OK?" she asked.

I groaned, "Paloma, you're literally too much."

We lay on our backs in separate beds, silently agreed not to interrupt our rest. In a short while she was asleep, but I lingered, spellbound by her soft breathing and the alluring contours of her head-to-foot profile. Alluring, but so innocent-appearing in sleep that I wound up feeling more abashed than lustful.

We got up, batteries charged, and I proposed the walk I'd planned, a popular proposal indeed. We hiked to the castle and enthused over vistas of old Lisbon and the Rio Tejo. We stepped down to the Museum of Decorative Arts and examined every room, my comrade devoting the expected attention to exhibits of needle, thread, and fabric work. Very interesting. Young as she was, Paloma was the best informed person I'd ever accompanied in such a place, well able to augment many of the museum's display captions. But only when asked—our visit was not turned into a tour. And she glowed as we left. "I guessed—no, I knew this would happen if I sent you ahead. I adore to have someone show me about, and, really, this museum was perfect." Now it was my turn to glow.

We stepped into the old Alfama quarter and found it a living museum. At first we were spectators quite apart, but we joined the flow of foot traffic and soon were immersed in the bustle and cries, flapping laundry, and tiny street markets overhung with the cloying odors of overripe fruit. I'd been there before, so the big fun for me was watching Paloma take it in. I was particularly touched by her delight in a miniature parade, two young women escorting a covey of blue-clad preschool girls holding hands, a waving rope of small bodies. Hair, skirts, and white aprons flounced as they skipped and tripped along, chirping brightly to the tune of *Frère Jacques*. My lady watched, enthralled, until they turned a distant corner.

By the time we doubled back to the hotel, the stroll I'd envisioned had become a constitutional. To recuperate, we returned to the promenade, ordered more *limonadas*, and sat gratefully in the shade. I looked Paloma over and for the first time appreciated her tasteful green pants suit and her flat hat, crisp and white. The woman has nice things, I thought. But it was the woman herself who had my attention, truly relaxed and happy — her eyes danced, fixed full upon me as was her custom. We said little for what seemed minutes until she looked around, gave me the biggest smile, and sort of hugged herself.

"This is great, just a few hours, but I get the best feelings from Portugal. It's all better than I hoped. And you knew it would be, and I think I knew that you knew. I can't wait for whatever's next."

"Great. I can't wait to be there with you."

Dinner was a simple treat. At the concierge's suggestion, we climbed the hillside behind our hotel to an intimate restaurant with turn-of-the-century decor, mirrored walls, and floors in alternate black and white tile. We were escorted to a quiet corner and seated at a small table with a red, red rose. It was a delight to have few choices and enjoy a delicious table d'hôte served by an inconspicuous waiter.

The girl across from me gushed in the wake of the day. "I must say, my cup runneth over. It's got so I don't expect a lot on flying days, even fairly short hops. It's usually an ordeal, you get there, you get settled, you eat something, and that's it, lights out. Not today. Look at all the neat stuff we've seen and done."

"Agreed, totally. But the big thing is, you turned out to be the person I'd hoped you were. We'd spent so little time together, honestly, this second round seemed like a dream, a dream I didn't dare count on to come true. Well, it has, you have, beautifully."

I sat back and tried to pretend that I was at peace with the world. But even I knew I was trying too hard, and I certainly hadn't pulled the wool over Paloma's eyes. As we ate our pear tart and sipped coffee, she reached over and touched my hand reassuringly.

"Don't push, Haley. You want us to know each other better than would be humanly possible. We're off to a wonderful start and we have two whole weeks to get acquainted. Just let it happen. Let's enjoy the whole process. All right?"

This seemed so wise that I cringed to think of the experiences that must lie behind it. "I suppose I am anxious. I haven't been in the position of breaking the ice with any woman in forty-some years — and never across such a divide in ages. I'm in the unenviable position of being nearly old and you have the assurance of youth — and the bloom. Those things really do matter."

She patted my hand smartly, her eyes snapped. "Look, I'm younger, sure, but I haven't done much, and you've done a lot. Doesn't that mean something? Besides, our differences aren't some grand canyon we can only wave across. Look, we're touching right now. We're speaking almost in whispers. How far apart can we possibly be?" Her touch was electric. I quaked like a plate of gelatin.

"Paloma, you're a gem, and I am trying to be better. But I'm in a situation I haven't even imagined for years. I don't know myself in this situation."

"Oh my goodness! I hope you're not worried about performing in bed. Relax. We can just crawl in together and all the rest of getting acquainted is easier. I know. I want you to know. You're very welcome."

There we were, doing a role reversal — I, the callow youth, she, the voice of experience. I sensed it, but all I could get out was, "I don't know what to say."

"Don't say anything. I just did. And I did it now because the closer it gets, the larger it looms. Better to break the ice up here and walk back arm in arm. You're with an admirer; if I were not, believe me, I wouldn't be here." And when we went out the door, she went right on making me feel welcome all the way down the hill and to our room.

Despite her assurances, I was deluged with feelings of inadequacy and unreality. I showered, then she showered and joined me in bed. I felt shy and awkward, but within an aura of incredible warmth. I began to touch, she touched back, and I plunged into a delirium of half-forgotten acts and sensations — skin on skin, lips, tongue, breasts, thighs, hands-on, mouth-on — all sweet, soft, but charged, my body charged. That irresistible rapture approached, grew, and burst its bounds — unique, yet echoing dreams and memories.

My ecstasy retreated, but I felt a rhythm unfulfilled and dropped down to add what I could. Seconds, then seconds more — she seemed to shiver, then squeezed my head. When I came up, she compounded my joys with a none-too-tidy kiss. I took a breath and blurted out, "Thank God for letting me know this one more time."

"Silly goose. See? Just as it should be. You're not as old as you choose to think."

Wednesday, October 16th

Light barely showed around the curtains when I rolled over, almost frightened to look for my improbable roommate. Paloma sat straight up, stretched, and grinned. There she was, real as could be, and wide awake.

She hopped up and peeked through the curtains. "Oh, let's take a walk in this first light—then perhaps your early morning coffee bar?"

"Are you always this chipper? How can you stay so up?"

"Get dressed and we'll go find lots of reasons for being up."

At that moment I knew I was completely lost. Old Haley, hopelessly in love.

Our map directed us to the Miradouro de São Pedro, an outlook point near the botanical garden I'd spurned. We arrived, out of breath, to take in a grand panorama of the castle ruin on its dominant hill and square miles of white buildings, most with red tile roofs, many with facades in ochre-colored tile—quintessential Lisbon. Paloma was impressed.

"One look, and you think, 'Oh, Italy, or perhaps southern France.' But notice all the details you don't find anywhere else. I see a thousand years of people waving for attention. And not just telling me they were here, telling me who they were."

She and I locked hands in unspoken accord, a friendly gesture, no more, but the feel of her strong, warm hand in mine had an electric effect. I flushed all over from a mix of pleasure and embarrassment. The cause of it all seemed not to notice.

The hillside produced no breakfast possibilities. We descended to the avenida and selected a bustling outdoor café resembling the classic bandstand-in-the-park. When we'd ordered breakfast and got drinks, I gazed over my cup and across the table. My tablemate peered back, bobbed her head from side to side, and gave me the cheeriest of grins. That look and that moment swept away the tension I'd accumulated in the hours since we made love. I'd felt possessive and, yes, resentful of Paloma's other "clients," but seeing her now, fresh, happy, and ready for the day, that all faded. If I chose, I could make myself miserable over other men, but I told myself, "You're here and they're not,' and that did it. I felt privileged and it was a day to live for. Our plates of melon, steamed eggs, and breads arrived, but I felt so fortunate and so fulfilled that I had a hard time making myself eat.

Breakfast over, we took a cab westward to Belém and to the door of the Museu de Arte Popular, a bit old-fashioned and shabby compared with The Espirito Santo Foundation, but offering compensations. At the Museu, Portugal's typical folk art is arranged region by region, hundreds of items collected in one place that otherwise would have to be searched out in every corner of the land. Once again, Paloma's knowledge left me shaking my head. Her first visit, and she knew everything? It seemed like a parlor trick, but that wasn't the time for probing questions.

As I'd expected, she lingered over the fabric work, took notes as she had the day before, and made a series of quick sketches. I peeked, admired the apt lines, and inquired about her artistic training. "Oh, just high school — art classes, biology fieldwork, that sort of thing. Now I record craft ideas. So often you can't take pictures."

"True," I agreed, but I was thinking, "I'd hate to bet she can't tap dance or bake a cherry pie, Billy-boy, Billy-boy."

As she finished up, I asked what triggered the notes and sketches. She reflected for a moment. "I'm trying to identify the elements that distinguish the work of individual artists or craftspeople operating within the same tradition. It's quite another problem, more personal and more difficult than learning to differentiate the crafts of distinct cultural groups, even close neighbors — say the pottery of adjacent Peruvian tribes."

She looked and sounded so thoughtful that I tried picturing her as the sober museum docent lecturing attentive visitors. That unlikely vision cost me a beat and I hurried to catch up. "Now that I think about it, I've chosen among craftsmen working in the same tradition dozens of times, you know, buying rugs, pottery, and whatnot. I must've made that distinction you're talking about every time. But I've never analyzed the reasons for my choices. Truthfully, I've never thought about them."

"Well then," she admonished, flipping her notebook shut and waving it under my nose, "from now on, be good and see that you do."

We emerged to a threatening sky and a rising wind. We cut across a spacious square, Praça do Imperio, climbed a slope to the Monastery of Santa Maria, and walked slowly through, craning our necks to inspect the great spaces. Neither of us knew much about the fanciful, florid Manueline style of old Lisbon, but we loved its cornucopia of carved stone—twisted columns, braided nautical cable motifs, anchors, and roses—especially given the day's dramatic weather. At times, we'd be dazzled by brilliant sun that shone through every elaborate window, and in another moment, we'd be shrouded by shadows of low, fast-moving clouds that darkened the chambers like gathering night. Or we'd be startled for a shuddering instant by the glare of lightning, and then shaken by a booming thunderclap reverberating through the vast chambers. One such effect was so proximate and uproarious that we and several French tourists were moved to applaud and cry "Bravo!"

We went outside to find the clouds moving away after shedding a mere scattering of giant drops. I peered at their pattern. "Imagine that, a six-inch rain." Paloma looked properly puzzled. "You know," I said, "the drops are six inches apart." How can I describe her look, that fine balance of appreciation and exasperation?

We stepped down to the waterfront and found a table at an outdoor café. Noon was at hand, and we split a chicken sandwich to go with iced tea. Talk turned back to crafts, and my curiosity got the better of me.

"Once upon a time, you assured me that I'd be surprised at the modesty of your education. I would indeed. In two days, you've put on two clinics in assessing and appreciating folk and popular arts. More than that, you react to every genre as if it were your heritage. Come on, no one can know that much even after flying around the world to visit the artists. How'd you get so smart?"

"Look, it's not a tenth as mysterious as you're trying to make it. I do some work at home for the folk art museum I told you about, the place where I have a friend on the board. They receive dozens of periodicals and the publications of other museums. The museum catalogs pertinent articles in a bibliographic database and makes it available to staff and members. Three years ago, when they were explaining it to me, they mentioned shortcomings reported by some of their users. I suggested keywording changes and the idea that new entries could be listed separately as well as entered in the composite file. That would give the users a handy way to keep up with the flow. The director said, 'Fine, you do it.' Now all the publications come to me, and I enter the bibliographic data and keyword each item. When I'm not traveling, I do a week's accumulation in perhaps two half-days. Every quarter, my update replaces the master at the museum and I provide the current list of new items. It's pretty simple now that I've got it organized, but I have to identify the articles to be indexed and select the keywords, so I do look pretty closely at what's reported worldwide, texts and pictures. That's it, no mystery."

"Right. Nothing to it. You remind me of J. S. Bach's reported explanation for his success. 'I worked hard. Anyone who worked as hard would do as well.' Uh huh. Let's face it, your onboard computer is a lulu—processor, memory, and data storage—and I don't mean the one you haul around in your luggage."

She twisted and looked away, a blush in pantomime. I gave her a gentle shove. She stuck her tongue out at me. We both laughed.

To wind up our outing, we took a cab to the Gulbenkian Museum to inspect its premiere collection of the craft of René Lalique—both of us had a soft spot for the self-conscious innocence of Art Nouveau. After forty minutes of fun with his playful contrivances in glass, ceramics, metal, and wood, we set out on foot, ignorant that our hotel was three miles away. No matter, we strode along tree-lined avenues, through two parks, and ended up coming to the Rossio by traversing the entire Avenida da Liberdade. We recouped with *limonadas* on the strip, but even so returned to our room warm and damp. I stripped and stepped into the shower. Soon the door opened and a little voice chirped, "Room for two?" Indeed there was.

She came equipped with a sponge, and we were soon scrubbing each other's backs. I gave in to the temptation to reach under her arms and cup the firm round forms of her high-set breasts, then give her and them a hug. There were other incidental contacts before it came to me that I was interfering with the supposed purpose of the exercise. I rinsed, got out, and started to dry off. Over the top of the shower door came, "You still there?"

"Nowhere else."

"Remember your platonic plan? See why I asked you to put it on hold?"

"Paloma, I never felt platonic. I just didn't want to force myself on you. I wanted you to know how much I liked the relationship we already had and the things we did back in Santa Fe and Taos."

The sound of the shower stopped and a delicious wet body emerged, still making a point. "Well, that was fine—then. But isn't it great when you stop talking and thinking, and just let go? Shall we let go some more?"

"Yes, milady." I retreated to my bed and, in a minute, I was joined, closely joined, and further aroused. Alas, I was also convinced that I was beyond the age for two days in a row. "Paloma," I half whispered and half groaned, "temptation and opportunity are not my problems. Old plumbing is my problem." Despite my pessimistic words, we were, by then, half engaged.

"You can pretend," she whispered back, "you can do no harm. I'm not a porcelain shepherdess."

"I've noticed."

In the end, I was right and she was right. I was teased to distraction before I could manage no more, but I did no harm. We did stop talking and thinking, and we took as much pleasure in partnership as in a tantalizing pursuit of rising and falling expectations. We stayed together as adjacent S-curves until and after she went to sleep, and so we stayed until time to dress for dinner.

For our final evening in Lisbon, we chose a more pretentious restaurant, one suggested by all the respected guidebooks. The place was nearby and it was a pleasure to stroll through the leisurely street scene after the rush hour. We were seated in a secluded corner, and ordered salads and salmon which, in due course, justified the good name of the house. Alas, for me, the cuisine hardly mattered. I sat across from Paloma, mesmerized by her eyes, her mouth as she spoke or ate, the modest décolletage of her simple dress, the potential of what it hid. My captivation must have been obvious. After I'd enjoyed but not reacted to a series of impish looks, she asked, "Should I feel like prey? Your salmon just sits, but you stare hungrily at me."

"Sorry. I'll need to be reprogrammed to prefer salmon to you."

"Good, we've made progress since dinner last night."

We ate, but I never escaped a surreal confusion of mouthfuls with other recent treats. In a delicious irony, I'd brought the unconsummated bedroom to the dinner table where its pleasures and frustrations overwhelmed the meal.

We skipped dessert, went forth among the firefly lights along the strip, sipped mineral water at our chosen stand, and returned to our room. Early, yes, but we were looking ahead to our first day on the road. We readied ourselves for the night and I turned in. Moments later, I looked up into eyes and a smile that came closer and closer until foreheads touched. She whispered, "There are days and days to come." "You're bad," I said, as she gently, gently, wagged her hair in my face.

She retired to her own bed, but I still ached for her touch, her glow, her promise. That day I'd learned more about me and my state. An orgasm was not what I'd been missing — that release can be had, do-it-yourself, in the profoundest solitude. What I had needed, and now found myself basking in, was the willing presence and response of a woman — mind, wit, sight, touch, and scent. I felt grateful and restored, so much so that I gave in to a compelling impulse. I slid down between our beds and silently examined my inamorata's face, innocent in sleep, her elegant lashes and parted lips. I felt like a thief with stolen art, and lay awake for ever so long trying to cope with my overflowing wonder and disbelief.

Thursday, October 17th

I'd planned our first day's drive to take us a bare hundred miles north on Portugal's nearest approach to a freeway, few curves and moderate traffic. With that in mind, we had a leisurely breakfast on the avenida and lingered with hot drinks to watch Lisbon come to life. At first, passersby were few and noises were occasional, but a cheerful hubbub grew. Cars soon streamed by, buses stopped to disgorge flows of store clerks and office workers, and groups of old men in black suits congregated on park benches and café seats. News stands opened, then flower stalls and hole-in-the-wall outlets for jewelry, tourist books, maps, and more. Paloma surveyed the activities, the setting, the tree-filtered light, and pronounced the scene downright Impressionist. We sauntered back to the hotel imagining ourselves in the Paris of the 1890s — an illusion shattered when the valet delivered our blatantly 1990s Opel.

After dealing with the desk and our luggage, we were off, I behind the wheel and Paloma skimming a *Michelin Guide*. I'd booked us into a *pousada* outside the city of Tomar, but we arrived at the indicated turnoff after less than three hours on an open highway with uninspired scenery. It was an easy decision to go on and spend our afternoon in and around Tomar itself.

The small city's core of old structures and narrow streets invited us to explore on foot, but we decided to start with something wet. A block or so from our parking spot, we found a café with an outdoor area defined by tubs of luxurious geraniums. As we sat enjoying the scene and our escape from the small car's cramped interior, I noticed that my companion's attention had wandered, but not far. At a table next to ours, two thirtyish women chatted over iced tea and salads. One had a baby buggy at her side that she constantly and unconsciously jiggled with her elbow, evidently contributing to the contentment of an unseen child. But Paloma had discovered, and been discovered by, the same woman's daughter, aged about three. This small person leaned against her mama's free side and regarded Paloma with a gaze as steadfast as her own. Paloma smiled and got a tentative return. She held out her arms and invited. The child peered up over her shoulder, seeking guidance, and her mother smiled and nodded affirmatively. The little girl took three steps and stood just beyond Paloma's outstretched arms. A little tentatively, she put out her arms, not to be lifted, but rather to hold hands. Paloma took them, and the big girl and the small one locked eyes and exchanged smiles. Paloma leaned over and in a soft voice sang a rollicking children's song, in Spanish, unmistakably centering on a cuckoo. That was popular indeed, received with grins. A suggestion was voiced by the mother, and the child responded softly but clearly, "*Obrigado.*" Then she retired to stand in front of her mother, but continued to regard Paloma.

We finished our drinks and stood. Paloma went to the other table, attempted a few words, and shook the hands of mother and child.

When she rejoined me, I remarked, "Surprise, surprise. I never expected to find anyone who could stare you down."

"It's true, I definitely met my match." Her eyes brimmed with tears, the first I'd seen. My concern must have showed, for she added, "She's just so secure, so whole. Sorry."

"For heaven's sake, Paloma, not sorry. Don't apologize. Something happened back there, and it got to me, too." She nodded and leaned against my shoulder as we started our turn around town. I recalled her rapt absorption in the tots we met marching in the Alfama, and I wondered, "Why so affected by children? Regrets over her lack of family? Echoes of shame over her occupation?" I said nothing about that, and we both confined our remarks to the sights at hand, the oh-so-Portuguese chimney pots and the vertical blue stripes on the corners of whitewashed buildings.

I drove us out of town and northwest to a hillside impressively decorated by a grand, arch-supported aqueduct built four centuries ago to bring water to a local convent. I didn't have to coax Paloma to stretch her legs, and after hiking an easy slope abuzz with insects, I posed her for a photo in the nearest of two hundred arches, dozens of others trailing away in vanishing perspective.

As I reloaded the camera, she took off her hat and skipped away, bending to pluck heads of grass as she went. I stood, mesmerized by her graceful turns and daydreaming of our amours, vivid in their abandon and recency. What strange visions out in that open field! I laughed at my pretensions—so delighted by Paloma's frank and frolicsome approach to sex, yet so woefully underqualified to evaluate such favors. After all, I'd had only a few clumsy attempts at sex before Marian, no extra-marital affairs, and damned few dalliances. As the dancer replaced her hat and walked toward me, I was overcome by a sense of gratitude. I reached for her hands and gave them a squeeze, but my impulse was to go to my knees.

After motoring the few miles to Castelo de Bode, site of the small Pousada de São Pedro, we tidied up in our modern room and reported to the lounge for much-needed tea. We were forgathering, it developed, with a van-load of enthusiastic, middle-aged English tourists having their first encounter with Portugal. Teatime began pleasantly enough, but gradually lost its serenity. Our fellow guests got merrier and merrier on port until the wine became stronger than that famous English restraint. One of the men came over to ask if my daughter and I would care to join them. In a stage-whisper, his wife wondered, "His daughter, or his secretary?" Another woman piped up, "You his Girl Friday then, ducks?"

My roommate turned to them in a languid fashion and stepped onto the English stage. "No, *no*, dahling. If you must know, I'm his veddy fahncy woman."

She smiled sweetly, turned back to me, and stayed in character to resume the conversation supposedly interrupted. "Well then! What about our plan for the new south terrace?" Silence overtook the revelers. We stood, wished them well, and retired to giggle in the garden.

"Great matinee," I said. "Sorry I have no bouquet for the star. Lousy foresight, as usual."

"Thank you, kind sir." She curtsied, then dropped the act to add, "Rude or not, they did see us quite clearly. I could just hear my Latin teacher, *'In vino, veritas.'*"

It was a truth I wasn't proud of. I turned to other matters as I showed her out the side gate for a stroll around the village, soft and gray in the light of day's end.

After supper we turned in early, I, more tired than expected, and Paloma behind in diary and letter writing. In short order, I was flat in bed, admiring the determined bobbing of her hair and the arch of her nightgowned back as she pecked at her laptop. Eventually she was satisfied, and it was lights out.

Tired as I was, I couldn't shut off my wonder at the presence in the next bed, the utter novelty of this adventure, the fascinating challenges that arose from spending day after day with a young woman so unlike any I'd ever known. But how many young women had I known? Certainly, our daughters didn't count. I knew them from birth, diapers, school days, and up, but at eighteen they left home to attend distant schools. By the time they were Paloma's age, they were married and living far from us. Only Marian was comparable. I hadn't known her in her growing-up years either, but when we did meet, we cultivated our acquaintance for two years before we spent days on end together.

This total immersion with Paloma was unimaginably different. From the first, Marian had a stand-back, wait-and-see reaction to new experiences. She took from travel largely visual images, a series of tableaux in light, shadow, and color. For Paloma, travel was a tour through history, seen as illustrations off its pages. Her approach was enthusiastic and physical; travel was an active experience that sparked verbal expression and playful uses of words. My last thought before I fell asleep was to marvel that I'd known so few people really well during what I had imagined was a full life.

Friday, October 18th

I woke, slowly for me, to the cheerful sounds of a shower in use. Shortly, it was turned off and I forced myself to get moving. I yawned a great, protracted yawn, "Hunh, hunh, hunhhh," hoping to sound like a bear coming out of hibernation.

"How was that?" issued from the toweling area.

I attempted to recreate the yawn, or at least the "Hunh, hunh, hunhhh," and added, "and I meant every word of it."

"Mmmm, deep. I'd better plan to take notes along with my eggs."

Company, blessed company. I lay back and mentally hugged myself. I recalled my typical waking mood during the past two years and offered up fervent thanks for my present state, however bizarre its basis. Then I rushed to catch up.

In fact, we both took notes with our eggs. The next leg of our trip would be new to me, and our waiter, a native of the area, noticed us poring over our map and offered to help. When we told him our day's destination, he recommended the scenery along minor roads leading north to reach an east-west highway. We thanked him and set out through amber hills on a ribbon of pavement that we shared with only the odd tractor, hay wagon, or pungent truckload of manure.

So there I was, new countryside, fine day, attractive scenery. Ordinarily I'd have focused on that, but I was bemused. There was nothing ordinary about this ongoing adventure. In some ways, it seemed an extension of our drive in New Mexico—the same mutual desires to relate what we saw to our experiences and to share enthusiasms and ideas. But now, added on, were my pleasure in our intimacies, and my amazement at the absence of negative aftereffects. The woman was in no way arch or patronizing, there were no references or leers, no evidences of regret. On the contrary, as we became in all ways more familiar, our relationship seemed to ripen and deepen. To my surprise, being with Paloma took me back to my early married days. Each time I looked at her I realized how happy I was. Somehow I was living a magical fantasy and I prayed that some genial spirit might keep me within its spell.

The rather humdrum scenery of the previous day had encouraged us to exchange anecdotes, make jokes, and speculate on the days ahead. But now our attention was drawn to vignettes of isolated villages, perched farms, and hillside agriculture, all overtopped by stony mountains. We shared speculations about people's lives in these places— now, and over the ages. Only during stops for refreshments did we revert to our accustomed joshing and small talk.

In mid-afternoon, we left the back road and headed northeast on a main route. Twenty minutes later, we parked at our inn for the night, just outside Oliveira do Hospital. As I checked in, Paloma stepped into the lounge and observed the tea things still out and being enjoyed. I got a pat and an unearned compliment, "I can't believe such scheduling!" Such scheduling indeed. Such pure dumb luck.

Pousada de Santa Bárbara was a delight, an elegant modern structure riding a ridge and overlooking a grand gorge. We took our refreshments out onto a terrace covered with trellised vines and affording dizzying views of plunging mountainsides and the abyss below. We lingered over tea, then stayed on with glasses of Madeira, courtesy of a charming English couple with whom we'd struck up a lively discourse.

Through this fourth day of our tour, we'd stayed mostly to ourselves, so I especially enjoyed this new social dynamic. I listened to the give and take and felt our new acquaintances drawn in by Paloma's ready charm and intelligent, sympathetic responses to all we discussed. I realized that I'd had many opportunities to see my companion turn heads in public, but not like this, shining in a casual exchange with peers. I heard sincerity in their regret that they'd accepted an earlier invitation to dinner, and that they'd be leaving at the crack of dawn. We were given a card and urged to visit should we ever come to Norfolk.

After an hour of rest and a change of clothes we were back on that enchanting balcony, all the more so after sunset and lit by a full moon. In the dim gorge below, white villages with sparkling lights dotted the slopes. Paloma was in a lovely white dress with a wide lace collar and, as we awaited supper, I was so overcome by the woman and the place that I speculated aloud, "Wouldn't this make a charming honeymoon spot?" Earlier daydreams clouded my vision and I maundered on, "Here I am, getting toward the end of this great journey, and here you are, just starting. How sad to be at the opposite ends of matrimony." Then, God help me, I dithered into a "What if?" scenario—until I raised my eyes and saw her looking stricken and shaking her head slowly, "No, no, no."

I flushed and tried to retreat. "I'm sorry! I'm such a bull in the china shop, so thoughtless. I promise, never, never again." She managed a wan smile, but the corners of her mouth were not as they should have been and I saw a welling of tears. Our dinner conversation was largely spoiled, but over coffee Paloma put her hand on mine and whispered, "Thank you." I supposed she was grateful that I backed off, but I'd have felt better with a hint that it was for the sentiment that underlay my bungling.

Back in our room, she remained subdued and soon excused herself to "wash my hair and take care of other things that need attention," leaving me to feel guilty and lonely. It was a huge relief when she finally came out, and over to me. I took her in my arms without words, and we exchanged small hugs and touched each other's faces with light fingers, trying to restore the rapport I'd disarrayed with my misdirected gallantry. Relaxation set in, the air cleared, and we parted on a gentle and hopeful note.

We parted, but I lay awake—"square-eyed," as Mexicans say—realizing how I'd come to take for granted Paloma's apparently unfailing good humor, and realizing what I should have seen long ago—no woman could be so employed and not have serious problems with self-respect and self-confidence. What other sensitivities had I missed or ignored? I felt low. I reminded myself how happy I'd been, how much she'd come to mean to me. What if I lost her now? What if she were to merely serve out her time with me?

In the midst of that nail biting, I thought back over my own recent emotional swings, uncertainties, and fears, and decided that I was going through something akin to a second adolescence and the throes of an adolescent crush. In that immature state, I trembled at the possibility of loss.

So, I tried to grow up. I reminded myself over and over, "This is more than a commercial encounter, this is a budding relationship with an intriguing person, intriguing in part because she is so responsive and aware. Stay awake, be alert to the signals she sends and the hints she drops." I thought guiltily of Marian, of how probable it was that I'd been lulled by familiarity and stopped being careful of her feelings. And of how probable it was that I was imposing bad old habits on a new relationship. I resolved to try to be better.

Saturday, October 19th

Paloma sat on the edge of my bed at first light. Would I care to climb down the great slope to reach an ancient, wind-sculpted pine we'd spotted before sunset? Sensing forgiveness in that, I leaped out and threw on my clothes. We held hands for support as we scrambled down a steep goat path toward several rewards—the moon large and low in the west, the pine splendid in the red light, and the pair of us reunited under its branches. We sat on a bed of fallen needles, head to head, wordless, until the sun struck the heights across the gorge. "Thank you," I whispered before we got to our feet and climbed to breakfast.

Our northeasterly drive took us from one world to another. On our right loomed the jagged crest and rugged skirts of the Serra da Estrela, the prominent mountain chain of north central Portugal. We passed harvest scenes in terraced vineyards — I say "passed," but Paloma could not. We stopped and walked in to watch strong men shoulder heavy, bulky baskets of grapes and labor up steep slopes to dump them into waiting wagons. Our route led on through landscapes cloaked by thick brush and evergreen trees, then took us up to mesas blanketed with dry grass and scattered with gnarled oaks. After a leisurely two hours, we entered a region of fortified towns, villages, and hilltop castles — the Portuguese-Spanish borderlands, fought over from the middle ages to the time of Napoleon.

Turning east, we wound through hills terraced with olives and dotted with clusters of white dwellings. The village of Pinhel's walls, churches, and castle reached down from their hill and tugged at Paloma, but I asked her to enjoy it in passing. "Trust me," I said, "I have something for you around the corner."

At the foot of a hill topped by tumbled ruins, we turned to the southeast, and in a few minutes, I pointed off to our left across oak-dotted fields and suggested that she look for something out of the ordinary.

Eventually, even though I knew what to expect, it was she who exclaimed, "I see some sort of ruin."

Two hundred yards from our narrow paved road, standing alone in a field of stubble, loomed a rectangular building about two stories tall constructed from blocks of the deep gold-beige local granite. I scouted out a faint dirt road, drove within fifty yards of the ruin, and we stepped out into the sun and the quiet and the still air.

I'd never seen mention of the ruin in a printed source, but on my previous trip I'd had the good fortune to notice it in passing and find a scholar at the site who knew part of its curious history. Its stout base was constructed as the platform for a Roman temple to Minerva, then, in medieval times, a nearby Cistercian monastery added on a two-story superstructure to create a combination watchtower and storehouse. Today, two-thirds of the external stonework remains. The craftsmanship from both eras is elegant, and the ruin is made more affecting by its lonely state.

Paloma was entranced. She paced slowly around, outside and in; she stroked the Roman stones and pressed her face to them. "I feel such an affinity—Latin roots, I guess. I close my eyes and I'm Minerva's handmaiden."

"Her polychromed caryatid come to life? Pity I have no bunch of grapes to nestle, one at a time, betwixt your carmined lips. Oh, and if you want more Roman, just remember, this very morn we watched the sunrise sitting under an Italian Stone Pine, the pine of the Appian Way."

"Yes. And half the words we're using came to us by Roman roads. Talk about echoes that never die!"

I posed her against the west wall, the cornice over her head, and took a picture of her wearing a look I'd seen so often, that puzzled expression that appeared to ask, "Whatever do you see in me?"

Paloma got out her pad and sketched the corner treatments of the basemold and cornice. She wanted to capture the entire treasure, and only our lack of lunch and the fast approaching time for tea enabled me to woo her away.

We had a quiet ten-mile drive to Almeida, a walled citadel constructed from the same golden granite. Ringed by unbreached and unrestored walls, entered by elaborate gates with graphically strong entablatures, and topped with crenelations and pennants, Almeida looks like the setting for a storybook, though a live village nestles within its walls. Underpublicized, like much else in Portugal, this anachronism brings gasps and disbelief because it is so unexpected. Paloma went into instant historical shock. Tea or no tea, she made me drive around the walls and within them so she could "Oh!" and "Ah!" at every turn.

The public rooms at Pousada de Senhora das Neves likewise appealed to my partner; she admired the aptness of the building's modern design located adjacent to eighteenth-century walls. And when we were seated in the lounge, she didn't have to fish in her purse for tea bags; some of her favorites were in the silver box on our tray. After taking tea with a foursome of sociable fellow tourists, we and they set out in golden light and a light breeze to stroll among Almeida's promenades, bulwarks, moats, and guard towers.

At dinner's end, Paloma leaned forward meaningfully. I leaned forward to match. "Haley, I'm sorry I was difficult last night. I overreacted."

"No, I bumbled in where angels fear to tread."

"I'm afraid I've cut myself off from angels, but in any event, I'm not proud of my performance."

"Paloma, you did me a favor precisely because it was not a performance. I deserved the comeuppance. I took the hurt on your face to heart and I'm trying to be better. But I do worry about what's making you unhappy, that I could be contributing to that."

She looked resigned. "Please, I'll never reproach you for your concern. And, take my word for it, you are not my problem. I know that sounds like a tease, but it's more complicated than you could possibly imagine. Try to be patient. I asked for your patience that first day in Lisbon."

"So you did. And you shall have it. Think of me as concerned and curious, not impatient."

She slid her chair closer to our small table, her voice low and her manner serious. "Thank you — for everything. This was a wonderful day, this is a wonderful tour. That's why I regret yesterday. I don't want anything to break this enchantment."

Once in bed, she repeated those sentiments in irresistible nonverbal terms.

Afterward, we lay in each other's arms through a long and pleasurable silence in which I luxuriated in the feel of velvet skin under my hands and a gently rising and falling breast within my arms. Finally a small voice pleaded, "Give us a hug?" She rolled on top of me, damp and glowing. After a prolonged squeeze and gentle attempts at lower back massage, I whispered, "Hug enough?"

Lips touched my ear, then a breathy, "Don't stop. I dote on this skin-on-skin — before sex, during it, rising from it — do you hear? Oh, hello! Do I detect something rising from it?"

"Miss Grey! Such a lapse of decorum."

"Decorum, sir, as you in particular should know, is redefined behind closed doors and between consenting adults."

"Minx! I love it when you talk dirty."

For the first time in close to fifty years, I was struck over the head with a bed pillow.

Sunday, October 20th

Dawn, or predawn, Paloma leaned over me, whispering, "Haley! The stars are still out and there's a rim of light over the hills. May we please go back to the ruin to see the sunrise?"

Why not? I'm a sucker for enthusiasm. We verged on the Spanish border, so I leaped up with a loud *"¡Nos vamos!"*

In reality, it was a great idea. We got there in twenty minutes and waited for the sun to rise and strike the walls of our pet antiquity. Dew rimed the fields. Partridges called from thickets. I felt youthful again, thanks to the ambience and my improbable comrade. She exulted in all else while I gloried in her.

Paloma kissed a Roman stone and patted her kiss. "I'm not the first," she insisted, "I felt someone stir in eternity." Someone closer was actively stirred and took her in a soft embrace. We enjoyed a quiet but contented ride to breakfast.

I had set this day aside to visit old fortified Portuguese border towns south of Almeida. In practice, perhaps I bit off too much, too many whirlwind hikes up hills to ivy-covered or bare-bones castles. In any event, by mid-afternoon we found ourselves catching our breath in Guarda, Portugal's highest city, and drinking iced tea in the square. I dared to remark that I had one more stop in mind, a place we'd pass on our way back to Almeida.

I was relieved that I'd saved my ace-in-the-hole for last. Tiny Castelo Mendo, not much more than the farm of an extended family, sits a dozen miles south of Almeida and a mile off the nearest pavement. On the dirt road, our way was littered with artifacts—long stone fences, a venerable stone cross, and a roadway worn so deeply in bedrock that it must date at least from the Roman occupation.

We parked outside Castelo Mendo's massive wall and walked up to its open gate and into an ancient past. No use looking around for a castle. Over the centuries, the "castelo" in the place-name had become a misnomer. As the border wars died down, villagers tore into the castle and converted its cut granite into useful structures within the medieval wall. Therefore, the miniature street we found inside was lined with modest homes built from massive stones.

"Look how they grow their herbs." Paloma pointed to lavender and stunted rosemary rooted between cobbles and in the crevices of walls. We peered at and touched so much of our medieval surroundings that an onlooker could have mistaken us for the near-blind groping our way along. We could imagine that we were alone until we heard the clanking of belled animals and a herd of goats streamed around a corner, driven home at day's end by an elderly man with a crook.

At the top of that curving lane, we came to a gate, passed through, and moved out onto a sloping stone knoll with an ancient chapel near its crest. We saw two older women standing on a large patch of exposed bedrock as they engaged in the ancient practice of winnowing. It seemed we'd entered a past age as we watched them toss dried bean plants high in the air and a strong breeze blow away the opened pods, leaves, and bits of stem while the heavier beans fell on spread cloths. Our timing was opportune. The day was winding down and the women left their aerie fifteen minutes after our arrival.

We gazed out through the stone-arched portal of the chapel ruins, out into a grand sun-swept canyon, its slopes checkered by cloud shadows moving with the wind. Paloma broke a silence long enough to have allowed several angels to pass over. "Haley, how do you envision God?"

For days we'd talked on and off about religious inspiration. She'd been moved by its role in the construction of cathedrals, and I by its influence on Bach, so her question wasn't entirely out of the blue. Actually, it seemed almost a caption for the scene with its ruinous chapel and vast landscape, and I knew as I opened my mouth that my words would never match the poetry of the moment.

"The truth is, I can't visualize abstract concepts, never could. You ask about God, and I think of the sun and the moon and the stars. I see the faces of flowers and small children. They're there and they're beautiful, and God is what made them and everything else. If I try to intellectualize God, or turn to the accepted authorities, I don't do any better. Organized faiths seem divisively provincial, but atheism doesn't work for me either — it's a denial of reason and order. My cosmology — if you'll pardon the grand title — is the observable universe, period. Everything I've ever known is made up of elements related to each other in an orderly fashion. And to me, order is not random, it's rational. I guess I see God as that order, and not as some mysterious being standing off to the side and pulling strings. I see God as the forces and relationships themselves, the stuff of the system."

"I'm surprised. I didn't expect your conception to parallel that of a teacher I had in a Catholic school."

"How so? Now you have me surprised."

"All right. Sister Eugenia believed that we see the hand of God and know Him through the observable rules of nature, and you see Him *as* the observable rules of nature."

"Paloma, there really is a significant difference."

"Haley, there really is a significant similarity."

I took her in my arms and waited for more, but she snuggled up, eyes closed, and I had the last words. "All else aside, I see God's order in you." Emboldened by isolation, I kissed her forehead and buried my face in her blowing hair. I'm sure the Creator appreciates a satisfied customer.

Monday, October 21st

Walking at dawn, we met a Spanish-speaking farmer delivering milk with his donkey-powered cart, and we had time to tag along and enjoy his slant on local lore because our beds that night would be a scant thirty miles away in the *parador* at Ciudad Rodrigo in Spain. When we finally loaded up our little red car and started east, those miles proved flat and colorless, the least interesting of our journey. Just one feature caught our eye. In each of several villages, an old stone church was capped by a massive stork's nest raggedly woven from gnarled twigs.

From afar, Ciudad Rodrigo presented a fairy-tale image, its towers and walls crowning a rounded hill rising from the plain. On approach, the composition became bolder and finally we could see our road cross the Río Agueda on a low Roman bridge and go up to enter the massive ramparts. Paloma was kept busy peering and exclaiming as we approached the citadel and then wound our way through medieval scenes to find Parador Enrique II, nestled into a fortress wall.

When we'd moved in, we set off on foot to see what lay around the beckoning curves of hillside streets. We roamed a small park and admired baronial arms cut into the facades of grand homes fashioned from the golden-brown granite we now knew so well. At teatime, we sought advice and took directions to the principal square, a *plaza mayor* on an intimate scale, lined with some of the city's finest architecture—and an arena for much of the city's public life.

We spotted our objective, Café An-Mai, its tables and chairs spilling out onto the broad sidewalk before its doors. Little did we guess that we'd stumbled onto the center of Ciudad Rodrigueño life, the place to meet people, watch the day begin, the day end, and the night come to life. For two days, thanks to An-Mai, we would do less and enjoy it more—but I'm anticipating. Our introduction was actually quite tame. We took seats and ordered iced tea, then traded bits of chitchat with folks at neighboring tables, possible now in Spanish as it had not been in Portuguese. Paloma's command of the idiom plainly puzzled a middle-aged couple who proved to be educators from Vigo. Evidently her accent in their tongue, as in English, has an indefinable quality that intrigues the ears of native speakers.

We happened in at the hour when businesses were reopening after the *comida-siesta* recess. Lines of cars and taxis filled the traffic lanes as drivers waited to discharge passengers. Presently An-Mai was full, people hovered for vacated seats, and we felt selfish. We quizzed our new acquaintances about restaurants, then walked down the block to a cheerful second-story bistro. After an unstylishly early supper, we explored side streets for an hour before circling back in gathering dusk to savor coffee and socialize at An-Mai.

Once more we were seated out front. Shops were lighted, street lamps were on, and each table glowed with a sheltered candle. The entire plaza imparted a sense of civic festivity, a quiet celebration enhanced by the cheerful attitudes of our fellow patrons, even the passersby. My partner was moved to ask, "What is it with Ciudad Rodrigo? These are the jolliest folk of our trip." So they would remain, and our question would remain unanswered.

Paloma was more than usually stimulated by the day and by her return to Spain and Spanish. After we prepared for the night, she was still perky, saucy even, and more inclined to bounce about than to recline. I took hold of her to restrain some of that energy or perchance to calm it down, but instead I was caught up in it and eventually wrung out by it. She, however, remained conversational and full of wit. My pensive mood struck her as odd, and she made inquisitive noises.

By then, you'd swear I'd have learned not to verbalize vague uncertainties over delicate matters. But no, I blurted out, "I feel as if I've made my way into the Garden of Eden under false pretenses. I can't fathom why a woman of your attainments and character is sleeping with a perfect stranger."

She got up and stood over me, now quite fierce. "You are so perverse! That's not sleeping we've been up to. You're not perfect and I do not consider you a stranger. What's bothering you is that you can't simply have fun. You have to be badgered by your conscience. Your conscience is telling you it'll be a little bit mollified if you can get me to be a little bit conscience-stricken. Well, I won't! Are we not consenting adults? It seems to me we were having great fun, and now you're trying to spoil it." There she was, nude and alluring, but sounding less like a courtesan than an injured party seeking redress in a court of reason.

I rolled out and took her in my arms. I whispered in her ear. "Oh God, Paloma. You don't understand at all. You've given me a reprieve from my years and I'm having the time of my life. But I still worry about the terms under which we travel."

She leaned back, her palms on my chest. "Would we be here under any other terms? Should I have lied to you? Should I have pretended to be what I'm not?"

"Of course not. I get your point, but you're dodging mine. Please see that I can love what you're doing for me, but still worry about what it's doing to you. I need to know more so I can worry less. Remember, in your first phone call, you apologized for your 'revelation' in Santa Fe, told me you'd never given that speech before. How come? If you have 'clients,' somebody had to tell them something." I lowered my arms and looked expectant. She put her hands on my shoulders.

"I'm sorry if I puzzled you. My words were poorly chosen — frankly, I had no idea they'd be so dissected. I did feel apologetic, but that wasn't the best thing for me to say." She sat down hard on the bed and let out a sigh. "Listen, I'll tell you almost anything, but not about my clients. You can understand that. Let's just say I hadn't given the speech before because I knew the rest of them from the start, and even before. Look, I invited you, so you were the first I ever had to spring the surprise on. Couldn't you be even a little bit flattered?"

"God, yes," I thought, and I nodded "yes," and dropped down to put my head on her lap while I wrestled with myself. Lord, what an enigma. How can I be so close to her, be every day more attracted to her and admire her in so many ways, and yet acknowledge that I'm here as a source of her income, that I'm getting what I paid for. But, if that's all that's involved, why can't I simply revel in her?

Then it hit me that I'd divided Paloma into alter egos. One I'd bought, and I was getting my money's worth — the feel of her thigh against my cheek was a reminder. But the other persona attracted me more, the friend with whom I shared so many enthusiasms. She was the one I was courting — and sighing over — even as I guiltily made love to the first. I stood up and gave the only Paloma at hand a chaste kiss on the forehead before we took to our beds.

I lay there, mulling it all over, when something else hit me. In her reluctant response to my query, she'd revealed that, as a rule, she doesn't solicit new clients, her patrons are limited. Her practice remained sordid, yes, but this was a glimmer of light. I breathed more easily. I relaxed. I slept.

Tuesday, October 22nd

I'd planned a day trip to see half-timbered architecture in nearby mountain villages. We kicked the idea around at breakfast and decided that since the next day would be all driving, we'd just poke around friendly Ciudad Rodrigo.

After plates of eggs, potatoes, and Manchego cheese, we got directions to the city's massive wall, strolled its sentry path, and enjoyed its sweeping views. Down by the river, we spotted what looked to be a small circus. Paloma was all eyes, so we got out the car, drove down, and joined the bustle that accompanied the erection of a carnival.

No acts or exhibits were open yet, the preparations were the show, and we were not the only spectators. We ambled around, watched work in progress, and rubbed shoulders with curious tourists and townspeople in festive moods. Concessionaires had opened stalls and were selling food, drink, and the sorts of souvenir gewgaws seen around the world. One vendor caught Paloma's eye, a solemn-faced girl about eight, looking quite Gypsy and clad in a threadbare purple dress. She sat at a rickety table hoping to sell lavender that had begun to wilt. My lady didn't hesitate. She went over, determined the price, took three bunches, and paid twice what was asked. Nothing was said, but dark eyes looked grateful.

We rounded a corner and heard the beguiling strains of a hurdy-gurdy. A second turn brought us face to face with the scarcely believable reality, in our day, of an organ grinder and his dancing monkey. The animal pirouetted dutifully on a petite wooden floor and captured the rapt attention of children and parents alike. One small boy was himself dancing, unmindful of his mates or anything other than the bewitching music. I chuckled, "Look, Paloma. He's an absolute rerun of our daughter Lys. She was like this when she was two, three, four, any time she'd hear music. Wherever she was, she'd go into a trance and dance away, all by herself, as if her life depended on it."

Paloma was puzzled. "Why did she stop?"

I could only shrug. "On to other arts, outgrew it, hard to say. Childhood is one long metamorphosis."

We walked off before she leaned against me and spoke. "I've had so little to compare. Honestly, your memories of family life are like radio from another planet."

"Sorry, Paloma. I'm not intentionally a salt-in-the-wounds kind of guy. Should I steer clear of family palaver?"

"No, don't stop. It's all part of the liberal education that I've missed." Her words were reassuring, but I guessed that they papered over a void I could never fill. I put my arm around her and we walked to the car with an occasional squeeze.

Paloma's lavender remained on the back seat until it was completely dry. The car smelled marvelous for days.

In our rambles around town, we had twice passed a guitar shop, closed on both occasions. As we walked by a third time, Paloma noticed lights on and someone inside. Suddenly she was twelve years old. "Oh, could we go take a look?" I could almost hear swallowed echoes of "could we, could we?" We went.

That guitar shop was wonderful, a turn-of-the-century period piece, the walls in dark wainscoting below and mirrors above, the floors in black and white hexagonal tile. Two old, walnut-colored ceiling fans turned lazily below the high ceiling, circulating a vague odor of furniture polish. Thirty to forty guitars, no more, were displayed under glass or behind glass. Each case had to be unlocked and each instrument individually and lovingly liberated. The proprietor was a man of indeterminate middle years, tall, balding, and with the grand hawk nose appropriate to guitar lore. He was very polite, very courtly, and, after a glance, very smitten with Paloma. In fairness, he remained a perfect gentleman, albeit one sorely tested. I was essentially ignored.

Paloma pretended not to notice the effect she had. She smiled shyly and asked if she might just poke around. She further pretended not to notice a look proclaiming that she could have the keys to the city or the mortal soul at hand, whichever she might prefer. She leaned over the flat cases and inspected every instrument, then stepped along and perused those upright along the walls. If she paused, she received a short treatise on maker and characteristics.

After a full circuit of the store, she pointed to a used instrument in apparently mint condition and asked if she might see and touch. Might the moon rise? She picked out a string of notes and commenced a short process of tuning that received the full, nodding-head approval of our host. She picked out a few more notes and began to play, at first tentatively, then with more assurance and a livelier pace. She played rather well. "Ah, the Sor prelude," the proprietor breathed. Clearly it was a performance among performances.

Paloma cradled the guitar and inquired whether he might have another in mind, a specimen that she, in her simplicity, would not discover or try without guidance? No, she was told, the instrument in her hands represented quality beyond its price, the best value in the house. Her perceptiveness was to be commended.

At that juncture, I interrupted this charming stage piece. I put the shopper on the spot by asking her, in Spanish, whether she wanted the guitar then and there. "Yes," she replied, and opened her handbag to produce a book of traveler's checks. The proprietor gave no evidence of surprise. He took the instrument and carefully slipped it into a plastic bag before putting it into a traditional black case. He busied himself with a bill and presented that, with his card, to Paloma. She paid, and he literally bowed. Would it be too great an imposition, she inquired, to pick up the instrument at a somewhat early hour tomorrow? Not at all, at the hour of madam's choice, she was assured. A time was fixed, he saw us to the door, and she shook his hand. I confess I was amazed that he didn't kiss hers. We smiled and headed for the Plaza Mayor.

"That was wonderful theater," I said admiringly, "with a surprise ending."

"I've coveted that Ramírez guitar for years. It's perfect, and half what they might ask in Los Angeles."

"Oh. You might've said. I'd have loved to get it for you."

"Thank you for a most generous thought, but this is way out of the keepsake category and you're already giving me more than I could've imagined. You don't need more brownie points, take my word."

After a snack, we hiked up to the *parador* for a rest. When we were down flat, some notion came to me and I broke a several-minute silence.

"Paloma.... Oh, dear, forgive me. I hear myself starting every sentence with your name. I love the sound of it. Ever since we met, it's been my talisman, my touchstone to keep you in my universe." My words were spoken to the ceiling, or to the skies above, and her reply took the same route.

"Forgive you for what? Saying 'Paloma'? I've spent so much time alone, I wait for a voice to call my name. Use it with my blessing."

The ceiling would no longer do. I went on hands and knees to the foot of her bed and kissed the bottoms of her feet, setting off the only real giggles I'd heard from her — nice, deep, resonant giggles. Even so, our rest did proceed.

We took a chance on overdoing it and walked again to An-Mai. Happy chance! Minutes after we got our tea, members of a party, people in Sunday-go-to-meeting clothes, began to arrive in groups of two up to six or more. Shortly, the word spread around that guests from a nearby wedding were gathering for an informal reception and the wedding party was on its way. A table next to us was taken by a mother, her adult son, and her daughter and son-in-law. Paloma questioned the mother, and when the family heard her Spanish, they vied with each other to tell us about the wedding and more.

It seems the groom's family acquired an old farm for the newlyweds at the edge of the nearby village of Conejera. The house proved to be in tumbledown condition, so kinfolk and friends of the young couple pitched in to help make it livable. As the costs of the restoration rose, funds for the wedding celebration dwindled. Moreover, most of the wedding guests had worked in their spare hours right up to the event. We scanned the gathering and saw the effects, the place was awash with the weary, including our informant's son, apprenticed to a roofer. Weeks before, he'd undertaken to renovate the farmhouse roof, then found many broken tiles and rotten support members. The job had taken twice the time and money reckoned, and the budding roofer was exhausted.

Before long, the bride and groom appeared and guests crowded around before gradually dispersing to talk, eat, and drink. The party, littered with the tired, was fairly sedate, except for the children, who were many. They were not exhausted, they were invigorated by each other's company. There were many comings and goings of elaborately dressed small bodies.

Paloma was caught up in the whole undertaking. After hobnobbing with our neighbors, she rose, beckoned to me, and led me around the corner to a store where she bought an oversized bottle of a good Spanish champagne. With that in hand, we marched back to the party and up to the bridal couple and their families. Paloma didn't have to ask for attention.

"Please excuse us for intruding. As you see, we're foreigners, but we hope you will understand that we are enchanted by Spain, and, today, by your wedding. We want to congratulate you and wish you long, happy lives, and all the children you wish. Please accept this token from us."

She presented the groom with the champagne and got an ovation from all around. An older man raised his voice to explain to a hard-of-hearing neighbor, "Daughter of the English ambassador. Saw her picture in the paper." Paloma gave me her best and broadest "Imagine that!" look.

We returned to our seats amid enough attention and handshaking to make us feel like part of the reception line. Even when we finally broke away, the apple of my eye remained exhilarated. Her wedding party glow carried through dinner, sherry in the lounge, and on into bed.

Wednesday, October 23rd

Back in our room after breakfast, I stepped into the dressing area, thinking Paloma was in the bath. But no, there she was, facing me and assiduously brushing her teeth, toothpaste much in evidence.

"Oh, sorry," I exclaimed, and backed out the door. But she pursued me, the toothbrush clamped in teeth exposed by an impish grin.

She removed the brush and spoke through white lips. "You're so weird. You can't wait to kiss me you-know-where — which is fine, of course — but then you turn around and get all flustered just seeing me clean my teeth. Is that Victorian, or what?"

"Sorry, Miss P. I don't know about Victorian, but it is a generational thing. We were trained, from toddlers on up, to try not to catch people unawares, especially in the bathroom — and to apologize if we did. It's the truth, you could look it up."

She frowned. "Ah, so. I guess my upbringing was not so couth. It seems to me you either know someone intimately, or you don't, and that sets the level of embarrassment." She returned to brushing teeth.

"Point taken, fairest one. And I admit, you weren't that great a shock, even foaming at the mouth. I've weathered it. So how about a compromise? If I can't kick my habits, I'll at least try not to overreact."

And that was that, other than vigorous nods and retreats to our respective spaces.

After a stop to pick up the redoubtable Ramírez guitar, we pulled away from Ciudad Rodrigo—with regrets. It was a good place, more than good to us, and also difficult to escape. Looking down from its high hill, its image pursued us for miles, if only in rearview mirrors.

My itinerary was simple. We would cruise all day on secondary roads leading to one of my favorite towns in Iberia, Castelo de Vide, back in Portugal. The open fields and farming centers along our way invited little study or speculation, so our talk pressed on from Paloma's guitar to music in general, important in my life, and, as I was learning, in hers as well. I described my one-sided romance with that art. I have no musical ability — hell, I can scarcely carry a tune — but even as a mere listener I'm profoundly affected. I told of my pleasure at live performances and in listening to my hundreds of disks. She asked how I got into it.

"Well, I was about thirty when it really hit me. I was laid up for months with a bad case of hepatitis and music was a wonderful pastime. That's when I discovered that J. S. Bach could take me out of myself and off to places I'd never imagined. He inspired me through what seemed like an awfully long ordeal — but that was only the beginning. That day to this, listening to Bach brings me a sense of the divine like nothing else. Strange, isn't it? Religion never reached me, but it reached him, and his inspiration moves me. But what about you? You mention music often, but all I know for sure is that you play the guitar very nicely, and you can really get into humming. How did you come to it, or how did it come to you?"

"You know, I can't remember a time without music. My mother was always singing to herself, and I had children's music on disks when I was small. Then I sang in the choir in my little school in London, but really, half the school did that. It meant something when I got into the chorus at my academy in Sevilla — tryouts, you know, and a more demanding repertory. When I was ten, my grandmother arranged that I take guitar, and my teacher coached me in singing songs to my own accompaniment, which I still do. After I came to live with my mother and stepfather, I was taken to concerts all over L.A., and later my stepfather took me to dozens of musical events in Europe. On top of that, he had a good sound system and his own hundreds of classical recordings. And yes, lots of Bach."

"So, what attracts you, what do you buy or perform?"

"I don't perform at all, except for myself. Songs and my guitar are rainy-day friends. I'm no virtuoso and I've had no real vocal training, so what I play for myself is pretty simple stuff. What composers?

Sort of a grab bag. Lately I've worked up pieces by, let's see, Sor, Sanz, and Carulli. And I'm working on a Martín y Soler song."

"Paloma, I don't know these guys well, but they're not my idea of simple stuff."

"Perhaps not what you've heard, but don't forget how important it was in their times to sell sheet music. Most of them wrote in a range of difficulty. You had to start somewhere and they wanted you to start with them."

"Right — you can tell that I never played anything. But I have sampled an awful lot of music and my own personal discovery has been minor composers. They save me from overplaying the geniuses, and better yet, some of their pieces are exquisite. I've got lots of stuff by Bach's sons, and, let's see, there's Barbara Strozzi, Michel Corrette, Antonio Soler — God, my list goes on and on. I'll bet I have disks by at least four dozen of the not-so-famous."

She nodded negatively. "Sorry. Most of the little I know about minor composers comes from snatches I've heard on classical radio."

"Might I lend you a few disks?"

"You might, and I'd thank you. I'm tempted to try things I see reviewed or notice in record stores, but I usually end up being more frugal than curious. I hate to spend money and be disappointed."

"OK. I'll send you some of my little-knowns. See how you react."

"Oh, I'll react. I love to hear other people's favorites — learn new music and learn about the recommenders. Never fails." She paused. "Did your wife love music?"

"Crazy about it, listened more than I did. Music was her companion, she always had it on in her studio — it occupied some part of her mind she didn't devote to getting her designs onto paper. She liked the piano, solo, or in almost any combination, especially the strong, positive stuff, like Mozart."

There was a pause. I looked over and saw that I'd lost my audience. We'd come over a low rise and were headed down a long slope. Off to our right, a dirt road paralleled ours, then swung toward us to make a junction. Near that turn, we saw a two-axled oxcart, its left front wheel visibly broken and askew, the ox still harnessed. The cart was stacked high with loose hay and the driver stood beside it, pondering his predicament. Paloma was affected.

"Please stop. Couldn't we go over there and see if we can help?"

I slowed way down and drove along the shoulder till we came to the junction. My spirit is less generous than hers and I voiced my skepticism.

"I hate to tell you, but the jack and the rest of the tools in this car won't help him one iota. That's a broken wheel."

"Yes, but perhaps there's something else we could do. Take him someplace. Tell somebody."

I turned up the dirt road and parked short of the breakdown to avoid spooking the ox. We walked up to a small, lean man, well into his seventies, who regarded us glumly and shrugged his shoulders. Paloma commiserated with him and asked what we could do. Nothing, he replied, there was nothing we could do. He acted embarrassed. Paloma persisted; she'd seen large squashes in a mesh bag next to the driver's seat. Might we not take the news of his plight to someone and deliver the vegetables at the same time? Well, the farmer decided, yes, those things might be done, and he'd be grateful. He described his house, which would be visible as we drew near the hamlet of Silos. Could we tell his wife that he'd broken down on the turnoff to Pedro Pablo Blanco's farm, and could she get in touch with their nephew Mateo? He leaned under the cart and fished out a basket covered by a cloth. And might we be kind enough to take this to his wife? He took it over to our car and I carried the squash. The man was now all smiles, cap in hand, as he directed effusive thanks, appropriately to Paloma.

I turned the car around, we waved and were off.

"You're a nice girl," I told my companion.

"Listen," she said. "I've been on the receiving end of lots of favors, and there's only the odd chance to do a good turn." She stared thoughtfully out the window, then harked back, "You were telling me about your wife and music. You mention her so seldom. Is that out of respect? Does it bother you to talk to me about her?"

That hit home—it recalled my shame over the feelings Paloma inflamed in me when we first met. But I dodged her question honestly enough. "No, that's not it. Marian would've hated the idea of being a lingering inhibition. I guess I've held back because you've mentioned your family mostly in terms of sorrow and losses. I know, the other day you told me not to avoid family talk, but I can be pretty careless, so I'm leery about taking chances, maybe opening old wounds or bounding blithely onto tender ground. Neither of us has really dredged up the past and I have no perception of your family."

"Lucky you. My past is complicated. Compared with most people, I've had only bits and pieces of family. But you and I are getting acquainted, *poco a poco*. I'm not in a hurry and I hope you're not. Don't hold back, and I won't hold back, and a lot of it'll come out along the way."

"There she goes," I thought, "closing that door on me again—but this time gently."

In less than ten minutes, we recognized the farmer's landmarks, turned into another country lane, and stopped at the second of two dwellings, a tidy house with an alarmingly swaybacked roof. Luckily, the señora was in. We delivered the messages and the goods, and she was grateful, but full of apologies that she was out of bottled gas for her stove and couldn't offer us a hot drink. Paloma took her hands, kissed her cheek, and told her not to worry, we understood. The woman lifted the cloth from the basket, exposed a stack of freshly dried raisins, and insisted on giving us a large bunch, which she wrapped in a napkin. When we took our leave, she followed us out, holding Paloma's arm and patting her repeatedly to emphasize her thanks. Then there was waving as we backed out and turned, our car full of the heady aromas of lavender and raisins.

We pushed on through increasingly hilly country and, after three hours, crossed back into Portugal. The morning's clear blue sky had given way to white, billowing clouds, softly gray on their shadow sides. The fortified castle of Marvão beckoned from its perch on a mountaintop to our right, but I drove resolutely past both of its approach roads. I'd chosen not to book its *pousada* because, despite its spectacular setting, the small village within its walls is not nearly so lively and rewarding a place as Castelo de Vide, four miles to the west. But when I caught my fellow traveler wistfully eyeing Marvão, I offered to return in the morning—perchance for breakfast! The promise of an early rise and a sunup view could be depended on to right Paloma's vessel whenever it threatened to capsize. An old dog can learn.

I suppose Castelo de Vide remained unspoiled because it is, as someone put it, on the road from nothing to nowhere. How fortunate for those who seek beyond big cities and bright lights. As we drove down from the mountains to the east, the afternoon sun thrust ruddy shafts through increasingly stormy clouds, and against that background rose a hill crowned by the ruins of a fort, the "castelo" of the town's name. Soon we could make out the higher, older parts of town spilling down from their castle apex, and then, lower and nearer, the more modern section. The whole scene, even the parts in shadow, glowed with sky light reflected off white plaster walls—a luminous image enhanced by the patterns of red tile roofs stepping down the hill and spreading onto the flats below.

After a wrong turn or two I found Hotel Sol e Serra, my lodging during my earlier visit. We moved right in, then took to the streets to see as much as possible before the onset of a threatened rain. In fifteen minutes we entered the castle, climbed its wall, and gazed out over the town, golden in the last rays of a sinking sun. We waved at our own images visible atop the fortress's shadow, then, as the light faded, we returned to the streets. Here, outside the castle wall, the town proper got its start, and we pushed along admiring old houses built within the protected neighborhood of the fort and its lord.

Before long, we came upon several carts in obvious need of repair. Next to them, in an open-doored workshop, an elderly man worked on an oxcart wheel by the light of a dangling clear bulb. He'd made two new spokes and was shaping a third with what I was taught to call a spokeshave, the first I'd ever seen put to its nominal use. Paloma was spellbound. "Oh, let's stay. Let's watch him finish this last one." I could tell that she saw some cosmic significance in the day's coincidence, our stricken oxcart's wheel with its three broken spokes, and now just such a wheel under repair. I knew that oxcarts were in daily use all over the region, but who was I to dash her poetic perceptions?

Actually, we'd both been affected by the feel of the land and the events of the day, and we shared our reactions as we walked back to our hotel, showered, and went down for an early dinner. After that it was a glass of Madeira in the bar, small talk with Americans and Japanese who had toured Marvão that day, general delight over the unexpected charms of the area, and general enthusiasm for Portugal and the Portuguese. Then it was off to bed at the behest of a woman already counting stars to be found in the morning sky. Fingers crossed by her partner, who cast sidelong glances at the cloud cover. The mingling of squeaky-clean bodies in bed, repairs to that cleanliness, lights out.

Thursday, October 24th

I awoke first and tried to envision a scheme to surprise Miss Gung Ho, asleep face down in the other bed. It came to me. I got up, leaned over the heavy head of hair, and whispered into its depths, "Up and at 'em!" Yawn, stretch, wriggle, sit up, recollect.

"How is the day?"

"Dark."

"Is there hope?"

"There's always hope. Let's go elsewhere to do our hoping."

The tall, trim body hit the deck and disappeared. Minutes passed, water ran in pipes, additional plumbing came to life. Outside the bathroom door, the team's other half donned garments and tied shoes. The door opened and situations were reversed. In minutes, two adventurers tiptoed downstairs, the night clerk waved, and we were out in the dark.

Wonders! Stars were clearly visible between the huge clouds scudding over our heads. We headed east up the grade, our lights showing the way. I sprang my surprise at the Marvão turnoff.

"What do you say we park here and hike up to Marvão? It's a thousand feet above us. Just imagine the vistas going and coming."

I knew it! This proposal was a total winner. Eyes shone with admiration for such an inspired notion. Oh Lord, I thought, I'll have to cudgel my poor head to conjure a follow-up for this one.

I parked the Opel off the road and we started our hike of some two miles. A coal-black skyline stood out in bold relief against an increasingly salmon-tinted sky, and nearby objects became visible. We pursued a path up and up, then around, then up some more—this is the kingdom of the winding road. Each glimpse revealed more detail in our view to the west, and, out of the gloom, Castelo de Vide appeared, now below us, with a great valley beyond and, yet farther, more mountains. We were determined to reach the summit by sunrise, so we tarried little and marched much. I noted with growing regret a succession of parking places thought out and prepared for a more prescient visitor. I reproached myself, why had I not driven the car halfway up? Paloma showed no penchant for hindsight, only for leaving me in the dust. I labored manfully, or at least old manfully, and in the end we arrived in a dead heat with the sun finding the distant mountains and, soon after, the intervening valley.

The eminence on which we stood casts a long shadow, which gave us a quarter of an hour to wait for the sun to strike Castelo de Vide, and time enough for my knees to quit wobbling. We climbed onto the wall, the grand show in our foreground began to unfold, and my stock reached its zenith for the day.

"I can't believe you planned this and pulled it off. It's perfect." I got patted and she held still to be kissed on the forehead, a rare concession in a populated area.

We stood side by side as the tide of morning light crept toward us. Paloma broke a long silence in a voice as soft as the breeze, "Sun at our backs, wind at our backs. Don't you feel projected out over hills and valleys? Gliding over the waves and troughs like the figurehead on a ship?"

The solemnity of her tone drew my eyes to her. I asked, "Palomita, what is it with you and the dawn, even the predawn? I've never known another soul so delighted to get up early and look over the world."

She took my hand in hers and intertwined our fingers; she gave our arms a little swing. "It is strange, a strange sensation. Early, before broad daylight, before people are really out and about, everything feels timeless, I could be back with my ancestors. You know I have no living family, but somehow, when I was sixteen and came back to Europe, I felt I'd rejoined my people. I don't care if that makes no sense. Early like this, I feel at home, as if this is where I belong." She pressed my hand to her cheek and smiled at me. "I love our dawn patrols. Bless you for humoring me."

"Bless you for sharing with me," was all I could think to say, but her words and the touch of her cheek left me feeling protective. I was relieved when we'd stepped over to the *pousada* and livened Paloma's spirits with savory eggscetera. Thus fortified, we took the comparatively easy downhill stroll to our car, waving as we went to the tour buses laboring up the hill.

We drove back to Sol e Serra to freshen up, and I got directions to a small museum of regional antiquities supported by the municipality and staffed by volunteers calling themselves Grupo de Arqueologia. On a previous visit, I'd seen their collection of local discoveries, Stone Age to Recent. These artifacts in bone, stone, ceramic, glass, wood, and fiber well illustrate the sequence of cultures lured by the region's warm mineral waters (curative of course), which, by Roman times were piped to public baths and became the basis for a community.

We walked to the museum and found it tended by a husband and wife I'd met before, people who responded immediately to Paloma and her devotion to the past. When they rose to show us around, I bowed out. "See everything," I suggested, "then come up the hill for lunch." She agreed, and I went back to our room to stretch out on the bed. My years were showing. Keeping up with May was putting a strain on November—I'd like to say "late October," but "late" has such an ominous ring.

In a couple of hours, May was back, thrilled to tell me that we had an invitation to go forth after lunch to inspect a dig at a Late Stone Age burial site not far from town. Accordingly, after our midday snack, we reported to the museum and tailed our guide's car five miles to the southwest. Near the village of Alagoa, we swung onto wheel tracks and crossed a pasture to a cleared spot on a slight incline. Several cars were parked, and eight or nine people labored in shallow pits making measurements, taking photographs, creating sketches and diagrams, or actually scraping dirt from the bottoms of trenches. I noted that the ages of the busy crew ranged downward from a contemporary of mine to some as young or younger than my companion.

The site had once been a burial ground. At a depth of four or more feet, the diggers had uncovered human bones laid out with various carefully arranged artifacts. In one pit, the bones had barely been exposed. A young woman with a wooden tool was expertly scraping hard soil from the figure of an animal, possibly a bear, carved from porous stone and embedded near the skeleton's abdominal region. A corresponding figure had been uncovered on the other side. Paloma examined it all and turned to me, "Doesn't this take you to other times? Just imagine! But it feels a little wrong, too, violating the dead."

"Yes," I affirmed in my soberest tones, "grave robbing is, after all, a form of skullduggery."

"Oh no!" she winced theatrically, "have you no shame?"

"None. Thanks for feeding me the straight line."

"Ha! If only I were so clever." But that was delivered with an admiring smile and a pat on the back.

I'd brought our napkinful of raisins from the car and, as we were shown around, my small offerings of the sweet bunches were well received and helped to surmount our language problems. We examined every part of the works and gleaned what we could, and what our guides, with limited English, could add. I'd seen digs before and a wealth of museum material, so I'll admit I wasn't as attentive as my protégée, who took a keen interest in everything. From our first encounter, I'd been attracted by Paloma's delightful sophistication, but further acquaintance was making plain that she was, after all, a relative newcomer to life. I watched her talk and laugh with a young couple as they explained their labors, and a stab of conscience reminded me that she should be spending time with her peers, not with an oldster. And watching young hands reveal old bones, I thought guiltily of young hands caressing a certain old body.

We drove back to town under gathering clouds and elected to walk again in the medieval quarter before we lost the light. We climbed the castle heights, then meandered north and east, keeping to the higher streets for better views. As we came off the hill, we looked into open windows on the second floor of a school. We stopped to hear a teacher and her students exchange questions and answers, then lingered for a unison recitation followed by a song. Paloma was transfixed, finally murmuring, "Really, eyes shut, I'm back in school in Sevilla."

"Not too amazing," I suggested. "Your old school is what, maybe two hundred miles away?" She said little more as we walked on, but she radiated a nostalgic joy I'd sensed building in her for days.

We arrived, thirsting, at the square, ordered drinks, and sat back to watch the towering clouds turn peach above and ever-darker gray below. As the sky show dimmed, a progression of lights winked on in the plaza, and when we decided we'd seen enough, a cozy restaurant beckoned, and we found seats at a candlelit table for two. We ordered, then Paloma thanked me for what she insisted was a perfect day. Feeling contented and expansive myself, I thanked her in return. I mentioned again the stress of Marian's final months and my inability to snap back afterward, my depression and constant state of fatigue. I squeezed her hands and added, "Thank God, we met — and I rejoined the living."

She squeezed back, her dark eyes luminous, reflecting the candle. "I can't pretend to imagine your state of mind, losing your lifetime partner, but I know more than enough about needing companionship. I needed you too. Someday you'll see that's not just talk." She looked down at our hands and turned shy. "Haley, I've been working up my courage to ask a big favor. You've been wanting to know more about me, and there are things I want you to know. I've thought about it a lot, last night and today especially." She looked up, all eagerness. "There's something about this place. Ever since we got here I've had visions of Sevilla and my friend Nourrit. Honestly, I half expect to see her wherever I look. Silly, I know, but she's always in my thoughts. Well, I know I have no right to ask this—it's not part of our bargain at all. But would you please think about taking me—no, taking us— to Sevilla? Perhaps a day's drive?"

I tried to answer, but got shushed.

"Please let me get this out. Ten years ago my grandmother died and I had to leave my home and the woman I'm talking about. For six years, she and my grandmother had been everything to me. And Nourrit's my stitchery friend, did I tell you? Since then, I've seen her only once, four years ago when I came to Sevilla with a client—he was fascinated by the big expo, you know, the one that celebrated the five hundred years since Columbus. Well, he wanted me with him every minute because of my Spanish, and I was new at this companion thing, and I didn't assert myself. It worked out that Nourrit and I met for only two or three hours and it didn't go well at all. It was as if we were saying good-bye again instead of getting reacquainted. I don't come over here on my own; it's so expensive and I try hard to save my money. Nourrit has no telephone, so I write to her, but that's never enough—she reads only a little and writes not at all. I can't tell you how hard it is to be this near and even imagine just turning away. Could you consider breaking your itinerary for a few days? I'm not asking you to pay for this."

"Paloma, the whole purpose of this tour was to spend time with you, and it's been wonderful, truly, but all we've done is sightseeing. I'd love to add something more personal. And not just for you; I'd love to meet your people. But promise you'll fill me in as we go—I don't want to stand around there like some dummy, I want to understand at least some of what happens."

"I promise! Whatever you like. Anything we can fit into the time."

The prospect of Sevilla animated Paloma. If such a thing is possible, she was more radiant and winning than usual. I sat like an old cat warming in front of a fire. As we walked up the hill, I felt her returning to Sevilla, reverting to the fourteen-year-old she was when she was forced to leave. She came to my bed, but I simply held her in my arms while talk slowed and she drifted off to sleep.

She slept, but I could not. I was on a rack, enthralled by her warmth and touch, torn by a conflicting melancholy. Fragrant hair pressed my cheek, a dear shoulder brushed my chest, an inviting hip lay under my hand, the whole of the woman I desperately loved, in my arms, yet totally, irrevocably out of my reach. I could not have her. I could never have had her. I shivered at that awareness and kissed that shoulder softly—a kind of farewell. I kissed it again to celebrate even this brief interlude of togetherness.

Buck up, I told myself, be thankful that we're together at all, and doing something for each other. Here I am, preparing for old age, but I've found in her a magical respite, a fountain of youth. But only a respite. The limits on our relationship underline the impossibility of turning back the clock. And what's in it for Paloma? There's the financial support, but is that all? Well, she *is* lonely, she *is* short on people. I seem to amuse her, and is it too much to hope that we share something beyond what she gets from other clients?

Eventually, her proximity became too sweet and too painful. I slid out and spent the night alone in her bed.

III Nourrit

Castelo de Vide, Portugal — Friday, October 25, 1996

We raised the blinds at daylight and peered out at dark skies and wet ground, neither a threat to our plan. Today it was up, pack, eat, and out. Paloma was cheerful enough, but preoccupied. "Behind the beyond?" I asked at breakfast.

"What, what?" she puzzled. "Oh, you mean am I off some place? Yes. In the night, I tried to think of what all you should know. Well, most of it I've never told anyone, not even in bits and pieces, and I lost track and drifted off. But now it's queuing up, waiting to get out. Think of a traffic officer, busy corner, signals not working."

"Relax. You're making it way too formal. Send your policeman home and I'll take whatever the traffic bears." I got a smile, and we carried our stuff to the car in a light rain and headed for the Spanish border as Paloma launched her tale.

"From the time I was born, we lived in Putney, west-central London, south side of the Thames, and just north of Richmond Park. My mother's name was Celia, but everyone close to her called her Chely, and that's what she had me call her too. She wasn't quite nineteen when I was born and I was told she liked to pretend I was her baby sister. We had a live-in housekeeper named Bessie Barr, and Bessie did all the things for me that a mother usually does, and I loved her and counted on her and thought of her as if she were my mother.

"Bessie lost a foot during the bombings in World War Two. She has a prosthesis that always looked to me like an old-fashioned high boot laced up around the calf of her leg. But losing her foot wasn't the worst of it. That bomb killed her mother and her father and her baby brother. Bessie was five, and after that she was reared in a Catholic home for girls, and then off and on in foster homes around London. When she was seventeen, my mother's father hired her to help a nanny in rearing my mother. That was because my grandmother died when Chely was born."

I interrupted, trying to keep track of the cast of characters. "Who *was* Chely's mother? And who was your mother's father?"

"Honestly, I can't tell you much about my grandmother. She was forty when she died, some complication of Chely's birth, and Chely was her only child. I have just one picture of her now, but I remember others. She was tall and blond and her name was Gwendolyn Williams. Chely told me she was from Wales, a village named Hawarden near Chester. That's about all I know except that she was a singer, very musical. I know more about George Inskip, he was Gwendolyn's husband, and from the late nineteen twenties on he was employed by the London office of a Spanish sherry broker. When my mother was ten, George took her with him when he was moved to Sevilla to supervise the English exports for the sherry people.

"My mother's married name was Grey, but you need to know that her husband Grey was not my father. My father was Francisco Utrera, and he was an heir to that sherry business. I was the child of Francisco, but there was no possibility of his marrying Chely, so she was married off to an older man in time to make me 'legitimate.' All that was worked out between Francisco's lawyer and George Inskip. After that, Francisco Utrera was responsible for supporting Chely and me.

"I'd just turned eight when I last saw my father. He brought me a gift at our place in Putney, came with a priest from Saint Vincent's— that's where Bessie and I attended Mass. He had to come with a priest every time, that was a condition of his visiting Chely and me. I didn't see them come, but I was herded out into the kitchen and I sat there with the priest and Bessie while my father talked to my mother—

I could hear them speaking Spanish in the parlor. After a while, my mother called me in and I recognized him from his visit two years before, but he looked bigger, more imposing than I'd remembered. He gave me a package and watched me open it. He said something in Spanish to Chely, and somehow I knew that I reminded him of his mother. Then he sat down and asked me questions in English. I remember being intrigued with his accent, but I had no trouble understanding him and I answered as best I could about school things. I mentioned studying French, and he asked Chely, 'Why does she not take Spanish?' My mother pointed out that there were only four teachers at the school, and none of them spoke Spanish. He asked my mother why she couldn't teach me, and then speak Spanish at home. I remember that my mother said she could try, but she acted tired of that subject and got onto something else."

"Strikes me as odd that your father, not married to your mother, and even restricted in seeing her, would come to England to give her a hard time because you weren't speaking Spanish. What was that all about?"

"Well, my father was a difficult man. I can't speak for him or tell you much about him and you'll see why. It all started on a Sunday morning, about a month after his last visit. My mother was on the telephone for a long time and then she called me down from my room and had me sit beside her. She sounded really upset. 'Paloma,' she told me, 'your father fell from his horse while he was playing polo. He was terribly hurt, and the doctors worked all night trying to give him a chance to live, but they couldn't, and he died. Your father is gone. You'll never see him again.' She squeezed me tight, and all I could think was that she didn't hug me or squeeze me much, so it must be important. But I didn't grieve for my father because I'd never known him. He was just a man who'd come to visit, perhaps two or three times that I could remember. I knew some of Chely's boyfriends ever so much better than that. They'd say hello if I answered the phone and they'd chat with me when they came around to take Chely off to wherever they were going. Of course Chely'd told me things about my father, but, at eight, none of it meant much to me.

"After that, terrible things began to happen. My mother got letters that made her furious or made her cry. She had long telephone conversations in Spanish, and while she was on, she'd weep and curse and call on God. After one of those sessions, she practically yelled at me that Francisco's family didn't want to admit that I existed, but they'd better get used to the idea. I had no idea what she was talking about. Then she told me that we must go to Spain, possibly for a long time, and that Bessie couldn't go. I'd never been separated from Bessie. I couldn't even imagine it. She'd been the center of my universe every way I knew or could think of.

"When the time came to say good-bye to Bessie, it was awful. That was the hardest, saddest thing I've ever done. I'll never forget how Bessie and I sat in our little kitchen and just groped for words and wiped away tears. I promised her things and she promised me things and we've both kept our promises. Bessie is a totally good person. She's as dear to me today as she was then, and I think of her and miss her every day. She's in my prayers and I write to her and she writes to me. But that didn't help the day we had to say good-bye. When we drove away, I thought I'd lost everything I could depend on in the whole world."

Through most of this, Paloma had sounded quite composed, but in the telling of that parting her voice dropped and, it seemed, her spirits as well. I put a hand on her arm and gave it a squeeze.

"Sorry," she said, "it was dreadful, really — but there was a bright side that I never could have imagined. I was on my way to Nourrit."

We crossed the high plain under dark clouds but dwindling rain, then, near the Spanish border and the old citadel of Badajoz, the morning sun broke through and dazzled our eyes. I had always loved the sweep of the western Spanish highlands, but this time I could add the excitement of a story itself headed into Spain. Border formalities were over in seconds and a stop for fuel took little longer, but I chafed at the enforced recess from eight-year-old Paloma's adventures, and rejoiced when we pulled back onto the road and she could resume.

"Anyway, that's how I left Bessie and the only home I'd ever known — I thought I was crushed then, but honestly, the nightmare was just beginning. We took a cab to an airport where it seemed to me we waited forever. I'd never been exposed to so much confusion, so much noise, so many people, so many languages, so many different-looking faces. By the time we got on that airplane, I didn't care if it was my first-ever flight, I was worn out and I went to sleep. I waked up when we were coming into Madrid, and there was the descent and all that long taxiing. Then there was more noise and more confusion in the terminal. I felt as if I'd died and gone to the Hell that some of the Sisters had talked about at school. And Chely was no help, she was just quiet and sad. I kept looking around and praying to see Bessie coming to save me. I wondered what God was thinking, or what I'd done wrong. It was getting dark, and that made it worse. I remember a curious illusion. We were in endless tunnels filled with thousands of strangers who didn't know we existed. I hung on to Chely as I never had before. She was all I had left.

"Then we had to go from desk to desk and line to line while Chely talked in Spanish to customs officers and waited for them to fill out papers. I dozed off and Chely had to pat me awake so we could board another plane. That flight was short, and after we'd got off and waited for our baggage, Chely found a taxi driver, and then it was a long drive with bright lights going by until we got to a little hotel on a dark side street and finally, finally came to rest in a tiny room. I went to sleep listening to Chely speaking Spanish while she tried to reach people by telephone.

"The next morning was worse. We had greasy eggs in a little, bare restaurant, then went back to the room and Chely made more calls, all the time acting tired and discouraged. At one point she began to cry, and I tried to put my arms around her, and she just turned away from me and slumped down on the bed and lay there crying. After a while, someone knocked on our door and Chely wiped off her face and let an old woman in. Chely told me the woman would stay with me while she went to see people in offices where children weren't permitted. Then she was gone. The woman spoke to me in Spanish, and of course I couldn't understand her or answer back. She turned on the telly and sat and smoked while she watched what I suppose were soap operas. At noon she took me to the same sad restaurant and ordered me something awful, nothing like the fresh food Bessie fixed at home.

"After lunch we were back in the room all afternoon. I had no books I could get to, and no paper, but I did find a pen. I made signs to the woman that I wanted paper, and she took me to the desk where another woman was glad to give me a few sheets of hotel stationery. The rest of the afternoon I wrote to Bessie in small writing so the paper would last. Then it was night, and we went back to that dingy restaurant. I asked for soup, and the waiter understood, so I had two big bowls of perfectly good potato and onion soup. I'll never forget how good it tasted — I'm reminded every time I make something like it for myself.

"I was half asleep by the time Chely came back. She'd been drinking. I knew because I'd seen her come home like that two or three times before, and Bessie had explained it to me. She paid the old woman and got undressed as soon as she left. Chely didn't want to talk, but I went over and sat on her bed and looked at her. When she'd got her nightgown on, she sat down and we hugged for a long time with my head over her shoulder. She began to cry again and shake all over. I was frightened, my worst fear was that she'd go off another time and leave me with that woman and not come back, ever. I went to bed and had the shakes myself."

Paloma was too good a storyteller. Her tale felt as if it flowed straight from the child she'd been. I took her hand and told her in all sincerity, "My heart goes out to that little girl."

She squeezed back and went on. "Well, Chely was better in the morning. We packed my things and got a cab to a neighborhood of grand apartment buildings, and Chely took me to a restaurant where I had what I thought was a great breakfast, but all I really remember is a hot milk drink with chocolate in it. Believe me, I'd rarely had such a thing. Anyhow, while we ate, Chely told me that we'd visit my father's mother, my grandmother. Her name was Amparo Vargas, but I was to call her 'Señora Utrera.' She was right, of course, but that Spanish maiden-name/married-name thing took some explaining to an eight-year-old English child. Then she broke the news that I might have to stay with my grandmother while she — Chely — made a long trip that might be necessary. I was shocked — panicked really — but all I could think to ask was who I'd be able to speak to since I had only English and a few phrases of French. She promised me my grandmother spoke English quite well.

"After breakfast, Chely carried two bags and I took one and we walked two blocks to a residence building so tall I thought it was a skyscraper. We rang a bell and a door opened and we went into a hall with an elevator. On the fourth floor we found a door and rang the bell. A man in a uniform opened it and showed us in, then a woman came into the hall and spoke to my mother.

"Haley, I give you my word, I had the strangest sensation the moment I saw that woman. She was the first person I'd laid eyes on since we left Putney who seemed altogether real, three dimensional, not just flickering by on a movie screen the way the others had seemed to do. I'd stepped into her world and she'd come into mine. She was tall and straight and she had on a pale blue dress of some linen-like goods, with a broad white collar and a long white apron from the waist down. I must say, she looked awfully foreign to me — probably her dark skin and her wavy black hair pulled into a bun — but the big thing was, she was so completely calm and dignified. I remember thinking that she moved and spoke in slow motion. Being there with her was an absolute counterbalance to all those nightmare people who'd flashed by since that awful trip began.

"She spoke a few words to my mother and then looked down at me. She raised her eyebrows and gave me a little smile, then she held out her hands and I took them and she swung me ever so gently in a circle toward an open door, swept me along at the end of her arms. It was magical. We spiraled across the room as if we were dancing, through a doorway, across a hall, through a second room, then faster through another door and into a huge great kitchen where she spun me around twice and brought me to a stop right in front of a chair. She stretched out her arms and let go — and there I was, sitting in the chair. All that time I'd looked into her eyes and she into mine. I knew she liked me, I could see it and feel it. And I liked her, so strong and so serene. She wasn't at all young but she had no wrinkles on her forehead, not a one. For the first time since I left Bessie, I wasn't frightened sick over what might happen next. I thought of Bessie and I said the little thanksgiving prayer she'd taught me.

"We couldn't speak to each other, but we still introduced ourselves. Her name was Nourrit, and she made my name sound more beautiful than I'd ever heard before. I felt stronger and better. Then she made lemonade, and it was better even than Bessie's. Another woman was there too, my grandmother's cook. She smiled and shook my hand

and I could tell she was apologizing for having no English—right there I learned the word *inglés*. Nourrit brought me big sheets of paper and crayons and I began to draw. I remember the time passed quickly, the kitchen was warm and light, and in the background I could hear a big pot of onions simmering away and an old-fashioned clock ticking. And I liked the sound of the women's voices and the looks on their faces. I knew they were saying things about me, but I could tell they approved of me. I felt welcome in the kitchen.

"After a while, Nourrit made signs to wait there, and she left. In a few minutes she was back and led me down a hall and into a room where we stood in front of my mother and a tall, older woman I knew must be my grandmother. I could tell there'd been some sort of trouble. Chely's eyes were red and her makeup was smeared. My grandmother looked stiff and had a frown on her face.

"I found myself looking at my grandmother. I had no idea what a grandmother would be like. I had no idea what any relative would be like because I'd never met any but my mother and my now-and-then father. Well, I saw a straight figure, all in black, and a handsome face with a severe expression. She turned toward me and acted uncertain about looking me in the eye, but she did. Then she leaned forward and put out her hands. I took them and we looked at each other for what felt like a long time. Finally my grandmother said in quite good English, 'Paloma, I am Amparo and we will talk.' She turned to my mother and spoke in Spanish. My mother told me she'd be back later, and she left. I looked around and Nourrit was gone as well.

"My grandmother had us sit in two chairs facing each other close up. First, she asked me about myself. She asked about my church and I told her about Saint Vincent's and Father Peter and the children's choir. I told her about Saint Anne's school and the Sisters who taught me. I told her about Bessie and her artificial foot, and about our home in Putney and how I missed Bessie and our home.

"My grandmother asked me what I liked to do to entertain myself. I answered that most of all I liked to help Bessie and talk to her and play games with her. I told her that Bessie used to read to me, but that for years now she'd had me read to her because her eyes were tired. My grandmother asked me whether I had friends, and I told her the truth. I had school friends, most of my classmates really, but no playmates away from school because no children my age lived near our house.

"My grandmother asked me if I ever told lies and I told her I did not. She asked if I ever picked up and took things that were not mine. I told her that stealing was a sin; it would hurt people, and it would hurt me most of all. She asked me whether I'd ever seen the Devil, and I explained that the Sisters told us the Devil could look like anybody he wished, so I had no idea whether I'd seen him or not. She asked me if anyone had ever tried to tempt me to do wrong things, and I said no. I told her Bessie had taught me to turn toward the light and the good always and not waste my time or thoughts on any sort of sin. My grandmother leaned forward and looked me in the eye when she asked what I knew about sin. I said I really knew nothing. Sin was a thing I'd heard about in church and from the Sisters, but I'd never actually seen any sin myself. My grandmother took my hands and asked me if I'd sing a song for her, so I began to sing *Adeste Fideles*. Before I could finish, my grandmother pulled me to her and hugged me, still sitting in her chair. She kissed me on the forehead and just held on. She started to tremble and cry, and it went on and I felt tears running down her cheeks. It frightened me that I made my mother and my grandmother cry. I wondered what I'd done.

"Well, she went on hugging me until she quieted down, then she held me out from her and said, 'Paloma, your mother has to go away on a long trip, and you will stay with me. I want you to feel at home with me. I want you to go to Mass with me and go to school here and learn to speak Spanish. I am sorry you will not have your friend Bessie, but we will do everything we can to give you a good home.'

"Then Chely came back and we had lunch. It wasn't exactly jolly, but everybody seemed more at peace. Chely and my grandmother spoke Spanish, but I knew a lot of it was about me. That afternoon a lawyer came and talked to them on and on. Then he and Chely left after she took me aside to say good-bye. She told me she'd be gone quite a while and she'd write to me regularly. But Chely was never very good about keeping promises."

We pulled off the road at Zafra and went to the *parador* for lunch. I opted for a *filete* and strong coffee. My partner satisfied herself with fruit, but declared herself less content with my insistence on doing all the driving. I admitted selfishness, that I wanted her to concentrate on her memoir and let me watch the road. On that basis, I pursued our way and she her narration.

"My grandmother's apartment was quite grand, a quarter of our floor in that large building. But even with four bedrooms to pick from, I always felt that I'd been given the best, the one that looked out on the front street. I loved looking down on the treetops and peeking between them. I could see people walking, shop awnings, taxis coming and going, our neighbors' cars, and delivery trucks and service people — such a contrast to our dull, quiet street in Putney.

"My grandmother's maid was a nice young woman named Celestina. She had a lot to do and she worked hard. In a day or two, I learned how to take care of my own room, and before long I was helping her with the other rooms and with washing up in the kitchen. We became great friends and she'd often take me out window shopping when she had time off in the afternoon.

"The cook's name was Consuelo, and she was my friend too. She taught me how to peel, pit, pare, or chop anything that came into the kitchen. And I watched Consuelo when she did special things, like slicing and stuffing chops, or pounding herbs into meat or chicken. I think of her often when I'm preparing meals.

"Every morning, I took breakfast to my grandmamá — that's what she had me call her, Grandmamá, the name I used before I was fluent in Spanish. I'd already eaten with Nourrit and Consuelo in the kitchen, so I'd sit and entertain her as she ate. Sometimes she asked me questions, but usually she wanted to hear my stories of school or my reading or what I'd done with Nourrit and the others. At night, I had supper with Grandmamá in the dining room, and then we'd talk about her life or she'd lecture me a little about serious subjects. She'd always know when I'd had letters. She'd seldom ask about the ones I had so often from Bessie, but she wanted to hear any news from Chely when I got one of her now-and-then notes. They were posted from all over Europe, and they were short and didn't tell me much. She never mentioned why she had to be gone so long."

Something seemed to be missing and I asked, "Where was Chely's father while all this was going on? Wasn't he involved?"

"Oh, I'm sorry, I forget about George. He died when I was in kindergarten and I'm not certain I even remember him. Later, I asked Chely what'd happened to him, and she claimed she'd heard no details because he'd lived in Spain all the time she was with me in England. Everyone was so vague about details, I've decided that it may've been a suicide. I know Bessie and Nourrit have no idea how he died."

Paloma was distracted by the sight of oxcarts being loaded in a muddy field, but when we'd gone by, she took up briskly on a different tack.

"You know, in a way I was an embarrassment to my grandmother just by existing—that makes me appreciate all the more the things she did for me, or tried to do, to build up my confidence. She'd always introduce me to any friends who came to her place. And when she was their guest, she'd often arrange to have me invited too. She told me, right from the start, that if she had a visitor, I was to present myself at her sitting room door to be introduced. I knew, or perhaps I just felt, that most of her friends looked at me as a real curiosity when we first met. But I must say, most of them became friendly, especially as I learned Spanish. And when we'd run into them later at church or around town, those people most often acted glad to see me and they'd introduce me to whoever might be with them.

"There was an English friend of Amparo's who visited twice a year—Paula Browne, a woman I liked a lot. When I was eleven or twelve, she came to our place as usual, and I walked in before she was seated. She saw me and called out, 'Oh, do come and sit, Paloma. I was about to ask your grandmother to let you come and visit us in Kent, perhaps go to school for a term.' Well, I felt as if I were onstage in the midst of a play. My grandmother acted entirely surprised, but she answered without taking time to think, something like, 'Oh, that's so kind of you and Henry'—Henry was Paula's husband—'but the truth is, my house can't spare Paloma. I can't spare her. We'd all feel lost.' I was embarrassed, but I was so pleased that she felt that way and said so right in front of me.

"My grandmamá showed her interest in me in lots of ways during the years we were together. She took me on drives out into the country, and sometimes she'd invite Nourrit to come along too. She took me shopping and got whatever she thought I needed and let me help to pick out clothes. Right from the start, she tried to do things for me. She'd come to my bedroom while I was getting dressed or undressed and brush my hair or try to arrange it even though she wasn't very good at it, or she'd suggest clothes to wear, or tell me how to take care of them. She liked to look over my shoulder into the mirror and smile at me, and more than once she told me she'd always wanted a daughter and never dreamed it could happen, but now she had one. I felt the same way, she was the grandmamá I'd never dared to imagine and I had her and I loved it. I just hope I let her know. I did try in a lot of ways, but I'm afraid I never came right out with it in so many words. I wish I had.

"But I think she knew, we shared so much. She even included me in some of her devotions. Every day, she read religious works and prayed at her bedroom shrine. I didn't bother her when she was reading or praying, but quite often she'd take me to kneel with her before the Virgin. Prayers were silent, and I had no trouble praying because there were people I wanted the Virgin to protect and I remembered them every time I prayed. Once Grandmamá asked me, 'Do you never lower your eyes before the Virgin?' I told her I felt closer to Our Lady when I looked into her eyes and into the eyes of her child. Sometimes my grandmamá asked me to sing for the Virgin. That almost always brought tears to her eyes, but she told me they were tears of joy and relief, and that I should be happy I could do that for her.

"But, to be honest, I had more fun with Nourrit. She must have been close to Amparo's age, but she acted more like a best friend than a grandmother, and a friend very different from Bessie. Bessie was more openly affectionate, but it seemed to me that she'd been satisfied to have me as a little girl. Nourrit's always had an eye out for any opportunity to show me ways to learn and grow. When school didn't interfere, she took me with her to shop for the things we needed at home, to take clothes to the cleaners or the tailor, or to find any of the tradesman or craftsman we needed at the time. Nourrit and I played a lot of games that didn't involve words. She was good at cards and checkers and dominoes, and it was a long time before I beat her at anything. The first time I did, she threw up her hands and smiled so, then she went to the larder and brought out some caramel nut candy as a special treat.

"I felt closer still when Nourrit invited me to help with her business. By then, she was partly retired, living with my grandmother but not working for her full time. She had a big room and a big wooden table so she could lay out the cloth for appliqué and embroidery pieces as large as five feet across. I was fascinated by her art when I was eight, and I still am. Some of her pieces were almost literal pictures of farms, or marshes, or riverbanks, or plants, or any sort of animal—bird, fish, insect, anything. Others were designs with similar elements, but more stylized and repeated in patterns that I'd call semi-geometric, you know, repetitive motifs that appear to flow or suggest motion. Some were quite abstract—I remember she called them 'spirits who will not reveal themselves.' All the designs were hers and no two were alike, but she often needed a lot of pieces that were alike, and that's where she had me start. She taught me to cut them out of two or three layers of fabric. Oh, and right from the start she taught me to sew, and I was making simple things for myself by the time I was ten. And she taught me to embroider, but not on the works she sold in the market.

"Nourrit had no interest in knitting, but she soon taught me how to crochet. She and I worked together for all the time it took to crochet the pieces for an openwork table cover for Grandmamá's sitting room. It was a big job, but what I most remember is all the trouble we had keeping my grandmother from knowing what we were doing. The problem was that she loved to come and sit wherever I was doing anything except homework. She'd sit in the parlor while Celestina and I picked up and dusted, especially if she heard Celestina singing and me doing harmony. And she'd come and chat with Consuelo and me when I was helping in the kitchen. But the problem was, she liked to sit down and listen and contribute while Nourrit and I were doing stitchery. To do all that crocheting, we had to keep another project at hand so we could pick it up the moment my grandmamá came to the door. Eventually we did finish the table cover, and Nourrit insisted that it be a gift from me, but I made sure to tell Amparo how much help I'd had.

"So there I was, busy, and basically happy with my new life. Besides missing Bessie, the only negative thing I felt at home was the sense that I'd come between my grandmother and my half sisters. Alicia and Marta are Francisco's children with his wife, a woman he lived with for only three or four years—they're about ten and twelve years older than I. They were young women when I arrived, and they didn't want to meet me or see me, ever. After a time, we were introduced, but on the odd occasion when they came to Amparo's, they'd pretend not to see me. Celestina disliked them, especially after she overheard them trying to persuade our grandmother that I had no claim on her and she should send me back to my mother. Once, I couldn't help overhearing Alicia raise her voice and accuse our grandmother of favoring a bastard child over them. I didn't hear the answer, but Alicia cried out again, 'Well, it's true, isn't it?' and then I heard Amparo telling her that God would punish her for judging her sister. And after that, my grandmother made me feel closer than ever.

"All through my first year in Sevilla, I thought it was so strange that my mother was gone so long. No one gave me any real reason, so I finally worked up the courage to ask my grandmother a direct question. I remember that it took her longer than usual to choose her words. She said Chely had to make a life of her own. She had to find something she could do, and then make a place for herself before she'd be able to take responsibility for me.

"My grandmother told me for the first time that she knew Chely'd had a difficult life and that she was sorry for her and prayed she would find happiness. But she also believed it would've been too hard for her to reorganize herself and take care of me all at once. Grandmamá explained how important it was for a child to have a stable home, and that was why she took me when my mother asked to leave me with her. She held me in her arms and told me she loved me. She thanked me for being a granddaughter any grandmother could love and be proud of. That gave me the oddest feeling because I didn't think of anything I did as good or bad. I was just me, the things I did felt like natural things to do with the people I did them with. But it was wonderful to have my grandmamá tell me that she was pleased with me."

I thought of the little I knew about Francisco Utrera and decided it was no wonder that Amparo took joyfully to her lovable granddaughter. I tossed in my two cents' worth.

"Look, I'll bet your grandmamá was more than pleased with you. I don't suppose that Francisco lived with her as an adult, so she'd been alone, except for household help, for a long time. You gave her company, family, and a sense of purpose. From what you've told me, I'd guess that your grandmother bargained to resume your mother's support payments on the condition that she leave you in Sevilla, and more than likely, get out of the country. I'm guessing that your father's support ended with his death because that would explain why Chely was forced to go to Spain. If she'd had any significant inheritance from her father, why would she have been so disturbed after Francisco's death? And why would she have had to break up your home in Putney?"

"Well, I'm sure you're right about part of it, but it wasn't quite that simple. Years later, when my mother was dying and suffering a lot of guilt over me, she told me that when she learned the Utrera payments would end, she decided to take me to Sevilla and tell them that I was their responsibility. That's why she had the confrontation with Amparo that first day. According to Chely, Amparo wanted to close the books on Francisco's life and not be reminded. Somehow she changed her mind and made an arrangement with Chely — that was all the lawyer talk that first afternoon. It did make sense. My grandmother was calm and thoughtful and old-fashioned. She must have seen that Chely was in no condition to rear me. But nobody ever breathed a word of that to me at the time, or even a year afterward when I asked about Chely."

"OK, that sounds like more of Amparo's kindness. She had a good idea how troubled your mother was, but she didn't want to demean her in your eyes by going into any embarrassing details. Your grandmamá concentrated on giving you the home she'd decided that you deserved. It sounds to me as if she and her household succeeded in that right from the start."

"They really did. I remember those first months in Sevilla as if I spent them in two wildly different worlds, home and school. I started as a total outsider both places, but the people were so different. At home, when I couldn't get the hang of something because it wasn't like anything I'd known, or because I couldn't understand the language, everyone got involved and encouraged me and made sure that somehow I did come to understand. At Academia de El Sagrado Corazón, I was an outsider, period. I felt lost. I wasn't exactly shunned, but with the language problem, few of my classmates made any effort to include me. All I could contribute was to help the Sister who taught English. Everyone studied English to some extent and I helped when

I was asked. In my other classes, I tried to read and follow what was spoken, but I couldn't make out much.

"In a few weeks, though, something magical began to happen. I began to make sense of what was said at home and in my classes and in the halls and on the playground, more every day. By Christmas, that first year, I no longer felt so lost. By Easter I could do most of my work myself and I was a little more accepted by the girls. But only at school. During my six years there, I was invited to other girls' homes only when Amparo knew the families. I'm almost sure my illegitimacy was the subject of rumors. My half sisters could have seen to that."

Paloma let out a deep breath and sat back. I needed the break. As soon as she mentioned social problems over her illegitimacy, my mind began racing. "OK," I thought to myself. "Here's a clue to those flashes of low self-esteem that keep popping up. Imagine what a burden that was for a child to bear." Of course, she'd told me about her irregular parentage first thing that morning, but she'd also mentioned the contrived marriage that made her legitimate. Now I could see, though, that her relatives in Sevilla knew the truth, and once she was there, she was vulnerable to the gossip they could start. Finally I pulled myself together and tried to commiserate. "Pretty tough to come in as a stranger and a foreigner and have a whispering campaign to contend with too. Was that a bitter pill?"

"Well, not exactly bitter. Of course I resented the stigma, that creepy feeling that people were pointing and whispering, and yes, I wanted to be like everyone else, but that didn't make me envy the other girls for their home lives. I never imagined that they felt more loved and included than I did, not as long as I had Amparo's household around me. And then, when I was ten, our home got a lot livelier with music and a new baby—I'll get to him later.

"Just before my tenth birthday, my grandmother decided that I should have music lessons, and she had teachers come to our place and let me choose among them. My favorite was a small, kind man named José María Tamaral who didn't smoke and seemed endlessly patient. He came every Saturday and worked with me. I love the guitar. I still have the one he picked out and Amparo paid for. It's had a couple of accidents and had to be mended, but it brings back wonderful memories."

My narrator's reminiscences were cut short as we turned off the highway to take a break in Santa Olalla. We got directions to a restaurant with a terrace where we joined a crowd from a Spanish tour bus taking afternoon sherry and cookies in fresh air and bright sun. We ordered drinks, sat and sipped, and found ourselves almost in unison describing how odd it felt to jump from the quiet and privacy of our car and Paloma's childhood into this genial hubbub. It was good to stop and then good to get on the road and back to the past.

"I know I've made it sound as if it were all joy under my grandmother's roof, and mostly it was, but I've made the transition sound easier than it was. I always missed Bessie, even with my new friends, and when I learned that Amparo and Bessie sometimes exchanged letters, I let myself dream that Bessie would come to live with us and we'd be all one family. I wanted it so badly that I honestly thought it was going to happen, and the hope took a long time to die. No matter what, I wrote to her every week. I was afraid that if I didn't tell her enough about my new world we'd be strangers with nothing to share. And she wrote back to tell me about her work, and the neighbors, and new acquaintances of hers. She always said that she loved me and prayed for me. I treasured her letters.

"I have to say that Grandmamá felt my loss of Bessie, and she was awfully kind about it. Right from the start, she'd ask me what I'd done with Bessie and what we'd talked about, and she tried to offer me the same kind of company. Of course, she couldn't do that. Her station in life and her background were so different that she talked about totally different things, and did different things, and then I was a different age, too. As I learned Spanish, Amparo would quiz me about that, and from time to time, she'd try me out on words or constructions she thought I ought to know. But it was obvious that she took pleasure in speaking English with me, and that's what we did unless someone else was present."

"Really! I guess I missed something. How come your grandmother was so devoted to English?"

"Oh, that came with the sherry business. Her people were in the wine trade too, that's how she met her husband, Ramón Utrera. All those sherry firms had ties to England, some going back generations. Amparo spent a year in England with friends of her parents when she was twelve or thirteen, then she studied for another year in Sussex when she was seventeen. She was proud of her English and read more books in English than in Spanish. The only times I saw Grandmamá showing off were at church when she made a point of speaking English with me in front of some people she knew, even after I could speak fairly respectable Spanish.

"As I got more fluent, I became closer and closer to everyone in the house and I learned more and more about them. Particularly Nourrit, because I spent so much time with her. She talked about herself very little, but I found myself curious and I had lots of questions. I asked about her family and her home. Little by little she told me her story, and it was so sad. And then she'd tell parts of it over again when I asked. I could tell that she was someone who understood loss and loneliness, and that made me feel closer to her. I came to feel as if her story were somehow part of mine, and I'll need to tell you part of it if you're to make any sense of Nourrit and our relationship."

I kept my eyes on the road, but nodded in vigorous assent. Paloma shifted about in her seat and started in as if she had memorized every word.

"Nourrit doesn't know where she was born. It was a farm near a village and a river somewhere in northwest Africa. Her father and mother were farmers who cultivated their own piece of land and kept a herd of goats. Nourrit had an older brother and two older sisters and she worked with them at the family's chores from the earliest time she can recall. She doesn't know exactly how old she was when she was separated forever from her people, but she supposes she was around eight, about the age I was when I left England. She knows so little because she never went to school or discussed things like maps or the names of cities or even the name of the country where she was born.

"One day her father took her to a town an hour's bus ride from their village. He'd saved some money and he was going to buy something the family needed—Nourrit remembers talk about tools. Once they got to town, her father left her at the house of a woman he knew while he went off to do business. He didn't come back that night, and the next day a man and woman drove up to the house and spoke to her father's acquaintance. She told Nourrit to get into the automobile with another young girl and this couple would take her to her father. Once they were on the road, the man and woman spoke to each other in a language the girls didn't know and they pretended not to understand the girls' questions. After that, they gave the girls things to eat and made stops for necessities, but they kept moving day and night, trading off on driving and sleeping. Nourrit waked the second day to see nothing but desert, and so it was till the day's end.

"At the end of the third day they drove into a huge city with lights and avenues and all sorts of things Nourrit had never seen or imagined. It was Casablanca, and she was turned over to a man and wife who served in a large house and put her to work helping them in the kitchen and the garden. She had to learn a completely new language and work hard all day every day, but she was accustomed to that. The couple didn't treat her badly, she said, and she was better fed than she'd been at home.

"She was terribly lonely, but then she befriended an old man who was partly blind and lived and worked in an abandoned garden on her street. She spent her evenings with him. He shared his tomatoes and onions with her, and she took him soup she made every day from onions and bones and vegetable trimmings while she worked in the kitchen. Nourrit told me he'd been a holy man in some other land, but he'd lost his place with his brother monks and was forced out to seek God among strangers. He told Nourrit important things and gave her good advice. He taught her to listen for true voices and to see things that other people ignore. He showed her that people try to deceive each other, but that one could stand aside and see around their deceptions — and that, in any event, no one deceives the God who resides in all. Nourrit was the friend and the pupil of the man in the garden for four years, then someone died in the house where she worked, and the building had to be cleared out to be sold. The man and woman who'd run the kitchen kept Nourrit busy for days on end packing up and crating all the household things. When they were finished and ready to be off, they told Nourrit she would go with them and she went to speak to her friend and found he was gone. The garden had been leveled and workmen were digging foundations for a new structure. No one knew a thing about the blind man. Nourrit believes he came there for her and left when she was ready to go on to other things."

"Young woman, this is right out of *The Arabian Nights*. Are you sure you're not Sheherazade?"

"Patience, My Lord. Hear my tale and render your verdict when you've met Nourrit. Now, where was I? Oh, after the blind man. Well, the gardener and the cook didn't take Nourrit where they were going. They took her to a woman in the bazaar who supplied domestic workers for homes and businesses. For weeks Nourrit slept on a hammock in a warehouse along with other girls and women. From time to time, someone would want to see her and speak to her, but nothing happened until the day she was called in to meet a Spanish woman. Nourrit told me many times how the Spanish woman, waiting in a room, watched her come through the door, greeted her, told her to take a seat, asked her name, and then asked her what she hoped to find in a place of work. Nourrit answered that she wanted a home, and in return she'd do whatever work was needed by her home. The Spanish woman turned to the agent and said, 'Nourrit is the person I've been looking for. She will come with me.' The woman took Nourrit to a house in Casablanca, and a few days later they boarded a ship and sailed to Cádiz. That was nineteen thirty-three, that woman was Amparo's mother, and she took Nourrit to Sevilla, where she did have a home—and, really, a family—for more than fifty years.

"When Nourrit came into the house, Amparo was off in Morocco with her husband, Ramón Utrera, who was an army officer. My father had just been born. Three years later, Amparo came back to Sevilla because her husband had taken his troops to join the Falange, the party of Francisco Franco. In nineteen thirty-eight, Ramón Utrera was killed in battle. He received lots of honors, and my father was reared with the pride and probably the burden of being the son of a national hero.

"When Amparo came back to live at her mother's home, Nourrit became her personal helper, but didn't have a lot to do directly with my father. She's told me that Amparo was jealous of her only child's attention, and she watched over him and fed him and was his first teacher while Nourrit kept his things in order and did whatever chores Amparo needed done.

"Nourrit's relationship with my father changed as he got older. When he was small, he'd ignore her except to give orders, sometimes so ridiculous that everyone laughed. When he was older, he resented her closeness to his mother. He called her an ignorant African woman and made all sorts of petty accusations against her. The strange thing was, in the next breath, he was likely to apologize. Nourrit's told me that, more than once, he brought her a gift after he'd said something rude or unfair. When he was nearly grown and went off to an English preparatory school, he came to her, shook her hand, and told her he would miss her.

"Nourrit never approved of my father and she never trusted him. She didn't tell me that directly, but it came out one way or another in her stories about him. From the time he was a young child, he seemed set on a contrary course. Nourrit thought Amparo was good to him and treated him as a child should be treated. But then he'd do everything imaginable to try his mother's patience. He lied to her, he stole things, he'd come home hours later than he was expected. Nourrit was fair and told me good things about my father, that he was a good student and had many friends, but she was convinced that some of them were bad influences."

I snorted. "Somebody was a bad influence on him. He got your mother pregnant but didn't marry her. Or was he married at the time?"

"Yes — married, but separated from his wife. Both families were traditional Catholics and my father was never divorced. But Nourrit didn't refer to his affairs with others; she based her objections to my father on her own experiences. Nourrit never welcomes gossip or second-hand opinions.

"Now something good — let me tell you how Nourrit herself is rearing a son. Two years after I came into the house, Nourrit brought home a newborn boy. For years, she'd gone to a certain market to get fruits and vegetables. I knew it well because I'd often go with her. There was a deaf-mute woman there who wove openwork totes that people used for shopping bags. Nourrit always stopped and bought a bag. Well, that woman became pregnant, and when Nourrit learned that she had no relatives and no way to care for a child, she went to Amparo and somehow got her permission to take the baby when it was born. That caused more trouble for Amparo. Francisco's proper daughters were as opposed to that baby as they were to accepting me in their grandmother's home.

"Nourrit named the child Benito, as his mother wished, and I came to think of him as my baby brother and I helped with him as much as I could. Consuelo and Celestina helped too, but they had regular duties and I had free time. Amparo didn't get around well—I think she must have had severe arthritis—but she joined us in doing things for baby Benito, and we all told each other stories of our experiences with him. We came to call ourselves *su tía por cinco*, 'his aunt times five.' I got to be quite the expert at changing diapers, and, believe me, after a few days with cloth diapers, I really appreciated the disposable ones my grandmother was kind enough to buy. I fed Benito morning and night. I played with him a lot and, when he was one, I began to read to him. That reminds me of another great thing that came out of all this. I had so much to write to Bessie about, things I knew she'd understand and relate to. Celestina had a camera and I'm afraid I pestered her to take pictures of me with Benito so I could send them with every other letter or so.

"A few months after we adopted Benito, his mother disappeared from the market and we soon heard she'd died. That made me feel more important and more appreciative of Nourrit. I remember hugging our baby and thanking God that he was with us, warm and happy and in my arms. I went on being big sister until Benito was four. Then Amparo died and our little family came completely to an end.

"I didn't know my grandmother had a heart condition. No one told me. One day she simply didn't get up, and Nourrit found her and closed her eyes. We all went in to see her and she looked as if she were asleep. I got on my knees and closed my eyes and prayed that she was only asleep, but it didn't do any good. Nourrit finally had to coax me away.

"Then it was like the events after my father's death, or worse. That time I had to leave Bessie. Now I'd lost my dear grandmamá forever and I was leaving the others who'd been my family. And it all happened so fast! We went to Amparo's service and then to the cemetery. I couldn't watch her go. I couldn't watch her lowered into the ground. I closed my eyes and thought of all she'd been to me. I thought of the day I looked up the word '*amparo*' and found that it wasn't just an abstract Christian virtue; it meant 'aid' and 'protection' and 'guardianship.' That had given me a mystical feeling about us, and now she was gone, and that was gone with her. I felt so alone. I couldn't cry. I stood there and shook, and my face felt stiff, like cramps. I can't remember going home or anything else that day."

Paloma stopped. I looked over, and she was dabbing her eyes and biting her lip. "Can't help it," she said brokenly, "it's still hard.... I was so young, I didn't understand all she'd been through, you know, her son and all. I didn't really understand what a huge step it'd been for her to accept me and take me in." Paloma clouded up again and there were tears. "And she didn't just do it, she took me into her heart. She loved me."

Paloma covered her face with both hands. I reached for our water bottle and offered her a drink, then devoted myself to driving. In a minute or two, she sat up straight, blew her nose, and went on, still a bit shaky.

"A lawyer came to us the morning after the funeral. I thought he was a wretched man, heartless. He gave me my grandmother's wedding ring and told us we all had to be out of her suite in two weeks. My half sisters were the heirs to the estate, and they'd given those instructions, or maybe agreed to them.

"By then, my mother had been in a stable relationship with an older man in Laguna Beach for more than three years. When I called her and told her my terrible news, she understood the fix I was in and promised to find a way out, but she said she needed time to talk it over with the man she was living with. That left me still frightened, but not for long. She called back that same day to tell me I would fly to join her while we worked out a new life for me.

"So that was that—the second time I had to say good-bye to my home and everybody I knew. Thank God Benito was so young. I pray he had no idea what all the good-byes were about."

"Amen to that! But at least you were lucky that Chely had found someone to support her when she had to reacquire a teenaged daughter."

"Well, yes, that's a long story."

By then, we were coming into Sevilla and Sheherazade's life took a back seat to finding a hotel. It was dusk, we saw the lighted logo of Hotel Meliá Sevilla from afar and decided we were too weary to search for more inspired quarters. We got a room, went for a snack, washed up, and gratefully placed heads to pillows.

The storyteller was gone in minutes and I was tired, but couldn't turn the motor off. I lay in the dark reviewing all I'd heard. No wonder my surprise at Paloma Grey. No wonder she reminded me of no one I'd ever known. But her story did have the outlandish air of *The Arabian Nights*, I wasn't imagining that. So why had I swallowed it, hook, line, and sinker? Paloma, that's why. There had always been something mysterious about her, but all my instincts accepted her look-you-in-the-eye honesty. I remembered my earlier doubts about her and my fears about being so attracted. Now I felt no threat—now my fears were for her.

As I lamented her sorry beginnings, I found myself giving thanks for my own untroubled childhood, something I'd taken too much for granted. True, I'd never felt all that close to my parents, but that was more a matter of dissimilar personalities and interests than of real conflicts. In contrast, I'd been extremely close to my mother's mother and my father's father, huge influences on my whole vision of the world. I had a sister too, so I was exposed early to the development of a woman and to at least some of the differences in society's messages to its boys and girls.

But I'd had no experience that could put me in Paloma's shoes. I couldn't imagine being illegitimate and so lacking in family. I lay there, shocked at her life and grateful for mine, but I was kept awake by something else—my attempts to envision Nourrit and our meeting. Could anyone match the expectations Paloma had raised? Eventually I did sleep, but the wait seemed very long.

Saturday, October 26th

Paloma didn't want to surprise Nourrit too early. She took time to wash her hair while I lolled around the room and even watched a little television. When we did leave, I glanced at my watch and shook my head. "Eight o'clock. Late for our team." The other half of the team was unrepentant. "Ten days, and it's a tradition?" But she did have the good grace to sigh.

We went to the hotel dining room and, over breakfast, I laid out my hopes for the day, foremost my desire to hear Nourrit's memories of their first meeting, and beyond that, to meet Consuelo and Celestina. Paloma told me that Consuelo had moved away, but that she'd planned to reach Celestina and see her, if possible. And Paloma was sure I'd have no problem with Nourrit — "You'll find her entirely forthcoming. Just wait and see." That said, she wrinkled her brow, an expression I was learning to interpret. I made an "Out with it!" gesture, and out with it she came.

"Yes, there is something else. I wanted to work it in yesterday but it just didn't happen. Remember, I told you about my reunion with Nourrit? How disappointing it was? Well, it wasn't just the lack of time or that I had a man with me. It was that I don't lie to Nourrit, and I tried to explain my decision to form these paid relationships. That would have been difficult and painful at best, but it was doubly hard then because I had to start from scratch on the whole thing. I hadn't written to Nourrit about any of it because she couldn't read and I was ashamed to spill it out for Celestina's eyes. So there I was with the whole load to get off my chest and it was a bad time to do it and I did it badly. Nourrit took it calmly, which is always her way, but I could see she was disturbed, even when she told me that she had faith in me and knew that I'd always try to do what was best. I went off feeling low. I'm telling you all this so you'll know what she knows. Please, no matter what, try to make allowances for her concern. Is there anything more I can tell you?"

"Paloma, we're here together in every way I can think of. I won't try to fool anyone or pretend anything. I'm not ashamed to be with you — I never will be. Let's just go and be us." She smiled, but I saw her dab at her eyes as we rose to go.

After getting directions at the hotel desk, we were off into the northeast quarter of the city, passing ever fewer modern buildings and more small businesses as we went. We parked near our destination and walked along a narrow street with many open doorways leading to enterprises or abodes that invited our eyes and imaginations, especially the small shops that yielded vignettes of artisans at work on everything from shoes to jewelry. We got more directions at a bakery that emitted an aroma of fresh breadstuffs laced with cinnamon, and half a block later, Paloma pointed up a short stair to an enameled number plate over an entry. We climbed the steps, the door opened quickly at our knock, and a slim, dark boy appeared, his face friendly and expectant.

"Benito? Surprise! Do you remember Paloma?" She held out her hands and the boy took them. He was quite overcome, his mouth smiling but tears welling in his eyes. Paloma tried to wipe them away but he completed the job with the backs of his hands. "Is Nourrit not here?" Benito held out his hand, palm down, twice patted the air, and disappeared. A moment later we were face to face with Nourrit.

I judged the woman to be more than seventy years of age, dark-skinned, sinewy, and tall — she stood eye to eye with Paloma. Her wavy hair was iron gray, pulled back into a bun set rather low on her neck and run through with a pair of what looked like short, stout knitting needles. Her head was long and narrow, her eyes close together and shallow set — if there is such a term. Her nose was long, high bridged, and narrow. Although her features otherwise reminded me of the desert folk of northwest Africa, her lips were unusually full. Her facial expression was benign, but slightly severe. There was no doubt in my mind that I was meeting a considerable person.

She and Paloma stood in the doorway holding each other's hands at arm's length and just perceptibly rocking back and forth as they gazed into each other's eyes. Time stopped as their figures and the moment radiated suppressed joy. Paloma brushed Nourrit's cheeks with hers and put her forefinger to Nourrit's lips. Nourrit returned the gestures and they embraced. In the exchanges that followed, I began to pick up the low-pitched cadence of Nourrit's slow, rhythmic Spanish. She turned to me as I was introduced, looked me in the eye, and acknowledged me with a nod. "Bring yourselves in," she said. We crossed the threshold into a light scent of dried rose petals.

Nourrit waved us down a short hall and through a doorway, saying, "Seat yourselves." Her small sitting room offered three chairs with laced leather seats and an L-shaped wooden bench designed for two to sit at right angles to each other. I chose a chair and Paloma sat on the bench, hand in hand with our hostess. The boy slipped in and perched on a stool brought from the adjacent kitchen.

Nourrit and Paloma leaned together, their heads almost touching. Paloma addressed her friend in such rapid-fire Spanish that I could not identify the topics, much less follow the train of thought. Nourrit replied in her more deliberate way, nodding a lot, and now and again glancing at me. Then they took turns recounting events, the telling embellished with stylized hand gestures, raised eyebrows, occasional mask-like expressions, and a few smiles. I got only part of it, but people and their lives were being discussed. Paloma stopped long enough to tell me, in Spanish, that even with regular correspondence, she and Nourrit needed to bring each other up to date on a few matters. I indicated that I understood, and privately found humor in the contrast between the women's conversational flurry and my slow, stilted New World Spanish.

For a busy half hour I watched these two remarkable figures and listened to their voices interact and entwine. And, as they spoke, smiled, and exchanged touches and thoughts, the boy followed every word, their contents reflected in his face. Finally, Paloma cocked her head, raised her hands palms out, dropped them to her lap, and sat back. Our hostess turned to me with a formal greeting. I was grateful that she spoke slowly and simply. She stated that I was welcome and would be welcome at all times—as Paloma's friend. (I noted that, as we talked, she called Paloma her patroness, her daughter, her sister, and if I'm not mistaken, her alter ego.) She thanked me for having a friend's concern for Paloma, and for joining her, Nourrit, in this concern, and thereby becoming part of a significant circle. All of this struck me as formal and ritualistic, the sort of preamble ascribed to Native American powwows. In keeping, I tried to look knowing and receptive.

But Nourrit had more in store for me. She turned to Paloma as if overtaken by a thought. Would it not be a good time to place a call to Celestina? She signaled Benito to show the way to a neighborhood telephone. Paloma rose and addressed me in English, "We'll be back soon. Nourrit wants to talk with you. I've told her that you're a real friend and that I trust you. And I do." She patted me on the back and joined the boy in the entry. I heard the door shut.

Nourrit didn't mince words. "Señor, it is true that you are welcome—to respect the wishes of our friend and family member. But I would wish to feel more contentment in greeting her companions. I would like to take more satisfaction in the ways she has chosen. I do not hide my fears for her. I wonder if you understand why all of this is true?"

I got the message. It was directed at a whole class of offenders, and I was the available representative, I was on the spot. I thanked my lucky stars for the day Paloma had spent preparing me, and I set out to explain—as well as I could with my bookish, halting Spanish—my situation and my view of the problem.

"Doña Nourrit, please hear me. Hear me because I believe I know and share your anxiety. I met Paloma only a month ago, but I knew in half a day that I wanted her as a friend. She is intelligent, caring, perceptive, good-natured, all things that I value. I was lonely. I lost my wife two years ago, my wife of more than forty years, my wife with whom I had two daughters and, through them, grandchildren. Paloma and I met at a hotel full of people interested in handcrafts such as yours. We spent two days together as no more than strangers becoming acquainted. When we had to part, she told me how she supported herself and how I could go on seeing her. I admit to you that I joined her on her own terms. But there is a crucial point that I hope you will recognize. I did not like those terms when I heard them and I do not like them today. I accepted her terms because I could not turn and walk away. I wanted her company, I needed it. And I am convinced, totally, that Paloma is a wonderful person with much potential and many gifts, some received from you. Our friendship grows every day we spend together, and, I can tell you now, her friendship is more important to me than any physical intimacy. So, no, I do not come before you with clean hands. I am part of the problem that troubles you. But I want to do the right thing, the best thing for her. I am trying to cultivate our friendship and learn what I will need to know if I am to be an influence. Do you see what I mean?"

"Oh yes, señor, I do. In the steps to a goal, 'to know' is placed before 'to act.' And I well understand why you stay. If you leave the circle, if you cannot share heartbeats, breaths, and whispers, your influence leaves with you. So it is with me. I can guide my Benito. I can only worry for my Paloma."

"Doña Nourrit, you do more than you may know or guess. You are part of Paloma's fiber. That could be her salvation."

She regarded me gravely, not satisfied with my portrayal of their relationship. "Señor, she and I are not bound by my cord alone. When our eyes first met, I became what she saw. From her, I learned to love."

I heard the key in the front door lock and I blurted out, "Thank you for receiving me, thank you for hearing me."

She rose, squared her shoulders, and ended our session by saying, "I had expectations as well as hopes. Without them, I would not have spoken."

Paloma's eyes sparkled. She'd reached Celestina, had a good talk, and Celestina would try to join us. It was high time; they'd made do with the occasional letter for ten years. She looked expectantly at Nourrit and me and I gave her an affirmative nod. Then I remarked that I had not raised the subject of their first encounter. Accordingly, she took up my cause as soon as we were seated.

"For some reason, Haley took an interest in my story, my life. I told him a few things about our household and my years in Sevilla, but he hoped to hear, from your lips, how you remember our first meeting, how I came into the circle at my grandmother's home."

Our hostess appeared willing, so I piped up to encourage her to tell the story in full, to include any details she could recollect. Nourrit watched me intently, nodding as I spoke. When I was through, she leaned back, put her hands on her knees, and appeared to rehearse from an unseen screen. She took a deep breath and released it in an audible "Ah!"

"That day was born among the darkest clouds and ended under clear sky and full moon. Mark that! We in the kitchen had heard stories of the Señorita Celia and her child. I remembered when her father brought her to our house as a very young woman, and I in particular knew how troubled our mistress was by the señorita's return. Señor Francisco was the only child of our mistress, and he was but a few weeks in his grave. The house was in mourning, and mourning wrapped our mistress's heart as it did her shoulders. She was fearful for her son's salvation, and she had reason. I knew him in all his years and I saw him try her in every way and fill each of her days with doubts and fears. He was handsome. He spoke well. He was successful in school, but, as I especially knew, he could be dishonorable and shameless. Also in Doña Amparo's heart were memories of what had been told. A golden-haired English woman had bewitched her son and led him into evil.

"For her own part, my mistress spent hours on her knees preparing herself to meet with the Señorita Celia, but she more feared to face Señor Francisco's child. She feared that the child was invested with sin, that she came to afflict our house with the evil that she bore. The day before they were to appear, she called me in and ordered me, when the time would come, to take the child to the servant's quarters, to keep her there, and to keep her quiet. She was not to wander by herself, she was not to see the family shrine, and she was not to be brought into my mistress's presence for any reason.

"When the visitors came to our door, the señorita requested my mistress. I asked her to wait until my mistress came and I told her that I was to watch over her child as they met. Then I looked down, and, *oh-eh!* In place of her child, I pictured my mistress as a child. That image passed, but the child fixed me with a look of such hope and trust that I knew she had measured my soul. I put forth my hands and she hers, their touch awoke my childhood and I swung her into a dance taught me when I was small. She bent to it like grass in the wind and missed not a step as we made circles through the rooms to the back of the house. We ended in the kitchen and I sat her down and offered her a drink, water, or it may have been the watered juice of limes. We shared no words, but she understood my signs and I went for the pitcher. Our cook stopped working and turned toward her and I too felt something and was made to turn. I saw a child at peace, her hands clasped and her eyes closed, sitting in the midst of many glowing spirits, all calm and hopeful. A shiver passed over me; I had never seen such a company of guardians, not even with a holy man. I feared to come near, but I was to take her the glass. She looked up, alone, but glowing herself, and I stepped forward and felt welcome. I sat down.

"I touched my breast and pronounced Noor–REET. She touched her breast and sounded Pa–LO–ma in the voice of the dove that she was. She spoke to me and I to her, nothing we could understand, but music to our ears. For an hour and more, we exchanged such sounds and played little games. I touched her lips and she smiled at me. I cannot forget that face; I felt chosen. From that moment, I took her eyes wherever I went.

"We found some paper and colored pens. In blue, she drew a seed around the letter N and grew it into a vine. She made a green seed around the letter P and trailed it too into a vine. The vines entwined and yielded flowers and fruits. While she drew, I asked the cook, 'What do you see in this child?' and the cook said, 'I see an angel,' and she crossed herself.

"Then I knew what I had been chosen to do and I heard what I was being told to do. I made signs to the child that she should remain in the kitchen. I went to the mistress's room. I saw and felt that the meeting between these women was not fortunate. The air was dark. Their faces were dark. I put that aside. I declared myself and asked to speak to my mistress. She seemed not to hear. She made no reply. I asked a second time, I entreated her to speak to me alone. She pointed to her bedroom. When the door was shut, I asked her pardon for interrupting. I asked her if I had not served her well and given her worthy and sincere opinions. I asked if I had not acted faithfully in her interests and those of her family. She nodded 'yes' to these, and I went on. 'Doña Amparo, I beg you to hear a plea that comes to me from without and within. See this child. Know this child. Do not turn this child away.' The mistress was impatient. She started to send me away. I went to my knees. I bowed my head. I could feel the child's eyes following me.

"My mistress heard me and raised me up. She sent me to bring the child, and she asked the Señorita Celia to leave her alone with the child. I flew to the kitchen and I beckoned to the child. I brought her before her grandmother, as we knew her to be. My mistress measured her up and down, then took her hands as those of a granddaughter and addressed her in the English tongue. I closed the door and left them together.

"They remained in my lady's day room for an hour and more. When the door opened, they stepped out hand in hand. My mistress appeared restored and happy for the first time since she was downcast by the death of her son. She looked at her granddaughter and her granddaughter looked at her. There was trust in their faces. Neither of them will forget that meeting. My mistress loved her granddaughter until the day she died and she loves her still."

Nourrit stopped, the silence was relieved only by the gentle hiss of a teakettle in the kitchen. I found myself holding my breath, and for what felt like a very long pause, I could not bring myself to break the spell Nourrit had cast. Her quiet voice and measured words had so heightened Paloma's telling that their private drama had become three-dimensional and glinted with clues and portents. When she did raise her eyes, I offered my thanks, all too aware of the inadequacy of words.

At some time during the tale, Nourrit and her adopted daughter had joined hands and the older woman softly stroked the hand of the younger. Our reverie was broken by the entrance of the boy Benito with a pot of sweet tea and four cups.

An awkward silence accompanied the taking of tea. I felt extraneous, an accessory to this homecoming; I'd tagged along and butted in. Well, at least I'd spoken to Nourrit and, I prayed, made my peace with her—now I should leave the women alone. I stood up when my cup was empty and insisted that I go for a walk while they made up for lost time. No one demurred. Nourrit glanced at Benito, who rose and offered to be my guide. We stepped to the door, leaving Paloma and Nourrit as they were, hand in hand.

Outside in the bright light and clear air, shops were opening, merchandise was being set out, and deliveries were being made—an ideal time to poke around and learn about local life and color, but I wasn't in the mood. I wanted to get acquainted with Benito. I asked him if there was a nearby park or square with seats. He nodded and led me past a church to an extended park-like area adjacent to the ruins of a medieval wall, a place dotted with seating and trees. I selected a bench with a pleasant outlook and invited the boy to sit at my side. I told him I was honored to be present for the women's first real get-together after years of separation, but also that I could see they needed time alone. I asked if he could recall the days when Paloma was with him as a sister. He nodded solemnly. "Oh yes, she was the light by which I saw. I waited for her whenever she was gone from our rooms." Benito paused with a faraway look in his eye, but I'd opened a floodgate.

"As Nourrit is my mother, the only mother I have known, Señorita Paloma is the sister I lost, more than a sister. At first, I knew only that she was gone, yet her place at our table was set for every meal. But Nourrit has taught me more. Before Paloma, Nourrit was no more than a servant and a friend in small things to her mistress and to the people in the kitchen of her house. Paloma appeared to Nourrit and threw her arms around her. Paloma gave to her, and took from her, and waked in her a woman and a mother. That is what my mother tells me to remember. She says that only then, in the middle of her life, did she learn the full meaning of 'give' and 'receive,' only then did she become whole. So it was, that when she reached out and gave to me, both of them gave to me.

"I have grown up with my sister's letters and pictures, which my mother Nourrit receives like the host of the Holy Communion. As young as I was, I remember the first day Paloma sent money and told us there would be something for us as long as she lived. Nourrit has told me how Doña Amparo's family shut their hearts to us, how we were so poor that she begged jobs from door to door, and we sometimes slept in those same doorways. Now, with Paloma's help and my mother's needlework, we have a home, I attend school, and I am apprenticed to a chef. But Nourrit misses her Paloma every day. She does not know where she goes, and she does not know the people among whom she moves. My mother prays for my sister in her own way, which is not that of the church."

I asked the boy if his mother professed Islam. "No. No one knows the faith of her childhood, not Moslem or Christian. For her own reasons she does not wish to be received into the church, but she has brought me since I was small. I was baptized and I have been confirmed. She has always wanted me within the walls, not outside."

I supposed this situation must be abnormal and I wondered aloud if it hadn't created problems. Benito seemed surprised.

"No, señor, Nourrit is Nourrit. Everyone welcomes her as she is, I cannot explain. Everyone trusts her. Padre Jaime trusts her, and he is her friend even though she is not Christian. He believes that people have value and bring gifts other than their faiths. To me and to others he has said, 'In the long run, Nourrit has the wind at her back.' I thank God to be blown along with her in that wind."

Benito tickled me. Here he was, fourteen years old, concerning himself with adult matters, understanding much, and engaging in proto-philosophical observations — a sage in the making. I asked myself if such a mind would be satisfied with a chef's kitchen. But then, why not? Cuisine is a vital part of life — why should it exclude philosophers? Meanwhile, the philosopher waited patiently on my pleasure.

I asked where we could get coffee, and the boy hopped up and led the way back to the south along another street. After two or three blocks, he stopped in front of a modest-sized bakery and café, motioned me toward a tiny table under an Indian Laurel tree, and in short order, we had Turkish-style coffee and baklava. Still thinking of Benito's calling, I inquired about his apprenticeship. He told me he went to work at four in the afternoon, five days a week, at a nearby restaurant, a place popular with city dwellers from outside this neighborhood, which I took to be something of a North African enclave. He assured me that he'd resolved to master everything, and that he too would one day be a chef. In response to my questions, he revealed an impressive range of cooking knowledge, including the character of many ingredients, their affinities and contrasts. I decided he must be in remarkably good hands, and encouraged him by observing that the world would never suffer from a glut of great cooking.

As we chatted, I cooked up a plan. I'd go back and suggest that Paloma extend her visit while I went to the Archivo General de Indias. This would appear perfectly logical, since that monumental archive is the prime source for original documents pertaining to Spain in the New World. Actually, the archive was unlikely to be open on Saturday afternoon, but I could still enjoy a visit to the principal plaza, home not only to the Archivo, but also to the Alcázar and the Giralda, world-famous Moorish monuments. I asked Benito to take me back to his home.

The women were seated in a space I hadn't seen, a room with a wide table covered with fabrics, threads, and yarns in an array of earth tones and other muted colors. Nourrit was stitching, peering intently through some archaic-looking steel-rimmed spectacles as she overcast a series of expert loops to fix a small piece of fabric to her field material.

I was disappointed but not surprised to find none of Nourrit's completed pieces on display, but I could examine the work in progress. Laid out on the table was an indigo background, about three feet square, decorated with what, at first glance, appeared to be the moon and a pattern of stars filling a sky over a body of water broken up by a pattern of rushes. On closer inspection, the stars proved to be tiny, chunky fish cut from palest blue goods and affixed so that their silver thread stitching furnished the details of eyes, gills, and fins. The "moon" turned out to be a fish as well, larger and head-on, which accounted for its near-circular outline. The piece struck me not only as a handsome design, boldly realized, but also deft in craftsmanship and subtle in details.

As soon as my curiosity was satisfied, I told Paloma my plan, and I'm sure she understood exactly what I was up to. She and Nourrit conferred, then instructed me to return at seven for the supper our hosts insisted on preparing. I thanked them for the welcome prospect, and left. Paloma waved her free arm, the other encircling Benito. Her last look spoke volumes.

Back at the hotel, the room was made up and the bed looked inviting. I realized that I was weary and my head was spinning. I lay down to unwind, to cope with the feeling that I'd been thrust into a heightened reality. Paloma had exaggerated nothing. Nourrit was more than real, and that hour or two in her presence was enough to put her on my short list of impressive people I'd been privileged to meet. Doubly impressive, I decided, because she was one of those rare individuals who rise from the least likely beginnings, have no perceptible advantages, but appear to belong in any company and to be equal to any occasion. Somehow, even my inklings of Nourrit made the reality of Paloma easier to accept and comprehend.

And Benito had partially accounted for Paloma's curious reluctance to fly over and cultivate her cherished connection to Nourrit. She had alluded to the high cost, but it had never occurred to me that Nourrit, and possibly Bessie, might be financially dependent on her. Now the money issue made more sense. I could feel my point of view shifting, but then I drifted off.

When I next checked my watch, it was two. I rallied sufficiently to go down for a bite, but after a bowl of soup, I returned to the room, the bed, and my contemplation of the ceiling. I sifted through everything that had come to me in the past two days, reassessing, and seeing Paloma anew. I was discovering that she'd been sorely tried and with that came a growing sense that she was born, or chosen, to flourish, regardless of obstacles.

But thinking over her gifts and accomplishments made her "profession" all the more haunting, a perversion of the blessings she'd received, a dead end to the progress she'd made. And what about my role? My disapproval of her choice of occupations sharpened the focus on my own moral choice. Here I was, blaming Paloma for an alarming misstep or weakness at the same time that I continued to play her game. I was offering no helping hand, I was exploiting her situation.

As I struggled with that burden, I also had to contend with what I hadn't confessed to Nourrit, the most romantic notions a man my age could possibly entertain. I was in love, an incredibly blissful state, but also a state in which I hungered unbearably for every contour of Paloma's mind and body.

Aside from that, I thought as I lay there, I have no problems at all.

When I roused myself from a fitful nap, I decided not to go downtown at all. It was high tourist season and the key attractions on the grand plaza guaranteed traffic and parking crunches. Instead, I set out on foot to watch the doings along the Río Guadalquivir. That proved to be a fairly humdrum exercise, but it was exercise, and it lasted long enough that I ended by hurrying to be on time for dinner.

I was surprised, then enchanted, by the scene greeting me inside Nourrit's door. It was dusk, and the interior darkness was punctuated by enough burning candles to fill a side chapel at a cathedral—the rose-scented air now suggested incense. On top of that, I was greeted by two identical small boys. Benito cleared up my puzzlement, explaining that the electric power had been shut off in the neighborhood, and that the five-year-old twins belonged to Celestina, present for supper despite the short notice.

We had a captivating evening, much reminiscing and much catching up, the faces and the talk charming in the warm, flickering candlelight. Fair-skinned, brown-haired Celestina Campillo was the most voluble contributor and the most animated. She explained, mostly for me, how her husband was developing a local and regional delivery business using trucks, motorcycles, and even bicycles. She also gave us news of Consuelo Esteves, Amparo's cook, who had moved the ninety miles to Córdoba to be near her son and his family. Paloma had kept up a bit through Christmas letters, but admitted that Consuelo typically had little to report. Celestina told us that Consuelo had lost a lot of weight through daily exercises with her daughter-in-law. All three women laughed affectionately at this mental picture.

Celestina was bright and appealing. It was hard to picture her as a housemaid; there was nothing subservient about her. In her mid-thirties, she'd lost the bloom of youth, but looked fit, had a nice face, an excellent humor, and a frank form of address—very Spanish. I was irresistibly tempted to ask her for a third recollection of Paloma's entry to the Utrera home. When I got the chance, I told Paloma.

Her reply, "Why not? You're one of the party, and there's been little enough for you. Look, I'm going to take her boys down the street for some ice cream. And we'll walk around for a while, it'll give us a few minutes to get acquainted. Why don't you wait till then? Celestina will be less inhibited if I'm not sitting there."

Presently, Paloma bustled the twins to the door, Celestina reminded them about their manners, and they were off. She rejoined our group, addressing me. "And so, señor, Paloma tells me you wish to hear how she came into our midst in the home of Señora Utrera. She told me I should wring out my head for details. All right, I will try, but it was long ago." Nourrit and Benito acted as if cued; they rose and went off to wash the dishes. I looked expectant and Celestina went on.

"First, you must know that the kitchen somehow heard of the visit of Señorita Celia and her child some days before they came. Believe me, there was much talk. Juan Diego—Señora Utrera's chauffeur—he remembered ugly rumors about Señor Jorge, the Señorita Celia's father. This man was said to have been a *maricón*, a fellow who escorted young men for his social pleasure. And we all knew more than enough about Señor Francisco and his affairs. No one had to tell me what a rascal he could be. I came to the house only months before he was killed, but he had put his hands all over me and was constantly urging me to go off with him. Nourrit walked in once when he was trying to corner me; it was the only time I ever saw her furious. She gave him a tongue-lashing you would not believe, especially over some promise he had made to her. Then she went to her room and tore him out of a photograph he had given her, a picture of himself with her and his mother. But even with all that, we were careful not to hurt the feelings of Doña Amparo, whom we all loved and who was always good to us.

"As I said, I was new, but Nourrit and Consuelo and Juan Diego had been there for years. They had all heard bits of family secrets connecting Francisco and the Señorita Celia in some shameful affair that resulted in her child. No one really knew Señorita Celia, but the belief was that she and her family were as bad a lot as our mistress's son. With those parents, this illegitimate child could prove to be the Devil's own spawn.

"It happened that they came on a Friday and I had that day and the weekend off. On Monday I walked in and found everything very strange. I went to the kitchen and ran into Consuelo. I asked, 'So, did they come? What were they like?' Consuelo answered me in her mock-serious way. 'You will not believe what you will see and hear.' Nourrit came in, and I asked her about the visitors, and she got that odd look in her eye and that little smile on her face and she said, 'Our house has changed.'

"I did not know what to think. I knew Consuelo and Nourrit well. They would not tease me as a prank. Just then Señorita Paloma came into the kitchen, so slim and straight, with her big round eyes and a bow in her hair. She stood there smiling at me, so I stepped up and offered my hand and told her my name. She shook my hand and told me hers, meeting my eye and more. Right then, I thought, 'I know what is going on. This child is going to stay with us and she is none of the things we imagined, and Consuelo and Nourrit are already in love with her.'

"And Nourrit was right, our house was changed. Señorita Paloma was such a ray of light, such a help, so *simpática*. As soon as I went to work, she joined in to do whatever she could. In no time at all she showed me that she knew how to make beds and sweep and dust. She took care of her own room from the very start and lent me a hand with the others. Mind you, this was before we could actually converse, though she and I from the beginning were using a few words and sign language. We even made jokes and laughed at them together. But you know, she mastered the Castilian tongue so soon we were amazed. Each day she added a long list of new words. At first we made remarks right in front of her without worrying that she might know what we said, but I tell you, that ended in a hurry. A few weeks after she came, she was off to school for the day and we all felt the difference, the loss. When she returned, our house lighted up. We waited for her to tell us what she had learned or what had happened during her day. Before she came, we were all friends under that roof, but she came among us and bound us more closely. Señorita Paloma made the biggest difference in her grandmother's life. Doña Amparo came out of her rooms, she spent time with us. She was a different woman—no more black clothes, so much happier. She had finally discovered why God put Señor Francisco on this earth.

"So, there we were, all a sort of family, except that I, of course, came in by the day. And everything went along beautifully for years until the terrible moment when Doña Amparo died. One day we were happy and all together, the next we were torn apart and scattered. To this day, I cannot forgive the jealousy of Señor Francisco's other daughters. The attention their grandmother gave to Señorita Paloma ate at their hearts. Their mother had good relations with Doña Amparo, and those young women were invited to everything, but they would not come. They would not even go to Mass with their grandmother because she took Señorita Paloma."

At that point, the ice cream detail returned with sticky hands and faces. Celestina cut short her recollections to go and supervise the washing up. Nourrit and Benito reappeared, talk became general, and shortly the party broke up. Our farewells were brief because we'd arranged to come by in the morning on our way out of town. I thanked Celestina liberally for her memories, and she was gracious in her farewells. But I wondered what she made of me.

As we drove away, I thanked Paloma for letting me butt in on her homecoming. I told her how impatient I was for more, but she was still harking back.

"Something wonderful came out today," she said, "and you and I were let in on it together. Remember, on our way down, I told you how Amparo changed her mind about me that first day and I didn't quite know why? Well, Nourrit never breathed a word about interceding for me with my grandmother, not till now. I know Amparo referred to it once in a letter to Chely, but only in general terms, not as a specific event. Nourrit must have decided it was time that I knew what happened, and you gave her the perfect opportunity to tell it in its natural place. That is *so* Nourrit. It also shows that she trusts you."

Paloma smiled and raised her eyebrows, but she wasn't done. "And speaking of you — are you listening? — it's wonderful having you involved, such a happy surprise. I mean it! Back in Castelo de Vide, we were having such a good time and getting on so well, I dared to ask you to bring me here. I hoped I might take advantage of your good nature and that you'd humor me. But I never dreamed you'd join in so, or what it would mean to me. Now you've met some of my people, and more and more I have someone with whom I can share."

Great, I thought, she too feels something new in our relationship. I couldn't imagine trying to discuss that yet, but I prayed she'd become more conscious of our shift from business and casual pleasure to deeper friendship and mutual understanding. And then and there, I resolved not to suggest or imply further physical intimacy. Of course, if she invited, I would respond—I couldn't imagine risking a misunderstanding by appearing disinterested.

We reminisced all the way back to the hotel, let it trail off in the impersonal air of the lobby, then enjoyed further exchanges as we got ready for bed. After a big hug, we turned in, and Paloma had the final thought as we lay in the dark, "I miss Nourrit, but I know I could never again be part of this world. And I don't see how she could be part of mine. That makes me sad."

I, the wise old man, replied, "Listen, my treasure, never is a long time. Sweet dreams."

Sunday, October 27th

Benito and Nourrit had hot drinks waiting for our farewell breakfast. We sat down to melon, then just-out-of-the-oven sweet cakes layered with honey and almonds. Benito was shyly pleased as we relished his craft, but our conversation was less successful. The obvious catching up had been done the day before and none of us was able to make a fresh start. Our awkwardness became so palpable that Nourrit finally put a finger to her lips. If we could stay for days, she said, matters of common interest would rise from our activities and become grist for our mill. As it was, however, we were too aware that only minutes remained. We were not clever enough to fit our pent-up thoughts and emotions into that small space. Now we must acknowledge our frailty and not spoil the memories already created. It was time, she concluded, to embrace, shed a tear, and let go. And we did just that.

I folded Benito's slim form into one of the bear hugs I give my grandsons. I took Nourrit's hands and kissed the backs of each. She acted shy, but not displeased—my hands were squeezed in return. I whispered an apology that my Spanish could not do justice to my gratitude for her role in Paloma's life, and that I prayed my message would reach her by other means. She nodded and told me that she had done what she was able to do. I, however, had but begun my part of our shared mission — and she did say "our."

I went outside so I wouldn't inhibit the farewells, and in a moment Benito joined me. Before long the women emerged, but parting was not easy — Paloma returned from halfway down the steps to embrace the boy once again. And even then, she and I turned at each step to add words and gestures. In my last glimpse, Benito waved and Nourrit stood behind, her arms around him.

As we neared the car, Paloma, despite her emotional state, felt compelled to clarify Nourrit's allusion to my unfinished duties. That was, she assured me, simply Nourrit's way of saying that I was out there in Paloma's world, and she was not. I said nothing about my contrary belief that I'd been deputized, sworn in, and that my efforts would be reviewed.

IV SCHOOLING

Sevilla, Spain — Sunday, October 27, 1996

My plan for the day was to head for the Portuguese city of Évora and there resume our interrupted itinerary. At least that was my geographical plan; my first priority was to tune in the next chapter in The Life of Paloma. As soon as we'd worked through Sevilla's traffic and reached the relative calm of the highway, I made my plea and Paloma took up her tale.

"Where were we on Friday? Oh, I was leaving Sevilla, a terrible time. I'd just lost my grandmamá and I was still in shock when the lawyers ordered us out of our home. I know it was two weeks after the funeral, but I was so miserable and confused that it felt as if I had only the time to hug my people and let them go. I still felt like a child, and they were my family, my world. I was in a panic. How could I live without Nourrit? I loved her, she was my counselor. I told her my thoughts and my worries, and she'd listen and understand and have ideas that seemed to help. And I was losing my baby brother. He was four and he followed me everywhere, usually with a book he wanted me to read. How could I say good-bye to Benito?

"So, yes, I was in a low state, but not as lost as I'd been leaving Putney. I was older after all, fourteen, and flying off to new places wasn't so threatening. And it was easier to give up a school where

I'd never felt accepted. Señor Tamaral came over for one last lesson, his gift to me, and when we said good-bye, he kissed my hand and told me he would miss me. He said I might never be a great guitarist, but I had an affinity for music that I mustn't let wither.

"The morning I left Sevilla, I got up thinking about Chely because I was on my way to her and because she'd been with me on that awful first flight. Haley, I can't tell you how painful it was to imagine living with her. Since she left me with Amparo, I'd seen her only the few times when she'd come through Spain on her way to somewhere else. And when I did see her, she acted depressed and nervous, apologetic as could be, and she'd never really answer my questions. Why did she have to be gone so long? Why could she stay only a few hours when she did come? She wrote seldom enough, and, God knows, her letters were short, but she said more and sounded happier in them than she did when we got together. The only time she'd brightened up and acted happy to see me and talk to me was on her last visit, just months before. That was when she was so surprised to find me nearly as tall as she and beginning to fill out.

"I thought about all that while I dressed, and I put on my school uniform, partly because she'd seen me in it — actually, I'd worn it for the school picture I'd just sent to her. I studied myself in the mirror, and there I was, looking the way I felt, frightened and excited all at once. Nourrit went with me to the airport and stayed while I checked in a mountain of baggage. We said good-bye, and I've never held on to anyone so long or had such a hard time letting go. I know it sounds silly, but I pulled away from her feeling that I was leaving my childhood in her arms. Then, as I said, I screwed up my courage and went in to face the big ordeal — but really, it wasn't so bad. The short hop to Madrid was nothing, and I felt quite grown up when I read the screens and made it over to my international flight all on my own.

"You know how endless the flights seem when you're going west? Well, that was my first, and I had the hardest time believing it when we landed in Dallas that same day and then went on and got into Los Angeles, still in daylight. Customs was slow, especially for me. There I was with all my worldly possessions, hundreds of dollars in extra fare, and the officials went to the bottom of every bag and box. I needed a huge cart to take it away.

"I pushed my stuff out into the waiting area and looked around. No sign of Chely, but before I had a chance to worry, a tall, slim, older man came up to me holding the same school picture I'd remembered that morning—and that was how I met Gustaf Grevilius, the man who'd brought my mother to Laguna. In fact, the first thing he said was that my mother wasn't well but that we'd go directly to her. He pushed my cart out front, and I waited with it while he went for his auto—would you believe, the same white Volvo I have now? You'd have laughed to see us stuffing in all my things. We had the trunk crammed full and the backseat piled to the roof.

"When we got on the freeway, Gustaf told me that my mother had cancer of the liver and might have only a year to live. He apologized for meeting me with such bad news, but I must say, he put it in as kind and unfrightening a way as he could. He warned me that I'd find her in a state of shock; she'd only had the diagnosis a week or so. He said she'd immediately had a bad reaction to chemotherapy and, so far, couldn't face talking about her condition. And he made a real point of how nervous she was about seeing me. We talked some more, and it came out that he knew all about Francisco Utrera and how I'd come into the world, but I could tell that he didn't realize how little I knew my mother.

"Gustaf begged me not to question her about the big issues in our lives. He'd been her only confidant, and he told me that he'd seen how overwhelmed she was when she realized she had to prepare for the end of her life. He thought she'd begun to cope, but he said she needed time to work into a relationship with me. He asked me to keep our conversations light and not get into personal problems unless Chely brought them up. He offered to help any way he could and told me to ask him anything, any time I wished.

"I remember that first drive with Gustaf so well. He fascinated me. I'm sure part of it was simply that he was a man. Haley, you can't imagine how little contact I'd had with men in any of my fourteen years. But there I was, alone with a man, a total stranger, and feeling that we were communicating rather well. And remember too, for years I'd spoken English regularly only with my grandmother, and hers was mostly from reading, not talking. Even so, I could tell that Gustaf spoke in a clear, sophisticated way. Anyhow, from that night on, he and I had a remarkable capacity to communicate. Looking back, that seems ironic—I'll get to that later.

"We were in the heaviest traffic on the biggest roads I'd ever seen—believe me, Sevilla was not Los Angeles—but even so, it was only an hour till we drove up to Gustaf's home. When we went in, I was amazed at the view out his windows. I was looking down on a blanket of winking lights draped over those coastal hills, and beyond that, coming right at me, was a long path of moonlight reflected in the ocean. I'd never seen such a thing except in films.

"Gustaf's housekeeper gave us a hand with my things and Gustaf took me up to my bedroom. That was amazing too, that same great view—and it was love at first sight, just like my room in Sevilla. I was still looking out the window when Chely came in. I ran over and put my arms around her, and she hugged me, and we held on for a long time, not looking at each other, just hugging. I heard Chely ask, 'Does she know?' I didn't hear an answer, but Chely started to cry. Then she pulled herself together and started what sounded like a speech she'd worked on but hadn't had time to polish up. Even so, I'll never forget it—the first time in my life that my mother talked to me as an equal. 'Paloma,' she said, 'more than anything in the world I wanted to be here for you and try to catch up for all the time we've missed and all the things we haven't shared. Forgive me, I'm doing badly. I can't control my feelings. But no matter what, or how badly I do, I want you to know that I love you and I want you near me. Please be patient and I'll do the best I can.'

"I'd been awake a ridiculous number of hours and I was worn out. Gustaf rescued me, and my mother, by sending me off to bed. I slept and slept and I didn't wake till after the sun was up—late for me, you'll agree.

"In those next days I kept Gustaf's request in mind, and when I sat down with Chely, I tried to keep our talk light and stay away from anything she might find threatening. I'd ask her things about our life in Putney, homely things I'd never heard or couldn't recall, and she acted pleased that I was interested in the years when we lived together. Before long, I remembered something I'd always wondered about and never got around to asking—where did my name come from?

"Honestly, I remember Chely's laugh—she didn't do it that much, and it was a clear sign that I hadn't raised a painful subject. She described the small hospital in Virginia where I was born, and told me how she first saw me in the arms of a young black nurse, or perhaps a nurse's aide, a woman with a nice face and a big smile. As she brought me in to my mother, she was wagging her face at me and smiling and calling me 'Dovey.' Then it happened that the same woman brought me to Chely just before she needed to give a name to put on my birth certificate. The nurse was still calling me Dovey. My mamá asked her, 'Do you call all the babies Dovey?' The woman laughed, and said, 'Oh no, just your little daughter. When she wants attention, she frowns and purses her lips and coos like a little dove.' Well, when Chely heard 'dove,' 'Paloma' popped into her head and she couldn't get rid of it. She told me that whenever she tried to imagine another name, it seemed as if I were already Paloma. So she registered me as Paloma Grey, no middle name.

"I loved her story, and I told her that I loved my name and that I'd always considered it a gift from her. I told her I couldn't imagine being anybody but Paloma. Which was true. Poor Chely, she seemed so happy to make a lighthearted connection with me. I think we just chattered awhile and got into funny memories of Bessie. I wish we'd had more moments like that."

Paloma was lost in thought, staring straight ahead, her hands folded in her lap.

We passed through Santa Olalla and turned off to the northwest and Portugal. Our road wound through rolling hills, the steeper slopes dotted with sheep and the gentler with agriculture. For some minutes, my storyteller peered out the windows without comment, but in the village of Arroyomolinos de León she noticed a group of girls in school uniforms. She seemed to take that as a cue.

"The truth was, my reunion with Chely really didn't work out. She tried, and she kept on trying as best she could, and she had her good moments, but she couldn't cope with having me around day after day. After a couple of weeks, Gustaf told me the strain was wearing her out, and it wasn't just her weakness or her remorse over her failings with me—he said she was agonizing because I had no life. She saw me as caged up, and she felt responsible. Gustaf told me he'd looked into the school situation and found Saint Brigid's, a Catholic girls' school forty minutes away in the town of Orange. He said he'd take me to see it and meet the people, and then, if I liked it, he'd arrange for me to enroll.

"The school made a good impression even though it was rather crammed into an old mansion. At least, that made it feel homey and less institutional than my school in Sevilla. It was a middle school and high school combined, and it had fewer than forty girls in each grade, mostly day students. The quarters for boarders were next door in a more modern building, and I thought the kitchen was great, butcher block work surfaces and a lot of new stainless steel equipment. The gym was an old utility building, pretty minimum, but the playing fields were all grass and nicely tended. All in all, it was a lot more inviting than the dirt and concrete play areas we'd had at the Academia.

"School wasn't in session yet, so most of the teachers weren't around, but we were lucky to find one in her classroom, and the Sister who was guiding us took us in and introduced us. Sister Eugenia taught biology, and she sat down with us and took our questions, really Gustaf's questions. He amused me no end. He commenced as if he were naive about education. Well, I knew better. Twenty years earlier, he'd designed and implemented the Western Civilization program at a college in the Midwest. Sister Eugenia amused me too. She seemed to guess he was engaged in some game, and she played to it. She answered his questions, each at its own level, but in a few minutes both of them dropped all that pretense and got to talking about the school's basic approach to secondary education. I didn't learn much, except to admire what you might call the cut of Sister Eugenia's jib, but Gustaf walked away saying he was confident he'd met an outstanding teacher, better than many college instructors he'd worked with. All in all, we went home feeling pretty good about Saint Brigid's.

"For the next two weeks there was a lot of driving back and forth and I enrolled as a boarder and they put me in a double room. The school had given me some placement tests and decided to split me between ninth and tenth grades — English literature and history in tenth, math and science in ninth. Gustaf took me to buy uniforms and I went for fairly large sizes — good thing, because I grew a lot that year.

"I was told my roommate would be María Cristina Kappelman from Tegucigalpa, Honduras. I suppose the Sisters put us together because we shared Spanish—they must have figured I could help Cris adjust to school. She was from a devout Catholic family, but her paternal grandfather was a Jew who emigrated from Austria before World War Two. Cris had already taken up service to mankind as her cause, and she was dedicated to medicine, I mean dedicated. You can't imagine how she threw herself into her studies! Just picture her wearing blinders, staring up a narrow path at her Holy Grail, medical school, and seeing her course work as the hurdles she'd have to jump. But she was tidy and quiet, and we shared the room chores and our time together with no problems. We also shared what you might call the stigma of being foreigners on campus. Well, I wasn't quite as foreign, and I could contribute to her school transition—lots of tips on English—but she wasn't a quick study for language. She picked up the math and science vocabularies all right, but otherwise she'd have reminded you of an outsider looking in.

"Another thing, though, because I had Cris as a roommate, I was still speaking a lot of Spanish. And that meant that I didn't pick up the nuances of spoken English as fast as I might. I took a lot of kidding from my classmates and I noticed that my pronunciations and my word choices tickled Sister Grace, my English teacher. Sometimes she had a hard time keeping a straight face. Later, when we were better acquainted, we talked it over and tried to add up what all had caused the oddities in my speech. First was Bessie. I'd learned to speak mostly from her, and she'd started her schooling in a London orphanage and, after that, I guess it was pretty hit-or-miss while she lived in a hodgepodge of inner-city foster homes. Also, I picked up things from the children's TV programs that Bessie let me watch, and there were my teachers in Putney, two or three different U.K. dialects there. And then I had those six years in Sevilla where I spoke Spanish most of the time and used English only with my grandmother and two teaching Sisters. But that wasn't the whole story. Outside my schoolwork, I read Spanish only in the newspaper and a few magazines, but I went on reading tons of books in English, every book in English I could find. Some of my grandmother's English friends sent me piles of books they'd decided I should read, children's classics, grown-up classics, P. G. Wodehouse, you name it! I read 'em all, good, bad, and indifferent.

"So, from all that, I learned thousands of English words I'd never heard spoken, and when I got to the U.S., I used them perfectly innocently in everyday speech, including all sorts of perfectly good words that most people recognize, but never, ever use in conversation. I can still see the looks on the other girls' faces when I announced that the dessert at the end of a large meal was 'superfluous.' I must have sounded like a real prig. Once, I managed to use 'inculcate' and 'eleemosynary' in an oral report on *Oliver Twist.* Sister Grace told me later that if she'd had her wits about her, she'd have recorded my book reports and made a best-selling comedy tape. It's long enough ago now that I wish she had. We'd both get a good laugh, believe me! Anyhow, *poco a poco*, I figured out my worst gaffes. But I must say, Gustaf was no help. His English was fluent and precise, but he'd first learned it in Swedish classrooms. He'd always correct me if I made out-and-out errors, but he'd never question a high-flown word as long as I used it accurately. Anyhow, it's still part of me. I was the green twig and, as you see, I was bent."

We felt the need to stretch our legs and pulled off at a natural vista point. A path before us led along a fence toward a knoll crowned with pines. Paloma turned to me. "Race you to the top?"

"No thanks. You run along and I'll get my jollies watching."

"Sure?"

I nodded, and she handed me her hat and was off. As her loping figure grew smaller, she looked like a graceful teenager, and I thought, "Paloma, you will never know how I'd love to frolic at your side." I felt sorrier than ever that her bizarre life had discouraged normal relations with young men.

I strode along at a more sedate pace and joined her at the top of the knoll. A light breeze rustled leaves overhead and we gazed off toward Portugal, wondering as we did at the isolation our few steps had provided. We separated to relieve ourselves in the privacy of the little grove and Paloma returned holding a long-stemmed purple wildflower, her eyes sparkling with tears.

I made a sorry face. "Sad at leaving Spain?"

"No. You'll think me silly, spilling over like this. It's those feelings I tried to describe yesterday, how happy I am that you took me to Sevilla and shared my reunion. And I waked up today with such a strong feeling that we're going together, you and I, to some lovely, lighthearted place. Just a feeling, no details."

"Listen, I'll go to the ends of the earth with you. But right now you'll have to be content with Évora."

"Sir, I will consider Évora the next step. You may take my arm." I tremble to recall the further regrets stirred up by that offer.

For me, back to our Opel meant back to Paloma's life. "What was it like," I asked, " to come to Saint Brigid's in California from that academy in Spain?" She thought that over for more than a moment.

"Well, it was a real change, and mostly pleasant. I suppose Sagrado Corazón was a fairly typical, old-fashioned European school — short on classroom discussion, long on drills and repetition, lots of recitation in the lower grades. Saint Brigid's was less structured and I made the transition all right, especially into physical education and the life sciences, mostly because of the women who taught them.

"For P.E., I had Sister Barbara. Just imagine a bundle of energy all channeled into spreading the gospel of physical fitness. Some girls hated her and complained and tried to stay out of sight and out of her clutches, but she fascinated me. She believed we were all underdeveloped, and that we'd learn and reason better if our bodies were in better condition. 'A sound mind in a sound body' put to practice, not just parroted in Latin class. Sister had us run a mile every day, and she ran along behind us. Believe me, if you lagged, you heard about it.

"Sister divided us into teams and had us compete in a different sport every day of the week — five days, five sports. I liked volleyball and softball best because I'd played them at the Academia. But not with the same intensity. It took me a while to adjust to the competitive attitude that I found in American girls. That was one reason I was surprised to learn that I could pitch the softball better than most. Sister Barbara noticed though, and she recruited me for after-school competition with teams from other P.E. classes. After that, I was picked for Saint Brigid's team in a league with other private schools in the district. I'm afraid I'm making it sound as if I were rather a star, but it was more that I was a boarder—it was always easier to get boarders involved in that after-school stuff."

"So, you were a pitcher, but you still came to bat. How did that go?"

"Oh, I got my hits—lots of singles, mostly ground balls. I was too cautious to take big swings, I'd always wait as long as I could and then chop at the ball. They batted me first because I got on base a lot but didn't drive in many runs."

"Paloma, you're apologizing for being the classic lead-off hitter. I know, I know, it's your 'modesty is the best policy.' OK, enough softball, but please, more of Paloma's School Days."

"Actually, something else came out of softball. Sister Barbara invited me to join a few girls who worked out early every morning. I did, and we used weights and exercises to develop good posture and general fitness. I grew taller that year and I was thin, but I got stronger and I felt better, the best I'd ever felt. At home, I still use weights during my daily walk. Anyhow, besides the exercise, I liked being with the other students and the two Sisters who helped run the after-school programs.

"My other love was my life science class with Sister Eugenia. I'd never had a teacher who combined course work with real life and such an evangelical passion. Believe me, Sister Eugenia was on a mission. We needed what she could teach, and what she could teach would improve our lives—save them even. You should have heard her lectures on smoking—God! She showed us how delicate lung tissue is, and then horrified us with stories of autopsies she'd witnessed during her education. She had appalling photographs of smokers' lungs, that evil, glistening black. I'll tell you, I always hated the smell of tobacco on people, but what I learned from her made me even less tolerant.

"And everything I've learned since convinces me that Sister Eugenia gave us a good background in diet and nutrition. She went about it in a practical way and she made me wary about all sorts of additives and overly processed foods. She'd have approved of you, Haley. You usually reach for the right things, I notice.

"But her lessons weren't all impersonal like that. You know how you've kidded me about always covering up when I go out in the sun? OK, it was Sister Eugenia who noticed me getting burned during an all-day picnic and warned me about the consequences and told me how to protect myself. And she shared her ideas about things outside science — one of them sticks in my mind, something of her own, I'm sure. 'The trick is not in learning to distinguish right from wrong — most children can do that. The trick is in bringing yourself to believe that there's a life-saving difference between them.' Good, huh? Actually, from day one, I didn't doubt the accuracy or the wisdom of one thing she said. Quite the contrary, ¡Viva Eugenia!

"And I'll always be grateful to Sister Grace. She was the one who noticed how lopsided my reading had been, so limited to English authors. I'll never forget the look on her face when I told her I had not read a word of Mark Twain. Then and there, she started me on Americans, and I really got into them, as you've been kind enough to notice."

I listened to Paloma's School Days and reflected on my own classroom experiences. "You know, I've been a student and I've been a teacher, but I'm hearing you describe student/teacher relationships that sound more intimate, more familial, than those I recall. Was that typical?"

"No, I wouldn't say typical. I wasn't that close to most teachers, I just had something special with Sister Eugenia. I'm sure I counted on her so much because I'd lost Nourrit, and Chely was so focused on her own predicament that we couldn't just chat. The funny thing about Sister Eugenia was that she had a way of hiding her friendliness behind formal language. I think she felt she could get closer to us and be more personal without being misconstrued if her feelings were all couched in proper phrases. Now don't take offense, but you've reminded me of her more than once. In fact, that came to me just after we first sat down with each other. I thought, 'This person is a lot warmer underneath than his speech suggests.' And then I thought of Sister Eugenia."

"Funny thing, Paloma. In those first minutes, I give you my word, I was puzzling away trying to guess your speech background, and you came across as warm yourself." I looked over and winked. "Too warm for comfort."

"Really, Haley, and at your age, too. Don't adolescent boys ever grow up?"

"Oh God, I hope not. But sorry, I'm short-circuiting your memoir."

"Well.... I'm afraid I've painted an awfully rosy picture of life at school. I was lonely there, doubly lonely. I couldn't go home at night to a loving family—I tell you, I missed Nourrit as if some great big piece of me was just gone. And the other part of it was that I never really felt at home with my schoolmates—you know, my odd speech and different background—but I must say, that kind of isolation was easier to take than what I'd been through at the Academia. There I felt shunned. I felt like the untouchable that parents fear and warn their daughters about. At Saint Brigid's I was different, but hardly a scandal. I'm sure my classmates thought I was odd because I sought out the teachers—probably thought I was looking for attention or trying to be inappropriately adult. Well, whatever, I went right on being an outsider. I had no best friend and I wasn't part of any pair, or trio, or clique."

I had trouble picturing Paloma as such an outsider. How could such an open, accessible person have trouble making friends? I asked, "Didn't you get invited home for the weekend? Wasn't there some way to cultivate friendships?"

She heaved a sigh. "I suppose there were things I could've done. I know I didn't pursue friendships the way I went after some other things. But mostly I was at a big disadvantage because of my home situation, Chely's illness and all. I spent weekends trying to console her. I couldn't very well accept invitations, and I couldn't invite anyone to my home. Anyhow, I did what I could, and I must have been pretty transparent in going after the positive elements in anything we did—one Sister called me "Pollyanna." I'm not sure what her message might have been, but I took it as a compliment. Actually, I'm one of the few people I know who's read *Pollyanna*. I never considered her unflagging optimism the least bit odd."

At that point, I slowed down so we could enjoy a few miles of particularly winding and scenic road. Paloma was silent while we took in the views, and when we emerged on a plain, she handed me the microphone, so to speak.

"Haley, you haven't told me a thing about your growing-up years, you've just kept after mine."

"Gosh, I wouldn't know where to start. Nothing that all exciting. Let's see. OK, one thing for sure, when I was a little kid, I was shy and timid. The Depression was on and we moved a lot to get the cheapest rent, and it worked out that I was in a different school every year. It was hard to make friends, and then I'd lose them, so I always felt like an outsider, too. My father worked as the engineer and foreman in a salmon cannery in Alaska, and he was gone nearly half of each year, so I was my mother's primary companion. She was very verbal and rather pretentious in her speech, and I'm told I was a carbon copy of her by the time I was six or seven. I'm sure I don't have to tell you that I'm like you, still carrying around the aftereffects.

"I'd have to say my first real social success came when I was eleven or twelve. There was a vacant lot next to our rented house, and I decided to build what we came to call 'the clubhouse.' At most, the thing was seven feet square and maybe the same height, and I was less than a novice carpenter, and my box was ugly. But the boys in the neighborhood noticed it, and two or three hung around while I finished it up. And then it got to be the place to hang out, especially on rainy days. That gave me a sense of accomplishment like nothing I'd done before, and it got me off the ground socially. After that, we stayed put and I had a more normal school experience, and I suppose my social life was more normal, too. But I went right on being an outsider in some ways. I hung onto my habit of retreating into books. That was the way I was."

"I know," Paloma agreed, "me too." Then she settled back for more.

"Young lady, I don't want to talk about me. You've done a helluva job getting me into your story and I wish it could last a thousand and one nights, so couldn't you weave a bit more magic before Évora? Am I too demanding?"

"No, of course not, I promised. But I never dreamed it'd go on so, or be so self-centered. I'm embarrassed."

"Don't be. You're what it's all about. Carry on. Tell me about life outside school, tell me about weekends."

"School and home? Alpha and omega, poles apart. My time at Saint Brigid's was fairly impersonal but basically cheerful. Weekends were a mixed bag, though—going home to face my mother's illness and our awkward relationship. Gustaf was my weekend savior. He'd pick me up, usually Friday afternoon, and bring me home. Then he'd coordinate Saturday shopping and errand runs with Chely's naps, and he'd take me with him. We both needed company. He spent a lot of time with my mamá and he had to supply all the energy—there couldn't have been much give and take. He spent the rest of his time working on his retirement project—it was a history/genealogy of the Grevilius family, something to chronicle their contributions to Swedish cultural life, all in Swedish and he was using Swedish sources. It must have been a difficult passion to share back then with no Internet.

"So, from the day I joined them, Gustaf rather seized on me as a diversion; I was an excuse to get out of the house. He loved construction sites, and down the hill from us a crew was starting to form up the foundations for a new home. We'd walk down every two weeks or so and he'd take me through the job and explain what was going on. He told the owner I was going to study architecture, so the man got out a set of drawings and explained the steps in their planning and design. I'd have to say the concept wasn't specially original or clever, but the job gave us a year's worth of fun and made a great schoolroom for me.

Also when I first came, Gustaf taught me a game that was traditional in his family. Whenever we went out, and especially when we sat down for a break, we'd take turns describing what we saw around us, and I mean in great detail. Whoever's turn it was would pick out an activity to speculate about, a construction job, a repair, upkeep, decoration, a delivery in progress, the creation of a window display, anything like that. Gustaf called them 'purposeful activities.' The observer would analyze the activity and account for it in as many ways as he could. What was the purpose? Who planned the activity, and why? Who was carrying it out? What education and experience would be needed by the various people involved? What materials would be needed? Where did they come from? And on and on—you can imagine."

"Yes, I can imagine. I'm thinking of our first walk up Avenida de Liberdade, the way you analyzed our surroundings. You were playing your game—with another old man."

"I guess—and I told you at the time that it was an old habit. Anyhow, when Gustaf and I played and I'd finish my turn, he'd quiz me about things I'd overlooked, questions I hadn't raised or hadn't answered. And when we came across something I couldn't possibly have known, he'd take me to a hardware store or a lumber company or a machine shop so I could learn about tools and materials and industrial processes. After months of doing that every time we went out, we got to be quick studies, really alert to the things that were going on. Along the way, I added something of my own, the search for things that needed to be done. Gustaf pretended to be impressed and he complimented me. He said he'd have to tell some of his relatives.

"Even though I was fourteen when Gustaf and I began to interact, I was slow to see what he was up to. Right from the start, I knew he liked to spend time with me — he was always watching my reactions — but it wasn't till later that I realized that he'd been schooling me in his own way. I'd equated learning with books and teachers, not with the world outside. But don't imagine that Gustaf downplayed schools or academic learning. Contrariwise. During our games, he'd praise me any time I drew on my book learning. He'd give me a big smile, and shake his finger at me, and say, 'See what you just did!' He was clever to work fun and education into the companionship I so badly needed."

We crossed the Portuguese border and headed for Évora, forty miles away. I'd been lazy and hadn't called ahead for a reservation, counting on the late season to bail me out by leaving a room for us at the last minute. Now I was worried, and that somewhat spoiled my anticipation of this little-known jewel.

Évora's many antiquities date from times Roman through Medieval, Renaissance, and Baroque, a mélange so fetching that a passerby is virtually compelled to stop and tarry. Paloma was no exception. As we twisted and turned through the narrow streets to reach the elegant Pousada dos Lóios in the town center, she lost her heart to four street scenes and a temple. I sent her off to explore on foot while I initiated the room-for-the-night process.

A formidable presence greeted me at the reception desk, a woman about thirty, only a touch shorter than Paloma and more than generously endowed with feminine form, abundant dark hair, large eyes, a large smile, and a large voice. Happily, all those out-sized assets belonged to a consummate desk manager.

I explained our need and she smiled and held out hope. She had one as-yet-unoccupied room, booked, but the guest had not arrived or telephoned. She took pains to describe it as a small room with one double bed, and promised that if the guest did not arrive by six o'clock, it was mine. She leaned forward and lowered her voice. "Be patient, have a drink in the bar. I will say a small prayer for you."

As I received this intelligence, my informant billowed across the narrow counter. Was I being offered the opportunity to admire her barely contained cleavage? It was a warm business.

Precisely then, Paloma swept in, sized up the situation, pulled me to one side, and whispered, absolutely deadpan, "You're sure you still need me then?"

"Oh, oh!" I repented, "caught with my eyes in the cookie jar. Please, gracious lady, overlook this and I shall try to be better."

I turned to the Venus of Évora and assured her that we would wait for the room and could be found in the bar. I offered Paloma my arm, we stepped in and sat down at a table well placed by a window at the far end of the lounge. We ordered Madeira and, once served, I raised my glass and announced, "Now, I *am* better." Paloma looked dubious.

"What is it with this 'trying to be better' line? Do you know that you trot it out like a mantra, perhaps two or three times a day?"

"Really? Bad habit, shouldn't burden the world with family jargon. But that one, I give you my word, is ingrained. We all use it. Partly, it's a handy closing line, I suppose, but mostly because we all remember how it started."

"Started?"

"Yeah, it started with Jack the Pup, a family character—hell, a family classic."

"And.... ?"

"Jack was a Queensland Blue Heeler, Australian cow dog, you know, part dingo, shaggy gray, brown, and white hair with black spots? My son-in-law Will brought him home as a wee pup a few years after he and Lys were married. Jack grew into fifty pounds of overeager readiness, readiness to do Will's bidding in all things, ready to learn any trick or retrieve any object or chase any quarry. But nobody could keep up with him, so Jack was underchallenged by life, and that left him anxious. Now and then his eagerness led him into error—the forbidden step into the street—or even sin—the punctured ball, the broken stick, the perforated Frisbee. When one of these transgressions was called to his attention, he'd crawl up to Will on his stomach, put his head between his paws, and show life only by tracking his radar ears and rolling his ever-peeled eyeballs. There he'd lie, quivering, every fiber thirsting for redemption, and Will would say, 'Look, he wants to be better. He's trying to be better.'

And that line was so apt, it so fitted Jack's yearning for pardon and reemployment. From that day to this, we all try to acknowledge our shortcomings and then go forth, like Jack the Pup, and try to be better."

"You all loved this dog?"

"He was our mute child."

"And did he achieve betterness?"

"Only to a degree. There he was, lusting after perfection and full employment, and never getting either. He tried to be better right up to a sad, early death — cancer. We all know he went on to a higher calling."

Paloma examined her nails. "I've never had a dog. I've never known anyone who did."

I took her hand in mine and ventured to kiss it. When will I learn? My prize was withdrawn and I got the message, "not here and now." I muttered, "Sorry," in a penitent voice and was permitted to live to err another day.

After a bit, a stir ran through the crowded lounge. The Grande Dame of the Desk was making her way toward us, parting the crowd as she came. She held center stage in our amphitheater as a magnet does to scattered iron filings — randomness ceased as every eye was drawn our way. She swept up to our table, delivered her message, turned, acknowledged the crowd with a smile, and gathered momentum for her return voyage. Randomness was slowly restored, but many conversations were forever sidetracked and many more started afresh.

She had come to tell us we could have the small room. Would we take it? "Yes, indeed!" we chorused. It had been a long day and we were happy to go no farther. We passed arm in arm to the dining room, my companion attracting her own following among the assembled eyes.

Long day or no, Paloma was unusually animated at dinner, on a tear, recalling our visit in Sevilla, reviewing parts of our trip, and revising her assessments of others. I found myself torn between her spirited analysis and the show she made of it — eyebrows, shoulders, hands, all busy, busy, busy. I fell to studying those hands that I must not touch in public — so skillful at massage, so electric in touch. The owner of said hands came to wonder at all this examination, and my quiet. Her raised eyebrows asked, "What?"

"Oh," I responded, "just admiring Barbara and Eugenia's handiwork."

Once we did retire to our room, we came to appreciate the desk's use of the word "small." It was very small, and interior as well — no window and no opening to the outside beyond an exhaust fan in the bath. The lone bed was an adventure, a carry-over from an age of more petite guests. And not flat. When we attempted to retire early, we rolled straightway to the middle of the bed, hooted, and got up to address the problem. Fortunately, the mattress was fine, the difficulty stemmed from slumping springs that we could level with folded blankets. Finally, I took a luggage stand and topped it with a pillow to create a perch for my overhanging feet. Of all our nights together, this was the coziest.

Monday, October 28th

At five in the morning, my bundling partner lost all patience with our cramped quarters. Évora called, and her response was magnified by having foregone her predawn hike for three days. Nothing would do but hit the street and I knew better than to drag my feet. Presto! We were up, dressed, and out of there. We found the front door unlocked and slipped out into a pleasant chill and an intriguing setting.

The *pousada* occupies a remodeled convent on the square that crowns the city heights, and shares that plaza with a major Roman edifice, today called The Temple of Diana. We stepped outdoors to be greeted by Corinthian columns softly illuminated by the door lamps of our inn and tinted by the rosy glow of dawn. A hushed silence was broken only by the shimmering notes of a distant chanticleer greeting the day. We shared temple and square with the enduring past — not a bad way to start a Monday.

Nothing would be open for hours, but Miss Get-Up-and-Go had concocted a plan to march eastside, westside, and all around the town, deciding as we went what we'd return to inspect later. I stifled an impulse to point out that she might be making two walks out of one. Why bother? My reward for that piece of intelligence would have been raised eyebrows and a questioning, "So?"

We strode up and down quiet streets, past churches, palaces, monuments, and mansions, across stately squares with elaborate black and white mosaic paving, through a handsome municipal park, and on to a gate in the city's fortified perimeter wall. We had only to peek through to find, sweeping right up to our feet, fields dotted with grazing animals and emitting abundant pastoral sounds and smells, a transition from urban to rural that can take Americans by surprise.

It was now broad daylight. The higher parts of buildings reflected the sun, people began to emerge, and our appetites announced themselves. Paloma allowed me to put my forehead to hers and whisper "breakfast" in my most seductive tones. Feeling like the Pied Piper, I led our return to civilization as we knew it. Our rewards included a basket of fresh-baked bread and cake goods, complemented by rich, dark coffee.

That morning we did everything on every page of the travel guide to Évora, or so it seemed. The old town center displays a bewildering assortment of sixteenth- to eighteenth-century buildings, some strong and refined, others awkwardly designed and over-decorated—all pictorially effective. Their cumulative charm beguiled us to stride on, block after block, gawking at such a concentration of Old World wonders.

Midday found us back at our lodgings, the spell finally broken. I offered up thanks to Diana—and to the *pousada* desk—for relocating us to a two-bedded room twice the size of the one in which we'd just bunked. How welcome it was. After lunch, both May and November lay down and shut their eyes, regenerating from many steps on unyielding stone.

Later, as we sat in the lounge with aperitifs, Paloma used "trying to be better" unconsciously; it dawned on her as I stared in mock surprise.

"Oh," she reacted, "you did that to me with your Jack story. All right, I see why you like the 'trying to be better' line, but I still don't see what Jack did that left you all so impressed. You mentioned tricks, but I'd think tricks would've got old in a hurry."

"No, no! You're off the mark. Let me tell you how it was with the Pup. He was so intense—sort of the way you can be at times. Now, now, don't overreact.... Anyhow, his stunts weren't parlor tricks so much as proof of the rapport he had with Will. Will could get young Jack Cardwell to do damn near anything he asked."

"Why Cardwell?"

"He was an Australian pioneer of some kind. It's a thing, down under, to name Blue Heelers after frontier characters, or maybe use the names of friends or neighbors as a means of joshing them. I met an Aussie who told me his Heeler was named for a great uncle of his. I asked what his uncle was famous for, and the fellow said, 'Spinning comical yarns, but with family, mostly for being a falling-down drunk.'"

Paloma was pathetically grateful for this edification. "Haley, have I mentioned how educational this trip has been, and how appreciative I am? Truly, I assure you, not Gustaf nor anyone else I've ever known has exposed me, even remotely, to the sort of enlightenment I now enjoy every day." She rested her chin on the knuckles of both hands and smiled sweetly.

"My pleasure. Glad to be of service. Any time."

It was our last dinner on the road. We raised ceremonial glasses, then took our time over leisurely courses, coffee, and port. We, or rather Paloma, reminisced, first with lively recollections of Lisbon's Avenida da Liberdade, and on to fond memories of our secret temple in the fields and our happy times at Café An-Mai. Then she rested her chin on her fists again and looked expectantly at me. I didn't perjure myself when I singled out our meetings with her people in Sevilla. But neither did I confess that she'd given me my greatest reward by admitting me to her past—thereby allowing me to understand her better.

We returned to our upgraded room and she prepared for the night while I lay back, still reliving our odyssey. We'd gone together to Sevilla for Paloma's treasured visit, but that hadn't changed her vision of herself, nor of me, nor of our relationship. It was I who had been changed by seeing her in this new light. And when my vision of her changed, our relations changed. Now I focused on a whole person, and that person was coming to look more like a friend in need than a willing sex object. When she emerged, ready for the night, I seated her on the bed, kissed her hands, and whispered, "Thank you for being the 'you' you are."

"How could I not?" she puzzled, but I swear she blushed.

Tuesday, October 29th

Our last day on the road. We started with a brisk walk to a couple of lookout points in old Évora. To and fro, we enjoyed a continuing profusion of geraniums, their pots set on ledges, sills, or in iron rings fixed to walls. Outside a door, we brushed by four small birdcages suspended from just such rings, each occupied by a songbird, silent but for ceaseless pacings and hoppings within its prison. Paloma turned away pained and walked for a block staring straight ahead, fists clenched. I said nothing, but added caged creatures to my list of her sensitivities.

We approached the *pousada*, gave the temple columns farewell pats, then went in to take breakfast and round up our things. We found the Venus of Évora more modestly draped in the morning but as full of bonhomie as ever. We shared her hearty handshakes and took our leave.

Vistas along the highway to Lisbon were uninspired and so were we. We fell silent. I glanced over at Paloma who sat expressionless, gazing straight up the road. I reached over and waved my hand before her face. "Hello, pilot to copilot. What is our attitude, please?"

She turned, looking distressed, not playing games at all. "Haley, I feel empty, alone — as if all the world's had a life that's passed me by. What can I do?"

"O God," I thought, "she's hurting. What can I say?" I pulled myself together and tried to be careful. "Paloma, your life humbles me and makes me cautious about offering advice. Your problems are tangled up in your very existence — something you wouldn't want to undo even if you could. But you're here and the past isn't. Why not look forward and try to fill your void with other things? Look at the possible. Look at Bessie and Nourrit. They might have missed out on more than you did, but they pitched in and gave you things they never had. Weren't they showing you that giving can push aside the hurt of not receiving?"

I felt inadequate as my words died away. I heard them sounding glib and not as consoling as I'd have liked. Fortunately they seemed to leave Paloma more thoughtful than troubled.

"You're right, Bessie and Nourrit were wonderful with me. And look at Nourrit with Benito. But I don't have the confidence to get so involved in anyone's life. I don't have that much to offer."

Oh, how I wanted to argue that point, but this wasn't the time. She needed comforting, not contrary opinions.

"Listen, when you're feeling blue is not the time to anguish over what might've been. Plan ahead, set your heart on something, and go for it. I learned in my teaching days to look at the signals sent out by young people with problems. The ones who abused themselves — tobacco, alcohol, drugs, unprotected sex—those were the ones with seriously low morale and headed for big trouble. It may not be easy for you to cope, but you can—and you will. It's in you, it shows. You're strong and you have a lot of self-respect—you eat right, you stay fit, you stay mentally active, you have a lively curiosity. Those are signs of a winner."

No response. She sat back and closed her eyes. I hated to see her so low, but what to say or do? I yearned for morning tea, but there wasn't a hamlet in sight. Then something popped into my head, something I'd been meaning to ask.

"Paloma, remember early on, you mentioned a job you had, not the folk art bibliography, something to do with supervising rental units? What's that all about?"

"Oh that. Well, I misled you if I called it a job." She sounded a little startled, perhaps the total change of subject. "It's like my museum chores, it's a fraction of a job. One of my clients owns four units in a condominium complex. I'm in one, and I 'manage' the others. Actually, I stand in for the owner in any way possible. It's all pretty routine, most of it by mail and telephone, and it doesn't require a lot of time, just due diligence. I do it in exchange for half my rent. It's a good deal for me, another thing I can do when I'd otherwise be rather at loose ends."

All this was delivered in dutiful tones, evidence that I'd stumbled onto a topic not near and dear to her heart. But, to my surprise, she brightened up and went on.

"Property management has it's moments though. It's a great teacher, so many things you need to know or learn. Gustaf had a real interest in the trades and their workers, but he wasn't handy at all. He hired people to come in to fix or adjust any little thing that wasn't right. I amazed him when I watched our routine repairs and adjustments and started doing some of the easy ones myself. Well, I still do that. I try to do anything I can to avoid those fifty-to-eighty dollar house calls for even simple things. And I do some of the same things for an older couple in one of the units. They can barely take care of themselves and they appreciate my efforts."

We might have had quite an exchange on the subject of home maintenance, but by that time we turned off for a late lunch at the baronial Pousada de Palmela. We entered that noble pile and passed through grand interiors on our way to a cheery dining room where I managed to steer the conversation onto more effervescent topics — a shift in which I had good and willing cooperation.

After lunch, I took a wrong turn trying to get back on the highway and we found ourselves skirting a lively street market. After a glance, Paloma asked me to let her out. "Just a moment," she said, "I have business to do." I did so, then looked around for a parking place. The only open space was behind a bus stop, and marked "Reservado." "No problem," I decided, "it's only minutes," and I pulled in to the curb and left the motor running. Minutes passed and no Paloma. I fidgeted, but not for long. I heard tapping on my roof and saw a figure outside. I rolled down my window and was confronted by a slim, straight-backed policeman wearing an immaculate uniform and an admonitory expression. He pointed to the sign, spoke feelingly — I assume about the law and the chaos that results from its disregard — and tore off a citation he'd filled out prior to approaching me. I took it — not much I could say, and I certainly wasn't going to make the mistake of speaking Spanish. Just then I heard Paloma's voice from the curb side, speaking across the top of the car. I caught a word or two of Portuguese and some English. The officer stepped deliberately around the front of our car and faced her on the sidewalk — they stood in a place where I could see only chests to knees. There was talk, and Paloma showed off a bundle of marigolds. I saw her point back into the street market. More talk. The officer reached down and opened her door for her, she got in and rolled down her window. He ceremoniously tore up his copy of the citation and dropped it in a convenient trash can. As I pulled away from the curb, Paloma blew him a kiss and he gave her a snappy salute.

"I'm sorry, Haley. I never imagined I'd be so long. But, I must say, what a nice man."

"For you, I foresee a lifetime of nice men. You bring out the best in us."

"Quite gallant. Did you notice, he tipped his hat? Anyway, thank you for humoring me. You had flowers for me when I arrived, and I saw those pails and pails of them there, and I had to get some for us for our last day. Then I looked down one of those narrow lanes and I was sure I saw that little girl and her mother I spoke to in Tomar. I paid for the flowers and ran after them, and it took a minute or so to catch up, and when I did, I saw that I was wholly mistaken; I'd found another nice mother and her pretty girl child. I suppose I was wishing for that closure to our circle, seeing them on the way out and then on the way in. Oh well, now I have another pair of bright eyes to remember, and that little girl has three marigolds to put in a glass."

I negotiated that final twenty-five miles in under an hour, city traffic and all. We checked into the Metrópole, then set out for our open-air bar where we sat side by side under autumnal elms, sipping Madeira as the sun went down and leaning together often. I was feeling a strong sense of impending loss when Paloma suddenly blurted out, "I hate journey's end, going home to that emptiness. I hate it this time more than ever. I'm terribly spoiled. I've had a terribly good time and I'm not being a terribly good sport." She burst into tears, real tears, and lots of them. I put an arm around her quaking shoulders.

"Please, Paloma, don't cry! Nothing's ending that can't be restarted. Think of next time."

She turned away from me, out of my grasp. "No. I'm missing this time. I'm missing every step we took. I want it all forever." More tears. I pulled up a chair in front of her and leaned forward, still hoping to console.

Pretty soon, she wiped her eyes with her fists as if she were a child and gave me a reproachful look. "Why is it when someone needs to cry, wants to grieve over anything, men can't think of anything to do but try to talk you out of it? I'm trying to hold onto something, and this makes it easier. D'you mind?"

It was a fair question and a good point, but I wasn't so stupid as to essay an answer. I put my elbows on my knees, cupped my face in my hands, and waited. Soon a handkerchief was out and put to use, then it was displayed to me.

"See why I don't use makeup?" I saw. "And it's quicker — notice how much time we save in the morning?" The look on her face and that wet hanky tugged at my heartstrings.

"Paloma, I didn't mean to squelch you. You gave me the sincerest compliment I could hope for. I'm going to hold onto it forever. I don't want this to end either, but things just do." I held her hand gently until she finally spoke up.

"I'm hungry. Let's go back to that little place we went the first night."

We did. We revisited all the places we'd gone that first night, and none of them disappointed us.

Wednesday, October 30th

Our last day. Our time together down to hours, and most of those on a jet. We walked out and did easy, enjoyable things that lay close at hand — a jaunt up La Liberdade, breakfast on the strip, a little shopping for family and friends. We had tea and coffee, shielded from a bustling sidewalk by a row of humorous topiary creatures carved out of potted Podocarpus.

When our time ran out, we loaded up the car, bade farewell to the Metrópole, and wended our way through the hills to the airport. We checked our luggage, returned the car, passed through the inspection area, and located our departure gate. We ambled around making fun of tacky tourist trifles in hole-in-the-wall shops. At last, we ran out of things to say and simply sat, side by side, from time to time smiling wanly at each other. At last we boarded and, in due time, felt lucky when the door of the plane closed and no one had claimed the third seat in our row. The flight attendants did their "abandon ship" demonstration, and we lived through takeoff, peanuts, drinks, a desultory dinner, and a slapstick film that was probably better as we experienced it—no sound.

Eventually the hubbub abated as fewer passengers needed restrooms, traffic in flight attendants slowed, and overhead lights were turned out. Paloma and I lay back and dozed. I suppose I managed to be half asleep for an hour, then it was over. I turned my head and encountered a very dear pair of wide-open, dark eyes.

"Hi," I whispered.

"Hi, yourself." Continued steady gaze while the lips below shaped a question, "A penny?"

I turned to really face her. "For my thoughts? You. And more you. You've gone from friendly stranger to fascinating study. I've been wondering not just where you've been, but where you'd like to go and how you're going to get there."

She came back in her own low tones, "You and your burrowing questions! Yes, I've thought about my future, and I've looked every which way at things I might get into. But I'm not making decisions, not now. Before I do that, I need to have the means to feel confident. The good part is, my plan for the means is working, but it takes time. In a few years, I'll be independent and I'll be ready to get on with the rest of my life. But sitting here this minute, I admit that's all pretty nebulous."

I thought she sounded dutiful and a little defensive, but I was feeling upbeat.

"You mention the rest of your life—well, I want you to know that, thanks to you, mine's not as nebulous as it was. When I met you, I had no plan and I was lonely and discouraged and half lost. Marian and I'd been married all those years and shared all sorts of adventures, but we were still active and felt creative and we were best friends. Sure, we thought we'd worked out the survivor's strategy if one of us went early, but not really, not seriously. We were going to go on together till our time here ended, and then we'd say good-bye as gracefully as we could, and leave. But when she went, I wasn't ready at all…"

Cabin lights blinked on and we were warned to check seat belts, turbulence ahead. No surprise there; the plane had just gone through elevator-like rises and falls.

Paloma shook her head. "How could you possibly have been 'ready' to lose the most important person in your life?"

"I'll never know. I just didn't face it. I was the ostrich with head in sand. And when she was gone, everything really went to hell. My work didn't go better because I had more time, it went badly, if at all. I needed someone to share things with. Our daughters did everything they could. They really did. But they couldn't be Marian. They had homes, husbands, children to raise, and careers of their own.

"Then, just like that, you were there and I snapped out of it. You can't imagine the effect you had on me, even those trite words we exchanged outside the coffee shop. Believe me, you fired up all my circuits and convinced me that I was still alive. And you've given me something to look forward to. You're a treasure I could never have imagined."

"Haley, all I did was walk down a hall and enter into a polite conversation. You're the one perceiving all those blessings and you're the one defining the treasure. It's great fun to be along, but don't give me the credit."

"Ah! My depression just vanished. My outlook just hauled off and turned itself around—overnight. I should be so clever. Miss Modesty, you've outdone yourself. You're the most damnably difficult person to praise I've ever met. Won't you hold still for any sort of stroking?"

"Listen to yourself. Imagine the sprightly little ways I could reply to that!"

"You're bad. That was intended to be heartfelt 'thank you' and I got too fancy."

"All right, you're welcome—and let me be grateful too. How about the ways you've made me happy? You've thrown yourself into making this our trip—really, it ended up revolving around me. That's incredibly flattering. And right from the day we met, you've been positive and forthcoming. Honestly, this trip's gone by faster than any I remember." She sounded a little blue, and she slumped down.

I raised an invisible champagne glass. "Well then, here's to more and better."

"Not yet. You don't get to shut the door on this one yet—it's still magic to me. I can't believe how short a time we've been 'we.' Two weeks? Is it possible? All right, I'm not really that surprised. Even in

Santa Fe I knew you were different. I'm sure it all started because I was alone and away from home, new for me. Sounds odd, I guess, but I've never traveled alone. I was used to deferring to someone else, but when you first spoke, I felt free to just be me, and I was, and you fell right in step. It was fun and I liked you straight off—your way, direct, no circling around. I was sure, spot on, you weren't playing any sort of game. I love wordplay, and you're always there with your up-and-down puns—grins to groans. I'll miss that."

Her eyes were smiling again and I wanted to go right on amusing her. "Listen, grins and groans are my game. And banter and chitchat. But that takes two, and you give as good as you get. Every bit as good. Do you think I'm not going to feel down—way down—when this is over?"

Paloma blushed and picked at a non-existent hangnail. She caught my eye and smiled. "That's what's so great—us together. And not just silly fun. Sometimes you put me on the spot, made me question my ideas, even some I was pretty set on. But you've been supportive through it all and made me feel comfortable. You can't imagine how important that approval is to me. I'm so insecure that any kind of silence or tension feels like a reproach, a signal that I've done wrong, or at least that I haven't done right. Well, you've haven't left me guessing. Not once."

"Paloma, I can't imagine who would be unkind to you. You're a complete delight. And I hate hearing you say, 'I'm so insecure.' Somehow you've got to shed that feeling, put it behind you."

She sighed and stared up at the array of switches and lights above her seat.

"That's so easy to say. But there's a lot of my past I'd have to forget to just 'shed that feeling,' as you say. How do you forget who you really are? And how do I get the big, bad world to accept a lot of things about me. Ever since I was eight I've known that something about me was supposed to be shameful, that I was being hidden away. Now I guess you could say the hidden-away child is hiding herself. But I'm working on one shelter I can depend on; everything's easier to face when you have financial independence. You can't imagine the boost I get going over my brokerage statement. As I said, it won't be that long before I can go where I want and do what I want."

There was a hard bump, as if we'd hit ground and skipped off. Cabin lights dimmed and some sort of electronic gong sounded. But in a moment, the lights came up and there was stirring in the cabin. We expected more turbulence, but after a few rising and falling sensations, Paloma continued.

"Anyway ... in the meantime things aren't all that bad. Don't forget the company and entertainment I get from my clients — you all treat me as a lady. Well, I know I'm no lady, but all of you are wonderful at making me feel that I belong in your company. That's important. It's when I'm alone that I feel vulnerable."

"Paloma, for God's sweet sake! A lady doesn't earn or lose her status by way of her private affairs. Not as long as they are private. A lady is a lady because of the generosity of her thoughts and actions and her treatment of others. In our time together, you've been ladylike to a fault. If you feel like slipping up a time or two, go ahead, you've earned it. And did it ever occur to you that you might belong in better company?"

"Now you're making fun of me — but kind fun, thank you. Even so, Haley, what you have to accept is that witty arguments are one thing, and self-confidence is another. It's that simple."

A host of objections declared themselves in my head. Who in the world would not take her to be a lady? No one — unless he knew her circumstances. So why, in the name of heaven, doesn't she turn to a proper vocation and start afresh elsewhere, any of an infinite number of elsewheres where people would instinctively accept her for the superior person she is? Don't ask, I decided, it's late and we're tired. Better to squirrel away such questions for a more promising occasion.

I reached over and took her hand, relaxed, but imparting a sense of its capable but curiously confined owner. I raised that hand to my cheek, overcome by a welter of divergent emotions — my unconditional affection, pity for her sad self-image and the choices that had arisen from it and fed it, and my shame for having purchased the right to be there and take her hand in mine. My road was hell because I had nothing to offer but good intentions.

In the next hour Paloma and I said our farewells. We knew it was better here, relaxed and with plenty of time, than later in the midst of airport confusion, or worse, in that always awkward moment of parting. At last she closed her eyes, but remained in mine as I mused. She and our trip remained a dream come true, and in dimensions I could not have imagined. Only at a time like that, when she withdrew, could I contemplate the shameful basis of our relationship — and even so, gazing at her sleeping profile, I had the hardest time coming to grips with my dilemma.

We came into New York and endured the rigamarole of customs, changing airlines, waiting, flying some more, and landing in Los Angeles. I rented a car and took Paloma to her condominium. I helped her to the door with her things and we shook hands. I walked toward the car, but turned at the sound of my name. Her soft "Stay in touch?" skirted on the edge of forlorn. I nodded an emphatic "yes," got in, and drove away. My amazing, eventful, tantalizing journey of discovery, delights, and doubts had come to an end, but not to a resolution. I went home to regroup.

157

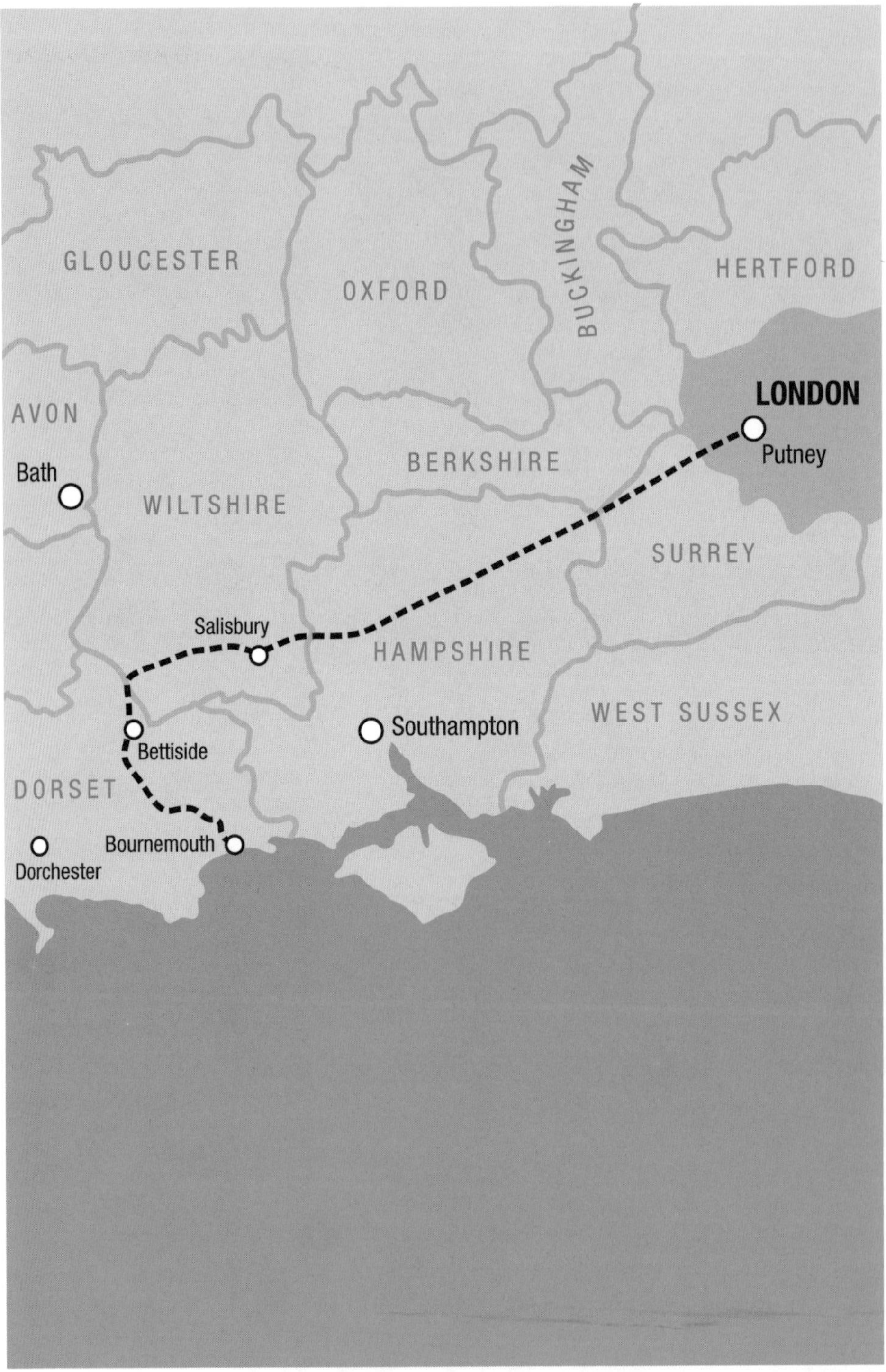
GLOUCESTER
OXFORD
BUCKINGHAM
HERTFORD
LONDON
Putney
AVON
Bath
BERKSHIRE
WILTSHIRE
SURREY
Salisbury
HAMPSHIRE
WEST SUSSEX
Southampton
Bettiside
DORSET
Bournemouth
Dorchester

V Bessie

San Diego, California — Thursday, October 31, 1996

I got home tired and stayed tired for days, worn down by the pleasures and the exertions of keeping up with such an exuberant partner. I'd paid dearly for every one of my forty-four extra years.

So my homecoming brought a kind of relief, a decompression. I lay in bed late and catnapped as needed. I returned calls, answered mail, visited family, and had coffee with friends. But after five or six days, when I was over jet lag and accumulated fatigue, withdrawal set in. I hated eating alone. I hated having no one with whom I could share a word, a touch, or a joke.

But I couldn't share that with family. When we got together, I rattled off the highlights of my trip and answered questions, but I trivialized the role of my companion, "the Spanish woman." I hated to hold out on Lys and Gwyn, but how could I describe or justify what Paloma meant to me? How could they understand that an older man might feel fortunate to have such a relationship despite its social unacceptability? How could I explain that I was willing to share her with others? That an older person might not have the jealous need for proprietorial exclusivity that younger people seem to feel?

All right, I could hoodwink the family, but not my conscience — I'd promised myself, and I'd promised Nourrit, that I'd work to get Paloma out of relationships such as ours. And that was good, and it was right, and, paradoxically, I needed that achievement as much as I needed her. But when would I actually take the step? When would I propose to Paloma that we end our contracted closeness as provider and consumer? I shuddered, and took refuge in some quixotic limbo where I could argue that we continue as friends and lovers. After all, the better I knew her, the easier it should be to persuade her that she sacrificed too much on the altar of financial security. There I was, prolonging a tantalizing interlude in which it seemed possible to have it both ways.

But, damn it, that's all it would be, an interlude, not a cure for my ills. My relatively happy state was a fool's paradise. Each night I'd toss and turn, foreseeing Paloma going on to better things—and me going to pieces in her wake.

So, what about alternatives to this doomed relationship? Why, for example, hadn't I accepted more help from friends? Because it just didn't work, I argued. Marian and I, together, had socialized with those friends, most of them old married couples like us. With Marian gone, our get-togethers were awkward. We either talked about happier times—with Marian's spirit tangibly present—or we avoided references to anything in which she'd been involved, and suffered the strain of that. I felt like a wet blanket at every gathering.

And what about cultivating new people? I remembered my weary sense that each attempt to connect with strangers required great efforts and endless bridge-building. We'd always wind up returning to our pasts, the very thing I needed to put out of my mind. Each such encounter left me emotionally fatigued.

In the end, none of my answers was convincing. My failure to adjust to single life spotlighted a kind of petulance in me, an unwillingness to accommodate and play the game. I acknowledged that I'd been truly spoiled and I'd taken for granted the relationship that spoiled me. My treasured companion had also been cook, housekeeper, social organizer, and keeper of the family flame. When she left, I was deprived of all those vital services and reacted in a sadly immature way. I suppose I even resented having so many chores, and my mind balked at the idea of training and having to live around a housekeeper. I'd never given marriage a thought. Who could replace Marian? Who could supply any part of what she took with her?

Now I faced all those realities and I didn't much like me. My appreciation for my wife seemed petty and self-centered, not what she deserved, and not what I should be capable of. I walked around the house and stopped at her regular haunts — studio, kitchen, bedroom, dressing area. I had little talks with her and I felt a little better. I did not talk about Paloma. She was not a Marian substitute and never would be. She was a glorious fluke, a visitation sent to startle me back to life. I loved her for it — hell, I loved her, period. So there I was, scared to death by uncertainties, but still enchanted.

Two weeks dragged by like a month before I stopped agonizing over my future, or Paloma's, and simply focused on another trip. What a relief to stop chasing my tail and do something! I recalled my magical visit with Paloma's people in Sevilla and hoped that she'd jump at a chance to see Bessie — and that I could tag along.

Paloma had said she'd be busy in November and December, and for me, the week leading to Christmas would be family time. January? I'd never traveled in northern Europe in mid-winter; I'd always supposed it would be wet and raw. On the other hand, spring was far off and I couldn't face the agony of so long a wait.

I sketched out a proposal and felt my load lighten as I took the phone and punched up Paloma's number. I reached her machine and left a message, "Paloma, this is Haley in urgent need of a conference. Please call." She must have been right there; my phone rang in less than two minutes.

"Haley, silly man, it is not I who arranges conferences. You are the conference king. If you need one, find one — and I'll go with you!"

"OK, I walked into that one. I said the wrong thing again."

"Well you might've said, 'Paloma, I'd love to talk to you.'"

"I know, I know. Once a pedant, always a pedant."

"There, there. Emulate the noble Pup. 'Try to be better.'"

"Paloma, I need more than this sort of counseling. I need to spirit you away. How about Merry Olde England? Down here, it's family togetherness through Christmas, but I could fly the next day. Could I send you on ahead for a Christmas with Bessie? But then you'll have to get me in on it — I must meet Bessie."

"Oh, Haley, what a dear, generous offer! If Bessie's able, I'd be thrilled. Let me call her. As far as I know, she goes each Christmas to the home for orphans that took her in as a child, but that's not far from her place. May I get back to you on this?"

"Yes, but listen, I don't want you two to feel rushed. I've got a bunch of editing to do. I could book some nice country inn, get over travel fatigue, and tap on the keyboard while I wait for you two to be ready. We can keep in touch, you know."

"Of course. And your 'country inn' strikes a chord. I know a great place run by the nicest people. It would be a treat to be their guest again and I'll be surprised if you don't agree. Fine food and lovely grounds, not particularly near London, but it's in Dorset, not a long, long drive. Bettiswood Hall—it's spelled B-E-T-T-I-S-W-O-O-D, but pronounce it 'Bettswood'—just up the valley from the sweet little village of Bettiside. I can see you absolutely eating it up."

"Shucks, Ma'am, sounds to me like it'll do just fine."

"Great! And I'll get back to you about Bessie and Christmas and all. I'm excited, and I have my fingers crossed, but now I must run."

"I kiss your hand, Madame."

"Well, that will have to do for now. Better arrangements will be made. Be good!"

So there I was, all a-twitter again.

Four days later, I had a fax sent from Area Code 808. (Don't ask, don't look it up, don't think about it.)

> *Bessie is thrilled. We will have Christmas Eve together and the next day we go to her Christmas party. I've booked me over there to arrive the 23rd and my return is open. Could you take care of your flight and Bettiswood Hall? (You will find their numbers below.) Call me when you arrive and we'll make plans, or perhaps we'll talk before we leave. See ya!*

I winced. The "See ya," like her earlier reference to Jack the Pup, was her way of kidding me about family in-jokes and stories that creep into my speech. Or maybe the wistful touch of one who has only adopted family, and that scattered.

I had to dig deeply for a flight so soon after Christmas and gladly settled for December twenty-seventh. Paloma and I didn't speak to each other again, but I got a bill for her tickets along with the briefest of notes.

Season's Greetings!
Take care of the airfare and accommodations
and you get me in the bargain
(the only thing I can remember
that you mentioned wanting).

Very interesting. I sat down with that in my hand and more in my head. "Wonderful!" I exulted. "Change — or at least stirrings."

Meanwhile, I called the number for Bettiswood Hall. The man I reached spoke cultivated but foreign-accented English. He was relieved to hear that I was inquiring about a stay after Christmas and offered to book through January sixth to be sure we'd have enough time. I found him so civil and helpful that I asked him to recommend an additional inn, preferably off to the west. He laughed, begged me to question someone better acquainted with the area, then told me he was a would-be hotelier from Italy, had been at Bettiswood only four months, and would not care to misadvise me. I enjoyed our exchange and the idea that we would meet.

My preparations made, I needed to maintain some sort of contact — anything but the telephone, since I feared that constant calls would nag. Paloma must have felt the same. In the next two months, we faxed each other a flurry of chatty notes with questions, jokes, random thoughts, small things that made me, at least, feel less lonely. She was also prompt to acknowledge the things I'd sent as soon as I returned — copies of my books, prints of our travel photos, and a dozen or more compact discs. Especially dear to me was her response to a gift, a disk of flute sonatas composed by an obscure sixteen-year-old woman. Anna Bon was born in Venice around 1740 and moved with her musical parents to Germany where she obtained posts in two court orchestras. Nothing is known of her after 1767.

Haley dear,

What a blessing you bestowed, Anna Bon di Venezia ringing down from a Tiepolo sky! And your letter. You care about her. I put on Opus 1 and listened. I listened again the following day. I listen now, and now I care. Anna Bon, where did you go? Where is the rest of your music and the rest of your life?

May we go looking for her? We could search from the Veneto to Bayreuth and back. We could get lost in the 18th century and never be heard of again! When could we leave?

An immeasurably richer Paloma

When I read this, I longed to find Mephisto at my door, to see his offer on my table. It must be that I had nothing he wanted.

Writing my article and creating its detailed map kept my nose to the grindstone and reduced the sense of emptiness around me — at last, I was accomplishing something! I remembered how it was before Paloma, how difficult to concentrate on anything, how difficult even to make myself sit down and try. I gave thanks each day to find myself still aglow from our first liaison and buoyed up by the prospect of another. What a blessing is anticipation.

Our daughters' extended families have complicated traditions involving gifts and feasts at the several homes on a rotating basis, much effort in the making, and much to enjoy as a result. Fortunately, it was all easier this year than it had been for the last two when Marian's death had cast a pall over even the grandchildren's enthusiasm. This time, I got into it with unusual energy, but also with the uneasy realization that part of my lightheartedness had nothing to do with family or Christmas.

Nothing detracted from my pleasure in our daughters. Inevitably, I contrasted Gwyn and Lys with Paloma. They were older — by ten and thirteen years — married, and in the midst of motherhood, homemaking, and home-based professional pursuits. But the most apparent difference was in their perceptions of their lives. They'd been able to take parents for granted, especially their mother who had always been home and put their interests first. When choices were to be made, they made them (not always flawlessly) and worked out the consequences (not without bumps). Neither of them reminded me specifically of Marian, but she lived on in both in the security that arises from knowing what one is about, and why.

In a flash of insight, I saw that in certain ways my daughters no longer needed me, and that I'd gravitated to Paloma for more than sex and more than friendship, though both were deeply involved. I was irresistibly drawn to an opportunity to intervene, to meddle, if you wish. She was not only a siren, she was a project, a project in which I might be actively useful, not just an adjunct. I counted the days until I could pick up where I'd left off.

Saturday, December 28th

Christmas passed, and I flew. I arrived at Heathrow, picked up a rental car, and was on the M3 by noon. I cruised along, thinking of Bettiswood and Paloma's previous visits, and it came to me that my role on this jaunt would be different, I'd be on her turf to visit people she knew. This time, I needed to sit back and let her guide me. Meanwhile, I'd keep my eyes open for ways to insinuate my new agenda, and, as always, take pleasure in her company.

As I drove, I repeated, "Bett-side, Bett-side," to fix the village's name in my head with just the two syllables, and that set me to musing over the English practice of contracting names. Suddenly, I was seized with inspiration. Bettiswood Hall might just as easily have been named Bettiside Manor — and then, of course, it would be an obvious destination for medical conferences. I tucked that away, already counting on a hearty groan from Paloma.

Three or so hours later I drove my small Rover into Bettiside, stopped for directions, and headed up the pretty valley. The day was sunny, but it was a hazy winter sun. At higher speeds on the throughway I'd had little sense of season, but now, on a rural byway, the muted hues of winter were apparent. The forms of bare trees dominated gray-brown slopes, mist lay in low places, smoke rose from a few chimneys, and leftover Christmas decorations soldiered on.

I rolled up before Bettiswood Hall just in time for tea. In the best fashion of upscale hostelries, the instant porter stepped forward to fetch and carry. He was followed by a tall, fit-looking young man who was expecting me and introduced himself as Carlo Giordano. I, in turn, recognized his voice and accent from our telephone encounter. As we chatted about my flight and the weather prospects, I was amused at the contrast between Giordano and the man I'd visualized. The real thing looked about thirty and stood over six feet tall, a more vibrant presence than the smaller, older man I'd imagined. Carlo was concerned that I might have expected a different reception committee. He explained that he was filling in for the Hilliers, the proprietors, while they spent Christmas with her relatives in Holland. He checked me in and sent me up to my room with an invitation to join him for tea, which I did as soon as I determined that no one was answering Bessie's phone.

We'd no more than begun to nibble when Giordano informed me that he'd volunteered to work as assistant manager in order to use Bettiswood Hall as a textbook. He and his sister had inherited a somewhat rundown rural villa fifteen miles north of Florence, a place they planned to restore and remodel into an inn of their own. He'd chosen Bettiswood for its reputation and because its configuration was similar to the one he wished to create. His description of his villa and its farmhouse adjuncts jogged my memory.

"Carlo, let me interrupt. Years ago, I spent a lot of time in Mexico, and down in Guanajuato I met a countryman of yours who was working wonders reconstructing big eighteenth and nineteenth century stone buildings—"

"My God," Carlo burst out, "you knew Giorgio Belloli!"

"Right. But how could you? Giorgio must've died when you were a child."

"University. I studied for a degree in architecture many things about the business of restoring and preserving historic buildings. One of my professors, another Carlo, Carlo Cavalli, was a Venetian, like Belloli. This Cavalli visited Belloli in Mexico, he followed his workings every way you imagine, he wrote to him, he collected photographs, magazine stories, anything. I did my big report, my thesis, all about Giorgio Belloli, and this Cavalli was my sponsor. Now you are here with this news. It is what they say, a small world."

"I guess! And the truth is, I knew Giorgio well, spent time with him and Louise off and on for several years. Once, I and an architect friend took Giorgio out for days in my Land Rover to see backwoods villages that Giorgio hadn't been able to reach. He was a wonderful man, an inspired artist. I never met his equal in reinventing buildings and salvaging materials. He's in my pantheon for sure."

After that, Carlo and I found much to exchange that only started with architectural design and construction. We finished tea having but scratched the surface and he generously invited me to join him for dinner.

I was particularly glad to have company for my first meal at Bettiswood. It was Saturday, the dining room was decorated for the holidays, and the weekend crowd was festive. I was not. A half-hour before dinner, Paloma had reached me with the sad news that Bessie had come down with what she herself called "a wretched chest." She had a fever and her doctor had put her on an antibiotic. Paloma told me the obvious: She would stay with Bessie until she could cope or until someone could be found to help her. She promised to keep in touch, then asked about a big envelope she'd sent to me at Bettiswood. "Not here," I replied. She sounded let down, but told me not to worry, she had the file on her laptop. I wished her and Bessie the best, but when we'd hung up, I felt disappointed and lonely.

At dinner that evening and on further acquaintance, Carlo provided thoughtful and engaging company. In repose, he had the look of a college don—intellectual, with a high forehead, prominent nose, and what I believe is often called "a piercing gaze." A laugh or smile transformed his features, gave him the air of a popular actor or athlete, open, jovial, very much at ease—I noticed his tendency to stress his sober side in his hotel duties. I also observed that he was on familiar terms with Bettiswood's owners. The other employees referred to them as Mr. and Mrs. Hillier, but Carlo unselfconsciously called them Bill and Anneke.

Sunday, December 29th

My encounter with Carlo Giordano resulted in four engrossing days during which I did less editing than I'd anticipated. During our conversations, I'd made plain that I had no formal background in architecture, but I did respond to Carlo's interest by telling him about the three houses I'd designed and built from scratch. That led him to ask if I'd care to see his project in detail, and then, with my encouragement, he laid out photographs, plans, and elevations of Villa Vigliano — the existing buildings, and those he and his sister proposed to develop. I appreciated the time and skill he'd employed to create detailed plans that allowed me to visualize his entire property.

A grand main house sat on a south-facing slope overlooking a valley and distant mountains. Five other structures were scattered off to the west, three lesser dwellings and two large storage buildings, all of stone and mortar in the more-than-substantial style of the region. Much work had already been done on the greater site — road building, and the gutting and stripping of all the structures to provide a clean start for Carlo's improvements.

Once I had the lay of the land, he took me through the steps of his agenda. First would be a remodel of the grand hall with administrative quarters, lobby, kitchen, dining room, bar, and a large public room located on its ground floor. For the second level, he had designed suites for himself and his sister, and several luxurious rooms for guests. Immediately to the west, a new structure would house a pool and exercise facilities, and next to that he planned two tennis courts and areas for lawn games. He proposed to remodel his five other buildings into a dozen suites.

Carlo sketched out the problems he foresaw, I raised some points that we kicked around, and he then asked me to review the whole project. That led to three days in which I fear that I occupied all the hours he could spare from his duties. And I accepted a further favor — Carlo was a bachelor and accustomed to eating alone, but now he was kind enough to take his meals with me.

Inevitably, our discussions broadened to include our lives and families — a survey in which I did not include my absent companion. Carlo gradually disclosed his sadness at how little of his family remained. He mentioned a brief marriage. Neither he nor his wife had been mature enough for such a commitment, they grew apart, their marriage was annulled, and they became strangers. He sounded pessimistic about marriage and family in his future. I got the impression that Carlo saw Villa Vigliano as the hearth and home he had not managed in the traditional way.

He also showed me two excellent photographs of a handsome woman much resembling him, radiant while smiling, rather pensive in repose.

"My sister Giulia, the last relative in my world. Really, Giulia has been to me a mother and a sister. She is only three years and one half older than my age, but all her life she has stepped in where our mother did not see what she needed to do, or probably did not have time for it. Our mother was a fine woman, really, very intellectual, always devoted to good works. My father was a structural engineer, and both of my parents were involved in historic preservation, very much active in ProFirenze, that is a group of people who work for preservation of historic parts of our city. Our mother was the real motor, so busy. When I had childish problems, it was so many times Giulia who put her arms around me or talked to me or did things with me to take me away from bad humors.

"In those times while we grew up, my sister and I, one of my father's most close friends had a son, Aldo his name, five years older than Giulia. Often he was in our home and so familiar that he was like one of us. He taught me to play tennis, he encouraged my swimming, and I worked hard and did well at these things, even in competitions. Aldo grew up to take an important position in the factory of his family. They made fine furniture, especially the best wooden chairs. When Giulia was nineteen, Aldo asked her to be his wife and our families were so happy and the next year they were married. Giulia seemed to all of us happy for five years, and they lived near us and visited us and included us in their social life.

"I was in my last year of study when our mother and father were killed, no, really it must have been my father's fault, driving off a mountain road in Udine. We were devastated of course, but another terrible thing came to us so short a time after that. Giulia's husband spent much time in other cities, he worked in those places with distributors and attended trade shows. Each year it seemed to all of us that he traveled more and more. When my parents were buried, right then, people began to bring me rumors, Aldo was traveling and sharing rooms with one young man, then it was another one. I could not keep these stories from Giulia, they came to her also from others. She was like someone frozen, she shivered, she did not eat or see people, only me. My father was gone, it was my job in every way to go to Aldo to make him end this double life that was killing Giulia. He saw me and he made no defense. He did not want to look at me. He agreed to turn this over to a lawyer and, I can tell you, we arranged an annulment and a settlement.

My sister locked herself away, she would see only two or three people, but she began to recoup and I began to see her smile again. Then it was, as you say, the rug was pulled from under her feet one more time. Two years after they separated, Giulia learned that Aldo was HIV-positive, really, he had AIDS. Giulia was again depressed — it is what you call 'shock'—all the time she waited to find out how it was with her. Finally they came to decide she was not infected, I thank God and all the saints, but I tell you it was a nightmare. Then, it was almost two years ago, this news came to us that Aldo put a shotgun in his mouth. I do not condemn this man for being homosexual, but he was a trusted friend of our family, and I confess, Mr. Talbot, I am not enough a Christian man to forgive him for what he did to Giulia. But I must add to this, he did send one type of message to my sister. He left to her whatever he had, not so much, really, because he had earned only a part of the business he might have owned.

"It was strange that our aunt and uncle died also that year, and Villa Vigliano came to us. It was so important to both of us. I was only a month or two separated from the woman who had been my wife. I can tell you, Giulia and I thanked our fortunes to have each other and before long we made jokes about being both of us married quite happily to the villa. It is the way we are now."

Apparently Carlo and his sister had always cherished the villa. They'd spent part of their youth on the grounds, visiting or staying with the childless uncle and aunt who eventually bequeathed it to them. The estate was once a grand family's country home and headquarters for a farm that raised cattle and sheep and forage. A majority of the original property had been sold off before the recent inheritance, leaving something under a hundred acres, much of it steep hillsides.

Carlo was studying Bettiswood because it too had a great house and outbuildings developed into desirable rental units. He'd introduced himself to the Hilliers and offered his services in return for the opportunity to study their practices and observe how they'd improved their holdings. I was fortunate to have caught him when I did. In a week or so he would finish his stint at Bettiswood, head back to Florence, and reassemble his remodeling crew.

Carlo and his sister hoped to do all the construction in one phase, but their finances might dictate a stepwise approach — first, the principal structure and the proposed gym plus the nearest farmhouse, and later the more distant buildings. We commiserated over the inevitable difficulties of funding new projects.

On the whole, I considered his program well conceived and his solutions intelligent. But after poring over Carlo's plans for hours, I felt that he was under-employing the grand area that lay before his hall and I had questions about access and the proportions and ceiling heights of some proposed rooms. I was flattered when Signor Giordano was more than polite in hearing me out, asked perceptive questions, took notes, and made quick sketches.

The morning after I arrived, I'd had a second call from Putney. Bessie was feeling better. Paloma apologized unnecessarily for the delay and, when I told her I was having a good time, I suspect she concluded that I was being a good scout — no real harm in that. She sounded cheerful and reported that she and Bessie were making up for lost time. Thereafter, she called regularly and opened her New Year's Day call by saying Bessie was much recovered, and I should come the following morning. A neighbor would give Bessie a hand so we could get away the day after and commence our travels.

Thursday, January 2nd

Carlo arranged an early breakfast, and when I presented myself in the quiet dining room, he joined me for a parting chat. Then I was off and into central London with no more or less travail than you expect in such a vast metropolis.

Bessie's neighborhood proved to be clean but amazingly barren, an extended vista of poles, wires, and similar small apartment buildings. Paloma must have been watching; she flew out the door and into my arms.

"Right here in the street?" I whispered in her ear.

She squeezed harder and told my shoulder, "Rules are made to be broken." We went in.

Bessie was an instant surprise. I had envisioned a large, motherly figure, walking with difficulty, but when we entered her small living room, she stood right up and stepped forward, a trim, sixtyish woman of medium height. Indeed, she had a trace of a limp, but her prosthesis had a remarkably functional ankle and I noticed later that she negotiated stairs with little difficulty. Beyond that, I soon observed that Bessie's personality fitted her sharp features, plain clothes, and severe hairdo. She came across as a bit of a stoic and not inclined to get or keep attention by means of disability or illness. She was well on the road to recovery and determined to send Paloma and me on our way.

Alas, I soon sensed that she was grimly determined. Evidently Paloma had kept her informed on most fronts, probably better informed than I'd care to know. She was polite, but it was plain that my presence made her uncomfortable, certainly my relationship with Paloma made her very uncomfortable. I was forcibly reminded of the similar awkwardness in meeting Nourrit, and from that I took my cue — if Bessie wouldn't take the bull by the horns, I must.

Before long she excused herself and I was able to remind Paloma of the rapport I'd gained with Nourrit, and to ask for an hour alone with Bessie. Accordingly, when Bessie returned, Paloma announced that she was off to pick up travel items she'd overlooked in packing, I fished out the car keys, and she took flight. Bessie acted neither surprised nor disturbed by Paloma's sudden departure, but neither did it loosen her tongue. "Very well," I thought, "here goes." I perched myself on the sofa facing her chair and dove in.

"Miss Barr, I'm at a disadvantage, or we're at a disadvantage — we don't know each other. Please let me use these minutes to tell you things I want you to know but I'm not ready to share with Paloma. I'm sure she's told you something about how and why she and I are together. I'm sure this doesn't please you and it may be worrying you. I'd be disappointed if it didn't."

Bessie acted more pained at each word. She kneaded her hands in her lap; she wasn't looking me in the eye, but when I paused, she opened up in a rush.

"Talk about me worrying. Worrying? Makes me that sick, and nothing to be done. The way Miss Paloma carries on with you and them others, what can I say? She's the most important thing for me, always has, but she's been gone too long and too far off for me to be any use. I pray for her, but how do I tell her what I think? Make a fuss and maybe lose her for good? And one of her men comes around, how'm I s'posed to feel? Try and be polite? Hide me feelings? It makes me proper sick to think of her carrying on with the likes of you. She was an angel child, but look what you're doing to her—the lot of you!"

Bessie sat stiffly and appeared ready for tears. Something needed to be done, and quickly, to right the ship.

"Please understand, I'm not here to make excuses. I'm a man, one of the men involved with Paloma, no argument. But things may not be exactly as you imagine. I first met Paloma last September. I had nothing to do with leading her astray, I found her that way. It's easy to say that I shouldn't have taken up with her, but I lost my wife two years ago after forty years of marriage. I was lonely and when I got acquainted with Paloma, it was all innocent. But when she told me how I could go on seeing her, I took the step. And listen, I'll never regret that. You know and I know Paloma's a valuable person even if she is off course. After we met, I traveled with her—you must know about that—and I learned more about her, a lot more. And that changed my feelings and my thinking. I got to the point where I wanted to help Paloma, not take advantage of her. Now I'm trying to figure out how to steer her into something she can enjoy and be proud of. Coming to see you was my idea. I wanted to know you because I need your help, Paloma needs your help. She needs to make big changes. I know it's hard for you to trust me—after all, I'm one of 'them'—but I'll bet I'm the only one trying to do what I'm sure you want. I'm looking you in the eye and promising to try to get her to see that this goal of hers, this financial independence thing, is what's keeping her from having a real life."

I was surprised at Bessie's calm. After a moment to take it all in, she sounded almost apologetic.

"I never expected to hear this from a living soul, never. I'm thanking you, and I pray it's all true and there's something can be done. It's hurt, all this time not knowing what to do meself, and nobody to turn to. What she's doing is wrong, and all these men ought to know better, she should know better! It's the same sort of thing her mum did, or something like, it seems to me, and she had a terrible time of it. But what's somebody in my place do? Miss Paloma's men are the sort that gets looked up to. She's sent me things about 'em cut out of papers and magazines, and she brought me a book you did. But that don't make it right. That chap she had here two years back, I'm no fool, he was smart and educated, polite too, chatted me up nice as you please, treated me like a lady — but I hated meself after, me smiling and pretending everything was fine." Bessie looked as if she'd bitten into a lemon.

"No question, Paloma put you in a tough spot, and what else could you have done? Human relations aren't easy, especially this kind, the absentee parent kind. Nobody has to tell me that all these years apart have been long and lonely for you."

For a moment she seemed faraway, but she snapped back. "Last time she left, it was like she'd been here trying me out. Second time I'd set eyes on her since she she'd been eight, and here she was, like the first time, a man with her. This time's different, her coming alone and more like she is when she writes. I feel that much better about her and me, except this makes it harder yet to say what I think."

Bessie had relaxed, her unclenched hands and her tone suggested that I was now tolerated, provisionally perhaps, but tolerated. I tried to reassure her further. "Look, there's no need for you to go into this with her, not now. I'm still figuring out my arguments and how to sell them to her. Why don't you let me make a start and I'll let you know how it goes. That'll help you to decide what you could do to push her along. It's not going to be easy to change her mind, though. Her plans are all based on what she's doing now."

Bessie shook her head. "That's so. She's sent me money six years now, says it's out of what come to her when her mum and that Swedish fella died. She must need it herself though, else why's she's doing what she's doing? I've tried to get her to stop sending it, though, mind you, it's a help. Take this place. I'd never be living here without, but I'd get by, needs must. But she won't have it. Says if I won't let her chip in now, she'll just save it up for me. There it is then, daft, me part of the problem."

As she spoke, I could hear her thinking shift, hear her joining me. I looked her in the eye and offered my sympathy, but in my head it was, "Thank you, Bessie Barr. Thank you for not shutting me out."

"Listen," I rejoined, "Paloma's let me know a dozen different ways how much she loves you and how grateful she is. It's the same with her friend in Spain. You can't stop that, and you wouldn't want to. If we're going to talk her out of this way of living, we don't want to be against the things that make her feel useful. We need to go after the things she's not happy about. It's a good sign, Paloma bringing me to meet you and Nourrit. It's as if she's putting the tools in my hands. Now you can help. When she's back, tell me more about the years you were together."

"Mr. Talbot, I'll do what I can. It's a comfort, somebody else thinking all this. That's something. Like I said, I'll pray it works out right. I'll pray for you as well."

"Thank you. We need all the help we can get. And could you call me 'Haley'? May I call you 'Bessie'?" She nodded and might even have looked pleased.

By then I was fidgeting over the time; I wanted to get on to some less loaded topic before Paloma got back. I asked about Bessie's current affairs. She wanted to pass that off with a few words, but after a bit of prompting she got down to cases, first with her budding career as a bookkeeper, "minding the books," she called it. She started with a local bakery, then parlayed her success into a similar one-day-a-week job with a florist-garden shop. More recently, she'd added two days with a local landlord and was as busy as she cared to be, since she also was doing volunteer work for her church. It was this innocuous talk to which Paloma returned, so my grand deception worked.

Oddly, with Paloma back, our conversation went awkwardly. Paloma and Bessie shared years of togetherness and correspondence, Paloma and I had laid in a surprising store of shared ideas and experiences, but regardless of our best intentions, we had little potential for a three-cornered exchange. Luckily, it was time for Paloma to put the finishing touches on the lunch she'd been preparing when I arrived.

We all crowded into the miniature kitchen-breakfast room, talk was blessedly low key and domestic, and before long we sat down to adeptly seasoned aspic salads and expertly roasted vegetables. I was amused to find myself thinking of Paloma's years with Consuelo, and feeling like something of an insider.

When we'd eaten, the cook went to wash up in the kitchen and I sat with Bessie and asked her to tell me about getting started with the infant Paloma. She gave me a conspiratorial look, almost a wink, and took up her tale.

"The first I knew, Mr. George Inskip rung me up from Spain, told me Miss Celia needed me to help when she'd come to Putney with a new baby. I said I might do, nevermind I had work at a bakery — didn't pay much, that, and me missing Miss Celia. Y'see, it'd been eight years since they was off to Spain and she'd come to see me only that once he brought her, some affair of his. So I said yes to Mr. George and he sent someone over with keys to the old place and I went straight around to put it in order after the last renters. There was boxes stored up from what we'd had before, none of 'em Miss Celia's baby things, but no matter that. I had Mr. George's orders and I guessed what they'd need and got everything ready as I could.

"Well, he called the day before and told me Miss Celia'd be coming in, she'd be brought to the house but he didn't say the time, so I was there hours till they finally come, three of 'em, some woman my age or so, Miss Celia, and Miss Paloma in a basket. The woman didn't stay long. Handed Miss Celia a briefcase, give her a hug, and then picked up the baby and held her up to her face and smiled at her and told her to have a good life. Shook me hand, she did, and said, like she knew me, she was glad to see me getting on so well, then she left. A bit rum, that, sticks in me mind. And all that time, Miss Celia looked worn out, like she needed to get to bed, so I packed her straight off.

"Then it was downstairs for the baby, me thinking how she'd never made a peep. Well, surprise of me life! Waiting, she was, those huge great eyes looking right at me. The second we saw each other, she smiled a big smile. Ten days old and me ten feet off! I'll tell you, the hair on me neck stood up and I went over and took her up and we was together for good and all.

"Right off, I could see it'd be me to bring her up, but I tried not to think of meself as her mum, that'd be wrong. I'd always call her 'Miss Paloma' to keep a distance. Well, that might sound proper to others, but it didn't work, y'know. Fact was, 'Miss Paloma' just got to be a pet name. She'd smile and bat her eyes at me and I'd sit there and crow, 'Oh, Miss Paloma, Miss Paloma,' and she'd grin and chuckle so."

The subject of all this rejoined us and the look on Bessie's face suggested that she still saw that happy baby when her eyes fell on the grown woman. The grown woman, however, declined to sit. "Look," she announced, "you two are better off alone and I'm feeling a bit housebound. Carry on, and I'm off for a walk. Back shortly." She got her wrap and let herself out.

"Bless her," Bessie sighed, "been fussing over me for days here, all cooped up. And her so active, I guess you know." I admitted that I did, then leaned forward and looked expectant. Bessie had no trouble picking up her story.

"So that's the way it was, the three of us together, but Miss Celia didn't do much of nothing, didn't want to be the baby's mum, didn't want to do the things that needed doing, didn't even care for the good things neither, like playing or reading with baby. It wasn't she didn't love her, deep down I think she did, but she was just a girl yet and couldn't bear to have charge of baby, specially by herself. She'd come up when we'd be doing things, she'd chat and watch, or I'd be holding Miss Paloma and Miss Celia'd tickle her and seem glad to hear her giggle or squeak, the way she'd do. Anyhow, way it was, I had to be the mum. And then Miss Celia was gone a lot, off with those friends of hers, sometimes weekends, sometimes weeks on end."

Bessie's story made me wonder about Chely's influence on Paloma. Everything I'd heard about Paloma's mother made her sound frivolous. Doubtless she deserved anything she got from the Utrera family, but it sounded as if she settled for that and little else. As Bessie had said, Chely had been a kept woman herself, or at best, not much more than a plaything for men. But that wasn't the time for questions, Bessie's tale was far from done.

"All that time, I knew Miss Paloma was s'posed to've come out of some devilment, but she was the angel child, I swear. All that time she's growing and changing so, no mischief never, never lied nor held nothing back, never pouted or cried unless she'd be hurt, and not much then. And she always tried to help out, and she was quick to learn.

"When it come time for her to start over at playgroup, I was the one to go make out her papers and then I'd see she got there every day and had what she'd need. I'd be the one when it come time for parents' days, or go to see programs. Then she was off to real school and there was more to do, more meetings and so. But y'see, I never minded. I'd been doing it so long it felt like me job, and it was just part of me and her. And I'd be so proud, I tell you, there was times I'd be fit to burst. I'd go to those parents' evenings and there'd be mothers there, but I'd know I was getting the best reports. The Sisters was all glad to have me little girl and they praised her for more'n good work, said she never tried to look clever, never made another girl look bad. On rainy days, Sister Marie Clare — she's the one like me, hurt in the bombing — she'd have the children inside, dancing in lines and circles like they did way back. With Miss Paloma, that first year at school, Sister noticed how quick she'd pick up those fancy moves and pretty soon figured she could be a help with the rest. Sister called Paloma her 'right hand,' but it was more like her left, y'see that's the one hurt so bad. The tall Sister, I forget her name, the one as ran the choir, she told me she'd always hear Paloma's voice, 'Strong,' she'd say, 'in tune, and on time.' All those years at Saint Anne's, never a sister told me one problem or wanted changes made. I felt blessed and I was so proud of her, the way I said.

"Mr. Talbot — sorry, Haley — talking like this about how it was with me and Miss Paloma puts me all atremble. I might sound like an old fool, but, y'know, it's all true. Saddest thing ever for me was her father dying, and her and Miss Celia having to go off like that. The bottom dropped out of me world, it was like I'd lost me own child and best friend, all rolled up in one. It was true, you know. We'd come to chat like grownups, she being such a wise little owl."

Bessie stopped for a moment, thinking. "You want to see something? I'll show you how it was." She stood and headed up to her bedroom. She beckoned me in and pointed to a small oil painting on her best-lighted wall, clearly a portrait of Paloma as a child — a beautiful child holding a blond doll. "Miss Daphne, she was a friend of Miss Celia's right along, she painted that when Miss Paloma was six, had her to keep her mouth shut 'cuz she had front teeth out. Well, that day they was off to Spain, I couldn't stand to see that picture. I put it out of sight, but that was worse. So you know what I done? Took it to the kitchen we had in that place and put it on the table. And Paloma'd left me Helen to be me little girl in her place — Helen's her doll you see in the picture. So I propped Helen up on the table too, and I'd take tea with her and the picture, just like Paloma had Helen to take tea with us when she was small. So that's how it was with me — they was all I had."

Bessie headed back down to the parlor, and when we were seated, she went on.

"So, they was gone and I was that lost, but what's the good of mistrusting God's will? I looked around for work, but even so I'd be so lonely I'd go to the orphanage and volunteer to fill up the time I wasn't at me job. But it was children and I was some use, I expect. Not that long after, they gave me a job and I was there two years till I began to get over missing me little girl every minute, every day."

She was fighting back tears and I wished I could comfort her. I wanted to say, "Bless you, Bessie, you gave Paloma everything Celia couldn't, and a lot more.' But all I could do was try to look sympathetic, and she did pull herself together.

"D'you know she's written most every week, sixteen years now? Real letters, long ones, some goes on for pages? Day she left, she looked me in the eye and promised to write. Can you see an eight-year-old setting out to do that? I've got every one, and y'know, these last years it seems like they've come from every place on earth. It might sound daft, but I read 'em over and over. I expect that's what you do with no child of your own.

"And she was that cheerful, every letter, telling me about her grandma and that African woman and all the help she was. I was jealous of her first off, but I ended up grateful, and she's in me prayers. It was months before Miss Paloma sent a picture of her with that woman, all that time me thinking she'd be like the West Indians we'd been getting round here, but there she was, tall and dignified like she was some queen of the Nile. I'll tell you, not what I expected at all."

There was a moment of silence, and before I could offer proper thanks, Bessie stood up and stretched. "I'm going to make tea," she announced, and headed for the kitchen. I followed, and before it was brewed, Paloma was back. That was it for intense reminiscences. We devoted the remainder of the day to an excursion the two of them had planned, and to a dinner out. Back home, the ladies excused themselves and left me to open the sofa into a bed.

    I composed myself, but couldn't sleep, and not because of the murmurs drifting down from the bedroom. Bessie was another milestone in my journey, a sympathetic person, resolute, principled, and plucky beyond belief. I'd been fascinated and touched by her story, but as I lay there thinking back, it became more personal. Especially the gut-wrenching picture of Paloma being taken away from her, forever, and the haunting thought of Bessie's solitude. Here was a woman with no family and precious little else, who was entrusted with a newborn child, raised her devotedly for eight years, then, without warning, found herself bereft. I recalled my own placid, almost detached experiences with parenthood. I thought, probably for the first time, about the degree to which Marian had raised our children, and to which I'd been an appreciative audience, accepting our daughters as a matter of course, but seldom volunteering to take much responsibility. All those years later, I lay on a couch in a foreign land and felt negligent and remorseful over those lost opportunities.

    Before I went to sleep, something else nagged at me, something about Paloma's evolution. Bessie, for all her virtues, struck me as a rather limited person, not full of curiosity, not probing in her thoughts. I realized that just when those shortcomings might have begun to inhibit Paloma's development, she was taken away from Bessie and delivered to Nourrit—or, as Nourrit would have it, they were delivered to each other. I thought of Nourrit, all I'd seen and heard, and what an open window she had proved, open to this world and beyond. Was all that a coincidence, a happenstance? I thought not. It reinforced my conviction that, in some unaccountable way, Paloma really was destiny's child.

Friday, January 3rd

We all got up early. The kitchen was again hard-pressed to accommodate the three of us, but no way would I miss the fun. I sat as observer and sipped coffee while the reunited twosome whipped up breakfast, much clatter, and many smiles. While we ate and cleaned up, a pale winter sun came up over a bank of haze and transformed the look of the day. Paloma gazed out approvingly — she'd found shortages in the larder, and today she was going to fill the gaps. She'd planned to take us too, but when she saw my interest in Bessie's stories, she decided that we should stay home to talk. I handed over the car keys and she was gone.

Bessie made us a fresh pot of tea, brought it to the sitting room, and took her chair with the air of one preparing to visit with an old acquaintance. I felt promoted, and decided it was the time to learn more about Paloma's mother.

"Bessie, yesterday you told me how Miss Celia didn't get involved with raising Paloma, not in the day-to-day chores, not in school, and not in church. What I wondered was, what did she do? You've mentioned she had men friends, but was that all she did, go out and socialize with them?"

"Not all, no. Miss Celia had some girl friends all right, and she'd go off with 'em, shopping and lunch and the like, but they was mostly the same crowd as the young fellas. Sometimes they'd all get together and go off somewhere. It was sad, y'see, Miss Celia having a baby before she'd had time to be a proper young woman. Had it hard right from the start, really, her mum dying when she was born and all. Mr. George brought her home and give her to that nanny woman, Mrs. Kinkead, then I come in a week or two after, and we tried to be her mum together, you might say. Mr. George wouldn't stay around that much and didn't do much when he was. Lots of nights, he never come home — stayed at that club of his, he said. He was an odd one. No interest in the house as long as it was properly cleaned, no interest in his daughter — well, we thought she was his — except she'd be kept sweet-smelling and proper dressed up. Took no interest till she got into school, then he'd ask her what she did all day and listen to as much as she'd tell. That last year before they went off to Spain, he'd take her out to lunch some weekends, then it'd be the zoo or some museum. But he mostly left it up to Miss Fairley—she was the second nanny—then me. All the last three years, the only live-in was me.

"I didn't get into school things with Miss Celia the way I did with Miss Paloma—it weren't me place when Miss Celia started. Mr. George, he sometimes went to school and met teachers and all, but neither of us, him or me, really kept up. Miss Celia just went and that was that. She must've done well enough—no real complaints come home, only now and then a suggestion. I can't say what happened with Miss Celia's school in Spain, but I s'pose that was all right too. She got through, but it took her that extra year, I s'pose to take up Spanish. Now, Miss Paloma went over there and never a problem. But y'see, she was a whole different story right from the start.

"Miss Celia and I always got on good, but she didn't seem that upset when she left, and I hardly heard from her—Mr. George neither—I guess I had half a dozen cards and notes in the eight years from her going off, then coming back with Miss Paloma. But we took up again all right, and she was glad to have me here to help, but, like I said, she mostly wanted to get out of the house and go off to play with her friends. Or more like play acting, really, pretending she wasn't a mum and hadn't a baby at home. But I was sorry for her, even not knowing back then what all had happened."

"That's kind of you, Bessie. Lots of others would've condemned Miss Celia for not getting more involved with her baby."

"P'raps so, but the truth is, I needed the job and it was a place to live, and then, first I knew, Miss Paloma was me life. I'm not ashamed to say it was no time till I didn't feel too bad when Miss Celia went out and left us be."

She paused to sip tea, then hesitated. "Am I going on too much?"

"Bessie, you were Paloma's real mother and I'd like to hear anything you can tell me. As long as we've got the time, nothing's too much. It'd be a great story for anybody who's cared for a small child." She seemed encouraged.

"Fact is, something happened right off, happened when Miss Celia come down with a fever just days after she was back to Putney, and they took her to hospital and left me alone with baby. The place was that quiet, I'd feel Miss Paloma's heart beat whilst I give her the bottle. Then she'd spit it out, seem restless like, roll her head around and nuzzle up to me. It got me thinking how she'd never been suckled, that not being to Miss Celia's liking. I hugged her to me and, not really thinking that much, I opened me dress and let her get to me. She took hold straight off and started to look at me sidewise right in the eye while she sucked away. Even when she'd be real sleepy, she'd open her eyes now and again to catch my look." Bessie sat up and appeared to check my reaction. I leaned forward and tried to look as receptive as I felt.

"Well, she took to it so, and seemed like there'd be no harm in it, so I let her have a go every time we sat down to the bottle. She'd take that awhile and then root for me. A few days more and I started these odd feelings. One morning, it pained me like I'd swelled up and was going to burst. The baby started in and gulped away. Bless me, that had me floored. I didn't know such a thing could happen, it was like being there for a miracle, that, and all the feelings she stirred up. First off, I felt like I'd done wrong. But every time, she'd just settle in and keep her eyes on me, and I felt better, lovely, really, and somehow I knew it couldn't be so wrong.

"First chance, I went to ask 'em at the clinic and I got a regular lecture from a woman there as wanted every baby on mother's milk. She changed me diet, changed me ways, really, it's been vegetables and more vegetables ever since. Well, Miss Paloma nursed eight months or so till she took to solid food and mostly lost interest. It'd got so I looked forward to it — it felt good, the whole thing, and made me feel a different position in the house, though that's hard to explain. The odd part was, when Miss Celia come back from the hospital and saw me nursing — I had no place to hide, y'see — she didn't seem to find it strange. I think she was too innocent to know what to make of it. I found out, though, that it don't happen much, what happened to me, most people don't know such things can be. But it did, right enough, and I figure it was part of the thing with me and Miss Paloma. Always her way to make things happen.

"Queer thing, this. For years now, me not telling a soul, and here it is, second time in a week. Y'see, just this visit, Miss Paloma and me chatting here, it all come out. Before now I'd never brought it up, wouldn't have been right, her so young and all, and then all them years of letter writing it never seemed like something to go back to. Who'd have thought she'd be so taken with it? She hugged me and made me feel more like her mum than I've ever hoped."

Alas, I hadn't learned much about Chely's ways, and before I could get back to that, Paloma stepped in with bags of kitchen miscellany. But when she started to look for places to put it all away, Bessie would have none of it. She knew our trip hadn't started and she ordered us out, said she wanted to store things herself anyhow. So we made a final round to collect our gear, and exchanged a flurry of last-minute thoughts during our goings and comings.

When all our things were in the entry, I held out my arms to Bessie. She hesitated, then held up hers, and I gave her a long, gentle hug and whispered "thank you" in her ear. I thanked her aloud for receiving me and sharing her memories. She reached up and patted me on the chest, a friendly pat, and one I took as a reminder of our unfinished business. I imagined what her next feelings might be, when she said good-bye to Paloma and watched her go, the emotions of one who has lost a lot, had little, and made do—another sort of survivor. The two of them were long in parting. Paloma came out with wet eyes and left Bessie in the same state. Then it was waves all around and we were off.

Paloma was quiet as we worked our way out of Putney. Finally, we stopped at a light and she caught my eye.

"Haley, thank you. Thank you for Christmas. The people I know best all have family commitments around the holidays. The last three or four years, I've spent Christmas eve and Christmas day in my complex with two women who have no families, my counterparts but older. That's all right, but it's a little sad. I hope you have some idea how much this get-together meant to me and Bessie."

She sounded a bit down, so I took a new tack. "You're so welcome. You know how taken I was with your people in Sevilla—well, I'm hooked on your past, and this step was a must. And I haven't thanked you for your gift to me, or my new status, if that's what it is. You *were* all I wanted this holiday season. Little Jack Horner couldn't be more pleased." That took her by surprise and she was flustered.

"No, it's embarrassing to call my presence a gift, what can I say? But I wanted you to know how special our times together have been. Couldn't we let it go at that, and just get on with the fun we were having?"

"Listen, I never stopped having fun. And with your past thrown in, I'm having more fun than humans are usually allowed. Let's press our luck and go for more." I swept my arm to the west.

Once we were launched on the M3 and the going was open and smooth, Paloma's reflections returned to Putney. "I got to Bessie's early afternoon on Christmas Eve. Of course we were glad to see each other, and we had a bite with tea and sat around, but I didn't feel we'd truly got together. Bessie seemed so stiff, so contained, that it didn't feel as if we were family or even friends. Her speech was in that overly respectful form, as if she were 'addressing her betters,' as they used to say. So I asked her what was wrong. 'Oh, nothing wrong,' she said, and she insisted she was thrilled to see me, but I could tell I'd made her more uncomfortable by asking. So now everything was wrong. It was as if we had a glass wall between us, like the ones between inmates and visitors in old prison movies. That brought tears to my eyes. I sat down on the sofa and took her in my arms and just sort of burst out with 'Something's wrong and it hurts me something hijjus!' *Just So Stories* was the last thing I read to her before I was dragged off to Spain."

"'The Elephant's Child,' right?"

"Exactly. So then I was well and truly in tears. Bessie just sat there all stiff, then she came apart too, and we cried on each other's shoulders for I don't know how long. Finally she pulled back and touched my cheek ever so lightly. Strange, she looked younger, all her wrinkles had smoothed out and she had a new little smile that came to her off and on the rest of my stay. She told me that all those years since I was taken away, she'd had no life, she'd just gone through the motions every day. She said she knew I wasn't hers, she had no right to me, but I was all she'd ever had and all she ever loved. It broke my heart. Then she got a little hysterical telling me how she'd turned on God and asked him how he could take away all she had a second time. It came out that she then considered herself a great sinner. She said Father Peter had been wonderful about that, told her God still loved her and His house would be poorer without her.

"When she'd calmed down, I told her I'd never left her in spirit, I was her little girl returned, and somehow we'd be together in the future. I meant it, even if I don't know how to make it happen. Then I said we should go to pray and celebrate the birth of Jesus. So we went to Mass. And that night we slept together and I held her in my arms.

"The next day I tried to think and act as much like her Miss Paloma as I could without being maudlin or silly. We had a great day. We toasted the cake she'd got for my visit, we exchanged gifts, and then we took the bus down to the orphanage for the Christmas party. I met young people she'd tended when they were small, and everybody was sweet to her and the whole thing was a big success.

"The next day Bessie was down sick, but it only meant that we had to visit between naps. Two days of that and Bessie took my hand and told me she hadn't really believed I was back for her, but now she truly did. And then she seemed to get better every hour. By the time you came, she was back to normal, or nearly so. Anyhow, I'm so grateful for this opportunity. That first day, I was just crushed. I was afraid we'd never reach each other again. Now that's past and we've finally got back to a face-to-face relationship. I suppose I'll never feel entirely whole separated from Bessie and Nourrit, but I do feel better."

We set Putney aside and I told her about my sessions with Carlo. She concluded that he'd done his homework when he sought out the owners of Bettiswood Hall, people she admired.

We rolled up to the Hall in time for a late lunch. Carlo was off someplace, the porter had no idea where. We followed our bags to the room, which I was looking forward to showing off. When we turned into the short hall, Paloma stopped, put her hands on her hips, and mounted a great frown. "Can you believe it? Eighteen rooms and I get the same one all three times! Good thing it's so nice, but even so, a girl doesn't like to be pigeonholed."

We had a sandwich in the sunroom, then went our ways, I to check on a rumor that Carlo was supervising work on a cottage, she to our room to put her things away. I ran Carlo down and found him not just supervising, but applying two-part filling materials a step ahead of a painter. We arranged to meet later. Back at the Hall, near the reception desk, I came upon a large, blond, open-faced woman I'd seen in a photograph, Anneke Hillier. We introduced ourselves and she shifted to confidential tones.

"I understand you're here with Paloma. Thank God you *are* with her. You wouldn't believe how bowled over I was—stepped into the lobby and there she was, all by herself. I thought, 'My God, she's come back for whatever bit of Bill she didn't spirit away last time!' Imagine my relief when I heard she was firmly in tow."

"Whoa, you're way ahead of me. When has Paloma been vamping Bill?"

"Oh, she needn't do a thing. Has him twisted around her little finger just by being here. No, just by existing, I think."

I chuckled, "Believe me, I relate to that. But isn't it a trifle hard on you?"

"Oh, not really. I'll grant you it's sobering for a not-so-young wife to have some stunner simply walk in and take over, but I can live without his attention a few days now and again. And seriously, Mr. Talbot, we love Paloma, and I feel literally in her debt."

I raised my eyebrows and Anneke plunged on. "Her first time here, Bill hovered over her in scandalous fashion—had his fun and it seemed to flatter her gentleman friend. But you know Paloma, how blunt she can be. She pushed Bill back a couple of feet when he was being attentive, and she made pointed remarks, all very sweetly, about her distaste for tobacco breath. Well, you wouldn't know, and she didn't know, but I and all Bill's friends had worked away for ages to get him to quit smoking. I dropped it twenty years ago. As God is my witness, after Paloma'd had her say, Bill never took another puff, that day to this. She came back the year after, and we'd only had a few words when she held out her hand and congratulated him. She knew straight off! Bill asked, 'Don't I get a kiss then?' And Paloma said, 'Just one,' and she leaned forward and puckered up. My Bill thought he'd died and gone to heaven. Now he's out showing off the garden she helped him plan. Turned out rather well, you know."

Before I had a chance to wonder at Paloma laying out gardens, Anneke invited me to join them for tea and hauled me off to the sunroom. We'd no more than seated ourselves when Paloma and Bill trooped in. It was windy outside and Paloma's hair was blown about. Anneke treated Bill to a growl and reproached him for tousling maidens behind the greenhouse. We all had a chuckle, and then the three of them traded news of their recent lives and saw to it that I was drawn in and brought up to speed—great fun all around. These were manifestly bright, good-natured people who knew how to direct a fine kitchen and a gracious inn. Furthermore, our little get-together made me realize that I'd come over so focused on meeting Bessie that I'd lost sight of the conventional pleasures you associate with a vacation abroad.

Back in our room, Paloma became persuasively amorous and wanted attention. A vision of all my high resolve flashed before me, but I felt helpless, caught off base. I had seen no opportunity to broach the subject of a changed relationship, much less persuade the woman holding the cards. Well, the timing was bad, but the prospect was irresistible, heightened in some perverse way by my unease. We stripped where we stood and took each other in a tender embrace, at first promising, then tantalizing, then simply ecstatic—the pinnacle of our brief affair, but a guilty bliss that left me disoriented. I confess my reluctance to break our satisfied entwinement and dress for dinner. Thereafter, along with twinges from my nagging conscience, I felt, and imagined I sensed in her, a soft carry-over of contentment that lingered the entire evening. My resolve and my campaign had suffered a double setback.

Dinner was a congenial affair celebrating our hosts' return from Holland and Paloma's return to their hospitality. Carlo joined us and I introduced him to Paloma, but he then acted subdued throughout the meal, odd for him and difficult to equate with his imminent return to Italy. After dessert and coffee, our hosts pled travel weariness and excused themselves. Our busy day caught up with us too, and we soon climbed the stairs and began to peel.

Minutes later, I looked into the dressing area and found my ladylove in her nightgown posturing in front of the mirror.

She laughed. "Caught in the act, projecting, sort of like you all and your Pup."

I looked expectant and she went on.

"This goes back to little me in Putney, the day Bessie took me to my mamá's tall mirror and asked me, 'Who do you see then?' 'Paloma,' I said. 'No,' she said, 'that's not Paloma, you're Paloma, you're out here in this room and she's in another room you can only look into. But she's your best friend. If you smile, she'll smile. If you sneak up and peek in, she'll be sneaking up and peeking back. She'll never leave you." Bessie told me I must take care of my best friend, and I'd do that by taking care of myself. As long as I was well and happy, so she would be. If I were lonesome, she'd understand and be lonesome too.

"Well, I already knew about reflections, but after that I thought about how I was responsible for that other little girl. Whenever anything bad happened or I felt threatened, I'd look in the mirror to see whether she was all right. Sometimes she was the only one I had to talk to, and even if she looked sad, she stood there solid and whole, and it cheered me up to see her. I'd say, 'We're still here, we're going to carry on, and things will get better.'

"And I share my joys with her too — look at today! I left Bessie feeling we'd finally got back together, you and I had a lively tea and dinner with friends, and we made love. So I looked in to see if she's as happy as I feel."

"Well, she certainly looked delighted last I saw. And, cross my heart, I'll never flirt with her behind your back."

I got a not too little-girl kiss before she hopped into her bed.

"Good night!"

Almost an hour later, I awoke to see Paloma motionless before her computer. She yawned and headed for the bathroom. On an impulse, I rolled out, grabbed my glasses, and peeked at the tail end of her work, three lines at the top of an otherwise blank screen.

> part of me waiting, suffused, expectant. Yes. Right to the heart of it. Lightly. Lightly. Gentle trigger, great waves. Here's your only-imagined art object, under your touch, enshrined, inflamed. That's special. I'll never lose it. Don't you.

I read it again, trying to memorize the enigmatic words but terrified of being caught. I retreated to bed, and none too soon. There was a sound of running water, Paloma emerged, turned off her machine, and promptly drifted off. But I lay trembling for some time. A young woman's poetry? A message for me? An arrow shot into the air? Regardless, I promised myself that I would never lose it — never.

Saturday, January 4th

I can't say I was surprised to wake and find Paloma leaning over me.

"Guess what? Before I march you around my favorite paths, I can show you where the predawn coffee lurks. Like some?"

As a matter of fact, recognizing the inevitable when it's set before me, I would like coffee first. Minutes later, two bundled up guests moved stealthily down the stair, through the public rooms, and into the kitchen. Surprise! The lights were on, and sitting at an ample table were Carlo and a junior cook. After a word and a gesture, we were seated and sipping some of the good, strong, start-the-day stuff. Carlo appeared to have shaken off whatever blues had afflicted him the night before, and as we hobnobbed, we invited him to breakfast with us, and he invited us — Paloma, really — to look over his plans. We drained our mugs and went our ways, minus the cook, who stayed behind to conjure his admirable morning magic.

Paloma and I stepped out into a brisk, barely dawn outside world, and she led me down the road, off to the west, and up a ridge, all on a neatly kept footpath. I admired stone-and-mortar culverts, low walls, and other conveniences put in place for the walkers, birdwatchers, botanists, and so forth among Bettiswood's guests. We made our way up an easy slope soaking up rural charm — the faint crow of a rooster, the odor of wood smoke hanging in the air, the sweet, distant pealing of church bells.

On the ridge, after some minutes of cold-nosed, hands-in-pockets waiting, we witnessed the winter sunrise, the apparition of a glowing, rosy ball hovering over an otherwise black and white world. I was allowed to stand behind a most appreciative audience, encircle her with my arms, and breathe the air resident in cold hair. When the spectacle no longer justified the chill, we retraced our steps to the warmth and cheer of the slowly filling dining room.

Carlo came in, I urged him to lay out his vision for Villa Vigliano, and he proceeded with the gusto that his project stimulated. In fact, I noticed that his new audience elicited details I had not yet heard. When we'd eaten, we picked up our cups and moved on to Carlo's office for Paloma's further indoctrination. He began with an aerial layout of the entire acreage, then photos of existing structures and other parts of the property to be developed. He followed with plots of the various groups of buildings, and plans and elevations of individual structures, and finally walked us, room by room, through a large plan of his main building.

Paloma cut in, surprising Carlo. "I see what you've done for pantry and kitchen storage, but what about housekeeping? What about spaces for things like linens on each floor? And what do you propose for cleaning equipment and mop basins and all that?"

Carlo smiled and relaxed, delighted to get into specifics. He pointed out locations and outlined his plans for storage and service facilities. When Paloma tried to pin him down on yet more details, he admitted a little vagueness on some of the minutia. He asked her how she would answer her own questions, and when she gave him an idea or two, he characteristically took notes. I could see how tickled he was to find his project interesting another newcomer. And then he treated us like friends or colleagues as he went into the pros and cons of developing the inn step by step. He added insights into the difficulties of borrowing money for their venture. He and Giulia would have to enlist investors to provide nearly a third of the two million dollars they would need in hand to get the loan that would finish the job.

Before we knew it, an hour had passed and Carlo and I were sidetracked with details he'd worked up while I was off to Putney. Paloma tolerated that like a sport for a few minutes, then excused herself to go looking for Anneke. Carlo watched her retreat, observed softly, "Magnificent woman," and returned to our deliberations. In another half hour, he had to excuse himself. Duty called, and he had chores of his own to complete before his morning-after-next departure.

Paloma was not to be seen downstairs and our room was vacant. Lacking other diversions, I pulled out my neglected manuscript and tried to re-immerse myself. Shortly before noon, my roommate reappeared, her face flushed.

"*¿Qué pasó?*" I asked.

"The stovehouse," she said, "you know, the greenhouse, glasshouse."

"What about it?"

"We started to clean it up. Anneke lent me a smock and I gave her a hand. We emptied some of last year's pots out, brushed 'em, 'n stacked 'em. Even took down some shade material left up from summer and had a go at washing algae off the insides of the glass. Unbelievable fun. Now it's time to dress for a meal I've actually earned. Care to join me then?"

I tried to look slighted. "I was hoping you'd ask. Ever so kind of you."

"Least I could do," she said, and dived for the shower.

We had a quiet lunch and a quieter afternoon as we worked at our laptops, did a little reading, and shared a visit to the Jacuzzi. At one point, Anneke called Paloma away to discuss menu planning, but before long she returned with the news that we'd be joining a couple from a neighboring estate at the Hilliers' table for dinner. Moreover, she whispered, she and Bill had cooked up some sort of surprise. "Surprise?" I puzzled. "Yes," she said, "don't ask." So it was that we prepared for the cocktail hour by getting into our best garb — smashing in her case, barely adequate in mine. As dinner progressed, we welcomed the neighbors' addition to the give and take we already enjoyed with our hosts, the rapport so easily developed between people who travel widely and take a lively interest in all they see.

When the dessert dishes were empty, Bill invited our table and the twelve or fifteen other guests for after-dinner drinks in the sitting room next to the bar. When everyone was served and settled down, Bill rose to speak.

"Dear guests, ladies and gentlemen, let me introduce our friend Paloma Grey. She's visited us before and proved she can tune my old guitar. If we encourage her, perhaps she'll show us how it sounds." A smattering of polite applause followed, and Paloma smiled and stepped over to a tall stool under a downlight. She accepted the guitar from Bill, and sat.

Well, I'd been warned that something was afoot, but I must say I was surprised. I thought to myself, "Good for you, Bill, for getting Paloma out of her shell."

After looking down at the instrument during an almost uncomfortably long pause, Paloma looked up and spoke in her rich voice, "I was giving thanks to José María Tamaral, a good and patient man who tried to teach me to play. He left us a few weeks ago. God keep him."

The first of four brief numbers was simple, quite slow, but very Spanish. I thought it sounded familiar, then I recognized it as the Sor prelude Paloma played in the Ciudad Rodrigo guitar shop. The second had an opening run, then Paloma began to sing, the first time I'd heard her musical voice since she played cuckoo for the small girl in Tomar. Her tones were vibrant and lilting, her singing unstudied but beautifully and simply enlaced with the notes of the guitar. I recalled what the school choir mistress had said of her, "In tune, and on time." Everyone applauded softly but spontaneously as the song ended. When she looked up to acknowledge their appreciation, I realized she hadn't raised her head since she began. We were seeing her just as she played for herself, alone with her thoughts.

The next song was pensive, the longest of her pieces. Paloma looked detached, even lonely, partly the result of her classic sheath dress in the darkest of greens and her hair drawn up on top of her head, and partly from her isolation in the overhead illumination. I found myself distracted by the light playing on her hair, on the curves of her back and shoulders, on her arms, hands, and the guitar. I was reminded how much she covered up and hid away beneath her perpetual long sleeves, long slacks, or long skirts. I glanced around the room and noticed Carlo standing behind the seated guests, a step in from the lobby. The man was transfixed, a statue, his eyes riveted on Paloma. "Poor fellow," I thought. "I know how you feel. She's out of reach for both of us. I'm too old and you're in another world."

Her final song surprised me with its vigorous rhythm and aggressive lyrics. I'd admired her discretion in choosing the previous lovely but relatively undemanding works, but I'd underestimated her ability — she carried off the fierceness of the words and chords in a most convincing manner. People were warm in their appreciation, but she took no bow, only raising her head to meet everyone's eyes as she said, "thank you." Then she turned to shush the ecstatic Bill who was urging more applause.

When Paloma came back to our table with Bill trailing behind, Anneke greeted her with soft handclaps and a kiss. The rest of us made do with pats and handshakes, then resumed our visiting. As the women chatted animatedly, I sat there musing, "One English, one Dutch, one International, different backgrounds, but see how they fit together. It's a small world for the elite."

When the neighbors took their leave, Paloma tried in vain to enlist the Hilliers for a morning walk, and then we retired. That is, I retired and drifted off as Paloma added to her diary.

Sunday, January 5th

Sunday breakfast at Bettiswood Hall is an occasion to savor and one could be tempted to linger. In our case, one could, but the other could not. We bundled up to strike out for what even the less enthusiastic partner remembers as an inspiring walk. The day was sunny and windless. Overnight, winter's magic had turned leaden clouds into an airy blanket of frost on meadows and hillsides and left the bare trees sparkling with myriad crystals. After a glorious hour, in which the chill dictated a brisk pace and put roses in our cheeks, we were back in the sunroom taking tea, and wondering whether my photos could have captured any part of our experience.

Housekeeping was at its low point for the week, but Anneke and Paloma, for reasons best known to themselves, took a tour of the Hall to review the entire checklist of daily, weekly, monthly, and annual chores. I'd heard Paloma ask questions and seen her interest, and I supposed it stemmed from her curiosity to see how her duties as overseer of Gustaf's mansion, or in her condominium job, compared with those of the manager of a larger place. In any event, it was not my cup of tea. I worked up an appetite for lunch by picking away at my endless manuscript.

Shortly after lunch, I took myself downstairs to say farewell to Carlo, finally on his way, sharing a ride to the airport with a departing guest. I fished out my card and asked him to send me news of his progress and of his opening, and promised to be an early guest. Carlo was warm in his thanks and I watched him leave with the very real hope that we had said farewell and not good-bye.

At three, we allowed our curiosity to lure us to the recreation room for a peek at a Bettiswood tradition, charades before teatime. The participants were few, scarcely adequate for a satisfactory session, so we were enlisted on the spot and wound up having fun. For the first time, I saw Paloma being a bit naughty in public, but only in response to theatrical demands. It was heartening to see her so socially involved and so accepted. Too many of her days were spent cooped up within the confines of her gated community and her strangely gated mind.

When Anneke and Bill joined us for an aperitif, I was flushed from the lighthearted charades and emboldened to mention an opportunity they'd passed up.

"Hilliers, both, are you aware that you could have had this place crawling with doctors if you'd just selected the obvious name?"

Bill looked at Anneke, Anneke looked at Bill. Both groaned. Bill sniffed, "I say, do you detect that doddering 'Bettiside Manor' gag around a corner somewhere?"

"I do," Anneke deadpanned. "Who'd believe it? We thought it'd died of old age, but damned if it isn't still stirring. It's got more lives than a cat."

I put on my best crestfallen face and retired from the fray for a full minute and a half.

Monday, January 6th

Anneke had errands to run in the village and she desired company, mostly Paloma's I suspect, but she was kind enough to include me. Bill would like to have come, but stayed behind rather grumpily to resume the tasks Carlo had shouldered for the past months. Accordingly, the breakfast table was a mixed arena. The women ate with one eye on a growing shopping list, their heads together over such wonders as paper napkin colors, the limited seasonal fruit choices, and materials for dry arrangements in the halls and public rooms. They also reviewed an astonishing list of items in short supply because of holidays or the owners' recent absence. We men turned to the commonplaces of male ritual — weather, sports, stock markets, politics — all totally impersonal and beyond our reach.

We needed no onboard audio system as Anneke drove us to Bettiside. She launched into song, mostly folk and old pop standards, and Paloma sang harmony. Sometimes it worked famously and everyone applauded, sometimes not and all groaned. The audience was jealous that the Creator hadn't given him the means to participate, but he tried not to be a sore loser.

At our first stop, we addressed the question of fruit for the Hall's morning menus, a headache in winter, what with short supplies, limited choices, and high prices. When we'd put an assortment of grapefruit, pineapple, bananas, and Down Under grapes in the trunk of the car, Anneke proclaimed that her clients, at least her regular clients, were tolerant folk who would not harbor unreasonable expectations. But why, I wondered, the heavenward roll of her eyes?

Next, we stepped around a corner to a shop offering tasteful selections of housewares and decorations. The ladies had come to inspect dried plant materials ranging from grasses to tree limbs, from leaves to giant gourds. In this quest, I was the odd man out, and never did manage to fathom the rationale underlying the many careful and thoroughly discussed choices. Nonetheless, I rejoiced in my companions' gusto at the prospect of arrangements to be designed and executed. Everyone needs a hobby.

Paloma came to need a bathroom, asked, and marched off. Anneke sidled up to me with a gruff whisper, "D'ja see our proprietor hanging about with his pencil and clipboard? Never jotted down a thing and no eyes for his stock either? Hmph! He's got your friend memorized, chapter and verse." Then she spoke more matter-of-factly, "That happens a lot, doesn't it, when you travel with a thing of beauty?"

"More than a bit," I admitted, "but as a good and philosophical Mexican friend put it, 'At times, one is called upon to suffer.'"

"Yes, poor dear Mr. Talbot, but that's why God gave you broad shoulders." Anneke cleared her throat to signal more to come. "Pity you couldn't have looked in on five minutes of Paloma's first stay with us — she wasn't much more than a girl. We had a thirtyish dandy, very full of himself, he was, and here with his dreadful parents. One evening, I can't imagine why, Paloma and her escort invited this fellow to join them for a drink. The fool patted Paloma on her bum as they went to a table. She swung around and gave him a slap so loud it turned every head in the room. My, it was still! She said, 'Little man, not in your wildest dreams,' said it loud enough to reach the far corners and out into the hall. Well, a young miss a table or two away started to clap and went on for must have been ten seconds, and the place still that quiet. The boob went scarlet and froze right there. Stock-still! He finally slunk off with his tail between his legs as he damn well should've. Mater and Pater just evaporated, and they all cleared out before breakfast. We never saw 'em leave." Anneke was in stitches and her eyes swam. "End of 'em," she gasped, "God's truth!"

While we were in the shop, a delegation of women from the church came to pick up items of decoration for that evening's Epiphany service — and when we showed interest, they invited us to see their work. When we'd completed our purchases, we drove to the church, peeked in, and found the place lavishly adorned with dried arrangements, not to mention pieces of antique farm equipment. In my ignorance, I wondered aloud about the numerous handsome oaken kegs and was reminded that Epiphany celebrates not only the coming of the Magi, but also the Wedding at Cana with its miracle of water to wine. Silly me. And I was further informed that two kegs were full of wine — no one was satisfied to leave the success of the after-service party to the passing of a new miracle. Our informants quickly added an invitation to the evening's activities. Anneke had to decline, citing hostess duties, but Paloma, Catholic background and all, expressed ecumenical enthusiasm for this Church of England celebration, and that was good enough for me. Excitement mounted when she spotted sheets of music prepared for the evening and found hymns and songs she'd sung at her schools in London, Sevilla, and California. Music is ecumenical indeed.

After lunch back at the Hall, I needed a rest. It was curtains drawn for me and comfy under my coverlet. I hope I didn't snore. When I stirred, I learned that my roommate had been thinking again. Nothing would do but we dress for the evening before reporting for tea — dinner might be so close to church time that we should sit down with the first tone of the dinner gong. As it happened, she was clairvoyant; we skipped dessert, and still just made it for the opening hymn.

The nice old church cast a spell with its rustic decor, soft candlelight, and sea of happy faces. Paloma sang all the songs she knew and all those she did not, since she'd picked up the tune every time before the start of the second verse. I felt privileged to stand beside her, feel her vitality, and hear the songs come from her in a joyous rush.

With its heartfelt hymns and short readings, the service proceeded briskly. In what seemed very little time indeed, we were milling about, talking to people, and sipping mugs of mulled wine. Everyone was full of high spirits and bonhomie, especially a middle-aged gentleman who introduced himself to Paloma and attempted to enlist her for the choir. I saw in him a kindred spirit, especially when his desire to chat was not dampened by the news that she was a transient. Quite the contrary, he positively flowered in the glow of her gracious response. Was I any different when I came upon her?

All in all, the place, the people, and the event fused into a warm, memorable occasion. We walked out happy, drove back happy, and carried the glow into our beds and our dreams.

VI GUSTAF

Bettiswood Hall, Dorset — Tuesday, January 7, 1997

We rose to dark skies and rain, and the forecast of a major storm made us doubly grateful for the Hall with its friendly owners and cozy amenities. When we reported for breakfast, the outside gloom still had the appearance of night and we were the only guests in attendance. We soon fell to reliving the previous evening, the beauty and joy of the community service.

"Palomita, you fairly reveled in church last night. You were raised Catholic as could be, so I wonder, now what? Why don't I hear references to regular church attendance, or any attendance, for that matter?"

I sensed her pulling up her socks, so to speak, and taking deep breaths.

"Haley, you are the nosiest man. I have to remind myself now and then that part of the reason you're fun to be around is that you're forever trying to get to the bottom of things. The trouble is, I'm often the thing you're determined to get to the bottom of... and you will please let that line lie right there, thank you." I attempted to look angelic and she carried on.

"Honestly, I can't categorize my religious beliefs. As you say, I was born Catholic, reared Catholic, educated Catholic, and I suppose I see myself as Catholic. But only if I don't ask too many questions. I'm also

Nourrit's daughter and I'm likely to be with her, outside in the open air, rather than joining the faithful in their tidy, prescribed temples, running through their tidy, prescribed routines.

"I'm finally realizing that Nourrit, most of all, has been my spiritual guide. She never preached a faith nor belittled the church, but her ideas about everyday matters wind up, in my mind, competing with the beliefs that my family and my classmates seemed to accept without question. Funny that you should ask. You took me to Nourrit, and when you left us alone, I brought up my uncertainties about faith and prayer and asked for her views. I had no idea what she'd say; we'd never had such discussions while I was growing up. So that's when I finally learned how skeptical she is of any authority that's not part of her immediate community. And I'm sure you've guessed that her community is her whole environment — creatures, plants, earth, water, sky, sun, stars — everything. In her mind, it's all before us. We contain bits of the original essence, we're mortal and immortal, everything is permanent but undergoes constant change. Though we won't be here long, we have absolute powers to affect what will be forever after us. I see Nourrit as a great ecologist even if she has no idea that such a discipline exists."

My cheeks burned. I'd never wondered what Paloma and Nourrit might have discussed when they got together in Sevilla. If I'd been asked, I suppose my answer would have been something dismissive, like "Oh, you know, girl talk." I covered my chagrin with a question about Nourrit's beliefs — and got a thoughtful reply.

"Well, she sees all creation as continuous and related. That's a theme in her art, and I look back and see it in everything — her stories of her childhood or, for that matter, what she perceived on a drive in the country. I feel such a connection with Nourrit when I travel, get out, see living things and sky and land and sea.

"I suppose it's because her community is all around her that she doesn't relate to absent authority, any of it, Rome, Madrid, or dictates handed down in ancient writings. She doesn't perceive people as saints and sinners, or as saved or damned; she sees all of us as equal parts of creation and believes we teach each other and learn from each other. The years I was with Nourrit, she'd point out people and tell me what she'd learned from them. She led me to study them, to learn where they stood. Who was happy? Who was miserable? Who was useful?

Who had special insights? Who was a burden? And why? Especially why. As teachers, they show us what they've learned and what it's done for them or to them. As students, we have to decide what to take and what to reject. And all our lives, we have to learn enough to be the people we want to be, or are capable of being. And through all of that, we serve as examples for others."

I had to cut in. "That hits close to home, Nourrit's recognition of people who are burdens, I assume she means burdens on society. I've always believed that each of us has a primary responsibility to prepare himself to live a fulfilling life and contribute to the greater community, or at least not detract from it. But don't let me sidetrack you, I just wanted to concur with Nourrit."

"Believe me, you two would concur on so much—try this. Last fall I told her how vital prayer is to me and I asked how she sees it. Believe it or not, she started with the Virgin. To her, Mary represents the mother we've all lost. I asked her about people who haven't lost mothers. 'Oh no,' she said, 'we've all lost a mother, the mother who nurtured us when we were helpless, who provided for every need, who held us and comforted us and reassured us. When we grew out of her arms and stepped out of her reach, she was lost to us, but we never forget. When we need the things she bestowed—and all of us do, and some desperately—we reach out for her with prayer.' Nourrit believes that is how we appeal to our origins, our creation, for solace or guidance.

"And Nourrit is convinced that prayer is universal. She can't imagine a soul who doesn't have the need to pray, and she pities those who have lost the hope that prayer matters. She sees prayer as an amalgam of petitions and promises, a way of reassessing and rededicating ourselves as we face the terrors of life. She believes we don't grow by having our prayers answered, we grow when our need for prayer leads us to try to be worthy of a response. It's simple. Prayer implies a listener, and also a deserving or at least a repentant petitioner. I was proud to come back, grown up, and take up things with Nourrit that we'd never discussed and find her thoughts so *simpático* and challenging— frankly, way ahead of me. I felt so close to her; she'd added something new to what we had from before."

"Paloma, this is one of those moments when we should be down on our knees to express wonder and give thanks. Try to imagine the odds on finding a philosopher working for your grandmother, and a non-Christian to boot. Imagine getting that perspective on prayer."

"Mmm, and a lot more than prayer. When things aren't going well, if I'm rather floundering about, I feel her behind me like a pillar, I lean on her and she puts her arms around me. When we talked this over, I didn't tell her everything. I didn't tell her that she's often the Mary I see when I pray."

I saw Paloma sincerely affected, but I had to bite my tongue. I burned to ask, "How can you be so obtuse and so willful? If Nourrit is your Mary and means so much to you, why don't you answer her prayers? Why don't you see her distress? And Bessie's?" But no telepathy did the job for me; Paloma pushed on with other aspects of faith.

"So, it's simple, right? That's my religion, or at least the tip of its iceberg. But it's not so simple. I look at Bessie and my grandmother. Their orthodox beliefs did wonders for them and I know some of that rubbed off on me. So where does that leave me?"

"I guess I don't quite see the problem. Do you feel you're missing something by not being more orthodox?"

"No, not really. I've learned too much about what goes on outside any orthodoxy to suppose I'll ever be a full-on 'true believer.' I guess what I'm really saying is that I'm not sure religion lends itself to logic or argument. Each of us has something of his own, but can it be explained or defended, or should it be? I end up feeling there are no answers, only a choice between faith and questions. But, whatever, I appreciate what the church experience does for others — and it's a great art form and social event. Look at last night. Whatever the state of my faith, I got something wonderful just by taking part."

"Paloma, your way is a book of wonder — is, was, and always will be. My question was prompted by an Epiphany service in an English village — and look where I was taken."

She nodded, but her attention had turned to eggscetera.

After breakfast, Paloma left to join our hostess in further list-making and I sat down to play editor. In a half hour or so, she was back with the news that Anneke wanted her to go to Bournemouth on a shopping run. She said she'd accepted Anneke's invitation so I'd have time alone to read the contents of a large envelope which she handed me as she spoke, the material I was supposed to find waiting when I first got to Bettiswood. She'd picked it up at the desk when she arrived because she was afraid it would interfere with our get-together with the Hilliers. Then, she admitted, she had second thoughts about delivering it at all. In the end, she decided I should have it, but she sounded still hesitant as she explained.

I squeezed her around the shoulders and went with her to the Hall's formal entry. She took my hands in hers, whispered, "Remember, it's all in the past," then she and Anneke drove off in the downpour.

I found a place in the sunroom to sit with my envelope, but when I discovered what I had, I sought the quiet and privacy of our room.

A handwritten letter introduced many printed pages.

> *Haley dear,*
>
> *In Portugal I promised you the rest of my story, but no opportunity presented itself. As soon as we had more plans, I sat down to do something about it. You plainly were having problems with what you had heard, and my intuition tells me that if you know the rest you will be more comfortable and we will be closer. One thing in particular I have wanted to tell you ever since we parted in Santa Fe, and I just could not manage. I have sold myself, yes, but I have not been impressively promiscuous. As you will see, I have shared beds with five men—you are the fifth.*
>
> *All of this is less embarrassing for me to write out than it would have been to extemporize as we drove, or as we sat face to face and necessarily off by ourselves in a private room. In fact, writing this for you gets me started on a project I have put off too long. As you know, I have kept a journal for years, but I have not previously attempted to organize and rationalize it. This part breaks the ice and I plan to put it all in coherent form. I like to imagine that those efforts and that accomplishment will help me to cope with the troubles I inherited from my past and my people.*
>
> *Affectionately, Paloma*

204 • *Portrait of Paloma*

Next I came upon three pages of photographs scanned in black and white. The first showed both sides of a snapshot, a man in his forties in a military uniform standing beside and with one arm around a woman as tall or taller than he. The man was homely, with big ears and a long nose. The woman was striking, very blond, strong and handsome in the face, and had a good figure, as far as her shapeless dress allowed one to judge. Most notable were her large, wideset eyes. On the reverse was written in pencil "George Robert Inskip," and under that "Gwen Williams Inskip, Aug. 1942." Paloma had added, "My only picture of my grandmother Gwendolyn."

The next sheet was devoted to four photos of Celia Inskip, "Chely." I scanned them and noted that her eyes, too, were large, and always imparted a look of surprise. I found her attractive in each view, but less distinguished in appearance than her mother or her daughter. In the first photo, Chely appeared about sixteen and already inclining to buxom. In the second, she was dressed in a short, snug dress, revealing her shapely figure as she somewhat awkwardly held Paloma, aged around eight to ten months. Paloma's hair was quite light, at least in the photo, and she looked straight into the camera, her intense gaze already evident. In the third snap, Chely stood arm in arm with two good-looking young men, all three attired for some winter sport and standing at an overview point with Alps or similar peaks in the background. In the fourth photo, Chely and Gustaf Grevilius stood with their backs to the rail of a cruise ship at sea. It must have been taken before Chely was ill, for she appeared happy and relaxed. Gustaf towered over her, a straight, slim-figured man with graying dark hair. He must have been quite handsome; in his sixties, he had the air of a patrician celebrity.

The last sheet reproduced four snapshots that included Paloma, each time gazing directly into the camera. In the first, she must have been around six, the age she was when her portrait was painted, and she was posed before a row house beside Bessie, then in her forties and looking happy and motherly. The second picture showed Paloma at ten or so standing in front of Amparo Vargas. Both looked resolute, but the grandmother's arms were draped around the child in a relaxed manner that appeared both protective and affectionate. The third captured Paloma, about twelve, and Nourrit, the pair surprisingly in matching white dresses, sitting side by side on a white wall. Whereas the girl sat up straight, hands folded in her lap, and gazed at the photographer, the older woman regarded the younger with a look surprisingly maternal for such a naturally austere face. In the last photo on the third page, Paloma, Chely, and Gustaf stood rather stiffly, apparently in his garden. I'd guess Paloma was fourteen because she was still skinny and all legs.

I set the pictures aside and picked up the typed text.

(Haley, the following begins during my second year at St. Brigid's.)

    Every weekend I went home to find my mother increasingly weak, and also increasingly anxious to relate to me. But when I urged her to talk, she still had a hard time bridging the gap that I felt she had deliberately created from the start of my life. I remembered her returns from her many trips with friends when I was little, how she always came back with a gift for me but not the desire to spend time and do things with me. All the time I had known her I could tell that even talking to me made her uncomfortable. I was puzzled and I was hurt. What had I done? I look back now and feel guilty that I didn't have more sympathy for her difficulties, but then I didn't know as much about her as I was soon to learn.

    One day, she asked me to sit with her at her favorite window, and she pulled herself together and began to talk. She had Gustaf on her mind and she wanted me to understand their relationship. I then knew only a basic chronology, plus a few anecdotes that had cropped up in our conversations.

    Chely started by telling me how she met Gustaf the year after she left me in Sevilla. He and a colleague were guests at a house party in a villa overlooking Lago Maggiore. She had come escorted by Franco Reni, one of her boyfriends for several years but tiring of her just then and finding many reasons to spend his days with the boys. Gustaf's wife had died two years before and he was lonely. He and Chely lunched together, took walks, played croquet, enjoyed each other's company, and exchanged addresses. During the next year, Chely's affairs took a serious turn for the worse. She lost her job at a perfume shop in Milano, she had no beaux, and much of her income from Amparo was spent on liquor and the amphetamines she had taken up to fight depression. She was frightened and wrote to Gustaf, telling him at least some of the truth about her plight. He arranged for her to fly to California. That was the end of 1982 and Chely was about to turn thirty.

Once she was in Gustaf's home, Chely became his lover and the manager of his house. She admitted she brought few skills to the job, but she said she pitched in and learned. Gustaf worked with her on her problems and paid for months of counseling, and luckily Chely was in the early stages of addiction and determined to escape. Her new security relieved her of enough anxiety that she relaxed, recuperated, and accepted what was actually a pleasant situation. She and Gustaf traveled the world as well as cultivating a few local acquaintances.

As Chely told her story, she called Gustaf the most honest, trustworthy man she had ever known, and she touched again and again on the points of his patience and kindness and particularly his gentleness. I was touched. I had never heard my mother express such sentiments. With the immature, romantic viewpoint of a sheltered almost-sixteen-year-old, I imagined my mother truly in love, possibly for the first time.

One evening while the three of us were at dinner, Gustaf and Chely joined hands and told me they were going to marry. Chely kissed his hand and said it had been her dream and it would simplify my position in the house after she was gone. At that point, nothing surprised me. The world looked bleak and uncertain. If this could help in any way, I was for it, and I could see the prospect made my mother happy. On the following weekend, I attended a simple ceremony on Gustaf's wonderful deck with its ocean and sky backdrop. A judge Gustaf knew performed the ceremony and two friends acted as witnesses. Wine was served, we all sat down to talk for half an hour, then the guests went home. That was the last time I saw my mother with any energy.

When Gustaf came to get me at the end of the school year, I still could not really comprehend what was happening. Each weekend I had come home and seen Chely in poorer condition, but I could not relate it to death. Now as we drove back to Laguna, he told me she was very fragile and very depressed, she needed to talk to me, and she felt guilty about the way she had treated me. He asked me to be patient and help him make the end of her life as happy as possible.

"She is your mother," he reminded me, "but she is also a young woman—sometimes she seems to me just a girl—and she has things on her mind that make facing death even more difficult." I was certain that Gustaf sincerely cared for my mother; in no way did he sound like a man just going through the motions or trying to say the right things.

When I came into the living room, Chely was sitting near the picture window. She looked at me and put out her arms. I went to her, dropped to my knees, and we really embraced. She had not said a word, but when I put my arms around her, she started to sob, great big, convulsive sobs. I just held on and it was terrible. For the first time in my life, I knew I was important to my mother, but I also had a frightening feeling of power over her. There I was, whole and strong, still in my school uniform the day after I pitched six innings of softball; strange thoughts like that were running through my head.

When she finally spoke, she just repeated over and over, "I love you, Paloma, I love you. I love you, I love you so." She was tiring, running down as if she were a windup toy.

The nurse stepped in and patted us both and separated us. She said my mamá needed to rest and I could see her and talk to her later. When I looked in that afternoon, I found her asleep, and the nurse said she was tired out, but would be better in the morning. Then she told me Chely had got herself all worked up over my homecoming. She had asked to have her hair brushed and her face fixed up, and for a while she had been quite animated. I suppose we were too long getting there and she had too much time to worry about our meeting. I lay on my bed that night remembering Chely as far back as I could, and I recalled no time when she had told me she loved me with that much conviction, and few times when she had even said the words. They would have done more good, I thought, if they had come earlier, a lot earlier. But I was not so heartless or so ignorant that I did not see why they were important to her now. My mamá was dying, she would be gone forever. That still seemed impossible.

She was better the next day and most of the two weeks after. I would come and sit with her, just the two of us, and she gradually brought up things we had never discussed, things about my life and hers. She told me how Bessie had come into her father's home as a teenaged babysitter when she herself was tiny. She described her earliest memories of Bessie and their relationship. It all sounded familiar to me and, at the same time, strange. It was not easy to picture the woman I knew as the fixture of my childhood doing the same things for my mother when she was just as young. Chely told me how vital Bessie's help was to her when I was a baby. She admitted she had no idea how to care for me and was almost frightened to touch me, but she trusted Bessie and turned me over to her.

One day I asked why it had been so difficult for her to accept me and learn how to handle me. I knew right away this was going to be a painful subject. My mother got choked up and weepy and I tried to get away from the idea, tell her it wasn't that important, but she insisted on staying with it. She told me that was what she most wanted to explain and have me understand. She said she needed to feel closer to me and she needed me to feel closer to her, and this question was at the heart of the problem.

Chely started out by saying she was not quite nineteen when I was born. In a single year, she had gone from being a student at a finishing school in Madrid to being pregnant, traveling to Virginia in the United States, marrying an old, sick man she scarcely knew, giving birth to me, and being moved, with me, back to her childhood home in Putney. She said she nearly went mad she was so frightened, confused, and frustrated. At that point, her story rather died away into details of those same sad events.

Days later when she was having a particularly strong morning, my mother apologized and told me she had not been able to face me with the whole truth, but now she was ready. This time she began with the night I was conceived. She had come home to Sevilla during a week off from her school in Madrid and discovered that George, her father, had gone on a fishing trip. Well, the place was empty and she had nothing to do, so she telephoned a girlfriend with whom she had grown up in Sevilla. The two girls arranged a date with two boys they had known a long time, boys their ages or perhaps a year older. They had gone on such double dates before; the plan was to stay together and if any of the fun and games started to get out of hand, the girl in trouble would sing out. The other, and presumably her partner, would intercede, and order would be restored.

The other girl and the two boys came to the Inskip place and they all danced and had a few drinks. Chely recalled that they had stripped off some of their clothes and done some fairly sexy dancing and some heavy petting, but nothing serious had happened and they were barely tipsy, not drunk.

Suddenly, she said, one of her father's business associates, Francisco Utrera—"El Paco," he was called—burst into the room and yelled at them like a madman. He was a big, strong man and he intimidated the boys. He threatened to call up the other girl's father and have him come over. Then he told Chely's friends to get out and go home. They left.

As soon as they were gone, Utrera began to scold Chely and call her a whore. She was crying and trying to get into her clothes but he pulled her to him and fondled her and, in short order, he raped her. But that was not the end. Before she could get her clothes or get away from El Paco, the same door he had come in opened again; it was the police and the father of one of the boys. Chely was hysterical, but she accused Utrera of assaulting her and, before long, sat down with a policewoman and made a statement about the entire affair.

In a day or two George Inskip was back and he was told what had happened and immediately went to his lawyer. When lawyers for the Utrera business were notified, and after they had consulted with their clients, they declined to defend Francisco or to take any responsibility for his actions. So Francisco hired his own advocate to respond to George's proposed lawsuit. After that, my mother remembered, there were weeks of off-and-on meetings with lawyers. Sometimes she had to attend, sometimes her father would go alone. In the end, Francisco Utrera was not prosecuted. George Inskip said that would create a scandal and do nothing for Chely. Inskip negotiated some sort of settlement with Francisco's lawyer. Chely did not see Utrera again, or hear from him, until the third year after I was born. After two months, Chely guessed she was pregnant and a test was taken at the direction of her father's lawyer. Chely said she was numb for weeks afterward. She felt completely helpless.

Inskip decided to handle her confinement by putting her in a convalescent facility accustomed to handling cases of awkward pregnancies in affluent families. It had a friendly, competent staff, beautiful grounds, and a secluded setting. Chely found friends in two other unwed mothers-to-be, and she told me that her time there was happier than it had been at home. She did a little reading about the responsibilities she would face and about the arguments for and against putting her child up for adoption, which she became determined to do.

When she was seven months pregnant, her father came to see her, one of his very few visits. He came to her room and shut the door, saying he had private matters to discuss. To start, he opened a briefcase and got out a pile of letters. He handed her a photograph of a couple standing arm in arm before a seawall; one she knew was her mother, but she did not recognize the other, a slim, boyish youth with dark hair. George then gave her the letters and asked her to look them over and read as many as she wished. At first, Chely didn't grasp anything about the letters. They were in English, all in the same hand, and most on the same stationery. They were addressed to "My Goddess of the Open Door," "Sweetness and Light," "Candy Cane," and other pet names.

When she was still baffled, her father handed her the envelopes, and the paper, ink, and handwriting all matched the letters. All were addressed in 1952 to Gwendolyn Inskip at a post office in a village just south of London. Chely began to read and found they were youthful, passionate letters written in broken English but plain as to intent. They described or implied a lot of consummated trysts and they anticipated more. Most of them were signed "El Paco."

Then it dawned on my mamá what this might mean. She met George's eye, but he did not look fatherly, he looked grim. She was born in 1953. These letters were to her mother who had died just days after Chely's birth. They had been written by the man, then not much more than a boy, who had raped her and was the father of the child she was now carrying. All she could say to George Inskip was "My God."

Inskip told her that he had found these letters among her mother's things not long after she died. He told her he had always known he was not her father, but he had decided not to make a public scandal of the matter. He called on the Utrera company's lawyer, told him about the affair, and showed him the letters and several pictures. The lawyer talked to Francisco and his uncles who directed the family affairs, and the uncles decided not to question the evidence. George worked out a settlement in which the Utreras paid the expenses of Chely's upbringing, the servants, schools, tutors, and so forth. In addition, George got some advantages for his part of the business. He told Chely he had held up his end of the bargain and reared her as his daughter. If he had done anything else, she would have gone off for adoption or been reared by the Utreras as a family bastard. George admitted that he did not know if he had done the right thing, but he had kept his word. He did not apologize for anything.

As George spoke, Chely realized that for the first time she was hearing an explanation for her distant relationship with the man she had thought her father, and for the little she had heard about her mother from George's lips. But those revelations were not the end of the ordeal. George had brought her what he expected her to accept as good news. He had negotiated—and Chely later came to suspect, dictated—a settlement whereby she and her baby would be supported by Francisco Utrera. His accounting firm would send Chely a fixed monthly allowance. In addition, Chely would submit bills pertinent to items like housekeeper, governess, schools, medical attention, etc., and she would be reimbursed. This plan was worked out in careful detail, including cost-of-living increases, and it added up to a sum that George calculated would allow Chely to live in a careful, upper middle-class style. However, it was all contingent on Chely keeping her baby—me.

Inskip had also worked out a scheme to ensure her baby's legitimacy. He told her the idea came to him as soon as he understood the position she would be in. He had an ex-employee named Harold Grey, an American who had worked for him for years. Grey was terminally ill and the firm had given him a retirement allowance so he could end his days at a nursing home in his native Virginia. Inskip and his lawyer devised an agreement whereby Utrera would pay Grey an additional sum to marry Chely. She would go to the United States, her child would be born there—giving me clear citizenship—then Chely could go where she pleased. George suggested that she rent his house in Putney.

George Inskip had displayed no emotions over any of his devastating revelations. Here he was with the young woman he had allowed to regard him as father all of her life. In her worst hour of need, he pulled that prop from under her without showing any qualms. When he left, he came over to Chely and gave her a kiss on the forehead, shook her hand, and told her she could call him any time she needed help or had questions for him or his lawyer. Then he was gone. ¡Así los ingleses!

A sheet of lightning flooded the room. My reading lamp flickered, then held steady. The punctuation seemed apt. I suppose I sound naive when I say that Paloma's telling of these brutal, shocking events had taken me totally by surprise—naive, because most of what I'd learned about her earlier lay outside any reality I'd ever known. But this! I sat there trying to envision a sixteen-year-old receiving news of these horrors from her dying mother who was, incidentally, her last blood relative. Suddenly I was vastly more tolerant of Paloma's subsequent actions. After what she'd been through, I should say "tut, tut," and lecture her on propriety? I felt low. I wished she were back so I could hold her in my arms. Well, she wasn't, but her manuscript had me on the edge of my seat.

After that long narration, my mother was exhausted but still fairly calm. She begged me to try to imagine the state she was in as she waited for me—she was going to give birth to her own half sibling, and she had just learned that she was not related to the man she had assumed to be her father. While Chely told me that, she did rather break down. She said, "God help me, Paloma, I'd decided to give you up already, and I knew from that minute how hard it would be to even look at you, but I couldn't fight George—I was afraid I'd lose him completely...and he was all I had." My mother had an awful time forming those words, then she went to pieces while I hugged her to me as best I could.

It took minutes for all that to sink in, and I am sure it was days before I realized all the implications. This frail woman in my arms really was my big sister as she had always so pathetically tried to suggest. But she was also my mother. Right there, for the first time, I began to understand her terrible difficulties in accepting me and dealing with me. I felt a rush of warmth and gratitude for Bessie. I was overwhelmed by a sense of her vital role in my early life, the mothering she lavished on me. I wished I could simply be Bessie's daughter, or Nourrit's daughter, and that none of the rest of this ugliness applied to me. But there it was. I could see that Francisco had been a monster, but I couldn't make it personal; he was gone and I had never known him. Just then, more than anything, I was troubled by terribly mixed feelings about myself and about Chely. I was an inexperienced girl, just sixteen, attempting to cope with a growing accumulation of burdens. How could I even begin to contemplate my parentage? What was I? I felt born out of Hell.

In a few minutes, Chely calmed herself and went on with her reaction to the awful news. For weeks after, she said, she saw no life worth living, no glimmer of hope. She told me she was numb, overwhelmed by the implications of the incest issue and by having to ready herself to be packed off to alien Virginia and face a series of ordeals among strangers. Only at the last moment did George seem to realize her bewilderment and provide a woman to accompany her and handle the arrangements for her marriage, hospital stay, and return to England.

Chely arrived in the U.S., and she and Harold Grey had a civil ceremony performed in Roanoke so there would be no question of my citizenship. While she waited for me, she heard from George that he had managed to hire Bessie and have her waiting. Chely told me those kindnesses made up for some of her bitterness toward her onetime father. But my mother told me that ultimately she felt completely betrayed. George may have come into this tangled affair as something of an innocent bystander, but she was convinced that he thereafter used it, and her, as opportunities for himself. She said she had later learned that he had not worked a day after he signed the agreement to drop the rape charge against Francisco Utrera in 1971.

And there was another surprise for me. Chely told me that as soon as she felt securely settled in Laguna she had written to Amparo to discuss the possibility of taking me back. She handed me three letters she had received in 1984, two years before my grandmother died. Here I translate most of the second (Amparo always spoke and wrote to Chely in Spanish and her handwriting was quite difficult).

> Dear Granddaughter Celia, you are blessedly generous to let me call you granddaughter after all the years I turned my back on you. I did not know of you until after you were born and I received the news in the worst ways. I can tell you God's truth, all this time later, that I did believe my son sinned with your mother, there were those letters and pictures, but I could not make myself believe that you were his daughter. For me, that was only a claim of Mr. George Inskip whom I did not like or trust. I believed he was using my son's mistakes to get money and advantages from our business. By the time I learned more about this man and had reason to believe you were not his daughter, we had accepted his arrangements to rear you as his, and I feared to make trouble.
>
> Now I know that I failed you and I failed myself and I failed my God when I did not acknowledge you and take you and rear you as the daughter I never had. God held out this opportunity and I looked the other way. I had no shred of the virtue for which I was named. May I be punished for eternity.
>
> But that is not all, that was not the worst of my sins. When my son wronged you so horribly, committed such a great crime on you and in the eyes of God, I was so horrified for him and so horrified at the idea of a child coming to us that way that I could only pray for the child to be taken away and reared by others to never know of all this crime and sin. I disapproved when Mr. Inskip worked out his settlement with Francisco, the business that would keep him tied to the baby. I felt my world threatened by

an unborn child. I am more shamed, far more, because
I condemned that baby, I saw her as marked by Satan.
I saw her as an embodiment of my son's sins.

Eight years later, when you brought her to me, I was
prepared to close my eyes and turn my back again. I did
not see that God was offering me another chance. I will
burn for this. God and Mary had to send Nourrit, who has
always been a better person than I, to plead with me, to
open my eyes. I did that, but, I confess, only for Nourrit's
sake. Through her, I found God's second gift at my door,
the work of His loving hand, all innocent of my wicked
imaginings. With her, I know at last the meaning of a love
that is shared and present, not felt only in prayers and
dreams. I am not good enough for her, but God has trusted
her to me and I have done the best I can. That is my
possible salvation.

Now I beg you for a mercy I do not deserve, I beg
you to leave Paloma here to carry out her mission. She
is my life and my hope and the heart of my household.
I will not live long, she will be yours again.

My grandmother had revealed none of this to me. Her letters showed her, and our relationship, in a new light; I felt as if she were speaking to me from the grave, and the burden of her message made me sad. On top of that, the letters reminded me that I'd grown up at the center of contradictions. I'd lived with Bessie's pet name, 'Angel Child,' and Amparo's insistence that I was a gift from God on the one hand, but on the other, I knew I was a bastard child, and now there was this disclosure that I was born out of incest. I was further confused because another side of me knew all of those things, but felt no part of them. What had they to do with me? Why couldn't everyone see me as a person with strengths and weaknesses like any other? A person just trying to be herself and grow up? Thank God, I thought of Nourrit who had always seen me as I saw myself and loved me anyhow. I felt better when I had written to her and tried to explain all that and thank her. I did not care if Celestina had to read it to her. I put in a note and asked Celestina to be my agent.

Amparo's letters suggested a new tack for relations with my mother. I tried to use what I had learned to make her feel less guilty for shunning me. I did not really know what I was talking about, but I referred to the grand plan that my grandmother perceived, and I asked my mother to accept her part in it and not blame herself for things over which she had no control. Chely seemed relieved and began to treat me as if she finally believed that I understood her problems and was capable of forgiving her. I saw her relax and become less anxious. I also must have relaxed. My understanding of my mother's plight was washing away my resentment for all those years of rejection. Gustaf noticed the change in both of us. He told me I had grown from a child to an adult before his eyes.

After that, Chely's time with us was mercifully brief. During the month after she told me the missing episodes of her life, she slept more and more, but Gustaf and I sat with her whenever she was awake. Gustaf was kind. I overheard him telling her all sorts of things to assuage her fears, or her sense of inadequacy, or simply to cheer her up. I added what I could.

When the doctor told us the end was near, Gustaf and I took turns sitting with Chely day and night. Early, early one morning I was there when she opened her eyes and tried to speak. I got down on my knees and leaned close to her mouth. I took her outstretched hand in mine. Then she pulled herself together. She looked me in the eye and started a monologue a little louder than a whisper and with pauses after almost every sentence. I can't guarantee I remember it word for word but it will be part of me as long as I live.

"Paloma, I love you more than anything I've known in this life. You're the best of all the things that happened to me. I didn't see this when it counted for you, but I thank God I found you in time. It's my punishment that I'm losing you just when I found you. You're everything I was not. You're strong and sensible. You're good. It hurts me more than dying to look back and see how good you've always been, and how you were right there under my nose, and I took you for granted and I did not appreciate what I had." My mamá seemed too tired to go on, but she was still looking right into my eyes and I was holding her hand and nodding to her almost mindlessly. Then she did go on.

"You'll have problems, but you'll overcome them. I know you will. I'd give you my blessing but I know it's not worth anything. I'll watch over you and pray for you, if it's possible. Paloma, you're all I have to leave to the world, all I ever accomplished with my life. Promise me to make the best of yours and I'll die happy. Promise me and forgive me, please forgive me. Paloma, I love you, I love you, I love you." Those were her last words ever.

I had never cried very much, but I learned to cry that day. It was a gift from my mamá and I have blessed her for it ever since. I wept, and she kissed some of my tears and clutched at my hand. I told her I loved her and I did forgive her with all my heart. I told her I would be careful and I would treasure the life she gave me. Then she held my hand more tightly and I kissed her face until she relaxed and went to sleep.

Gustaf came in toward the end of this and took my place so I could get something to eat. When I returned, my mother had a peaceful expression on her face and she was breathing, but she looked tiny and pathetic on her side with her knees tucked up. I stayed with her all day, sometimes holding her hand, sometimes touching her cheek or her forehead. I said good-bye to her every way I knew how. I found myself going back over her awful life, no parents, no home, nothing of her own. I realized how dependent she had been, and the callousness of most of those she depended on. I cried for her on my knees. I begged God to keep her. I knew she believed she was a bad person, but I saw her as frightened and lost; I had never seen in her the ability to be bad or deliberately hurt anyone.

As I thought of her and her life, I felt more vulnerable myself. I had no family and I was dependent on others. Feeling helpless added to my gloom. I shivered and felt closer to Chely than ever before. I began to sing all the songs I knew. Some of them felt right and I sang them over and over, relating them to a pendulum clock ticking away in the hall. The day passed. Chely went on breathing, but I knew her breaths were tiny and close together. As the sun went down, she left us without ever waking. My mamá was only thirty-five years old.

I finished the page holding my breath, then I wiped my eyes. Chely's whole life had been so pathetic, she'd had so little of anything. And there were Paloma's elegantly simple words—suddenly I longed to see every journal she'd ever kept. But most affecting was Paloma's state—sixteen, and losing the people closest to her for the third time. How could I respond? I wanted her back, but I almost feared the moment.

The phone rang and startled me out of my ruminations. "Yes," I answered, expecting it to be Bill.

"Haley, this is Anneke. We're in Bournemouth, but ready to pull out. I got away from Paloma for a tick and I'm calling to warn you. I don't know whether you two are having a tiff, or what's going on, but

I'm calling because she's apprehensive over something she's written to you. You see, apprehensive is not my vision of Paloma at all. Whatever's wrong, could you try to cheer her up or at least try not to aggravate her worries? I hate to meddle, but I thought you ought to know."

"Anneke, you're an absolute peach. Believe it or not, I'm sitting here trying to figure how to do exactly what you suggest. She has nothing to worry about here."

"Good! I'm relieved. See you for dinner."

I thanked her and dived back into the memoir that wouldn't let me go.

> When my mother had been buried, I did not feel "strong or sensible." I felt like the survivor of a third shipwreck. I have always loved the phrase "flotsam and jetsam," it's one of those things that make me love the English language. But it's no fun being flotsam and jetsam, wondering where you will wash ashore. I was terrified. Now what would become of me?
>
> All I had left in the world, or so it seemed to me, was Gustaf and his house. I would wake in the night and lie there appreciating how vital, how central, that place had become to me. I have told you about its vistas and gardens, but I wish you could have seen the interiors and Gustaf's collections. He was enchanted by Middle Eastern woven materials, particularly kilims, and had splendid specimens on most of the floors and many of the walls. On top of that, he had a great library, most of the classics of the English language, hundreds of books with reproductions of every type of art, and a huge collection of classical and folk music. And Gustaf himself was part of all that, he was the host and the guide and the only stable presence I had in this new life.
>
> All through the time we had been watching Chely die, Gustaf tried to cheer me up. We played our games when we went out. He took me to the library and to the video rental where he helped me make choices. He played anagrams with me and bought a deck of Authors Cards—a tough one with a lot of minor authors—and we played it a lot. When we sat around Chely's bed and talked to her, Gustaf constantly asked me questions or gave me other opportunities to show off my knowledge, something he knew pleased my mother.
>
> When she was gone, Gustaf changed the daily schedule and made it revolve more around me. He got the names of two guitar instructors and let me try each and pick the one with whom I

would study. He suggested shopping trips, some to buy things for me, and others to buy things we needed at the house. For the remaining two months of the summer, he was my companion and my teacher.

Shortly before school was to open, he brought up the subject of my future. He told me he would support me until I completed my final year at St. Brigid's School. After that, I could choose to go to college or get a job, but financially I would be on my own. He listed my assets, $60,000 that he had promised Chely he would give me, and another $60,000 left to me in trust by my grandmother's will, money I was hearing about for the first time. I suppose the lawyer in Sevilla did not tell me of it because I was a child and my mother was its designated trustee. (Gustaf had inherited that supervision at my mother's death.) Incidentally, I was greedy enough to wonder out loud why my obviously wealthy grandmother had left me so little. Gustaf imagined, and I am sure he was right, that Amparo feared a larger sum would be contested by her legitimate heirs, and without George and his documents it would have been difficult to prove in court that I was Francisco's daughter.

At any rate, Gustaf pointed out that all my monies, taken together, would support me through the usual four years at a public university. Then Gustaf told me he had another proposal. The cleaning woman had come in, so he suggested we go to his study to continue our talk. Actually, of course, it was his talk. The whole prospect of my future frightened me, all its uncertainties and discontinuities. I was reliving the emotions I'd had as I was taken away from Bessie and Putney when I was eight and when I lost Grandmamá and had to leave Nourrit and Sevilla. But this time there was no change of scene and there was Gustaf to help me with the transition. Something had happened to me in the last months of my mother's life and in the weeks since. I had adapted quite comfortably to having Gustaf as my daily companion. I had come to feel at ease spending every day in his airy home with its sweeping ocean views. Without realizing it, I had found in Gustaf what I had lost being torn away from Nourrit, a challenging comradeship that demanded effort on my part and gave me a feeling of intellectual togetherness and accomplishment.

We sat down and Gustaf laid out his cards. Oh yes, he certainly did. He reminded me that when I left, even to finish high school, he would be alone in the world. Chely was gone and he was somewhat estranged from his one child, a son, who, as I knew, was divorced, childless, and lived on the opposite coast.

Gustaf told me he was beginning to feel old and had never been able to face loneliness. That was why he had come to Chely's rescue as soon as she called for help. When they met, some spark between them told him she could relieve some of his problems even as he offered support to her. He said my mother had made a promise to him: She would try to escape her addictions and she would stand by him no matter what happened. Gustaf seemed quite affected when he described Chely as a good person who never had a chance in her life. She did her best to be the partner Gustaf needed, and for three years they were happy. Gustaf said he knew he was not my mother's Prince Charming, but by the time he knew her she was disillusioned about that sort of thing. Now he was worn out with the cares and the emotional drain of their last two years.

Gustaf told me I had come along at a crucial time to keep him from crumbling in the face of his daily ordeal. He said my weekend visits were a breath of fresh air for Chely and for him. "You know," he told me, "she didn't know how to talk to you. She was ashamed of her past failures with you, and she was afraid of you. She always believed that you knew what was going on inside her mind, and that you were judging her. But she did cherish you more than anything else in her life. She watched you and listened to you and was a different person. And it stayed with her through Monday morning after you went back to school. She felt your presence. Well, Paloma, I did too. I'm in love with you and I want you in my house. I need you now more than I needed your mother."

I must have looked agonized and I could not think of a thing to say. Gustaf saw my confusion and stood up. I remember him saying, "Please wait a moment, child. I will be back." I went to the window and off in the distance I saw gulls sailing above the cliffs, I saw trees bending in the wind. I felt as if I were holding my breath and all my senses were in suspense.

Gustaf came back with two cups of tea, no sugar and a dash of milk. He had noticed my routine and duplicated it perfectly. We sat, and he said, "I want to start by saying I have no right to approach you like this. You are only sixteen and now my stepdaughter. What I am going to offer you is probably illegal and it is certainly not socially acceptable. Nevertheless I ask you to weigh it carefully. I already feel the loneliness in this house when you go off to school. I offer you the position your mother filled. I invite you to learn to run the house, direct the indoor and outdoor staff, plan menus, learn to drive, assist with the shopping and, most of all, be my companion. If you decide to do this, it will interrupt your education and take a piece out of the first part of your adult life. I do not ask you to do this as a favor to me. I do not consider that you owe me anything. I offer you an endowment that will pay you well, very well, for your time and effort. I could discuss the details with you if you are interested. But Paloma, when I say I want you to be my companion, I mean companion in all things. If you have no experience with sex, you would let me show you how it works. It is a natural human function. We should not apologize for needing it."

I was shocked. Gustaf had never laid a hand on me or looked at me the way some men did. He had never walked in on me when I was undressed or spied on me in any way I knew or suspected. His proposal left me speechless. The first thing that came to my mind was what happened to my grandmother and my mother, unwanted pregnancy. I must have said something, I can't remember what. Gustaf's response was matter-of-fact. He told me he'd had a vasectomy years before when his wife feared another pregnancy.

Again I was speechless and I must have looked miserable. And again Gustaf responded by standing up. He said, "I am being unfair. I needed to talk to you and I went too far. Please think it over and don't worry. I will never put any pressure on you. We can talk about it any time before you go back to school."

I went to my room in a daze, if a daze means you have all manner of thoughts and images and questions wheeling around in your head and you can't stop them or sort them out or make sense of them. No one had ever presented me with any significant, major choice that I had to make. Nothing more than asking which piece of clothing I would prefer to own. I was overwhelmed. I put on clean sweat clothes, laced up my running shoes, and jogged down to the high school track where I went round and round wrestling with a problem I have never mentioned to you.

Right after I came to Laguna, I was agonizing over what I had left behind in Sevilla, and I rather broke down while I explained my concern for Nourrit and Benito. Gustaf reassured me and promised to allow me two hundred and fifty dollars a month to send to my friend. I was profoundly grateful and he knew it and soon raised the amount to three hundred. If I struck out on my own I would somehow have to shoulder that burden as well. I ran and ran, but nothing useful came into my head, nothing was resolved or even furthered, as far as I could tell.

Damned vulture! The man knew what she'd been through and how dependent and lonely and insecure she must feel. Now he'd made himself her prime companion and he was circling for the kill. I fervently wished he were alive and I might have a minute or two of his time. The whole picture left me cold, my stomach in knots. I hated to read on. I could see what was coming.

When I got back and showered and dressed, Gustaf insisted on taking me out to lunch, using the excuse that there was no privacy around the house on cleaning day. At lunch, he apologized for his abruptness that morning and asked me to take my time and not feel pressured. Plainly, though, his proposal was on his mind and he needed to dwell on it further. He told me I basically had two choices and he was confident I could succeed whichever I chose. He acknowledged that he was the wrong person to speak for one of my options, so he suggested I confer with a counselor at school about higher education and career opportunities. If I chose that route, he reminded me, I would be on my own. I would have a lot of expenses and day-to-day responsibilities. In the second, Gustaf's option, the routine would be more familiar and the outcome more secure. Then he said—as if to tempt me to argue, or at least to think—"If you go out on your own and succeed, as I am sure you eventually can, you will be more independent. If you stay with me, you will have a lot of catching up to do when I am finally gone. But you will still be a young woman and you will have the means to live comfortably while you make a transition. In my judgment, that's the gist of what you have to consider."

Right there I spoke up about the sex thing, an issue he had not raised again. He nodded and admitted the omission. "But," he added, "don't you forget that sex will be a concern in any life you lead. There are all sorts of men out there who will move heaven and earth to penetrate your defenses, lead you or cajole you into some position of dependence, and get you into a sexual relationship. I am being honest about my desires. Most of them will not."

Now, Haley, there's something you need to understand—my lack of self-confidence, whether it results from my origins, my lack of family, my inherent weakness, or whatever. In some fashion I always knew who I was, and I was true to myself, but I also had to live all those years with the knowledge that I was a bastard, that I had no real parents, that even my name, Grey, was a sham, a subterfuge. I discovered more and more about people's reactions to such cases. My sense of self-worth had been undermined even before I heard the worst part of my beginnings. Then, just before I faced Gustaf's proposal, I had to try to cope with the knowledge that I originated in an act of extraordinary cruelty, the incestuous rape of my mother. I already thought of myself as unacceptable to society, now I had to add that. Ever since my experiences as an outcast at the Academia in Sevilla, I've had in the back of my mind a fright that someone would find me out and expose me—and now that I knew everything, the threat of exposure seemed more frightening and somehow more probable. Sixteen is an emotional and melodramatic age.

In my panic I thought of Nourrit and Bessie; I wondered if they could somehow help me. But what could I ask them? If I told them the story, they would be horrified, but then what? I couldn't go to them, I was a minor and an American citizen. I couldn't imagine trying to get a permit to travel overseas to visit a non-relative. Besides, Nourrit was already dependent on the money I sent from Gustaf, and I knew Bessie was living almost hand-to-mouth with only a part time job and some help from the church. As I thought about it, neither of them seemed to have any relationship to the world I was in or to my problems. For the life of me, I could not imagine adding my woes to theirs, or even trying to explain them. I thought of Sister Eugenia, but as soon as school ended she had started a year's leave of absence to do some conservation thing in Alaska. So that was it. In my mind I had no one else to whom I could turn for solace or counseling, no one but the man who was reaching out for me and putting me to this test.

I simply did not have the experience or perhaps the character I would have needed to recognize that accepting Gustaf would compound my problems. Or that living with Nourrit or Bessie might be possible even if they were poor and lived far away. I felt safe behind the walls and gates of Gustaf's house high on the hill. And it was not only a haven, it was a place where I would continue to have his full attention. I remembered all too well the miseries of losing my home in Putney, and then of losing my home in Sevilla, the helplessness, the despair, the emptiness, the loneliness. I knew I was not the only one who had suffered, I knew how devastating it had been for Bessie, Chely, and Nourrit—each in her own way—to lose the stability of a nucleus of people and the walls that sheltered them. That made me more sympathetic to Gustaf. His way of life was also involved. I lived with those memories and many more as I attempted to decide how to answer him, but I think I lived even more with my fears, childish fears—but then I was a child. Of course I was unprepared to make such a decision. Of course I should never have had to make such a decision, but I thought I did, and I did, and I will live with it forever.

Please don't conclude that I simply gave up. I did try to use my education and my pathetically inadequate experiences. I outlined the things I would have to do in order to pursue Plan A, strike out on my own. I made a list for B, remain with Gustaf. Remember, I could only include things I could recall or imagine, and I had not lived a day of either alternative. As I went along, my decision seemed to make itself. Leaving Gustaf would expose me to the public I feared and would entail a life of responsibilities and uncertainties. I would have to arrange for living quarters, transportation, employment, schools, courses, and all sorts of other things. The responsibilities alone seemed scary but, in addition, all of it would cost money. I was terribly conscious of Nourrit's dependence on the monthly sum I was sending. How would I manage that, or how would she manage without it?

I was sixteen and I had learned enough to suppose that sexual relations were a normal part of adult life. Even with a man in his late sixties, that loomed as less threatening than the unknowns and turmoils of independent life. I looked around me and out to sea. I felt the serenity of Gustaf's house, his library, his art and music, and, yes, of the man himself. The more I pictured my situation, the more frightened I was to give it all up and return for a last year of school where I would not even have Sister Eugenia. Here in Gustaf's house, I would have the assurance of his full-time company, and I had not had anybody's full-time company since I was eight years old.

After two days I told Gustaf I would stay with him. He thanked me and said he would start making arrangements. He also told me I could change my mind at any point in the next month. Then our life together proceeded exactly as it had before.

At the end of a month, Gustaf announced that I needed to learn to drive. He had given me some tips, but now he proposed a trip to the desert. He drove us out on a dirt road north of Twenty-Nine Palms, put me behind the wheel and supervised while I went through a lot of stops and starts, turns, backing up, and signaling. We passed a couple of rusting oil drums and

Gustaf set them up so that I could practice parallel parking between them. A week later, he took me to a driving school, and after two lessons the instructor said I was a driver. I got a learner's permit and began driving. Gustaf was a good teacher and I was proud of myself.

Then he began to teach me about sex. At first, he talked. He described mutual gratification as the basis of ongoing man-woman relationships. I was not so naive that I had not heard all of this and understood it to some degree, but it had come to me in other terms—Sister Eugenia's blunt biology lectures and little insights derived from literature, jokes, and the talk of older girls at school.

One night Gustaf asked me to sit in his lap while we watched a film. It had a certain amount of sexual by-play in it and he touched me and hugged me at suggestive moments. Around the house, he began to embrace me, usually from behind. He would take a soft hold on my shoulders and then kiss my neck. Other times he would reach around me and place his hands over my breasts while he held me. None of this was especially exciting for me, but it was so gentle and low key that I was not frightened or disgusted. At no time did he attempt to kiss me on the mouth (actually, he never did in all our time together), but he did commence to kiss my hands, arms, and shoulders. After a few weeks of that, he asked me to his room and had me lie on his bed. He lay down at my side and embraced me from head to foot. He held me for a long time. He had music going and, strangely enough, I was more aware of that than of his fondling me.

Just before Christmas of 1988, he began to take off my clothes and make sexual contacts. He did this gently and none of it was painful. After that he lay with me and we had sex once or twice a week. He tried to give me pleasure with a variety of caresses and kisses. He did give me a sense of sexual response, but I was more aware of his stimulation than I was of my own. I had a feeling of accomplishment when he would pull away from me satisfied.

So, for two years we lived, as they say, as man and wife. No one appeared to suspect and I was aware of no outside repercussions. If I'd had access to Nourrit, I'd have told her my situation, but in those days I could reach her only through letters that Celestina read to her, so I described little more than our travels and other activities. I did send Nourrit pictures of Gustaf and me together, and Nourrit sent a gift to Gustaf, an old bronze seal such as might have been used with sealing wax. Gustaf admired the device that it printed, hands cupping a stylized heart.

From the time we met, Gustaf had used every possible occasion to teach me about money and its role in people's lives. He lectured me on capital formation and investments, interest, dividends, taxes, the whole picture. He showed me how to read bank and brokerage statements—no, he drilled me. Bessie and Nourrit had taught me a lot about frugality, but only at the level of daily purchases and petty change. Gustaf showed me the basis of financial success and the consequences of ignorance. (I am afraid he used my poor mamá as a warning about financial ineptitude.) He taught me to run the house, keep its books, and handle the bills. He transferred money to our household account and I paid everything with checks and a credit card with automatic payments taken from the same account. Gustaf supervised as I learned to deal with the tradespeople who provided needed services.

More fun for me were my times working with the cook and the gardener. The cook was a Belgian woman, well organized, and prepared to get me involved. She told me her needs and I did all the buying, but not until we had made shopping trips together so she could teach me a how to select meats and fruits and vegetables. Gustaf encouraged me to pick out the flowers we would grow. Our gardener was good about explaining which would do well in our soil conditions and coastal location, so I consulted with the him before I made selections. Gustaf suggested that I design an English garden for a sloping area we had off to the south of the house. We studied books and magazines, and then both of us helped to supervise the terracing and rock work. We enlisted the gardener as much as possible, and it was a great success for the last two years I was there.

But there was a lot more to our lives than domesticity. We went out to dinner twice a week on the cook's nights off, and went to concerts and traveling art shows all over the southland. And, best of all, we traveled abroad. Gustaf was starved for travel because my mother had not had the energy during her last two years. He and I went to Italy, England, and France twice, and also to Scandinavia, Germany, Switzerland, Greece, and Turkey—four long tours, six to ten weeks, all when I was sixteen and seventeen. Everywhere we went, he indulged his passion for shopping for fine specimens of Middle Eastern weavings. That was fun for me too. I loved the adventure, making the selections, and I found a lot of motifs and even a piece or two that I thought might interest Nourrit.

More significantly for me, Gustaf's travel plans included his choices of preeminent centers for educational and cultural experiences. Gustaf's ideas may have been old fashioned by today's standards, but remember, he had been considered an authority on undergraduate education in Western Culture. You could say I was exposed to the basic "Dead, White, Male" European cultural itinerary.

I lowered the pages and shut my eyes, weighing this revealing backdrop to Paloma's unusual attitudes and reactions. There were themes of wealth and shame. In Sevilla, she'd lived in her grandmother's fashionable apartment with servants, attended a private school, but also sensed that everyone around her knew her bastard status. In Laguna, she lived high on an exclusive hill and high on the hog, but she also lived in fear that judgmental outsiders would find her out and expose her to ridicule. And Gustaf evidently did nothing to allay her fears.

When, at sixteen, she learned that she was the product of incest and that Chely too was an illegitimate child, she must have felt more unacceptable and become more reclusive. Gustaf knew she was aware of her parentage and soon took advantage of her fears and insecurity. I didn't wonder that Paloma had such fond recollections of her time with Bessie and Nourrit, even Sister Eugenia. Those were days of innocence before the avalanche.

In 1990, I had my eighteenth birthday. I didn't think of it as a particular milestone, but I discovered that Gustaf did. He invited his lawyer, his doctor, his tax man, and his stockbroker to a private party at the Ritz Carlton. They were all somewhat younger than he and all lived alone—one divorced, two widowers, and one never married. In that adult company and wearing a sophisticated cocktail dress Gustaf had insisted on buying, I felt very exposed, very much on display, and very aware of everyone's elaborate politeness. And then even more on the spot when I learned that the observance of my birthday was also a celebration of Gustaf's escape from potential legal problems over me and my age. To make it worse, although I knew these men more or less understood the nature of our relationship, I had no preparation for facing them all at once with this knowledge lurking in the background. To be fair, everyone was kind and discreet and there was nothing overt to make me squirm.

Two months later Gustaf had a serious heart attack and there I was, my life in a turmoil again, not to mention Gustaf's. His son Robert flew from Connecticut all set to take over the household. Fortunately, Gustaf was mentally competent and backed by his lawyer and doctor. Instead of the dispositions Robert wanted to make, it was arranged that Gustaf's recovery take place at home with me and full-time trained nurses. Robert and Gustaf had little to say to each other, and in a few days Robert went home.

Here, my room phone jangled again. "Hello, Haley Talbot here."

"Hi. Paloma here. Have you looked outside? Are you in the midst of a gale?"

"Well, sort of, but it's inside my head. Why? Where are you?"

"Still in Bournemouth, and I'll tell you, lucky to have a room on the lee side in a snug hotel. You can't imagine the windstorm we're having! It's a scene, poles down, wires down, trees down. We were turned back before we could get on the throughroad north and we're here till further notice."

"Look, as long as you're safe, the rest is nothing. You're young, I'm retired, we have lots of time. The bummer for me is that I've read a lot of your story and I'm aching to take you in my arms."

There was a pause, then, "You're sweet. I'm getting a glow from your hug. And, thank you, I didn't know what to expect."

"At this end? Listen, Palomita, nothing but total gratitude that you've made it this far and that you're you. Now, just get back safely. Tell Anneke to relax and do it sensibly."

"We will. Keep your fingers crossed—and don't get eyestrain."

"Guaranteed to not. See ya!"

"Bye!"

The dial tone left me staring numbly at the page I'd been reading. I finally snapped to and hunted up the place where I'd broken off.

Our lawyer filled me in on Gustaf's affairs and my part in them. Gustaf had no great wealth. His wife had inherited a sizable fortune well after they were married, and when she died, half went to their son and Gustaf retained the income from the other half, but only for his lifetime—when he died the principal would revert to Robert. Gustaf's own estate consisted of savings from his income, and of his personal effects—art, books, furnishings, and the like. I would be the sole beneficiary of a life insurance policy that would pay $400,000 at Gustaf's death, and my claim to that could not be contested because all the premiums were being paid out of income. In addition I learned that I was indeed to receive the bequest of the $60,000 that Gustaf had promised two years earlier. The lawyer gave me his word that he foresaw no problems for me in obtaining my part. Eventually he was able to do more for me.

When Gustaf felt better, he began to work up his resolve to have the angioplasty his doctor and a specialist felt was necessary. That procedure was carried out after three weeks, and only then did I discover that the doctors had feared Gustaf might have a lethal episode at any moment. Thereafter, he needed physical therapy and massage on a daily basis. I worked with the practitioner, and she taught me enough in six months that I was able to take over. Gradually Gustaf returned to some semblance of normal life. He was back on his feet in two months and able to drive, but he did little walking or driving. Our traveling days were over since he lacked the energy to do the things that make travel a pleasure.

Haley, here I come to an important part of the story of my relationship with Gustaf Grevilius: His sense of responsibility for me and how it changed. Prior to his heart attack, Gustaf gave me no signs of misgivings over taking me sexually when I was so young. Once he was out of intensive care and we were alone, he could not wait to start apologizing and blaming himself for failing me, for failing the paternal responsibilities he might have shouldered. He recounted all I had done for him, and how much he appreciated my companionship. He begged for a chance to restore himself in my regard and he gave it his best till the day he died.

Gustaf lived nearly two years after they cleared his coronary blockage, and all that time he devoted himself to giving me a decent facsimile of an undergraduate college education—minus, I would have to say, mathematics and the physical sciences, fields outside his realm. He supervised my reading, and it was extensive, and we devoted hours a day to intensive discussions, question and answer sessions, lectures, some fascinating and illuminating, some long, dry exercises. We both worked hard at it, and it was a blessing because we were so cooped up in the house. About all we went out for were our twice-a-week dinners and as many good films as we could find locally.

Gustaf had never cultivated a circle of friends, nothing more than a couple of neighbors with whom we traded occasional hospitality. Gustaf's business associates, the men who came to celebrate my eighteenth birthday, were closer to him than any friends, and they became close to me. I took him to their offices, and he had me sit in while they foresaw and discussed contingencies relating to his death. I judged each of these men to be honest and frank. They treated me with respect and dealt with me as an adult. I liked all of them and I could tell they liked me.

Now that I ran the outside errands alone, I began to meet more people around town. That was not all good. I found that several young or youngish men knew about my solitary state. They approached me, but none of them interested me. I was surprised and somewhat upset at how persistent they could be and how uncomfortable they could make me feel. One day a plumber who was working at the house made advances that frightened me. After I reported him to his employer, I worried he might be lurking somewhere. When Gustaf died, I became more apprehensive about unwanted attention.

Gustaf died in 1992. His lawyer soon handed me a note in which Gustaf asked to be buried beside my mother so he could retain that contact with me. Somehow that made me feel even more alone. I was barely twenty, and again I was forced to deal with his son. Fortunately I had the lawyer to represent me and my interests. At first Robert Grevilius threatened to go to court to challenge my claim to anything pertaining to his father. He was particularly upset over the cash bequest and the number of furnishings and artworks left to me. All of this was reported to me, but my lawyer did not seem disturbed and he assured me that Robert had little chance if he chose to sue. In fact, the lawyer discouraged him so effectively that no suit was filed and I got everything that was spelled out, including Gustaf's Volvo, his hi-fi system, his collection of recorded music, and around a third of his paintings, furniture, and rugs and hangings—he had tagged the ones he knew I cared for. I got the entire contents of the kitchen and any of his books I cared to specify.

I also inherited Gustaf's cronies. For reasons that will become obvious, I will not name them. After Gustaf was buried, each of them contacted me to offer whatever assistance he could. I was grateful because I needed to become knowledgeable about my inheritance, its bookkeeping, investment, and taxes. I needed to learn about rentals in order to put a roof over my head. I needed to learn to budget since my income was now a small fraction of what I had been able to draw on before. Therefore I was soon closeted with my old acquaintance but new adviser, Gustaf's stockbroker. From previous discussions, he knew I was determined not only to conserve my inheritance, but to make it grow. I asked for advice.

His counsel sounded like variations on the old "good news/bad news" jokes. My half million dollars was a lot of money in 1992. However, he informed me that I would need two or three times that amount in order to feel independent, really secure. Moreover, if it were invested with an eye to growth, I would need all the income it would generate just to support me modestly and enable me to go on helping Nourrit and Bessie. (I had been increasing my support, trying to keep up with inflation and their needs.) I felt threatened and I asked myself: What might I do to earn a significant supplementary income? What were my options?

Keep in mind, I was twenty, but I had never held a paying job. I was not a high school graduate. In school I had received no employment counseling—such advice as I got was directed toward preparation for higher education. In my mind, the concept of getting out and competing in the job market loomed as a black cloud. I did not begin calmly to go out and assess the outside world, I huddled inside the walls of Gustaf's house, the walls that were about to be taken from me.

One day I had a call from one of Gustaf's circle of advisers. He asked me to dinner that night at a certain nice restaurant we both knew. He said he had news and ideas he wanted to discuss with me. I accepted and we met. As we were seated, he pointed out that our location would ensure a private conversation, my first clue that we would discuss out-of-the-ordinary matters.

This man had broad cultural interests and was my personal favorite of the group, and I suppose I was transparent enough that all of them may have realized that. We ordered, then, as we nibbled bread and ate our salads, we chatted over the timetable for settling Gustaf's estate and about my impending need for shelter, and such matters. When we had caught up on those, he got down to cases. First, he told me that all four of my advisers were concerned for me and wished to help assure my independence. Then he let me know they had reason to believe that Gustaf and I had not lived together as father and daughter. He did not mince words. He and the others wanted me to consider assuming a similar relationship with all of them. My jaw dropped but he went right on with his pitch. Each of them proposed to present me with the annual maximum tax-free gift, ten thousand dollars, plus his professional services without charge. For my part, some system would be worked out whereby I would spend time with each of them under mutually acceptable circumstances. They calculated their offer would provide me with the means to live well, conserve my capital, and invest my dividends and interest.

I had a few seconds to breathe and think when our entrees arrived, but when he reopened the subject and proceeded to point out the advantages of their proposal, I had to stop him cold. I told him the implications were monstrous and I was unprepared to go farther. I thanked him for his candor and for everyone's concern. I assured him I appreciated the services they had provided and that I was aware of my current dependence on them. I asked him whether I could rely on those services, regardless of my answer to their proposal. He assured me that all of them were prepared to accept a rebuff; they were realistic enough to see that I might not want to even consider it. It was, he said, an idea they had thought could give them what they wanted and me what I needed. This man has always been polite and solicitous toward me, before, then, and later. And then, in particular, I couldn't face making a break with any of them. We finished dinner and parted politely.

As I undressed at home, it came to me that I was living through Gustaf's original proposition for a second time. I looked at the little girl in the mirror, found her not so little, and began to wonder. How big a mistake had I made? I was whole, healthy, and had a small fortune. I had survived. However, living with Gustaf in this beautiful home was one thing, sneaking in and out of back doors or getting involved in a lot of tacky rendezvous in hotel rooms—that is all I saw in the great proposal—was altogether out of the question. I could not envision such a thing, ever! I went to bed.

I lay there, wide awake, and memories crowded into my mind. I recalled what fun Gustaf and I had on our grand tours, especially abroad. I realized I had not traveled for two years, and that I missed it. What if I arranged to travel with my old boys, one at a time? With that, the proposal sounded more acceptable. I reviewed my feelings for each of the individuals I would be dealing with, men between the ages of fifty-five and sixty-five. I had known them for several years and, in general, I saw them as calm, quiet, innately kind people with good manners and good taste. I could visualize relating to each in the environment of elegant travel. Why not? I had been through that before.

I see now that I wrote off the sex angle too easily. But in my mind, I had crossed that line with Gustaf long before. I was already tarnished. I had less sense of compounding an error than of accepting a reality. It had been two years since my last sexual contact and, in truth, it was a kind of attention that I missed. But most of all, my head was turned by the prospect of a tax-free $40,000 a year. I had no idea what it would cost me to live on my own. What I had learned running Gustaf's house was actually a disadvantage because he had always insisted on the best of everything, and that had given me exaggerated ideas about basic needs and their costs. That made the offer of money extra tempting because I saw it as necessary to allow me to help Nourrit and Bessie and still accumulate the capital I needed to feel secure. At any rate, I thought it all over as best I could, and decided to find out how my would-be sponsors would react to a counteroffer.

The next morning I began to write out specific things I would and would not do. My only sexual experiences were with Gustaf, and they were all acceptable, but I had heard stories of practices that disgusted me, things I would never do or allow to be done to me. It was not easy to get all that down on paper in even close to polite terms. You would have enjoyed my creative euphemisms!

After working on that for a day or so, I called my contact and asked him to come to the house. I went over it with him. He saw no problems with my limitations—he saw no need to discuss them—and he seemed sure the others would be more than happy with my counterproposal. He chuckled at my adamant refusal to "travel" with a smoker, saying that only one of the crew smoked, and he not that much. He supposed the offender might consider becoming an ex-smoker. Also, at least one of the group had never been abroad, so I might have to accept domestic travel. He also kidded me, said the group might insist I take up golf, since all of them played. (Little did they know I would soon be beating one of them.) He claimed he fully understood my provision that I could drop anyone altogether if I learned we could not travel and room together amiably. He took my paper— which I stressed was a working proposal, not a contract—and went to discuss it with what we all came to call "the syndicate."

There is no use going into details. Everyone agreed to my terms. Everyone agreed to put payment for the first year irrevocably into my hands. We agreed to a trial period and then an assessment, but that never came to pass. Once we began to travel, each man spent what I thought was an inordinate amount of time trying to ensure that I remained happy with him and our arrangements. I was spoiled. They all proved to be gentle lovers, except one, who, it developed, was incapable of sex—really, of any sort of intimate contact—but he desperately wanted me as a companion. (We have never even roomed together, but he is always good company and takes me everywhere absolutely first cabin.) Collectively, they occupy less than five months a year, so I have a lot of time to myself.

Haley, at this juncture I can just imagine you saying to yourself, "How could she even think of doing what she did?" Well, I have asked myself the same question a thousand times; here are some of the things then uppermost in my mind. I had little confidence in myself and I was frightened at what others knew or might learn about me, and I already thought of myself as a whore after my years with Gustaf. No, that's not quite it. I could rationalize my relationship with him; we had provided for each other's needs and I knew he cared for me. But I assumed the world would see me as a whore as well as misbegotten. So it all boiled down to my insecurity, my loneliness, and my determination to have the means to go on living as I had. That was one thing I felt I was owed, one thing that should come to me out of my messed-up life. I wanted to be independent and never again have to worry about losing everything as I had twice before.

There is another point I want you to understand. In my mind, the syndicate's proposition broke no really new ground, unless it was accepting four men instead of one. Otherwise I had done it all before and enjoyed a lot of it, the travel, the company—new places, new faces. In the course of my odd upbringing, I was not conditioned to be disgusted at the idea of sex without marriage or mutual love. I associated the only sex I knew with security and companionship because both were involved in my first sexual relationship. Once I accepted Gustaf as a patron, I opened the door to other patronage.

Haley, let's face it. What you have before you is damaged merchandise. You know I am not trying to paint myself as pathetic. Pathetic is not my nature. But I also can't be more self-reliant than I am, and I rely on my men for so much. Look at us. When I am with you, I feel wholly relaxed. You make, or we make, good and interesting things happen. We talk and have, for me, wonderful conversations. And I love the interest you have taken in me. How in the world could I reveal all this to someone I did not trust as I trust you? Someone who did not know me as you do?

Let me tell you something I have never discussed with anyone but myself, something I have only begun to recognize and accept. When I am not with one of you, I am lonely. Remember how I was at the end of our trip? I felt desolate. I missed the fellowship of the days just past and I dreaded the solitude of those ahead. As far as I'm concerned, that proves I don't have a lot of independent psychological or spiritual resources.

I have never found it easy to make friends, especially with people my own age. I *have* had my antennae out, I *know* I would be better off with a wider circle of friends. But do you know what has happened? I feel uncomfortable with my peers. Women seem to treat me as an automatic rival, and men are either hung up on talking about themselves, or on making rather transparent and undesirable passes at me. May I tell you who my few friends tend to be? Older women, your female counterparts. My best women friends, perhaps my only real women friends, live in the same complex and are retired from careers. We get together in twos and threes and have fun talking, shopping, lunching, and the like.

I have come to face the obvious: I relate best to older people. I find them wiser, more tolerant, funnier—good things that younger people often lack. I enjoy learning from people who have had lifetimes of worthwhile experiences, taken lessons from them, grown from them, and care to share them. In an admittedly odd way, those older women and the men with whom I travel have become my family and friends.

That was it, the end of Paloma's account, no signature.

I gathered the pages and pressed them to my heart, insufficient tribute to the most poignant message I'd ever received. I felt unworthy as I marveled at all she'd shared and what that said about the bond we'd formed in our four months. I put the pages in my lap and reread bits here and there, appreciating the light they shed on things I'd wondered about since the day we met. All along, I'd been plagued by one enigma, no matter that I'd posed it many ways. Why does this marvelous creature so undervalue herself and remain so immobilized? Why does she settle for so little? How can she be so self-protective, yet remain in such a precarious position? Finally I was seeing a larger picture and finding it bizarre, dramatic, ugly, and all too human.

No wonder my perplexity. Who could possibly have guessed any part of such a story? I'd been cataloguing Paloma's symptoms, but the roots of her problems were far below the surface. She was denied the usual family presences—no father figure, little contact with her mother—and all her life she'd been sustained by a series of fortuitous benefactors, the ward of a succession of people on whom she had no certain claim. With each new protector, she adjusted to another dependent position—and became yet more adept at consolidating relationships in which she was compliant, even submissive.

To make matters worse, she'd felt the shame of her origin since she was a child, and what she learned as she matured only added to it. All her life, that shame had been intensified by isolation, living behind the scenes, at first hidden from an inquiring world because of her origins, and later, hiding herself because of her relations with men. Her strange relations with men. In her childhood and youth, Paloma had entree to few homes and no intimate knowledge of functioning families. In her small exposure to men, older ones acted as priests or practiced professions, younger ones came and took her mother away. After her years with Gustaf, she accepted "adoption" by a bevy of older men at an age when most women engage in dating, love, marriage, and careers.

But she wrote "the men with whom I travel have become my family and my friends," and there was the rub. They were family or friends only as they traveled. In all, they occupied scattered blocks of time that added up to less than half of her year. During the remainder, she was a recluse.

Our casual meeting in Santa Fe somehow led her to choose someone for herself, apparently for the first time. I could only surmise that those canny instincts of hers told her I was someone she needed, a person with whom she felt comfortable, a person who might have something more to offer.

That thought led to another insight—and a flush of remorse and shame. I'd never attempted to analyze our association from her perspective. Now, at last, I faced the fact that Old Haley could not have had such an alliance with a young woman *unless* she had deep-rooted problems. Normal young women don't consummate relationships with their figurative grandfathers, they have better things to do.

I winced as I recalled the illusory pact with the Devil for which I had so fervently prayed. It wasn't a figment of romantic fantasy after all. I'd made that pact and got the deal one should expect from the Devil. I sold out my better instincts and my obligations to a daughter in distress. I took the bait of her mind and body, but in the best diabolic tradition I was denied the restoration of youth that would have let me enjoy my acquisition — and redeem it. Moreover, my acts had left me no high moral ground from which to advise her. I'd accepted and participated in her misguided affairs and offered her further psychological and financial justifications. My face should burn.

Suddenly I saw Paloma as the prisoner of a vicious circle, a victim of others, a victim of her own perceptions. I tried to imagine where that circle could be attacked, and thought of her admitted dependence on us old boys. I'd been dazzled by her vivid personality from day one, dazzled and drawn in. But the closer I got — and I now felt very close indeed — the more clearly I saw her spontaneity, her freedom to think and act, shrouded in this dependent behavior. Paloma needed to stop being so goddam amenable. There was fire in her, she could be positively electric, but the things that excited her always seemed safe and impersonal — love for music or art, for history or the countryside. In relations with her "clients," she apparently became tame and accommodating — delightful for them, but what was it doing to her? And she was not just submissive, she was protective of her dependence. That was the wall I was running into.

So, how to redirect Paloma? So far, I'd played by her rules, and that decision left me with no firm footing. Logically, I should've turned my back as soon as she revealed her, to say the least, unconventional lifestyle. But I wasn't then in a logical state, I was mesmerized, and even though I failed that test — which I did joyfully — why shouldn't I build on the relationship I did establish? Getting off on the wrong foot shouldn't doom me, or her, to compound our errors.

Fair enough, but, I asked myself, "How do I start? How do I diagram an end run around her rationalizations?" I was still empty — no strategy, no clue.

Wednesday, January 8th

The phone next to my ear rang at 7 A.M. I wasn't strictly asleep, but I wasn't awake either. "Paloma, is that you?"

"Yes, with teeth chattering. No heat and no lights in this modern hotel, pitch black, outside and in. Anneke and I are huddled here in one bed, bundled up in all the clothes we have. She's in her knit cap and I've got a shower cap, but my hair is too big for it. Anneke says it's definitely not me. She's just back from the lobby, lucky we're up only four floors, because of course there's no lift. No news on road conditions, but at least the wind's died down to what you like to call 'a dull roar.' Management offered her dry cereal and apples but they're as cold as everything else, not appealing at all. Haley, I'm worried. Will I ever be able to face another *limonada*? Right now I can't imagine such a thing. Please, please, have the kitchen make soup and keep it on the back burner till we get there. I promise to empty one tureen and Anneke is nodding her head for another. No, she says 'two.'"

"You poor child! If only there were a thing I could do, or suggest. All I can share is something that won't help at all and it'll sound pretty selfish into the bargain—I'm feeling disconnected too. I lived all night with your story and I have these overwhelming needs to console and embrace. The phone is nowhere. I need contact."

"You can't imagine how much I'd like to snuggle. Of course, it could cost your life to warm me up, but it does help to hear you're willing to pay the price. Listen, they tell us incoming calls are blocked, so don't try to reach us. When we know anything, we'll try to call. Now tell Bill all about it. We'll be careful, don't worry. Big squeeze!"

"I miss Miss Paloma."

"Miss you too."

I told Bill so we could bite our nails together. He'd been attending to both the tube and the radio and learned that the worst damage was east of Bournemouth. Specified major roads were expected to be cleared by midday, but no one mentioned the smaller ones our women would need to get home. The morning dragged on, wet and windy, with no further call. Neither of us felt like sitting down to a breakfast, so we picked away at cinnamon rolls all morning and drank coffee until I, at least, had a sour stomach.

At lunch, Bill and the seven guests hanging around the Hall drifted into telling a *Decameron*-like progression of tales, mostly about "great storms I've lived through." That passed a little time, but afterward, when we repaired to the recreation room and had a go at charades, the need to create a diversion poisoned the atmosphere. After a few desultory laughs, we bailed out, and before long the common rooms were dotted with readers. I withdrew to commune with my neglected manuscript, but no luck there either, I couldn't concentrate. I was soon rereading Paloma's letter and reliving my agonies of the previous day.

This time, though, my anger settled on "the old boys," the investment counselor in particular. What an ugly scene. That man knew full well how bright and capable Paloma was and what her earning power could be if she were properly educated. He knew that half a million dollars was a nest egg beyond most people's wildest dreams, knew that, but withheld the advice she needed. Driven by plain old lust, he callously scared her into thinking that his vicious offer was in her best interests. I had the bitterest thoughts as I pictured him playing on her past exposures to wealth to reinforce his arguments for greater financial gains. And his actions didn't excuse her other "clients," all sophisticated professional men. They had to realize that they were turning Paloma away from any path they would have wanted for daughters of their own. The whole thing was nauseating and left me thinking gloomily about the ways that men use their advantages to impose themselves on women. I included myself in the indictment.

Bill and I had dinner together and he told me how he'd met Anneke while they both worked as underlings at a posh London hotel. Their reported romance sounded less like a drama than an unbroken run of happiness and progress, with one sad exception. I felt for them after his painful account of their inability to have children, and the accompanying sorrows and frustrations. Paloma, I learned, was around the age a daughter of theirs would have been had she not been stillborn. That made me think of Anneke's obvious interest in Paloma and an earlier remark of Bill's that he found Paloma a provocative woman, but more attractive to idealize as the daughter he might have had. I was grateful that I hadn't dwelled on the subject of my daughters and grandchildren. In the end, we broke up and headed off to bed with no phone call, but reassured by benign weather reports.

Thursday, January 9th

The next morning, Bill proposed a grounds cleanup around the Hall. I volunteered as unskilled labor and was awarded a berth. He rolled out his Range Rover and a largish flatbed trailer and we proceeded to collect many fallen branches and to cut limbs off two trees that had blown over. We reduced our take to logs and kindling for the Hall, but the trunks had to wait for bigger chain saws and younger men. These exertions were carried out in brisk temperatures — coffee breaks were several — and lasted well nigh to lunch, a meal that Bill and I approached with some enthusiasm.

We'd no sooner buttered our rolls than who should walk in but our wayfarers, weary, windblown, but triumphant. I rushed for a reassuring hug.

"Are you still friz?"

"No. Anneke had this inspiration about her auto and its heater and a tankful of fuel. We ran out there and in twenty minutes we were de-iced, blessedly. It's such fun to be able to feel your fingers! Then Anneke ran in and learned that the road to the west was open. So we were off, all wrong you could say, till we could swing north. We passed through Dorchester — can you believe? — and came into the valley from the southwest. Long way around, but all's well that ends well. Here we are."

Bill sounded aggrieved. "No phone call? We were beside ourselves."

Anneke looked puckish. "Well, I did a Bill Hillier. Once we were underway and dodging fallen trees, I just kept moving. We're starved, we're thirsty, and we expect to potty, then sit down to the table you've got waiting for us." The women grinned and trooped off. Bill and I dashed to the kitchen. After a decent interval, the returnees appeared and we had ever so lighthearted and festive a lunch.

Afterward, Anneke and Paloma announced their intentions to take naps. Bill and I were invited to get what we needed from the affected rooms and keep the Hall quiet. We promised, and for two hours we did. When I popped in at five after a stroll, Anneke was on deck and bustling about her chores, but her traveling companion was nowhere to be seen. Anneke fixed me with a look, signaled me into her office, and shut the door.

"I know I'm being Mrs. Paul Pry, but there it is. We are who we are. Quite frankly, I'm concerned for Paloma. Bill and I are concerned. We like that girl even if we don't know her terribly well. She's such a winner — warmhearted, and every asset you could imagine — but then there's her circumstances, or the ones we think we see..." Anneke dropped her voice and her bluff manner and went on quietly. "We've just spent two days together and I'm frustrated. To begin with, being with her turned a nightmare into great fun, an absolute lark. There we were, in half a disaster, and she turned it into a sleepover with a best friend—but she didn't offer to share confidences. I tried to get her to talk, give me any clue of what she's up to, but all I got was the sweet assurance that she's fine, and everything's under control. I really don't want to pry, I don't want to get into your private affairs, but you're the only one I can turn to and I want you to tell me that everything *is* fine, and that she's going to be all right. Do I presume too much?"

"Anneke, you don't presume at all. You can't imagine how completely our concerns coincide. Don't ask for details, but I'll tell you that Paloma's life is not entirely fine and perfectly under control, at least not as you and I would see it. I'm trying to wiggle into a position where I'd have enough influence to get her to rethink what she's doing. Believe me, it's not simple and it's not going to be easy. She likes you guys, and if I see some way you could give her a nudge, I'll let you know. For now, though, I'll have to ask you to trust me. And believe me, I appreciate knowing how you feel."

"Well thank you for confiding. I do trust you. I had a hunch you weren't the problem; you and she are different together — she speaks of you as a dear friend. Do keep us posted, and our fingers are crossed, OK?"

I smoothed out the frown on Anneke's forehead and planted a light kiss in its place. I said, "Thank you," and we exited to the common rooms and went our ways, she to the kitchen and I to the library. No other guests happened to be in the room, but I found myself rejoicing in a company of spirits united in a common cause, our wayward foster daughter. I'd made promises to Nourrit, Bessie, and now the Hilliers. I was no longer in an ambivalent position. I was through being the vacillating occasional lover/would-be father figure. I was committed, and now I had to communicate with Paloma. The questions were how and when.

The problem child came down at six and she and I sipped Madeira and chatted about the storm. Eager as I was to get started, I'd concluded that wasn't the day to refer to her letter, but it wasn't long before Paloma brought it up.

"There we were, huddled together, Anneke and I entertaining each other. We got around to trading limericks, and I know a lot of them. Back in school, Sister Grace gave me a collection, knowing I'd be amused. Can you believe a whole little book of polite limericks? So, there we were, I, the bad girl, reciting clean ones, and Anneke, the good girl, reciting dirty ones — and both of us with chattering teeth. Anyhow, I knew you'd been reading my letter, and I remembered thinking of one limerick as I wrote to you, actually one I've thought about a lot. It goes,

> The Dachshund seems not to belong —
> Born under a bureau, all wrong.
>   You'll see him go by
>   Just a half a dog high,
> But a dog and a half or so long.

"I'll tell you, when I finally learned how my life really got started, I well and truly related to the poor dachshund. I too was born all wrong, viciously misbegotten in another sort of ungainly way. Perhaps I didn't look peculiar outside, but I felt deformed inside. That's part of what I was trying to tell you in my letter."

Lousy timing. Before I could do more than look receptive, Bill and Anneke marched in with two couples who'd heard Paloma perform and then followed the course of the storm adventure. My companion pulled herself together with no sign of strain, and she and Anneke proceeded to refine and amplify their eyewitness accounts of the big blow. Bill and I were surprised at all the colorful detail that had been passed over at lunch. We had a pleasant dinner, despite the renewed storm that sounded like an offstage wind machine even through double-hung windows. Paloma and I retired early after only guarded references to her manuscript; we were too busy rejoicing at the happy ending of what we would come to call "that time in Bournemouth."

Friday, January 10th

I was up and out with the first glints of day but Paloma uncharacteristically tarried in bed. It was eight before she came down to breakfast and we began to talk, or at least, to talk about talking. Breakfast done, we found the public rooms dotted with guests confined by the wet, chill weather, so we ordered a pot of tea and retired to our quarters.

I was impatient to get into some heart-to-heart talk and I pulled my chair up to the love seat on which she sat, up so close that we had to splice our knees. But physical closeness was not physical ease. She sat straight and looked uneasy as I plowed ahead.

"First off, thank you for making me a confidant—I feel privileged. Getting all that down on paper was a huge effort and you made an elegant job of it. But honestly, your story's the toughest thing I ever had to contemplate. Reading it was reliving it. No, that's not fair, I could only imagine what you went through, but that was bad enough. And all through reading it, I wished you'd never gone away. I needed you here so I could stop at the worst bits and we could console each other. Well, you weren't here, but you know what got me through? I thought about the you that I know, the you that made it through all those horrors, and I thanked the powers that be for your survival. The patient is flourishing and free to do as she pleases. And the patient is the apple of my eye." I took her hands in mine.

She dropped her head and showed me the part in her hair. She spoke to our clasped hands.

"Haley, dear Haley, you are the sweetest. You always know what to say to make me feel at ease, or to feel better, or to do whatever you want me to do. And I know you're not the least bit of a hypocrite, but I don't feel 'free to do anything I please,' and you do minimize problems. You're so sure they can all be solved or exorcised by adopting the right attitude, 'trying to be better.' I wish it were that simple."

I put a hand under her chin and raised her face. I waved the other hand for her attention. "How can you possibly know how difficult it might be? Sounds to me as if your idea of trying to be better is to look the other way. Well, my idea is to figure out the problem and take steps. You're an unusually animated person. I'm puzzled to see you so immobilized."

She let out a breath and slumped a bit, but sounded less dejected. "That's because you see only one side of me. I'm at my best when we're together. You see a lively me because we do things that I, and I suppose you, really enjoy. But I'm alone most of the time, and alone I'm not that happy. I do my museum job and my other chores, I read, I listen to music, I play my guitar and sing, but I can still feel empty and pointless. I walk, I run, I try to get tired, but nothing really works. I need someone to carry me off, involve me in something, get me out of myself."

Paloma seemed so downcast that I slid over and sat beside her and put an arm around her shoulders. "All right, you've got a ways to go. But don't forget how far you've come. You've overcome unbelievable obstacles to an unbelievable degree. Of course, you had love and guidance from Bessie and Nourrit and Amparo, but not the lifelong family support most of us had. You were a victim of things that happened before you were born and you've had to cope with the fallout ever since. Paloma, face it, you've done a hell of a job. So, now you're saying it wasn't a perfect job, something's missing — so let's work on that. In your letter, you called yourself 'damaged merchandise.' Let's start there. How do you feel the damage?"

A deep breath, then, "All right, this incest thing haunts me. I feel like a freak, like a humpback with the hump inside. Whatever is a person who was put together the way I was?"

"Lucky as hell," came to mind, and it was God's truth, but not sensitive to the moment—I turned to something less personal. "Paloma, please, please don't confuse societal judgments with science. Genetics is something I know a little about. I've made plant hybrids, taught biology, raised kids, read a lot. It's true, everyone recoils from incest—the implications are unspeakably ugly—but that's in human society. In animal husbandry, 'the way you were put together' is a favored procedure; it's called 'line breeding'—I know, I know, not exactly comforting news for a young woman, gently reared. But, on the evidence, you'd be threatened only if your father/grandfather carried a genetic defect—you could be subjected to double jeopardy. But look at yourself! You're living proof that no such thing happened. Chin up!" I reached over to elevate that chin. "Not convinced? OK, look at it another way. Pretend I'm Sister Eugenia. Are you ready?"

"Ready for what?"

"Ready to answer questions, honest and true, cross your heart or hope to die?"

"I suppose."

"OK. Think of all mankind. No, think of the segment of mankind that you admire and respect, your private picture of the best and brightest. Now, answer my questions in relation to them. Give me Outstanding, Above Average, Average, or Below Average. First, how is your health?"

"I suppose Above Average."

"Come on, Paloma, play the game. From what I've seen and what you've told me, your health has been damn near perfect. How about your intelligence?"

"Perhaps Average."

"OK, fair enough, but only assuming your control group is pretty high powered. How would you rate your strength and stamina?"

"Above Average?"

"You're asking me? I'd say Outstanding, no question, but you're the one who's supposed to be getting the message. How would you rate your appearance?"

"You're trying to embarrass me."

"The hell I am. I'm trying to make a legitimate point. I'll bet you didn't treat Sister Eugenia this way when she put you on the spot. So, how about it? Where do you fit in the greater world of physical beauty? How did you fare when they handed out things like will power or a sense of humor? How about coordination, language, or musical gifts? Paloma, how about any inherited trait you can imagine?"

Just then, I had no inkling what was going through her mind. Her look could have suggested irritation, so I was relieved when her tone was hopeful, not piqued.

"Don't give up on me. I see what you're driving at and I'll admit I've never looked at it exactly that way. The whole thing was so revolting that I suppose I just couldn't see anything acceptable coming out of it. You make a good Sister Eugenia, and I guess I do sound pretty silly worrying about inherited traits. But it's not just genetics. I feel as if I came from nowhere. I've had so little family, and most of that so hopelessly dysfunctional. Or criminally antisocial. If it weren't for Amparo, I'd feel like the product of a moral void."

"Only if you insist! Only the gloomiest, most narrow-minded old-fogey theologian could possibly hold with all that 'sins of the father visited on the children' crap. Those sins will be visited on you only if you take them on. Don't do it, it's that simple. We're all products of the past. Every family's had its sprinkling of immoral or criminal acts. Think of the blessings you got from your grandmother, and from Bessie and Nourrit, your real mothers. Together, you created families where there were none. You all deserve a lot of credit. Accept it, and give thanks."

"But I do! I've known for years that I owe body and soul to Bessie and Nourrit. I've thanked God that they could give me the kind of love and support they'd never had themselves. Can you imagine Bessie's childhood—no family beyond an institution and odd sets of foster parents? Or Nourrit, all those childhood years almost alone? They're my idea of miraculous survivors. How can I complain?"

"Please, Paloma, don't overreact either. You have profound reasons to feel shortchanged—don't pretend they're less compelling than they are. But why don't you go back to what you've always done so well— accept what can't be changed or avoided and go after the possible. Look at your assets, personal and financial, decide where you want to go, and how, and work on it. The answer could be something as obvious as education and then a job, a career. A program that would get you out among people your age, challenge you, make use of your intelligence, make you a contributing part of society."

That sounded pretty glib, even to me, and Paloma was not buying.

"You know, Professor Talbot, you talk about education as panacea and utopia combined. But here I am, already way behind. I'd have to begin by getting a high school equivalency just to enroll as a freshman. I'd be in classes with kids seven or eight years younger. I'd be a fish out of water socially and I'd be starting with no real notion of where I was headed. And by financing it all myself at the same time, I'd be giving up a big piece of my present income. The way I see it, when I have the funds, I can study whatever I like, wherever I like."

"Paloma, could we stop for a moment right there? You're talking about making changes years from now, but it's this minute that you're lonely and dissatisfied, and it's now that you need to get something started. Look, I'm not saying 'do as I did.' I bumbled around and wasted a lot of time before I figured out what I needed. But at least I was out there in the world doing things. I got a lot of experience simply by being involved. Why can't I try to plug that experience into your case?"

When I got a tiny, tentative affirmative nod, I plunged on. "OK, here's an opinion. If you want a career to match your talents, you'll probably have to invest some of your money, and you'll definitely have to invest some of yourself. Believe me, time is passing. If you try to ride it out on the sidelines, you'll wind up as an outsider riding out life."

Paloma had a way of fidgeting when the subject was close to home and the ball was in her court. Rather than give me the satisfaction of a hearty, "Hear, hear," she appeared to contemplate the window.

"Haley, speaking of where I want to go, look outside. The wind's died down. May we go for a walk? I need to feel fresh air in my face, stretch my legs, breathe deep, all that fitness stuff."

"Up and at 'em. We're out of here." Bettiswood Hall lent us two doorman-sized umbrellas and we hiked down the lane under the dripping trees, out into the fields, and around by the stream as I bragged about my part in clearing the paths. The air was fresh, and a half hour of it did dilute the tension of our cloistered morning. Once back in the hall, we ordered tea and got Anneke and Bill to join us before the fire in the lounge. Jolly repartee squandered the hour before the important business of lunch and, for me, the nap that served as *digestif.*

When my eyes opened again, three-ish, I was greeted by a low-angled sun and the long shadows of bare trees. That put me back on deck and my roommate into another insistent walking mood. And the great outdoors was exhilarating, the air still and sharp, the light brilliant, the sky blue. We got back with cold extremities, but a general feeling of physical and spiritual uplift. To our surprise, we found the lounge occupied by few patrons and no hosts, but we did find the perfect cap to our outing, small glasses of a delicious Amontillado, good enough, we agreed, to inspire Mr. Poe's masterpiece.

Neither of us broached Topic A, but as so often happens, one thing led to another. The subject of the syndicate arose because one of its members, as ever, unidentified, had brought Paloma here twice and enjoyed his time in this room. In a rare careless moment, she mentioned that, then caught herself and covered her mouth with both hands.

"You didn't hear that. Anyway, Haley, being with you is different because I found you — no, not true — we found each other. And you hadn't moved in on me to take advantage of the position I was in. I appreciated that, and then it was the best surprise to feel so at home with you in just minutes. And when it went on and got better, it rather tickled me to think that I could offer you something you probably didn't imagine possible."

"Paloma, I'm haunted by that offer and that I found it irresistible. But I had no experience with that level of temptation. You were so impressive to talk to, so beautiful — don't make depreciating gestures at me! You are intensely bright and beautiful — and you were so composed. Honestly, I got no inkling of your troubled past. I was too selfish to suspect that I needed to worry about you. All I was praying for was to find a place for me in your life."

"Well, you did, and as far as I'm concerned you did it for both of us. Look at us! Aren't we a success?"

"I love to hear you say that, and I treasure the 'us' you're talking about, but I won't lie to you. A young woman needs a broader life than hanging around with a man my age, much less a group of oldsters. You've got to admit, most young women have friends, they date, they enjoy romances..." Here I was interrupted and got a simultaneous, not-so-playful shove.

"Stop, and back up! Isn't all that mine to decide? Are you going to define romance for me? Tell me I can't see men unless I might marry them? Get me to a nunnery?"

"Come on, Paloma. I know you've given all sorts of hints that marriage is a role you don't feel worthy to play, but couldn't that be fallout from your—how can I say it—unorthodox financial plan? There's more to life than economic security. If you want a life, listen to your head *and* your heart. Wouldn't it make sense to get out into the world and at least expose yourself to the possibility of marriage? I'll grant you that sex can be fun without that symbolic commitment, but it's a lesser thing altogether. And marriage can be the stable unit in which you celebrate all the seasons of life. I know something about that."

"Oh come on, yourself! Look to marriage for security? Out of the frying pan, for God's sake! Half of all marriages fail."

"OK. Not now, maybe never. But give yourself a chance to be independent. Your way scares me—your social life—being squired around and into bed by affluent uncles. Life shouldn't be a choice between loneliness and wantonness."

"Haley, what is all this? What do I know about 'the dating game'? I *am* insecure about marriage and family. And the ugly world of commerce. You're so damned glib. 'Go out, get educated, get a job, get married.'"

"Paloma, why would I try to point you off in some wrong direction?"

"So why wouldn't I call it a wrong direction? You're telling me to abandon the things I've started and head off in directions I know nothing about."

Hell! Anneke and Bill trooped in with more "old friend" clients. Paloma's question died away unanswered and both of us had to relax our argumentative stances. Introductions all around led to more sherry, general conversation, and shortly, an invitation to the Hilliers' table for an evening meal advertised as a farewell party for us.

Dinner was a grand affair, and lengthy. Bill told stories on Anneke and Paloma, Anneke told stories on Bill and Paloma, and I told stories of Paloma and Haley in Portugal. The other two couples listened and reacted like real sports and I didn't feel apologetic. There was, after all, that splendid meal and the pleasure of our distinguished company! Just before eleven, we thanked our hosts, said our farewells, and headed off to bed. To my relief, sleep was uppermost in both our minds and I didn't have to further plead my case — nor feign a headache.

Saturday, January 11th

We rose early and organized our things. Paloma had arranged to spend that night with Bessie, and her flight was set for the following day, but I had to be at Heathrow by two-thirty that afternoon and preferred hours early to minutes late. We didn't wait for breakfast, just had coffee and hit the road, our way still strewn with debris and fallen trees and branches.

After an hour's driving, we pulled off for a perfectly decent English breakfast in a perfectly dreadful Anne Hathaway-cum-Disney cottage. After that, Paloma got behind the wheel to acquaint herself with the little Rover before we got into London traffic. In all that commotion, I made no attempt at substantive discussion. My first attempts to state my case had encountered resistance. Best not to push it, I thought, give her time to ponder. And she seemed glad to let serious matters rest. Indeed, she acted specially animated, at times even silly.

At the airport, I lifted her onto a curb and I stood in the gutter, our eyes at the same level. I brushed her nose with mine. I said, "Call me the minute you're home." And she said, "Yes, daddy," and I said, "I'll love you for all time," and she said, "You're impossible," and kissed me right on the mouth, right there in front of God and everybody. Then she was gone and I flew.

VII QUESTIONS

San Diego, California—Tuesday, January 14, 1997

Paloma called two days after I got home. All had gone well, she said, but, "Haley, we had too much fun. I'm lonely already. I really am. What can I do?"

Then I got brave. Too brave. "Come on down. There's more we could kick around and I'll show you my home and my things. And there's a ton of amenities within — are you ready for this? — walking distance!"

"When?"

"You name it."

"Wonderful! I'll get back to you, perhaps tomorrow. I'd love to come and the Volvo needs driving. See ya soon!" She sounded elated. That made me happy, but with misgivings. This time I'd have to confront her, but what strategy could I get in place in a day or two?

And by the time I put the phone down, I had more second thoughts. The junior family members come and go at my place as if it were theirs. But then again, maybe that wasn't such a problem. Gwyn and Ted were off to Tahoe to give their kids, leggy Lynne and intense Birk, a chance to play in the snow. Will was working out of town, and Lys and their active pair, Annelise and Jan, were occupied with all sorts of school and sports activities. Hell, let it happen! In a pinch, I could introduce Paloma to whomsoever. She was hardly an embarrassment.

The next evening, Paloma called again. "May I come tomorrow?"
"Name the hour and I'll fax you a map."
"Great, see you by eleven."
"Drive carefully, precious cargo."

I'd done my best to sound lighthearted and expectant, but panicked and paralyzed were closer to the mark. My attempted overtures at Bettiswood had been interrupted, inconclusive, and had generated resistance. Once again I was loaded with sweet reason, but how would I organize my arguments and lay out my plan? I'd never faced anything like that and, more by default than choice, I made the fateful decision to play more wait-and-see.

In the morning, shortly after ten, I heard wheels on the gravel of my off-street parking. I looked down and got my first glimpse of the white Volvo, amazingly mint for a ten-year-old car. I took the stairs two at a time and opened the front door before Paloma reached the bell. She reached instead for a hug, which she was in no hurry to break. "Thank you for having me" was whispered in my ear, and I murmured "Welcome to Casa Talbot" in hers.

I went to the car to unload bags, and the sight of them made me cringe. I hadn't considered sleeping arrangements, and I had no way to explain if I put her in the guest room downstairs. Damn. Now the whole business of a revised relationship had to be on the table long before bedtime — more pressure, and I was already sweating. I took her and her things upstairs to Marian's dressing area.

When she'd freshened up, we started the home tour with Marian's studio and some of her original art. Paloma took her time, examined and admired everything, and wished aloud that Nourrit could share the showing. I echoed that wish under my breath — for wildly different reasons.

We came to our gallery of family photos and Paloma finally examined the Talbot clan en masse. She remembered all the names and relationships and took my hand as she said, "You're all together, and you love them, and they love you," I thought of her perspective and felt deeply blessed and deeply sad, all at once.

It was easier to accept her compliments for our collection of furnishings and my design of the house, less emotionally charged subjects that loomed large in her interests and experiences. I was flattered when she recalled my remarks to Carlo Giordano about the desirability of cubelike rooms. She whirled slowly around in our living room and assured me that its ambience made my point.

At the hour for lunch, we stepped down the hill to a favorite restaurant, overlooking cliffs and bay. We sat side by side, I thought to share the view, but she was more inclined to hold my hand or lean on my shoulder. She soon brought up her loneliness and I seized the opportunity to tout schools as ready-made social centers. I tacked on another pitch for education, something more specific than a nebulous degree program.

"Why not go for courses in fiction or journalism? You could develop your writing, something you do daily and well."

"Oh," she said, with a dismissive wave of her hand, "That's more therapy than anything else. I keep the diary to record my thoughts and I write letters to stay in touch with the handful of people I really care about."

"So, why don't you expand on that handful? Get out there and find activities and groups connected with your interests, folk art, travel, music — innkeeping even. If you want to foster togetherness, go out and look for it in human contact. Right?"

So we kicked that around — without a lot of enthusiasm on her part. She seemed more interested in what she liked to call "communing," just being together and touching and talking in little bursts about memories or the trivia in front of us. So we did that during our after-lunch foot tour along the waterfront.

Back at the house, Paloma retired for repairs and I waited in the living room. In a few minutes I heard the bedroom door and looked up. There she was, coming through the portal from the hall, clad only in her shortest, most scant nightgown. Her hair was disarrayed. Her eyes shone. She'd wiped the lipstick from her mouth. With her first stride, I was overwhelmed by a fifty-year-old vision formed in a hall of the Louvre, my first encounter with the Winged Victory of Samothráki. Then, I'd been enthralled, but now I was frozen, an anguished appeal welling up inside. "O dear goddess, why do you advance on me more resolutely than ever just as I must withdraw?" Then she was upon me, her hands on my shoulders, speaking, and sending shivers down my spine.

"Everything came apart so badly there at Bettiswood — the storm, the delays, the partying — it so seldom felt really right and there was so little of just us together. You know, we made love only once the whole trip, but I felt closer to you than ever, and more and more as we went. I was afraid you'd think I was avoiding you. So see, I'm not. I'm here."

My vacillating, wait-and-see, non-strategy died on the spot. I had no strategy. She'd plunged me into the heart of the problem. My lofty, reasoned arguments were trumped before they could be laid on the table. I wanted to call time out. Overcome, I sank to my knees and put my arms around the fullness of her hips; I embraced the palpable essence of readiness and consent. Paloma was mine for the taking, captivating, delectable—I could so easily slip into that oblivion. But no, not again. I had to disengage, but for that moment I could not. I clung to the zephyr that had swept me out of my doldrums and back from the far edge of life, the femininity that had become for me the epitome of temptation and fulfillment. I sensed, in living flesh, ancient symbols of promise, fertility, and renewal.

But in the proper scheme of things none of that was mine, and I knew it. I let go. I withdrew my cheek and sat back, holding her hands in mine.

"Oh God, Paloma. Can't you see? If I make love to you now I'll be perpetuating old wrongs. Gustaf taught you that your time and your mind and your body could be traded for gold. Then it was his buddies. Any of them could've stood in as a father, but they all took the low road together. You know how distressed you are at the sight of caged birds? Well, haven't these men caged you up? I can't go on being part of that. Listen to me—the door is open. Spread your wings. Fly."

Tears came to her eyes, her hands were limp in mine, but she said nothing and I had to go on. "Don't you know how unbelievably dear you are to me? Crossing you is the most painful thing I've ever done; I hate it. I can't tell you how sweet it would be to simply make love, but that's not where we need to go."

My mouth had gone dry. Time seemed to stand still and the scene was preposterous. An intensely beautiful young woman stood before me like a statue. Her frozen look combined sorrow and bewilderment. One does not confront such a vision. One rises, embraces, and consoles in the most loving possible way. That is, one does these things if he's operating in his allotted time. I was not. I reminded myself in harsh terms that I was old, that I'd reached into another's time and meddled with the cosmos. Paloma did not realize these truths. She withdrew her hands.

"Haley, I don't get it. I spilled my guts so you could understand me, so you could accept me for what I am and stop being so tentative about us. You've told me over and over how our relationship was fulfilling and inspiring. Life giving, you said. Remember? So why this? And what about me? I've loved your company, I've loved our travels and our intimacy. It's all been a brilliant improvement on what I had before. Why are you so hell-bent to throw over what we have?"

I'd tried to rehearse for that. But how could I defend my earlier words and actions in the face of my new resolve? How could I mollify Paloma as she stood there humiliated, her offering rejected? I had no more wit than to plod on.

"I'm not throwing over our friendship, I'm only trying to change it. If I lie down with you now, I swear I'll relive Gustaf's betrayal every day of my life. I want you to feel free, be a girl again, proceed as you choose into a woman's life. I want you to turn your back on this submissive position Gustaf enticed you into."

Her cheeks flamed, her body tensed into a stunning sculpture of youthful indignation.

"I can't believe this! You blame Gustaf for whatever you find wrong with me. So he did impose sex on me. So I'm sorry about that and, take my word, he came to be sorry too. But no one else was so responsible for making me who I am. If you like the product so much, how about a little credit for its biggest influence? We've known each other just a few months and we've spent one month together — good time, great time — but how does that give you the right to demonize me or Gustaf?"

"Believe in yourself, Paloma. You're so much more than Gustaf's creation. Besides, I'm not denying what he gave you. He deserves credit, and he has that credit in you. But he betrayed you and you suffer the consequences. Nothing excuses him for stunting your emotional growth — and your social life. Paloma, please get out of this trap. Get out into the world. Meet people. Learn the things you've missed. Don't be satisfied to capitalize on the program Gustaf lured you into. Don't substitute that for the full life he steered you away from."

She pulled back and crossed her arms. "Oh, now I get it. You're condemning my financial plan. But damn it all, it's working! My investment counselor long ago made his point—keep my eye on my goal, don't waver, don't be influenced by short-term events. My estate has doubled, better than doubled. I've met my day-to-day expenses, including Bessie and Nourrit. I don't dip into my capital, I add to it. I'm going to be independent and I'll still be young and I intend to be healthy. And I know what I'm doing and where I stand. What's wrong with being independent before I set out to deal with the world?"

She looked so defiant, so young, but she was purposely missing my point. "Paloma, what's wrong comes through loud and clear. This independence you talk about is isolation. You insist that if you're not exactly happy, you're comfortable and on the right financial track. But it is wrong, even if you like some of the results. And look at the other consequences. You say you're lonely and I believe you. No wonder! Your world, your workplace is not a community, it's a series of one-on-one escapes. And you admit to being apprehensive over the way society might be seeing you. Listen, you may feel ostracized, but you're not branded. You can shed this stigma you've conditioned yourself to accept."

"OK, so I got my scarlet letter when I was sixteen and I don't like to wear it out in public. But damn it, Haley! We're not talking about me and society, we're talking about me and you. What happened to you? Sex is a natural part of the togetherness we've shared. You were satisfied to have a here-and-now relationship with me and you never fretted over my other activities, or at least you never gave a hint that it spoiled our time together. And what do you mean about shedding some stigma? Is it that bad? Do I show wear and tear from all my sexual bouts?" She spread her arms wide to invite an appraisal.

"Of course not, you couldn't be physically better and you know it. I'm talking about what this business of yours is doing to your head. Do you have any idea how often you make self-disparaging remarks? They're adding up, they're deforming your self-respect, and I can't just stand back and watch—bitter and apologetic is not you. Anyhow, what I've done bothers me. And what I haven't done. I want to feel right about being with you."

"You feel guilty, so I should feel guilty, right?"

"Whatever you want to call it. I'm just trying to get you to grab the wheel and steer your own course. Your men have the time and money to play, to dally around, and your whole life is their spare time. You're sidetracked, you're not going anywhere."

That made her bristle. She got up, paced toward the dining room, and turned back, her fists clenched. "I am going somewhere. And I'm going to get there. You can't imagine how threatened I'd feel if I gave up my guaranteed income and threw over my investment adviser. I don't have to take those chances."

"But you do have to, Paloma. This man may serve your pockets, but don't you see his built-in conflict of interests? He's got an insider's position to protect and he's the one who sold you on the idea that you needed an absolute fortune before you could feel secure. Hell, he was talking an amount of money that you or anyone else could retire on. Damn it all, you're not ready to retire. You haven't really started. Remember what Sister Eugenia said? Something like, 'The trick is in coming to believe that there's a life-saving difference between right and wrong.' You never intended such a thing, of course, but I think you wandered into 'wrong' and accepted it. Look at yourself! You're selling yourself a slice at a time like dessert at the end of the old boys' Dinner of Life. What a treat for them! But the point is, what about you?"

I hated what I was doing. I hated the sound of myself. I saw the strong, vibrant person before me shriveling. The tones and words of her reply carried a reproach that made my eyes fill.

"It's not like you to be cruel. How dare you! You make me feel even more lost just when I need you most. You want me to burn my plans and start all over. Well I have no idea how to start over, or what else to do, or if I even want to!"

She took a step and crumpled into a chair. She put her head down and wept. I didn't know what to do. I went over and knelt beside her. She was shivering.

"Paloma, I don't mean to scare you. I love you and I'm frightened for you. Lord knows, I'd give anything to be able to offer you marriage, family, a share in my future. But what a cruel illusion. I'd be offering you a job as nurse-companion. I'd be offering you a fatherless child. And a share in my future is a share in my will. I've already had a life and all I can offer now is love and experience. But those aren't nothing. Please, please take them and put them to use."

She wasn't looking at me, she wouldn't look at me. She'd shrunk into herself. I'll never understand why I pushed on, but I did.

"Look, I'm not speaking for me alone. Think of your grandmother. She called you her gift from God because she saw how good and promising you were, the polar opposite of her son. Think of Bessie and Nourrit, think how they feel about you, how they worry — no, it's worse than worry, they agonize. How can your plan be so right if it distresses everyone who loves you?"

She sat so still, head down, silent. I put my hands lightly on her shoulders and attempted to massage her rigid neck. She shook me off. I bowed my head and prayed she would respond.

At last she did, her voice low and constrained. "I called you and told you I was lonely and miserable. I asked for your understanding and support, and you invited me to come. This is your idea of a welcome? I loved what we've been to each other — now you're saying it was wrong. You make me feel dirty. I can't stand it." She rose and turned her back. "Don't say anything, just let me be, let me go."

I was numb. I couldn't raise my head until I heard the bedroom door close. It was over, further argument would be an insult. But I had to add something, forbidden to speak or not. I got a pad and wrote, *No matter what, I know you will do the right thing. H. T.*, and pinned it inside her hat and put it back on the table in the front hall.

I virtually held my breath for fifteen quiet minutes before she came out of the bedroom — but not to me. I heard her steps on the stair and the front door open and shut. I went to the window and looked down as she backed out and sped away, away from me, in her old but perfect white Volvo — a gesture from Gustaf's dead hand. It made me sick.

I felt spent and empty. I had failed the conditions attached to the great gift of my later years. The next hours burned into me the degree to which I was obsessed by Paloma, her story, her problems, her future. Worst of all, I missed her. I began to relive the emptiness that followed Marian's death.

Days later I pulled myself together enough to keep my promise to Bessie. I sent her a summary of my attempts at reform and the breakup that resulted. I never received a reply. I'd neglected to get Nourrit's address, but I faxed a note to Anneke and Bill.

I wish I had better news. I did my best to get Paloma redirected — and got the sack instead. I'm now out of the loop, persona non grata, but don't you give up, I haven't. There is good stuff there and it's going to assert itself. (But a few prayers and crossed fingers wouldn't hurt.) Good luck to us all!

And Anneke did get back to me, promising they'd keep their ears to the ground and send me any news. But that was the end of that.

Every sorry day, I dragged myself through this or that step leading up to my debacle, blaming myself for ineptitude and making endless attempts to imagine what I should've done instead. I decided that I'd over-assessed Paloma's maturity. When I attacked the basis of her livelihood, I'd made her feel that I was attacking her. I was so full of myself and my wonderful logic, my senior statesmanlike vision of the world, that I assumed she'd be convinced. I didn't allow for youthful resentment at being confronted. I made myself a threat — and she scarcely heard my arguments. She retreated instead to the arms of the more cooperative members of her coterie.

I decided that, bastard child and all, Paloma had always seen herself as a member of the privileged class, equated herself with Amparo and Gustaf, not with her beloved Bessie and Nourrit. Her interests and pursuits associated her with patricians. She had their ways, their tastes, their vocabulary, their point of view, and she identified with their freedom from drudgery — that was a perquisite of her curious life, and one she was not about to renounce. No years of required studies for her. No nine-to-five jobs or cut-and-dried career paths. I might as well have been baying at the moon as trying to sell those programs to her. She was spoiled, and that was the end of it.

But that argument collapsed on the spot. Blaming Paloma was like saying there'd never been any hope, and I asked myself, "Do you believe that? Paloma is hope personified. Blame yourself. Why were you in such a hurry? Why couldn't you take whatever time was needed, court her, enjoy her company, take every opportunity to introduce ideas and talk them up? She came to you, and you turned on her. Why?"

Selfish reasons, I'm afraid. My pride and my already-compromised principles were at stake and I was too petty to put them aside and be an effective mentor. Why, in God's name, had I been so self-righteous and so impatient? Why? Why? Why? I lay awake for hours each night bouncing hopeless questions off the unfeeling walls of my empty nest.

My phone rang at breakfast nearly three months after Paloma went out of my life. I was still in the chills-and-fever, jumpy-irritable stage of withdrawal, but, for once, I answered calmly enough. I was expecting a call from Gwyn, but it was an unfamiliar voice. "Am I speaking to Haley Talbot? This is Herb Knowland, M.D., Laguna Beach."

I practically leaped into the mouthpiece. "Paloma's doctor friend? Dear God, please don't tell me something's happened to Paloma."

"I have no idea. That's why we need to talk."

"Praises be, no news *is* good news. But I've got to tell you, we may be in the same boat."

"Maybe. But Paloma's gone missing, I'm hurting for info, and you're my only candidate. Is this a good time?"

"The best." I tried to sound nonchalant but my head was spinning. One of the old boys was in the same fix I was in—Paloma was gone from both our horizons. Hallelujah! She didn't fly back into the arms and beds of the syndicate! I was jubilant, but I wanted to hear the doctor out before I began to whoop.

He went on, "Did you get a note from her?"

"I sure did not."

"Seems odd.... Oh, right up front, I abused a confidence to track you down. I was the one who arranged for Leo Lachner. Remember, a doctor came to your place? His report had your name and number on it. Paloma'd called me for advice, she'd just met you. Well, that was a surprise, you being an outsider and all, but she didn't tell me another thing, and I didn't ask—that was our understanding from the word 'go.' So I'm bending the rules—but, hell, nowhere else to turn."

"Hey, don't sweat that, tell me about the note."

"Damndest thing, just four lines, very formal. Said she was off someplace until some issues were resolved and some decisions made. Asked for patience and said she'd get back to me when it was all cleared up."

"Sorry, that's all news to me. The question is, what's she up to?"

"Right, and I was hoping you could give me something to go on."

"OK, I'll tell you what I can, but let me ask, when did you or anybody see her last?"

The doctor brightened up. "End of November. I took her off for a week, but I was sick right from the start, all she did was play nurse, a real sport the way she always is. So I called some time late January, early February, to set up another jaunt, but she said she had an engagement. She sounded sort of detached, for her, not like herself. I took the trip anyhow, a real dud, it turned out — you know, no Paloma on the other side of the breakfast table. When I got back, I called to check her schedule for May/June, left a message, but nothing happened. I wrote to her and it was two weeks till I got that note. Well, I felt disconnected, big time. I figured something'd happened that had nothing to do with me. I know two of the others reasonably well, and they had no clue. They'd gone through the same routine and got the same note. I called the other man, Paloma's broker. I know him only a bit but I figured he had to know something, he's her landlord and he's got all her assets on his books. Well, that was frustrating as hell. He knows all right, but he ain't tellin'. I begged him, 'For God's sake, give me a hint, put me out of my misery.' He said there were damn few people he'd stonewall for, but too bad for me, Paloma was one of 'em. He said he wouldn't add a word or a letter to the note I got in the mail. 'Sorry.' That was it, he hung up on me. The whole thing didn't last two minutes."

"Doctor, I feel for you. I guess the only bright spot is the loyalty Paloma inspires — much good that does us! Anyhow, here's my side of it. I'll confess right up front I may've set off this disappearance thing. I don't know, but the timing's suspicious. She and I traveled a couple of times, the first before your November outing, and the other after Christmas. Nice, relaxed trips, I thought, but things changed as we went along. I got to know her better and that gave me cold feet about our agreement. The last thing in the world I wanted to do was break it off or lose her, so I told her as best I could that I wanted her as a friend instead of as a mistress. I thought I'd be doing us both a favor, but the fact is, it blew up in my face."

"Funny. I've never seen Paloma blow up or be all that emotional. What was it that got to her like that?"

"Well, you may decide I was meddling, but here it is — she and I fell out because I tried to persuade her to stop being dependent on you all, and me. I made a pitch for her to get into some studies, some employment, anything she could devote herself to and take pride in and use as a platform for a life."

"Mr. Talbot, I don't know how you handled it—not great I can see—but I'm sorry it didn't go better. If it comes to that, I'd say I'm at the point where I'd be more comfortable, happier really, to have Paloma as a friend, period. Believe it or not, I've always thought of her as a friend, and you're right, she did need to get something else going."

"Doctor, I'm glad you see that, you knowing her for years and all. I just couldn't stand by and watch her stagnate, much less help her do it. But I didn't see that she wasn't ready for that much change, or at least she wasn't ready to talk about it. She said so in no uncertain terms, then she left. And I've had no word since—believe me, I've gone through my own hell. But listen, do you realize what happens when we put your news and mine together? It shows that Paloma didn't just cut me off. I don't know how you'd interpret that, but it gives me the idea that she might be considering my arguments. Otherwise, why would she cut her ties to all of you? Weren't you her other sources of income?"

"You know, you're right. I didn't think of that. Hot damn! That could be it. But it's still hard to believe her leaving us to worry like this—that's not like her at all."

"Well, maybe she needs time to herself, time to think and not have to account for anything or make excuses. I try to visualize good things going for her. I'm not religious, but I'm learning to pray, if you know what I mean."

"Amen, brother!"

That was enough. I had Knowland on the line and I could have fished for more insight on the syndicate, but I let him go. I didn't want to know and I never want to know. Let them wrestle with their own demons.

In the months after, I was often tempted to call Bessie or try to reach Nourrit. Providentially, I held back and finally junked the idea altogether. If the stockbroker had instructions to stonewall, why would Paloma give free rein to the women in her inner circle? And why would I want to put them on the spot? If I were not cut off forever already, that might ensure it.

A maddening year dragged by in which I heard nothing. Then months more. Whenever I was most down in the dumps, I'd get out my photographs of our trips and play disks we'd shared and enthused over. I might have lost Paloma, but the pictures and music evoked the Paloma I'd known before my faux pas.

After those sessions, and under their influence, I'd write to her at her P.O. box. At first, it was apologies for the form my efforts had taken, but not for their substance. And no recriminations, only best wishes for whatever she might be doing. Then I took to writing as if no problem existed. I'd offer ideas and encouragement as if I knew she was in some sort of transition. I repeated my dreams for her and reminded her how capable she was. My letters weren't returned, but they weren't answered either. After months I'm afraid I rather lost hope and let a plaintive note creep into my writing, but I never dared to include the wistful postscript that I breathed with every mailing: "Paloma, I'll never forget. Don't you."

However, even in my worst moments, I remained grateful that Paloma had brought me back to life and given me months of high adventure. I remembered what a mess I'd been after losing Marian and I didn't let myself backslide into that abysmal state. Gradually, my feeling of bereavement lessened and, in some figurative sense, I divided myself into two parts. In one guise, I became productive, threw myself into research, writing, and everyday chores. I cultivated my kin and attended the events — family, school, and sports — that go with grandparenthood. I tried to get out more and socialize with the people I knew.

But, truth to tell, not everything returned to normal or progressed. The part of me that had grown and flourished with Paloma remained forlorn, holding its breath, and leaving me aware of the strain. My history of Spanish California grew, but I lagged behind, waiting, waiting, waiting for a sign from the life I'd lost — and struggling with a growing suspicion that I might wait forever.

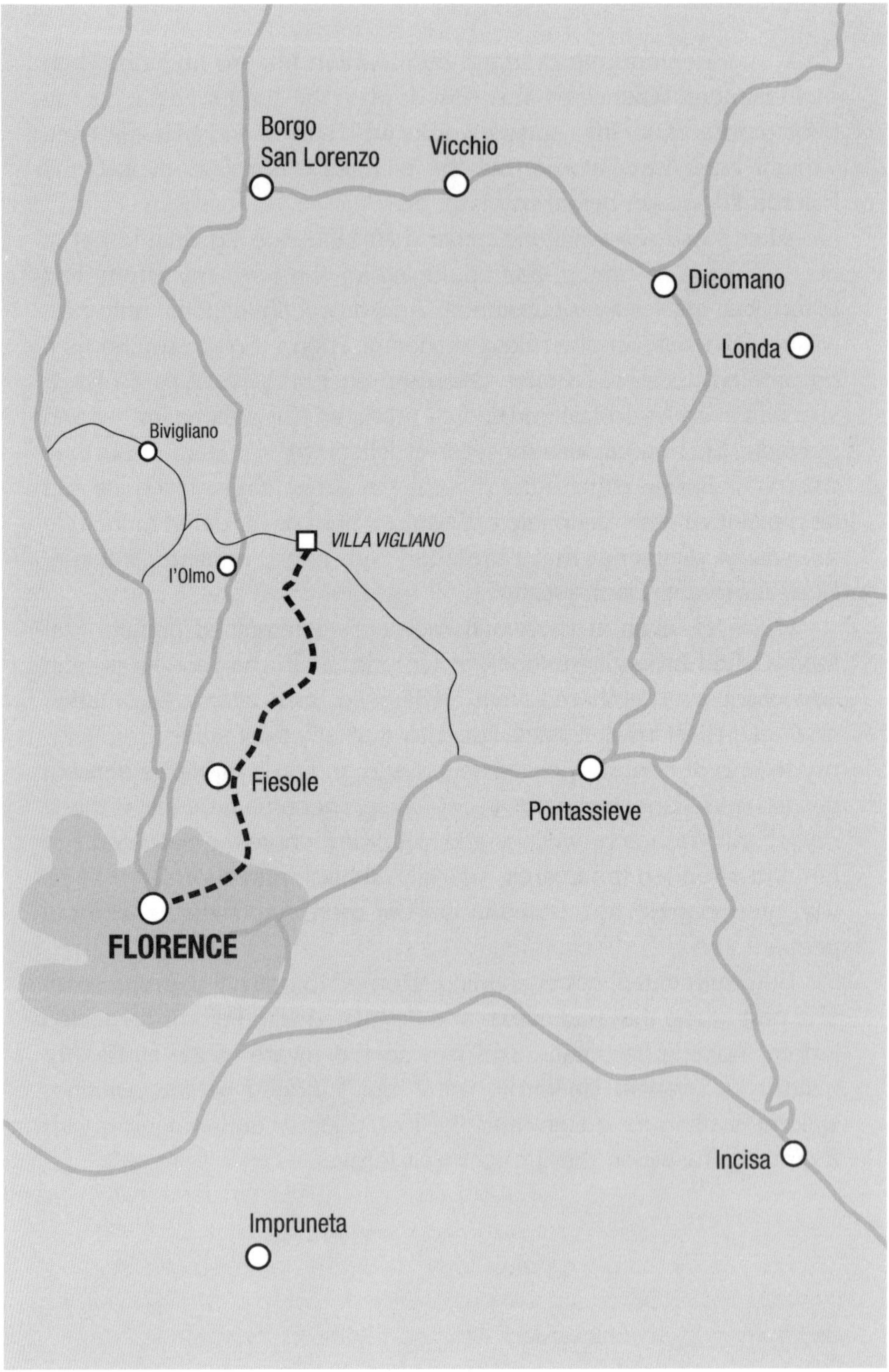
Borgo
San Lorenzo
Vicchio
Dicomano
Londa
Bivigliano
VILLA VIGLIANO
l'Olmo
Fiesole
Pontassieve
FLORENCE
Incisa
Impruneta

VIII ANSWERS

San Diego, California — Tuesday, August 5, 1998

Early in the day, almost nineteen months after Paloma drove away — and, yes, I was counting — my fax machine spluttered to life. In a few seconds I saw familiar handwriting and began to shake.

> *Dearest Haley, I am guilty of this long, cruel silence. I have no excuses, only reasons. Remember, you used to tell me I had no childhood, that I missed the vagaries and caprices of adolescence? You encouraged me to be a teenager once again and grow up my own way, and I fear I responded to that suggestion. Please try to forgive my childish need to keep you in the dark. I swore myself to silence until I had great news to impart. Now I am aghast. At long last, I make myself realize how much has happened, how much time has passed, and how unfair I have been. My first way to make amends is to tell you everything.*
>
> *Your Paloma, trying to be better.*

As I read, I could hear the machine whirring and clicking, creating other pages and spitting them out. I started to scan the printed lines and, blessedly, to feel broken ties being mended.

Haley,

When I left you I was as bitter as I have ever been. I felt you had turned me away—and attempted to destroy my confidence in my own decisions. I felt totally cut adrift because, as I realize now, I had come to depend on you as my confidant and counselor. Twice I found my idiot mind telling me to reach for the phone, call you, and ask you how I should cope. I was beside myself and I wanted it to be all your fault.

I was angry with you for recognizing and exposing the unease in me that I had long felt but wasn't addressing. Of course I was fighting like mad not to accept it, but in any case, it was not fair that you should confront me with it. Besides, where did you, a man, get the right to lecture a woman about sexual mores?

I was angry with you for suggesting that my plan wasn't working. I had comfortable relations with my old boys, and that let me rationalize about the ugly side that was so plain to Bessie and Nourrit—and you. I had stayed with my clients for four years and close to tripled my money. I saw myself as well over half way home, and then you came along and tried to spoil it. How dare you?

And there was the physical rejection. I was hurt, particularly hurt because I had felt that your touch was special and our physical closeness was precious. You were certainly clever, you certainly did get my attention, you certainly did make me think.

But not right away. I left your house vowing to go back to things as they were before Santa Fe. Perhaps the old boys could order me up like a *crème brûlée*, but I also had them wrapped around my little finger. But even if I wasn't admitting it, I had heard your warning. I knew I was frozen into four immature, artificial relationships. I would get nothing more from my partners than the money, and they nothing more from me than the fun and games they had bargained for. Going back to them was the easy way out, but you had ruined it for me. And, yes, I know that was your purpose all along.

After a bad night, I decided to hunt up Sister Eugenia and talk to her (which I had not done since she took her sabbatical). Years ago, I tried to get her address from St. Brigid's, hoping to send holiday greetings, but the school told me she had never returned to their employ and they had no address to give. This time, luckily, I found a woman in the office who knew her and had her telephone number. The next day I spoke to Sister herself, except now she is Jane Schmelzer. She had renounced her vows, married, had two children, and she and her husband were working for the World Wildlife Fund in Anchorage. She sounded pleased to hear from me and said I had been one of her better pupils. I tried to tell her how big and positive her influence had been, and she sounded almost apologetic, as if she needed to justify leaving the service of the church and taking a hiatus from teaching. She said something like, "Paloma, I came to realize that when I took the vow I denied a part of myself, and that devoting myself to teaching alone, always with children, would be a constant reminder of that unfulfilled part." Her news opened my eyes. I saw that one of the most committed choices a woman can make is not necessarily final, that while we breathe we retain the power to change. After that I did not attempt to discuss my life with her. She sounded busy and preoccupied with home and family, and I could see that my problems would be laborious to explain and sound quite bizarre, and besides we had talked long enough to pull me out of my self-centered whirlpool. We exchanged addresses, and then letters and photos last Christmas.

But I was still aimless in my dilemma. I began to recognize that Gustaf did only half the job of preparing me to be an adult. He taught me to observe and analyze. He taught me how the world works, but always as seen by an outsider. He taught me to be like him, a spectator, an audience, a critic, anything but a participant. Then, in my wild casting about, I knew I needed Nourrit.

I had never taken myself abroad all on my own. It felt odd to book a flight for just me and strange to send a telegram to Nourrit. More strange sensations came on the flight. It was night, but dawn was approaching—you know how fast it comes as you go east. I had a window seat and I stared out into the barest ghosts of clouds and felt myself tumbling over and over through the sky and my past, all sort of jumbled together. I was angry because you had called me spoiled and lazy. Underneath, I am sure I had some perverse pride in having coped with and overcome a lot. I had not seen it that way at all when I was a child, the idea did not come to me until I had crossed the Rubicon with Gustaf. I suppose that started me to rationalize, to project backward and decide that I had been a real Little Engine That Could. When you confronted me, I was not ready for the idea that ninety-nine percent of the world didn't have my material advantages, or that I was running away from work and responsibility by taking an easy way out. So even if I had hated having that thrown in my face, I came to hate even more the probability that I was paying a price for self-indulgence and perhaps was not the self I might have been. That was the first of your arguments that I accepted emotionally and resolved to face. I am not proud of that. It shows how self-centered I was. First should have been my responsibility to others, your question about what I was doing to Bessie and Nourrit—but it wasn't. Not till later. Anyhow, I watched the sunrise out the plane window and asked myself, "What do I do to put all that behind me?" I still had no answers, but at least I was looking.

I flew on from Madrid to Sevilla, went directly to Nourrit, and found her and her home just as we left them—but not Benito! You would not believe how he had grown; by now, he must be as tall as I. I was tired and Nourrit put me on a couch under a ceiling fan and massaged my neck and my back—I can still feel her rhythm becoming part of my prayers. Then I slept, and when I woke after dark it was as if I had broken a fever. I sat up considering challenges, not quandaries. It was very strange, I absolutely assure you.

Benito had made some wonderful onion soup and good bread. As we ate supper, I told them I had turned my back on the men I had been dealing with, actually on my whole way of life, and now I felt terribly lonely and detached. I spent that night on a cot in Nourrit's workroom.

The next day I sat down with Nourrit, counting on her, as I had years before, to have ideas that would help me. First she reminded me of her childhood on a farm near a river. She recalled her earliest memories, working in the fields with her family, and told me how she still felt rooted to that spot, even though her body and soul had been stretched to faraway places.

She described a patio in Casablanca. In it were four large pots and in each a tree had long ago been planted. The trees were small and stunted, she said, their earth depleted and salted out—that is, three were small and stunted, but the fourth tree's pot had cracked, its roots had escaped and taken hold in the soil. That tree was ten times the size of the others.

She said my roots were stunted, that I had been watered and fed by a parade of gardeners as I was carted around like a plant in a pot. She said I needed to grow, something she had prayed for, and now that my pot was broken, I could take root in the ground. My life had been arranged so I could know many lands, many people, many ways. Those experiences would guide me in placing myself.

A series of impressions washed over me. Nourrit was echoing you. Sister Eugenia had broken her pot and found a place to take root. All of you were sending fragments of a message that I was beginning to assemble. I found myself answering my own questions with decisions I had already made. Now that I look back, it is easy to see that I had digested your arguments and was imagining a future for which you had, to some extent, furnished a blueprint. But that's not the way I saw it then, and I was not ready to give you credit—far from it. I was determined to show you up by performing some miracle on my own.

(Haley, I must interrupt. My desk stands before a window in our drawing room. It has rained all morning but we are up so close under our wide eaves that I leave the window open to be part of the scene. This morning, a summer storm quite boiled up the valley and swept us with dark and showers. Minutes ago, the sun burst out and now shines on us and our forecourt while rain still falls. The most intense rainbow arches through it all. May I offer you one end of my rainbow? May we join hands once again?)

My second afternoon in Sevilla, I took a room at a hotel and called Carlo Giordano (I had one of the cards he gave us the month before). After some delays, I got through to his sister Giulia and learned that Carlo would be gone for days. I was impatient, so I asked her directly how their affairs were proceeding. She was cordial, but naturally not inclined to tell me much— I am not sure she had ever heard of me. Then I came right out with my idea. I told her how I met Carlo in Dorset and how he showed me his plans and drawings. I recalled how we had discussed the future of Villa Vigliano and the funds that would be needed. I told her I had money to invest, but that I must have a job to go with my investment. I asked her to discuss my proposal with her brother and begged them to call me as promptly as possible. I must say, Giulia was sweet. She promised to talk to Carlo as soon as she could arrange, and that one of them would call me in a day or two.

I lay on the bed and was lulled by the breeze of another ceiling fan. I assure you I had no premonition that I would really find a place at Villa Vigliano. The villa came to mind because it needed money, perhaps an associate, and, judging from Carlo, would be run by people I could imagine working with. I tried to see ahead into the swarm of my ideas and come up with a Plan B to pursue when I was turned down by the Giordanos. I was neither depressed nor holding my breath, which I proved by drifting off to sleep.

Imagine my surprise when the telephone rang in my ear. It was less than an hour since I had spoken with Giulia, but she was on the line again. "I talked to Carlo," she said, "he called minutes after you hung up. We both think you should come at once and see us and Villa Vigliano. Let us know when you will arrive and we will meet you." She sounded like an angel calling from the skies, and I told her so. "It is a villa," she laughed, "it is not the Kingdom of Heaven." I loved her immediately, as I will forever.

Here the page ended and the next was in Paloma's hand.

Haley, I have to interrupt. Carlo does not approve of my account of our meeting. He wants to help in bringing you up to date, and since we are married, we listen to each other. He will phone to explain.

Your Paloma

I swear, as I read those words, I recalled the magic that had hovered over my communications with Paloma. When my phone rang, I picked it up with, "Carlo! Is that you?"

"My God, it is!" he laughed. "Mr. Talbot? Haley? May I call you that? Good! I don't want to be kicked again by Paloma. Listen. We have so much to tell you and so much to show you, for me, the proper way is to have you here for some days and look you in the eye to better communicate. Can you come soon? The sooner the better!"

Well, I was shocked and I was thrilled. Since I read Paloma's line about their married state, I'd had no chance to reflect, but now I began to visualize the metamorphosis she might have made. And I was immensely grateful to Carlo for accepting me at all—knowing as I did that the ever-honest Paloma would long ago have told him whatever he hadn't guessed about her relations with me.

"Carlo, thank you both for a generous invitation. I can't wait to see you and hear what you're doing. I'm thrilled to hear your news, wonderful, wonderful news. I'll admit that I've been worried sick, but now I'm cured, more than cured."

Carlo sounded contrite. "I feel very wrong that you had to worry, so does Paloma. It was her problem, but it is past. We pray to put all this burden down and celebrate. We hope very much you will wish to celebrate. When can we do that?"

I'd been looking over my calendar. This was a Thursday. "How about next Tuesday?"

"Really? That is wonderful! Tell us, please, which is your flight and we will meet you. We cannot wait to see you and tell you and show you. Paloma hugs me to pass on to you. Our house is yours as long as you wish."

"Grazie mille!" I said.

"Ciao!"

The weight that had borne me down all those awful months lifted with the gathering force of a missile launch. Paloma is well! She's happy! She's with Carlo, a fine fellow, a prince among men. The *Et expecto* from Bach's *B Minor Mass* struck up in my giddy head, its outbursts of fearful joy sounding and resounding. I made my way to a nearby cliff-top path and wandered, staring out over the rolling surf. People must have thought me mad with my vacant eyes and foolish smile. I came home to lie flat and listen to myself exult.

That evening I received another fax, a single handwritten paragraph.

> *Haley dear, I have told Carlo and Giulia everything about everything. We have no secrets. We may discuss anything we wish and even tell war stories — as long, of course, as they are in reasonably good taste! And I have to tell you one thing more, there are no clouds on the horizon, none at all. There are no ifs, buts, or perhapses. I am so happy. You will see!*
>
> *A big hug from Paloma*

I had to dab at my eyes before I could read it again.

The next morning I sat and scanned the sea over rooftops, gratefully aware of a peace I hadn't known since the first shock of Marian's cancer. More than peace — actually, it was a lightheartedness I'd forgotten, something deeper than the welter of surprise and jubilation I'd gone through the day before. In those first hours, relief and gratitude drowned out details, but now I could laugh at myself as I pieced together what Paloma had done. Ever since the doctor revealed her break with the syndicate, I had pictured her taking steps toward a new life worthy of her abilities — as I saw them. But yesterday I'd learned that she pursued a less arduous and less ambitious route. I was the one who had invented some castle in the clouds and urged her to occupy it.

Her decision to break from her dependence on the old boys was another matter. I never presumed that I introduced that idea; all along, I'd seen shadows of reluctance and shame behind her defensive facade. But I could take pride in pushing her to make the break and go for some better thing — the timing and her own words attested to that. The more I kicked it around, the more I admired her direct response. She remembered Carlo and his project and that hotel keeping was at its heart. She not only took pleasure in fine hotels and inns, she was intrigued by the mechanics of their operation, and her friends Anneke and Bill had taken her behind the scenes. Carlo and his sister needed money. Paloma had some money. Carlo was an attractive man, maybe from her new perspective more than attractive. Florence? In a pinch, one could make do with Florence. Given the circumstances, the outcome seemed almost inevitable. Why hadn't I thought to step into Paloma's shoes and perhaps locate her a year ago? Well, better that I did not. I'd meddled enough. She needed to make her own choices — and take credit or blame for the results.

Curiously, I didn't find her less sympathetic because she'd gone for the quick fix — that was human and understandable. What I could not forgive her was putting me through such hell for so long. That was vindictive, not like her. Nevertheless, I said a prayer for Villa Vigliano, the seat of her new happiness. And I couldn't wait to get over there and see for myself.

I told my family I was invited to an Italian country hotel opened by old friends. "How gala," they said, and encouraged me to go, plainly welcoming my changed mood, regardless of how puzzling it might have been, or for that matter, how puzzling the long low period that went before.

The flight was a prolonged ordeal until I was on the local leg leaving Milano and could feel the end at hand. Minutes later, I was out of the plane and hurrying up to Paloma and Carlo, she stepping toward me, hands outstretched. I took them and pecked her cheeks before she placed one of my hands on her belly. It was large and firm. She swung me around with the order, "Say hello to the father of our child."

Carlo was all smiles. "Haley, Haley, it is good to see you again. I have much to show you, no, we have much to show you, much to talk about. We can't wait. Let's go." I shook the man's hand and gave him a big hug and pats on the back. While I waited for my luggage, my hosts went off for their car and I reacted to the biggest surprise thus far—Paloma, some six months pregnant. Lucky child. After two generations of shame and neglect, this one would have a father and, I guessed, about a mother and a half.

In a few minutes we were gliding along the road but stumbling in our attempts at conversation. We had much to catch up on and an array of new things to go over, but there'd been that long, awkward interlude, and that was not easy to ignore. "Too soon for probing exchanges," I thought, and inquired about the child. "Nearly seven months," said Paloma, then echoed my thoughts by referring to Baby Mystery as the first in three generations of her line to be wanted and waited for with great expectations.

"Let it be a girl," I hoped aloud. "No fair for a boy child to come along and be outrageously spoiled. Not after two girls in a row had to endure such grudging worlds."

"Aye, aye, sir," said Paloma.

Carlo beamed and chimed in, "I cannot wait. In my first marriage, I saw trouble when the woman who was my wife was not enthusiastic for children, she had difficulties to relate to them, even to talk to them. Paloma has enthusiasm for everyone and she can talk to everyone. I give you my word, since Paloma came to us, we are so popular! I need more training as the diplomat to get her away from every party, every group of people. All people want her attention and hang on her. It goes so far that we must budget our time for these things."

"Ah," I replied. "Were you not warned? Did you not know that Paloma casts spells with every glance? Has anyone been able to resist her?

Poor Carlo! You've joined the ranks of us lost souls. But who would have it any other way? Who needs lotus to eat when he can share the planet with Paloma?"

The subject of all this put the back of one hand to her forehead, gave a theatrical groan, and emoted in tones of lofty annoyance. "Carlo, haven't I warned you about Haley? And remember, he makes puns, can't restrain himself. Just wait and see." She made a face at me.

I did my best to blush. "Paloma gives me far too much credit."

I'd peeked at the odometer when I first got in, and now I saw that we must be nearing our goal. With another game in mind, I asked casually, "Carlo, tell me about Villa Vigliano."

He took my bait in all innocence. "Oh, much progress. Since Paloma came to take part, a big crew works with us what you call full time. We are finished remodeling the big house, much in accord with the plans you saw two years ago. Two of our farmhouses we have remodeled and made their grounds in good order. We have brilliant success to rent them by weeks and months, and we expect better when we offer more services in the big house. We complete work for two of the other three farms by the spring of the year that comes. I have confidence for that because we concentrated to make new roofs and now they are completed before the winter—that way we can work inside and not lose time with the weather. One of them will be the *gioia*—how is it? jewel? gem?—of our offerings. We have made it grand in the classic way and it has a view equal to the big house, also better trees all around, also more protection from our winds that blow down on us from the Alps. You will see, Paloma has done much planning and working on all of this. You will be surprised."

I scanned the hillsides at each turn, and finally spotted my objective. I pointed and asked, "Carlo, do I see Villa Vigliano up there?"

He was astonished. "How possibly can you know that?"

"Surely you remember showing me pictures taken from every angle."

Paloma cut in, still affecting mock irritation, "Carlo, you will get used to it. He remembers everything. It's really quite disgusting!"

As we pulled into the villa, I had to admire Carlo's management of the site. It's no small trick to operate a country inn and run a good-sized construction job as neighbors on a fairly steep slope. Necessarily, both operations utilized the same entry, but a fork in the road enabled crews, building equipment, and materials to go around a knoll that hid them from the manor house and its immediate grounds. Carlo drove directly to the villa parking where he summoned a porter for my bags. We trailed him up the stair and across the graceful plaza whose development Carlo and I had discussed and somewhat disagreed over. I turned to him and he winked. He was right; I was surprised. He'd let me discover for myself that it was principally my scheme he'd adopted. All right, I'll admit that I liked it, and I was soon to learn that he was grateful. "This," I reminded myself, "is not a petty man."

Odd sensations of déjà vu overtook me as I entered the main building. I had pored over the plans so thoroughly that I could literally have walked to any desired room. What I hadn't visualized, and what delighted me, was the elegance of the old stonework and the artistry of new plaster that somehow mimicked the patina of well-tended age. My inspection of this handsome work on a handsome structure gave me confidence that my friends would be offering an admirable product.

Inside, the Giordanos had another surprise. They'd said nothing, but there was Bessie Barr, living at the villa as a combination of guest and bookkeeper. I was delighted to give her a hug and get back pats and a "bless you!" in my ear. While I stood with my arm around her and made small talk, I imagined Nourrit in the next room, Consuelo in the kitchen, and Celestina in housekeeping. Not so, it turned out, but all through my stay I half-expected another surprise around any corner.

After a cursory tour of the main hall, I was ready for a nap and retired to the charming second-story room and view put at my disposal. When my eyes next opened, I enjoyed a valley panorama drenched in golden light as I straightened myself up to go downstairs.

Guests were assembling for afternoon drinks and discussions of their days. What a contrast with Bettiswood Hall, not only the grander scale of the structure and the room, but the cosmopolitan air of the whole enterprise. Bettiswood is near no major cultural center but London, hours away; Vigliano is a half hour from magnetic Florence, a proximity that affects every activity and the ambience itself.

Paloma was nowhere to be seen, but Carlo was there and introduced me around. In minutes I was embarrassed by wholesale exaggerations of my supposed input to the villa's planning and design. I had to take my host aside and remind him that, in one case, he'd credited me with an idea, actually his, which he and I had discussed only as an alternate to another of his own. He laughed, and said he was happy to have things as they were and glad to give credit to all involved.

"Haley," he added, "I owe you so much and for so much."

"Great," I said, "but couldn't we keep it to ourselves?"

"How is it Paloma says? 'Aye, aye, sir?' I will tell only what is true, I promise you." And that vow he largely, if not scrupulously, fulfilled.

Duty called Carlo away, but I mingled with the guests and had no trouble detecting a general enthusiasm for the villa and its hosts. I breathed more easily. After all, it was I who had advised Paloma to invest in something in which she could be involved.

I had dinner with the Giordanos and Bessie, but we didn't bring up the charged topic of the recent past. Talk was light, suitable to the start of a reunion and intended to entertain me and prepare me for planned activities. Dinner over, I passed up the sociability in the grand lounge and headed off to bed in a thoroughly contented frame of mind.

Morning light turned pink as I threw on my clothes. Carlo was in the kitchen when I showed up seeking coffee, and he led me, cup in hand, onto the terrace and over to a series of admirable tables, cast iron openwork topped with glass.

"Belgian, turn of the century. We were so fortunate to find six of them, all alike. Two were broken, but our welder does miracles. Look to find his mends."

"Thanks, Carlo, but I'm satisfied with what anybody would see. They're magnificent out here, and good, I'll bet, for another hundred years."

"Haley, let me change our subject. Let me tell you, Paloma needs to talk with you. She is so very nervous over this, she feels guilty for all the time she made you wait. She thinks about it and gets into sweats, real sweats, I tell you. She will be with us for breakfast, then I will take myself over to our construction for an hour—no, more, definitely more. I have tried to tell you how I feel guilty this same way. I agreed to keep you in the dark even when it felt wrong to me, so I was wrong, with Paloma. What troubles me most is—Paloma now admits this—you did nothing to deserve this to happen to you. It is the reverse. I am absolutely the most grateful for all you did, everything!

You did it for me even if you could not guess such a thing. You set Paloma on the path that brought her here, you got her to think about working and making her feel secure of herself to go into marriage. She told me how directly you opposed the way she lived and how you said these things to her. It is strange. She felt so very much rejected, and she went away from you so bitter for your judgments, but she remembers every word, and now they are to her like additions to the ten great orders from God, I ask pardon for blasphemy."

"Look, Carlo, I was worried sick over Paloma's disappearance, but I never believed she was off doing something stupid or self-destructive. She's a born survivor. And now I get to see my wishes for her come true, and sooner than I ever imagined. It's everything I've prayed for. Paloma was an inspiration to me when I wasn't facing the problems in my life — and when I saw that she needed help, I wanted to do something for her, whatever I could. That's what I was trying to get started when we met you in Dorset."

Carlo remembered all too well. "I had no idea of that. I knew only I could not permit myself look at Paloma for fear I would offend you. That was for me so difficult, I cannot really tell you."

"Well, I did notice that you admired her, but most people do, and I didn't give it much thought. I was too busy trying to figure out what moves I ought to make. Then, when I finally pinned her down and asked her to rethink her modus operandi, she ran away, and I was afraid I'd frightened her more than I'd persuaded her. Thank God she thought of you, and you offered her what she was missing, and your dream became hers. How wonderful that you were wise enough and tolerant enough to take her for her gifts and overlook the ugliness in her past."

Carlo did grin at that. "I find funny your suggestion that I was so wise. I was in love. It is wise to be in love, I agree, but that does not make wisdom and love the same. But, Haley, anything from before makes no difference. I knew the Hilliers' good opinion of Paloma even with her strange ways. They were not naive, and I myself booked you both into one room. But what is all of that? I myself have pursued women for little more than pleasure. I would feel bad to have on my conscience that I made them somehow no longer desirable. For me, it is people who count, not circumstances."

"Carlo, I fear you are doomed to be happy."

"No, no, much more. I have more than my greatest dream. You are more than my benefactor. I cannot put it in words."

"Don't try. You two needed each other, and Paloma needed a family. Now you've got it all going. Motherhood will be an enormous milestone in Paloma's life, in both of your lives, of course, but it has a mystical significance to her."

"To me, and to Giulia as well. You cannot imagine what this means to us. We grow with Paloma. We will burst with her. She will have much company, you will see!"

I'd never seen Carlo so elated. He made me feel like family as we went on to recall our days of trading experiences and opinions at Bettiswood. Who could've imagined how all that would work out?

Breakfast was not the most relaxed meal I ever shared with friends. During the fruit course, even our small talk was shrouded in an almost laughable pall, an anticipatory cloak of inhibition. Before long it was more than I could stand.

"Look, you guys, all this tiptoeing around is driving me nuts. We've had our difficulties and we're anxious to put it all straight, but couldn't it wait till after breakfast?"

My host got up and pounded me on the back and we all relaxed and polished off plates of, yes, eggs Florentine. Carlo soon left, as promised, and when fresh coffee was poured, Paloma asked me to give her a few minutes' head start and then come up to their suite. I took my cup to the farthest table on the terrace, sat, sipped, and frankly enjoyed the prospect of getting back on comfortable footing with my favorite project.

After what seemed an adequate interval, I tapped on the Giordano's massive door and heard a muffled "Coming!" from Paloma. Then I was in their salon, gawking at the indeed marvelous kilims she'd inherited from Gustaf. After I'd had a tour of the room, she sat carefully on a love seat and stuffed a pillow behind her back. I took the chair across the tea table, sensed her anxiety, and came right to the point.

"Paloma, I've talked to Carlo. He was upset because he thought you were upset. Well, I'm not upset, so don't worry. We may have things to regret, but we have the best of all reasons to put that behind us. We've all come out winners."

"Haley — damn you! — you're treating me just as you did when I needed to shed tears after our magical days in Portugal. I can't believe you're trying to keep me from speaking my piece." I shrank into the smallest, most penitent-looking ball I could manage, and she did her part by looking both severe and solicitous — a neat trick.

"Thank you. And don't act so crestfallen, be serious. We play so many games and have so much fun, I worry that something will get lost if one of us wants to be serious. So please attend. This is not something lost, this is something found." She glanced down, smoothed her skirt, and looked up, ready to go.

"I can only try to tell you how wonderful it is to have you here and have our separation behind us. You don't surprise me by being so good and understanding over my — how can I say it? — no-way-to-be-defended delay. But that shames me even more.

"It's hard to remember the way things were that awful day. Since then, everything's turned upside down; the thing I most hated when you confronted me is now the thing for which I most bless you. You shook me up so hard that all the pieces fell together — without that I would never have got here. Sometimes I wake in the night with that idea and I'm terrified. Or I'll be with Carlo or Giulia, even with my arms around them both, and get an awful chill just imagining a life without them. That's what you did for me. You got me going, got me on a road where I could relate to people. My great plan was going to work, I was going to be comfortable enough, but I'd never asked myself 'Then what?' Or faced up to the question, 'At what price?'

"So, you asked the questions for me, and why was I so put off? Well, I've been wrestling with that one. I think it had to do with the odd roles of men in my life, and in my mother's life, too — men were at the root of our problems. I suppose, deep down, I resented men in general. I wanted to use them somehow because of all that happened to her and to me. But what makes me sick now is that you were the last person I should have lashed out at. There you were, literally trying to undo the damage that'd been done to my head."

I straightened up and tried to get in a word, but she wouldn't have it.

"No, please. From the day we met, I knew that for some reason I never understood, I had your respect. I thought it was misplaced, but I loved it, and in the end it helped me to respect myself. It gave me courage to take the steps that got me here. Remember when you called me a caged bird and challenged me to open the door and fly away? Well, if I hadn't been so worked up, I'd have told you why I never released a caged bird. You know why? I was afraid it wouldn't be able to fend for itself. That was the point, you see — I was afraid I wouldn't be able to fend for myself. The funny thing was, even when I thought I hated you, I trusted your opinion about me and that helped me to fly away. Haley, I responded badly to having my cage rattled, but I pray that we still have each other, and always will."

"Paloma — sorry." I dabbed at my eyes. "Thank God for a good outcome, but it's ridiculous, your giving me credit for being so clever. I didn't set out to shake you up so hard. I had a terrible time getting started, and then I couldn't stop."

She was trying to get comfortable and tugging at her pillow, so I jumped up to help her rearrange. She took my hand in hers and I sank down beside her to finish my thought. "Besides, it wasn't all my doing. I may've spelled out a few hard truths and offered some options, but you had to weigh the arguments and decide what to do. Well, you may've pouted, but you did act."

She pressed my hand to her cheek. "I feel stupid that I couldn't put any of it together right there on the spot. But, you know, I didn't come to your door that day looking at any big picture. I felt guilty. I was thinking how our last trip had been all me, me, me. Me with Bessie, me with Anneke and Bill, me showing off with the guitar. And you'd made me nervous at Bettiswood with all that high-minded talk about changing my life. I'm sorry now, and I'm ashamed to admit it, but I didn't believe you were doing that for me. I was afraid that you were cutting me loose, and that I was losing you just when I was realizing what you meant to me, and counting on you to make my 'professional life' more of a pleasure and not just something to live through. So I showed up at your house hoping to patch everything up and I wasn't prepared for what I ran into. You questioned me and I felt backed into a corner, all defensive and cut adrift. It was crafty of you to push me away and shame me with talk that suddenly I should be your daughter."

"Crafty?" I leaned back in the love seat and stared, unseeing, at the ceiling. "You'll never, never know what that cost me. When you left, I was sure that I'd ended 'us.' It seemed like forever before I heard from you and could finally believe I might've done the right thing."

"You know you did the right thing! But you caught me at the worst time. You put me in a position where I had to grow up before I could accept what I am, or what I could be, or should be. And then I didn't grow up all at once. You'd pointed out how submissive I'd been, and got me to thinking about standing up for myself, and that made it really ironic when you were the first person I rebelled against."

She lowered her eyes, examined her hands, and appeared to be whipping up her resolve. She spoke quietly and slowly.

"Haley, all we've talked about goes back to me running away, and that's only the start. I'm still dragging my feet on why it's taken me so long to get back to you. I'm dragging my feet because I have no excuse. I can't justify it, I can only try to explain.

"I knew Carlo was taken with me as soon as I came here; he was a perfect gentleman in every way, but I could just tell. But right then, romance was the last thing on my mind; that wasn't the sort of fresh start I was looking for. I saw Villa Vigliano as a challenge, something I might help to make possible, and then something I could stay involved in. But it all got more personal when the three of us really got our heads together. Carlo and Giulia were open with me and made me feel welcome and I began to return Carlo's feelings. Before long, it was a romance and I knew it because I felt it right down to my bones.

"But I hardly knew Carlo, and he hardly knew me, and some of what he did know had to be — what can I say? — ugly and offputting. So I decided to tell him and Giulia everything, and I more or less did. But that's where it got hard. I was sensitive about you. I felt differently about you than about my other men, and you were the one that Carlo had met and seen me with. He'd seen us rooming together and enjoying each other's company. I downplayed you, and that was my mistake. I wanted Carlo to have time to really know me and not think about my past so much as about our present. I was afraid if I restarted any sort of relationship with you, he'd be jealous or feel uneasy about me. So I put off getting back to you; I was waiting for a point where I'd feel more secure and I'd know that Carlo felt secure. And let's face it, you had pushed me away, and I was still hurt. I wanted to rub it in a little and that made me greedy. I wanted everything to be perfect.

Even after Carlo and I were married, I wanted more things I could point to and show off. I wanted the villa to be farther along. I wanted our baby to be born. I figured that if I threw myself all day every day into all that needed doing, and worked really hard, I could justify leaving anything else on the back burner.

"So I led Carlo and Giulia to think that my breakup with you was just part of tearing myself away from that whole way of life. That added up to the worst lie I ever told, but it helped to justify not sending you our news. Your letters kept coming, but I didn't open them, partly out of plain old superstition. Everything was going so wonderfully well that I was afraid to rock the boat. And the other part was bad conscience. It was hard enough, not knowing what you were thinking, but I couldn't imagine reading your words and feeling what they might tell me.

"But I kept all your letters and didn't try to hide them. I had them in the big desk over there by the window. One day last month, Carlo noticed the whole lineup—my god, there must have been thirty of them, you were so faithful—and he asked me why I kept them at all. Well, I was sick of covering up, and by then I was feeling awful about keeping you in the dark and sort of lying to him. I told him that, and then I poured out the whole truth, everything, especially how you were the one who'd lighted the fire under me to get a life. Haley, you would've been proud of your friend, and that's what he is, you know. He gave me the worst scolding I've ever had, I mean it, especially about trying to spare his feelings. He asked me why he should resent another man admiring me or even loving me. He said that was the easiest thing in the world to understand. And he called you his friend and his benefactor and went on with all sorts of things that would've embarrassed you if you could've heard him. And then he told me to get busy and do something about bringing you up to date. He told me I would feel better right away, and, of course, he was so right.

"So I began to read your letters, and each one made me feel smaller and uglier, but the one that got me right here"—she crossed her hands on her heart—"do you remember the one where you asked for mercy and tweaked that line from Poe, 'For the love of God, Mon Trésor'? Well, to make it worse, I'd just been thinking of that Amontillado story while our wine cellar was being built down in what we call The Crypt. So there I was, 'your treasure,' showing no mercy, actually laying up the bricks and mortar to wall you off from all my joys that you deserved to share. I thought of the endless times I'd wondered what life would have been like if I'd had a father, and I admitted to myself that you'd abandoned part of our relationship to take on the job—and then done your best to give me paternal direction. And I'd rejected it.

"O God, Haley, I'm so ashamed. I sat there saying over and over, 'I wouldn't be here but for you!' I felt so low—I'd failed the simplest test of friendship, failed it over and over. I read all your letters that day and I blubbered a lot and never felt so unworthy in my whole life, not even close. All I could do was sit down and begin typing. I was at it all the next day and I faxed part of it that same night—and you know the rest."

She sighed and paused, looking at me contritely. I tried a smile, but she still looked uncomfortable. She waved me off.

"No, please, I lied, you don't know all the rest. I'm not through. Carlo made me promise to tell all, and there's another thing I'm not proud of. We've had Anneke and Bill here twice, to visit and to advise us. They were immensely helpful, believe me. Anneke told me about your letter to them, and I made her promise not to get back to you till I was ready. She hasn't been happy with that, she's lectured me and I should've listened, and that made it all the worse. And even before I took myself to Sevilla, I asked Bessie not to contact you, and I never told Nourrit how we broke up or what you did for me. So I got all my people involved in my pettiness. Please call me bad names or do something to let off steam, I really let you down and I want to be told off. I can't tell you how sick it's made me feel."

"OK, Paloma, I was hurt and I felt that I'd driven you off and I was lonely as hell. You said you were counting on me? Well, I was counting on you, and not just for now-and-then companionship. I loved the idea that we were friends, together or apart. I'd never seen any sort of mean streak in you and it was a cruel disappointment. It went on forever and you wouldn't give me the least little sign so I could stop worrying. But I don't have to tell you this. You're punishing yourself. I can't improve on that." I paused, but I wasn't done.

"And speaking of self-reproach, I've done some too. I didn't come into our relationship as any saint, so I guess when I heard about Gustaf,

I tried to push the blame onto him. I did use him as a whipping boy, just as you said, partly because I was ashamed of myself. If his sins were truly enormous, then mine were that much smaller. So, when you called me on that and stormed off, I mulled it over and finally admitted that I'd never been in his position—lonely, alone with you, and in complete control of your life. I saw that we both, he and I, responded to you in the same way, and we both failed part of our test. So, in the end, you shamed me with your defense of Gustaf. I'll never be able to forgive that man, but your assessment of him was less puritanical and more generous than mine and I thought better of you for it."

She got up with a bit of a hitch and came over, eyes brimming. She motioned me to stand, put her arms around my neck and her face to my chest. I could feel the roundness of her belly. She said, "God love you," in a tiny voice, and gave me a hug. It seemed minutes before she let go and retreated to her seat. She wiped her eyes, blew her nose, and spoke anew in a more buoyant fashion.

"Haley, it's such a relief to feel the sun come out. And to have something happy to share, something for us, something Giulia brought home to me and for which I owe her. You can't know, but Giulia has done so much for me. When she and I met, I was wrestling with myself over so many things. Over time, I told her most of it and, in the end, I told her about you and your advice and our breakup and how I felt afterward. And she asked me the oddest thing, she asked me how many times I'd been in love. I told her, 'Never, till I got together with Carlo here at the villa.' 'Wrong,' she said, 'you were in love with Haley. Haley was the first man you chose for yourself, he was the first one to whom you confided your past, and he was the one you came to count on for company and advice. Paloma, love may have sneaked up on you in disguise, but you were in love. You just had no experiences which you could compare.'

"At first I scoffed at her, please forgive me for that, but her words came back to me, over and over, and I knew she was right. And not only because I felt so lost when we parted. I know from the way it's been with me and Carlo. We go somewhere, we talk over things that interest us, we exchange ideas and I have such good feelings—and they're familiar, familiar because I had them when I was with you. I hope it makes you feel good too, to have been a young woman's first love."

I bit my tongue. I was touched all right, but also reminded that I had this place in her life only because of her abused and distorted coming of age. But whatever its history, our relationship, all of it, was dear to me and I wasn't about to dash her sweet illusion.

"Makes me feel good? That's pretty weak tea. Enchantment, that's more like it. Before I faced up to the big picture, I lay awake nights trying to dream up ways I might hang onto your company. How does it feel to have been an old man's last love?"

"Oh, don't put us in the past. Everything's changed, but nothing's changed. We'll always be man and woman to each other, so what if destiny makes us more like father and daughter? I should've been so lucky! I'm available for adoption."

"Paloma, you're a joy. And, ready for a secret? — I'm way ahead of you. I can't claim legal rights, but please be notified, I adopted you in spirit long ago, like it or not."

"Oh dear, I wish I could blush for modesty. But you know, we do belong to each other, it's been proved so many ways, even if I could never live up to your expectations. Haley, let's face it. I was never going to be Rachel Carson, or Barbara Tuchman, or whoever was the wonder woman of your fantasies. This is just Paloma here. Someday I hope to believe the stars in your eyes are for just me and not for this incredible Galatea of your inventions. Carlo is more comfortable. He loves me for me, the way I am."

That distinction made, she sat back with a self-satisfied air, and I nodded slowly and smiled and kept my eyes on her. After a few beats, she assumed an oversized frown, and demanded, "So, why do you look at me like that? You devil! I know you. You're going to ask why I care, why I make so much fuss about your high opinions. You know I'm flattered, you know I like to wonder whether any of that could be true. You love the idea that, in the end, you really did make me feel a little guilty, a lot guilty."

"Come on, I wasn't after guilt. I was trying for awareness. I wanted you to see your position clearly and make a real assessment."

"Oh, I have. Now I know what's going on. I'm the rebellious teenager who's seen the light. Daddy was not so wrong after all, perhaps he was right about some things. Perhaps I should let Daddy know, so he'll take me back."

With a wicked smile on her face, this large woman, now even larger, came over and sat on my knees, facing me. She put her arms around me and her head on my shoulder. She relaxed, all the swagger gone. In a moment, I felt more than heard a little voice, almost crooning. "How can I be so lucky in this life? Haley, I made it — can you believe it? I keep pinching me, and this is all real, and now you're here and every bit of it feels good. I never had a time in my life without some black cloud I had to work so hard to ignore, always, always. Now I have no cloud. I feel so free. I pray this is not too good to be true. Will you pray with me?"

That hit home. She'd never exposed the torments of her past so candidly — or showed them so plainly in eclipse. It was what I'd come to hear. Well, I heard it, and I replied, but there was no comparable poetry in my poor, plodding head. "Palomita, you've had the best prayers this old heathen could muster ever since he wandered into your orbit. And now they're answered...."

Suddenly I had a vision of the burdens Paloma had borne from childhood on, and all I could manage was a shaky whisper. "Sorry — can't help it. That voice... a brave little girl... finally finding her way out of the dark, finding her way home." Then I just squeezed and held on.

She pulled back gently, her hands cupping my face. She gave me a fond look, and for a second I thought she was going to kiss me. But no. She was letting me go. We were letting each other go; that's what we were there for. We were turning our backs on one relationship and taking up another. I was ready, but I lingered for a last, poignant wave of her presence — her heavy, glistening hair, those great eyes and full mouth, her ripening, rounded form, her warmth and glow. O Paloma, what did I ever do to deserve such a visitation? My boyish fantasies at first sight of Botticelli's Simonetta Vespucci, all come true, but richer, warmer, fragrant, three-dimensional — *The Birth of Venus* at a range closer than the Uffizzi allows. I put my hand to her cheek.

"Helen, Isolde, Beatrice, they are the breaths of others. You are mine. You must stay here forever, just as you are, or you must get up now before Carlo comes and forever ends my joy at anything."

She rose and tugged on the bell pull to signal the kitchen. I found my legs asleep and sighed. So much for romance. Carlo did show up, letting himself in as if on cue, and one look at his wife prompted a light-hearted salute. "Ah! What is the news from this meeting?"

"Oh," said Paloma airily, "Haley has decided he still likes me. And that it's time for morning tea."

At lunch, it was my great pleasure to meet Giulia Giordano, returned from a week with friends in Bologna. From a distance, she and Paloma had sisterly resemblances, similar stature, hair, and complexions. But Giulia's countenance was more aquiline, and she had the fine, high-bridged nose of Italy's northern aristocracy. Her excellent English spoke of her years of education in England, and within minutes — we sat together at lunch — I came to appreciate her considerable sense of humor and the role she'd chosen to play vis-a-vis her sister-in-law. I suspect Giulia had been accustomed to having Carlo defer to her in domestic and social matters and to depend on her assistance. That changed radically with the advent of Paloma. Giulia loved to poke hints of irony at her new sister, and at herself, all in good fun — a mood enhanced by her obvious affection for her acquired relative.

After lunch, Giulia and I repaired to the terrace to enlarge our acquaintance. Paloma and Bessie had come out with us but they tactfully excused themselves to pursue some errand. As Giulia and I watched them go, she sighed. "I am so very fortunate, I got a sister and a friend. She could have been a rival. She would be a formidable rival."

"How did you feel about her when she burst on the scene with her money and her enthusiasm?"

"I was fearful. She reached me first, it was by telephone, a day when Carlo was off to Bologna. She told me her idea for investing in the villa and I passed it along to Carlo. I could hear in him a new note. I thought, 'Oh, oh, something more than discussion happened in England.' I know Carlo so well. I knew this would not be just business. We waited for her to come, and he spent those two days like a clown making pantomime of waiting for the broken elevator. But, when she came, she was quiet, she wanted to listen. She asked to see everything and hear all our plans. We must have gone over the whole place three times before we sat down to our second supper."

"What were you thinking by then?"

"I was skeptical. We needed money, no question. But why did we need a partner in the construction and in our operations? That was Carlo's world, and mine. But it was strange, we walked around and talked of all that was to be done, and she understood so much. When we had been with her only hours, I remember feeling that she was here to stay, that she would not be leaving. I began to imagine how it would be to have her working alongside us. To my surprise, it did seem possible, and then I began to think I would enjoy it. When I felt myself hoping that she would not leave us, I thought to discuss it with Carlo, but he was already lost to reason. Then I knew I had a new partner and I had better get ready for a new sister-in-law. She is not bold, you know. She did not flirt with Carlo or me. She does not need to. She looks at you with those big, round eyes and makes you warm without even having to smile.

"But I must say, I made one big mistake of judgment. I guessed wrong about how she would take part. I expected her to bring money and stand back from the work and perhaps approve or not approve some of our details. But that was not her way. We made business together in a short time and she came to work with us. For a day or two she watched everybody, the masons, the painters, the carpenters, even the gardeners. Then she fell to talking over details with all of them in part-Spanish, part-Italian—Carlo called it "Espagniano." Then she became apprentice to all these craftsmen and lent a hand wherever she could. They adore her. The plasterer, God help us, is a Spaniard. She took him over at first sight. He will work all night for her. She has been I don't know how often to his house for dinners and fiestas. She is the godmother of his new son! I tell you, before long, I feared Carlo and I were being swept away by an avalanche. I feared, but Carlo could only look foolish.

"But you know, in only a short time, I could not imagine it all without her. It was as if she had come back to her childhood home. We were amazed to see her put down roots before she could really speak the language. She turned to me for advice. She opened a door, I could feel it, she took me into her life. Neither of us talked about ourselves but we knew each other. I cannot explain. Before long I was just as much in love with her as was Carlo—in quite another way, you understand."

I studied Giulia as she spoke, this handsome woman eight years Paloma's senior. I appreciated the open-hearted, generous way she'd responded to Paloma's intrusion. What a promising pair they made. I asked her what Paloma had actually done, what she'd worked at.

"Oh, looking back, it is a kaleidoscope—you cannot imagine the energy of this woman. She did silly things you can easily hire workmen to do. I can think of her painting, digging holes in the garden, even down on her knees, for God's sake, scrubbing stone floors with acid. It is too much melodrama! But, you know, there were important things. Two or three months after she came, the three of us stood out beyond the court—I think we were studying your idea to make it a meeting place—she looked up at the house and delivered a sentence as if she were a judge. The old storeroom had to go, had to be torn away. We were shocked. It was constructed of solid stone. It was added to the house, who knows, hundreds of years ago. And useful, it sat at the center of areas where we needed to have available maintenance tools and furniture for special times, and seasonal things like umbrellas. But Paloma was so certain. She sketched out with her hands and arms in the air the damage that room did to the symmetry of the great house. She made us for the first time see the house without that growth on its side. Now you see what happened. She was right.

"As soon as the old storeroom was pulled down and all that mess was carted away, the house looked so much finer, more noble. All of us were delighted, and Carlo proposed to Paloma just then when he hoped she felt important. He asked her in front of me! Can you imagine? I said, 'Paloma, this is his proposal, you understand, not our proposal. I did not put him up to this." And she said to me, 'I will say yes, but only if I have your blessing.' I put my arms around her and I said in her ear, 'Stay with us forever,' and she took Carlo's hands and kissed them and got down on her knees and said if he could accept all the evil in her past, she would be his forever. And Carlo got down on his knees and said it was the blessed past that brought them together. Both of them cried like babies. I had to walk away so that my tears would not trespass on their moment."

Now I had tears in my eyes and Giulia noticed. "Look what Paloma does to us. She is Circe, with a better heart."

"No," I replied slowly, "she was a good seed in a dark place. She sprouted under rocks but found her way to the sky. Her flower is fair, but you and I are moved by knowing the way by which she came."

"Signor Talbot, you amaze me. I thought we Italians are the hopeless romantics of this world."

Around three, Carlo and Paloma showed up in exercise outfits and walking shoes. "Come on, Haley, come see the two nearest farms." So I jumped up and we marched off to the west and around the shoulder of the hill. My hosts were in high spirits and I was impatient to see the works.

On the way, Paloma mused over their plans for our reunion. "Men are so different. Carlo didn't want me to start our rapprochement with talk or words on paper, he wanted to show you our progress on the villa, some of your ideas incorporated, and my fat stomach. He wanted to deal in the tangible. I knew you better than to believe that was the best way, but he does have a case. Words may be less sincere and more easily manipulated than stone and mortar. Anyhow, we hope you'll approve of our stone and mortar." Carlo nodded his assent.

I spent the next two hours enveloped by that sense of return to familiar ground, a walk through full-sized solutions to problems Carlo and I had pored over on paper. In all, the buildings and their improvements appealed to me. The entire complex had a splendidly solid, Old World atmosphere, something we typically don't achieve in the U.S. despite the best intentions. Credit a true son of Tuscany, an insider. We wound up our inspection looking at a ravishing view out a grand window in a second-floor suite, and I did my best to compliment Carlo and Paloma for their accomplishments. I took them both by the hand to make my point, but then they hung on, and Carlo turned the tables on me.

"Haley, you are part of this forever, please. Paloma and I have talked about this all the time you are here. We are most decided to have you and your family — really, all of them, everybody — to come next year when we open this farm. You will be the first guests, and that is the right thing. We will have a reception to welcome this place and you together. Now say that all of you will come to us!"

"My God, Carlo, what else could I say? My family will be delighted, and it'll round out my world when you all know each other. Thank you. Count on us to come and get in your way as much as possible." We ended with hugs all around.

On our walk back to the villa, we cut around on the north side and my hosts pointed out where the offending storeroom had adjoined the main building. I examined a grand portal and read an ancient inscription carved into the stones of its arched frame, *AD ASTRA PER ASPERA*. This was the once-principal entrance that had been bricked up and plastered over, along with its motto, at the time of the storeroom addition. Paloma had caused it to reappear.

I whistled. "To the Stars through Difficulties." That's eerie, the story of your life in a phrase. You really are Nourrit's daughter."

"Don't be silly," she said, but then turned away and vigorously blew her nose.

We split up and I went to my room to change, then down to the terrace and the table with the best view of the slopes. I found myself comparing the old Paloma with the new. This married, pregnant, Florence Paloma was so calm, so serene—it seemed impossible that only a year and a half separated her from her anxious and less happy predecessor. At twenty-four, the alluring woman I first met had proved emotionally underdeveloped and vulnerable, a combination that left her ill prepared to cope. At twenty-six, this new Paloma had lost none of her gifts, but had made an amazing leap in maturity and confidence. A wave of pleasure swept over me; she was becoming the person I had always imagined that she could be, or ought to be. I prayed that all she was building upon would prove substantial enough to last a lifetime.

Before long, she came and sat with me, glad to rest in this seventh month of her pregnancy. We hadn't discussed her condition since the day of my arrival. Now I asked her how it had gone and whether she'd had problems.

"Problems? No, but you may have saved me from one—pregnancy! You were so successful in my re-education and I became such a pillar of virtue that I made Carlo wait until we were properly married, in church and in the court. I told him it is good discipline for both of us. It's true, you may ask him! Since then it's been a different story, as you see."

"No, dear heart, I wasn't talking about getting pregnant. I'm asking about the course of your pregnancy."

"Cruise control, all the way. My doctor tells me I'm a brood mare. Each time she checks me over, she shakes her head. She makes jokes. When I have the children I need, I can be a surrogate mother for very high prices." Here a wicked grin. "Naturally, I say nothing about having charged high prices for related services."

"Paloma!"

"Don't 'Paloma' me! You were there. Who else can I joke with then? Besides, would we ever have got together had I not been a wicked, wicked woman?"

"Would you ever have needed me if you hadn't been a wicked, wicked woman?"

She made an elaborate pretense of surveying her belly, the house, the courtyard, and the panorama of Tuscany. "Do I need all this? Silly man! Answer your own question."

A day or two later, the three hotel keepers were engrossed all afternoon and evening in preparations and then a banquet ordered up by a prestigious cultural group from Florence—getting their custom had been a coup in itself, and the Giordanos hoped to secure its annual return. I used the opportunity to drop in on Bessie at her work, and she introduced me to Francesca, a middle-aged woman who shared the office space, answered the telephone, and kept an eye on incoming faxes and e-mails. She and Bessie were becoming friends and helping each other. As far as the bookkeeping itself was concerned, Bessie reported it as routine. Once the pattern was established on the computer, it was largely a matter of plugging in numbers. I looked at some of her work and saw that it was all in Italian. I whistled and quizzed her about that. She made that sound simple, too. She was no linguist, but she was methodically picking up a specialized Italian vocabulary, using a dictionary and Francesca and older records as her sources. I complimented her on her achievements, but that barely expressed my admiration for the larger transition made by this disadvantaged sixty-plus-year-old woman.

I asked Bessie to join me for dinner and later went to pick her up at her room. When she opened the door, I saw behind her the portrait of Paloma at six, now hung over a chest on which sat Helen, the self-same doll that appears in the painting. I said nothing, but marveled, "How magical! Paloma's life regrouping under this grand and friendly roof."

Once we were in place for our meal, I asked Bessie how difficult it had been to leave the city and country where she'd always lived, and take up a new life, mostly among strangers, and a new language. She paused, looked at me, then out the window or off to another place and time.

"Well, coming to the wedding was easy enough, I wouldn't have missed it for the world. I wasn't so sure about leaving home for good. Hard to think about, that. But now I look back, it seems 'twas harder to decide than 'twas to do."

She went on to describe how she looked around a changing Putney and thought of her years with Paloma, then decided it was worth a try to recover their relationship. As she said, "If it didn't work out, we'd hug each other, give it up, and stay close the way we were." So she got herself ready, physically and spiritually, to leave England for the first time, and possibly forever.

"I got up that last morning thinking how I first come to Putney, forty-four years back it was, me seventeen, and Mr. George hiring me to help with Miss Celia. I remembered my years with her and I hunted up the letters she sent me before she passed away. Made me cry to read Miss Celia thanking me for what I'd done and wanting me to forgive her for never saying much. I'd written back, but it was like I needed to tell her again, she didn't owe me, more like I owed her. I'd had more'n she'd ever had and most of it because of her. So I went over to pray for Miss Celia in Saint Vincent's, the way I had since nineteen fifty-three, and I thanked her for all she give me and I thanked God for His blessings. Then I was set to fly, first time ever for me.

"Well, 'twas strange. The wedding was the grandest thing, and me in it, standing up for Paloma right there with Miss Giulia and Nourrit and her boy. But those first days when it was over, I was sure it would never do, me out of place in all this grandness, these rich folks and hard-working Italians. But Paloma had things for me to do and I found a few meself, and first thing you know it seemed like I was fitting in. I've never had such a place, never in me life — so busy, but everybody friendly with always time for a smile and a word. It's warm, and you've seen how the food is. There's odd times, I feel like I'm back at the orphanage, the house so big and so many people, but the spirit's different, and Paloma's here, and that's all the difference. Living here means more than visits ever could do. You visit, and a few days you run out of things to say. Here, we never run out, it's heads together all the time, there's so much to do and new things coming up. I see now, at home I was always lonely. Here's the place to be."

Coffee was served and Bessie changed direction.

"You'll think me a bad person, it taking me so long to thank you for what you done for Paloma and me. It's only these last weeks she's said anything, but, believe me, it was a lot. Before that, you must've been on her mind, but she wouldn't talk about you, nor let me do, neither. I had your letter about the falling out you two had. I felt bad about it, but it weren't long before I could see, even with your troubles, you'd managed what we talked about. First, I could tell from things in her letters, and when I was here, it was plain. And all of it like answers to me prayers, years worth, I'll tell you. I'd have said, way back, but Paloma had me to wait, said she had a plan. I hoped so, but it was a worry and I felt better right off when she told me she'd be sending you the news."

I asked her to forget it, it was settled now, and besides, I wasn't the only one who had helped. I reminded Bessie that she'd launched the child Paloma. But I mentioned nothing about my romantic notion that all of Paloma's supporters were like me, under her spell the moment we met, enlisted by a higher power, and with no option but to help as best we could. That made perfect sense if you idealized her as a beneficence struggling for its place in an imperfect world — but I kept that to myself. It's not easy to share an epiphany.

I sat there, making small talk, but thinking of Bessie, all those years in London, making do with a portrait and a doll, and Paloma in California agonizing over their distant relationship. How wrong I was when I belittled Paloma's choice for a new life, when I decided she was taking an easy way out. I thought of all her joys and how they included giving Bessie room, board, job, and family. It was almost spooky. Bessie yawned discreetly, and the two oldest folks under the villa's roof bid each other goodnight and went to bed.

For a week, I was wined and dined, guided, introduced, and generally fussed over, then I began to feel that I'd learned and contributed what I could, and that my hosts needed to get back to their lives. I spoke to Paloma about it at lunch. She wasn't impressed.

"You are most certainly not in anyone's way. It's fun having you here. You entertain me. You entertain Bessie. You've enchanted Giulia.

Since you arrived, I've come up in her eyes, she better understands my naughtiness. Now she says she's in love with you! And look at Carlo. He was shaking his head just this morning, appreciating your idea for the balcony access over on Number Five. So spoil us. Get a book to read and stay as long as you can stand it."

So I calmed myself and settled down to a vacation with friends in an elegant place. I spent time poking around in the plans and the construction, and hours accompanying Carlo on his runs to Florence for odds and ends needed in the work — shades of my own career as "gofer" when I built our homes.

Most days, I dropped in for mid-morning tea with Bessie and Francesca in their back office. I'd met Francesca's son, a porter-handyman at the villa, and I'd often help him with his English for an hour or so before lunch. We laughed a lot over our own limited communication, but at one point I succeeded in asking his opinion of Paloma's growing command of Italian. He rolled his eyes and sighed. "When my English will be the same good like her *Italiano*, I will have employ in *il corpo diplomatico!*"

If Giulia expressed enthusiasm for me, I more than returned the sentiment. She appealed to me at once as an entirely sympathetic person and one of much wit and insight. But there was also about her an air of autumnal melancholy. She was only thirty-four when we met, but she seemed to have written off any prospects for marriage, children, or independent living. I worried that she might somehow have been eclipsed by Paloma's resounding presence. One morning I mentioned this privately to Carlo in his workroom, but he would have none of it.

"No," Carlo insisted, "Giulia is a new person since Paloma. They fell on each other so, for weeks, I feared there was no place for me. If you knew my Giulia and her life, that is a very big thing. I must tell you, I worried for my sister for years, but now she has so relaxed. We all breathe better every day."

To our chagrin, Giulia walked in just then and plainly had picked up Carlo's last thoughts. No matter, she acted unperturbed and got in her oar.

"Carlo, you were my dear friend and worried for me. Also, Haley, I worried for him. We worried too much. We spent too much time in the past. Paloma came here and brought a lightness, a joy. We laughed, we looked up, we looked forward. She did that for us, but also she says we did that for her, she had the same need for us. We are like your 'Rub-a-dub-dub' song for children, we are the three men in a tub! So, don't let Carlo tell you how much better I am. Villa Vigliano is better, all of it, everyone under its roof."

Carlo squeezed her about the shoulders and put his head to hers. She pretended to shrug him off, patted my cheek, and marched out with the bearing of one who has set the record straight.

I tried to rally each mid-afternoon on the terrace, and one or the other or both of the "sisters" would usually manage to hobnob and take tea. Around twelve days into my stay, on a particularly brilliant, flying cloud day, Paloma and I were reminiscing and trying to imagine the future. We had a rather hard time avoiding the fact that it was she who really had a future and I who had a greater stake in the past. I recalled the bewitching balcony at Pousada de Santa Bárbara and reminded her how I'd trampled on her emotions while I wrestled with the fact that I was in love, but past the time when I could do anything about it.

So there we sat, two years later on a balcony in Tuscany, seventy doing what he could to explain the burden of age to twenty-six, and twenty-six doing her best to inject new optimism and insights. Her job was not easy. This time the problem was mine, and there was no solution.

Luckily, a diversion was on its way. Paloma noticed it over my shoulder. "Ah! Here comes tea." Trailing a server was Giulia, and we welcomed her and the tea as life preservers tossed on the heavy waters into which we had drifted.

Signorina Giordano must have felt something in the air; as she seated herself, she hurriedly delivered a light-hearted report on the ongoing spat between two chambermaids who'd set their caps for the same painter. She'd just fended off one who wanted to know when next the villa would call back the painting crew.

"How," Giulia asked, "can I conspire with one and not the other? I told her I will put up a notice in the kitchen as soon as a decision is taken."

She laughed and poured tea and passed a selection of finger food. Then she waved her hand at the nicely arranged tray.

"Signor Talbot, in our former life you would not have had fresh fruits or cucumber sandwiches with your tea. We would have served you barbarous things like fruitcake, shortbread, chocolate, mints, such things. That was before Paloma."

She looked sternly at her sister-in-law, who clapped hands to her face and leaned forward in her best "Penitent Magdalene" pose. Giulia pressed on relentlessly with the grand sweep and aggrieved tones of a Greek chorus.

"You cannot begin to guess all she brought with her. It was our house, our land, our country, for the love of God!, and she came to us with almost nothing, that is, nothing we could see. But then she brought out her diet! Did she impose it on us? Certainly not, that is not Paloma's way. She ate it in front of us. She mentioned little things about it. Naturally, Carlo was, shall I say, receptive? He encouraged her to tell us more. Then he wanted to try. Now we eat differently than we have all our lives. Thank God, we are never smokers! Can you imagine? We would not have got her out of the airport that first day. I am amazed, really, she did not raise the subject on the telephone before she came. We have been subjugated by this woman in so many ways. Look at her, she grins, she has no shame! But, of course, you must guess the truth, we are better for it. We knew these things before, but she had to come and shame us to do our duty.

"But is she satisfied? Oh no, there is still the exercise! Paloma makes me work out with her and go on many fast walks, you cannot believe the uncivilized hours! I have never perspired so in all my former life. I tell you, it is a relief she is pregnant and we walk at a more sensible pace. In a few weeks, I will get some days of vacation, but they will be very few, you wait and see."

Paloma clasped Giulia's hand. She cleared her throat. "As Giulia says, this is her home, her land. But please know that I did not take it from her, she gave it to me." Paloma smiled and dropped the act. "When I came, I found this a beautiful place, but a place like others I'd touched upon before. Giulia took me by the hand, like this, and opened up so many small, hidden away wonders and introduced me to so many people I already cherish. But was that all? Oh no. Now she's giving me her language. She's my best teacher. And in all of this, she gives me herself, a treasure I could never have imagined. It's true that I have little to offer in return, but as she says, I do try." She and Giulia leaned together and touched foreheads. They leaned back with sister smiles.

One day in Bessie's office, I picked up a color brochure printed the previous year to announce the villa's opening, and found it signed by owners/hosts Giulia Giordano, Paloma Utrera, and Carlo Giordano. I quizzed Paloma at the first opportunity. "Utrera? When did that happen?"

"Oh, there's a story. Before I became Giordano, I was what you see there, Utrera, would you believe? It happened roundabout. By the time Carlo and I were engaged, he knew that Bessie and Nourrit and Benito were all the family I had. When we made plans to bring them to the wedding, he insisted that I ask them to stay on here and live with us. I wrote to Bessie, I wore her down with phone calls, and now she's here, I pray, forever. But I couldn't call Nourrit, no phone, and anyhow she's convinced that it filters out a lot of what people can communicate face to face. So I made plans to go to Sevilla. I told Giulia, and — pop! — she was with me on the plane. We sat in Nourrit's house and talked about everything, and she was her usual mysterious self, seeing all sorts of hidden meanings and, as usual, perceiving things quite as they were. I'd been sending letters for Benito to read to her, but now she was feeling my presence and measuring it, and she knew I'd not only broken my pot, but I was putting out roots. I've never seen her with more high spirits, and she was so taken with Giulia, I was almost jealous. I watched them together, so close even though they had to practically barter Spanish and Italian, and I said to myself, 'She'd like to adopt Giulia too, they'd like to adopt each other.' Nourrit said she was sorry she couldn't meet Carlo, but it wasn't necessary, Giulia was his bond, his guarantee. Oh dear, I'm afraid I paint Nourrit as a caricature of a Gypsy fortune teller, but you know the truth, they are the caricatures, Nourrit is real.

"So, she listened to my invitation and said she and Benito would come happily to our wedding, but they could not leave Sevilla. She was firm on that. Benito was — he still is — apprenticed to a chef who could open up a career. Nourrit is so patient; she said that if I would leave my door open, someday, when Benito was independent, she, or perhaps even they, would try to step into my world.

"Being in Sevilla brought back so many memories. We walked by Amparo's building, happy memories there, and I thought of my half-sisters, unhappy memories, but it did remind me that they were my last relatives. Well, we were there, and Alicia was in the directory, so I took a deep breath and called. I was surprised to learn they were living together. Marta had been married, but she's separated and has no children, and Alicia never married. But the big surprise was that they were willing to talk to me, and they invited me and Giulia to visit. We found them in a large, fine flat where they received us and treated us, I must say, in a very genteel fashion. I did tell them some things about my recent life — and you may be sure I glossed over many details along that road!

"They also told us their problems — Marta's separation and a romantic disappointment of Alicia's that wasn't described, just regretted. Oh, and a financial setback caused by a friend, someone they'd really trusted. Both of them had turned more to the church, and I must say they sounded sincerely concerned for their own salvation. They said they'd already resolved to contact me, and they regarded my reappearance as a sign to them. So, the upshot was, they wanted to end our estrangement and welcome me as a member of their family. It's true they could use another relative. Besides me, all they have left is their mother and an uncle, no cousins even.

"So, there it was, we met and we parted, all amicably enough. I think they were quite taken with me and Giulia. We even invited them to the Villa. And then, soon after I got back here, I got a letter from the sisters begging me to forgive them for sinful behavior toward me when I was a child. They asked me to take the name Utrera, if I chose. 'Why not,' I asked myself, 'who in the world is more Utrera than I?' Forgiveness was easy. I look around now and I have no problem with the past or anyone in it. It's added up to more than I ever hoped."

One afternoon it clouded up, the wind blew, and for two hours we could peer out to see a heavy and surprisingly cold summer rain fall and splash. Carlo was off to Florence and Paloma took me once more to their private salon. To ward off the chill, and for auld lang syne, she'd brought up a bottle of a Madeira we'd favored in Portugal. She seated herself on the sofa and patted it to call me to her side. When I showed the slightest hesitation, she laughed.

"Sit here so I can pat you and tweak your ear and, if need be, put my head on your shoulder. Don't look at me like that! What can you possibly be thinking? Have you no faith in my conversion?"

"That's not it. I guess I'm just old-fashioned. Having been where I've been and done what I've done, I worry over Carlo's feelings."

"Haley, you and I are going to be friends forever, I've decided that. We must act as friends do. You know perfectly well we were friends first, and lovers second. So, give up second and don't spoil first— otherwise, we part forever because we've sinned. Imagine! Well, I won't have it. Carlo and I trust each other, and we'll never let each other down. You watch!"

"My, how times have changed. I picture a very serious young woman standing in front of me and fiercely insisting that marriage was out of her reach and, anyhow, a risky proposition at best. I caught hell for advocating marriage."

"What am I to do with you? I've admitted my mistakes. I bowed to your judgment and I begged your forgiveness. Am I to get down on my knees? That's not as easy as it used to be." She shifted her weight and peered at me quizzically. She raised a hand and pointed to a dressing room. "Over there is something I want you to see. I thought I was too proud, but I'm not. It's a message to me that I pray I finally got. Look behind the right wing of my dressing table mirror."

All right, I was intrigued. I got up and followed orders. On the wall was a small laminated document, one handwritten line, the snippet I pinned to her hat the day we split. That gave me a shiver.

"Paloma, I'm flattered as hell. And no more apologies. Even our difficulties were high drama and excitement—and I haven't had much of either in my life." She smiled a crooked smile and appeared to contemplate some wicked possibility, so I hastened to tack on, "But calm yourself, please, I've had enough stimulation for this decade."

I sipped my wine and strayed into my habit of studying Paloma's hands. She responded by folding them primly in her lap and setting off in a new direction.

"Haley, I must tell you, it's been fascinating peeling back the layers of the Carlo onion—there's so much there and he's so different from anyone I've ever known, especially different from us. Is that a funny idea to you, us? Ever since that first day in Santa Fe, it's grown on me that you and I think alike, we're related. But Carlo is something else. He's 'old money,' really old—Renaissance. No rationalizing needed, it's in the breeding. And he knows, just by instinct. On the odd occasion when he's wrong, he's so chagrined that he's adorable—you can see he feels betrayed by his twenty-five centuries of culture. You and I have nothing like that to live up to. Your people banished themselves to the New World. And I? Well, I resulted from the flaws in those who stayed behind. We have to create do-it-yourself confidence, take the bull by the horns." She pinched my knee, hard, and I jumped and let out an "Ouch!"

"Sorry. Just showing you that I've joined you on your high ground of confidence. I used to envy you up there, it was an outlook you just had. Well, guess what! When I finally figured out how to get up alongside you, the view wasn't as different as I expected. It's not the perspective at all, it's the attitude you took up there with you."

"Palomita, we've come full circle. That was the attitude I wanted to induce in you from day one. Your life and all we've been through is right there in Mother Goose.

> For every evil under the sun
> There is a remedy or there is none
> If there be one, seek till you find it.
> If there be none, never you mind it."

She looked rapt. "Say it again?" I did, and she embraced it. "Honestly, that one must have gone right over my head. You're right, I've lived the whole thing, and that last line is me and my father. Do you know, I really don't mind? I have no feelings for him, no judgment. I exist in the real world. How can I regret the act of my creation? Remember our discussions of common sense?"

"Thanks, kiddo. Ain't it grand when our amateur philosophizing hits home? Of course I agree about your father. He fathered you, therefore you exist."

She raised her eyes and gave me the sweetest "thank-you" look. She settled back and folded her hands on her shrinking lap. I'd never known her to be more relaxed and contented. I gazed into those eyes and was transported back to the coffee shop on that first day of the rest of my life—Paloma in the same sort of shirt, hair the same, skin just as perfect, the same brown-red lipstick, the same quizzical smile. For me again, it was love at first sight. And I knew it was time to go.

The next day I made the rounds for farewells to acquaintances old and new. There was no sadness—after all, in a few short months, I'd be back with family. When it was time for Carlo to whisk me away, Paloma and I said our good-byes at the head of the terrace stairs. I was talked out. I took her hands and told her I'd be holding my breath and praying for her joyous and safe entry into the world of maternity. Maternity and Paloma! We chuckled together over the pilgrimage that concept had made. We hugged and parted.

I went home wrapped in the feeling that I'd carried out the miraculous assignment delivered to me in Santa Fe, carried out, still in the process, and yet to be enjoyed. And though I would never make the claim on either side of the water, I had added to my family. I rejoiced in all my daughters, sons-in-law, and grandchildren. I looked forward to all I would find at home, at all my homes.

But after six weeks I became nervous, Paloma should have delivered. Praise the Lord, my vigil ended on the morning of October twelfth when I stepped into my office and discovered a handwritten fax.

> *Haley, my angel,*
> *I have a baby of my own! Everything is perfect, but I will torment you one last time—for a few days. I will tell no more. You must see, not read.*
>
> *Every joy from Paloma*

My torment was to last six weeks. How many times was I tempted to call and ask what was happening—and each time lost my nerve? Paloma put me off as a lark, but there was the possibility of some mishap and I dared not butt in. At last I held in my hand an ivory-colored envelope bearing the crest of Villa Vigliano and emitting a light scent of lavender. I breathed a prayer and slit the seal.

I have the folded card before me as I write. It is elegantly printed in deep sepia and the Italian text announces Giulia Celia Giordano.

Above, is a superb, close photograph of Carlo and Paloma with Giulita in her mother's arms. Carlo beams adoringly at his beautiful daughter, and she and her mother fix me with identical wideset dark eyes. It is a look I treasure and know so well. Below is written,

Bless you! Bless you! Bless you! Paloma

Her open, airy script appears to fly from the page.

And Finally—

Top drawer thanks to daughter Bronle, my sole confidant, editor, and critic in the first year of the Paloma affair, often suggesting a better word or phrase, but usually inclined to point out muddles and let me write my way out of them. (Even, alas, when that led to countless readings and tested her gift for trenchant, piquant marginal notes.) And later I benefitted immensely from Jennifer Redmond's broad, tender, and understanding review.

Thanks as well to friends, colleagues, and professional advisors whose enthusiasm and suggestions contributed to my development as I essayed the daredevil leap from historical writing to fiction: Richard Farson, Susan Kleeman, Diana Lindsay, Catherine Mayo, Noel Greenwood, Debra Ginsberg, Tershia d'Elgin, Dana Monroe, Alfred JaCoby, Kathleen Wise, Julie Fitzgerald, and Verna Loy.

And to Joanne, my wife, for gracefully accepting a ménage à trois with newcomer Paloma.